Rumand

romises

DATE DUE

HERITAGE BEACON
F I C T I O N

RUMORS AND PROMISES BY KATHLEEN ROUSER
Published by Heritage Beacon Fiction
an imprint of Lighthouse Publishing of the Carolinas
2333 Barton Oaks Dr., Raleigh, NC, 27614

ISBN: 978-1-941103-66-1
Copyright © 2016 by Kathleen Rouser
Cover design by Elaina Lee
Interior design by AtriTeX Technologies P Ltd
Interior graphics by Susan F. Craft

Available in print from your local bookstore, online, or from the publisher at:
www.lighthousepublishingofthecarolinas.com

For more information on this book and the author visit: http://www.kathleenrouser.com

This is a work of fiction. Names, characters, and incidents are all products of the author's imagination or are used for fictional purposes. Any mentioned brand names, places, and trademarks remain the property of their respective owners, bear no association with the author or the publisher, and are used for fictional purposes only.

Scripture quotations from The Authorized (King James) Version. Rights in the Authorized Version in the United Kingdom are vested in the Crown. Reproduced by permission of the Crown's patentee, Cambridge University Press.

Brought to you by the creative team at Lighthouse Publishing of the Carolinas:
Eddie Jones, Ann Tatlock, Nancy J. Farrier, Brian Cross, Paige Boggs

Library of Congress Cataloging-in-Publication Data
Rouser, Kathleen.
Rumors and Promises / Kathleen Rouser 1st ed.

Printed in the United States of America

PRAISE FOR *RUMORS AND PROMISES*

Kathleen Rouser will entice booklovers with descriptive detail
and an engrossing storyline full of drama, hints of humor, and
plenty of romance in *Rumors and Promises*. They will also enjoy
the Bible verses sprinkled throughout and the message of hope
and redemption told in a non-preachy manner. An all-around
delightful read that I highly recommend!

~ **Sharlene MacLaren**
Author of 16 faith-based, bestselling novels
including the Tennessee Dreams series

Set in 1900 in a fictional Michigan town, *Rumors and Promises* is
a tender story of two people whose love is tested against difficult
and trying circumstances. Author Kathleen Rouser takes the reader
on a journey of betrayal and loss and rumors determined to ruin
the best of reputations.

~ **Jill Eileen Smith**
CBA best-selling author of *The Crimson Cord*
and The Wives of King David series

Rumors and Promises is a poignant story of God's mercy and
unconditional love. Kudos to Ms. Rouser for crafting a touching
and thought-provoking tale of forgiveness in all its forms.

~ **Marianne Evans**
Award-winning author of *Devotion*

Set in America's Heartland at the turn of the twentieth century,
Rumors and Promises is a story of one woman's journey toward love
and learning to trust. Author Kathleen Rouser offers a perennial
message of faith and forgiveness that is sure to inspire readers."

~ **Kate Breslin**
Award-winning author of *Not By Sight*

Rumors and Promises is a charming story of faith and trust, mistakes and redemption, of learning how not to run away from truth even when it's nearly too painful to face. Set in 1900 Michigan, the historical setting comes alive under the wonderful imagery penned by Kathleen Rouser. Ultimately this is an unforgettable love story with an exciting finish—a highly enjoyable read that will refresh your faith in God and in others.

~ **Maureen Lang**
Award-winning author of *Whisper on the Wind*

Acknowledgments

First of all, thank you, Lord Jesus, for putting such a story on my heart and giving me the tenacity to write to the end. And for the mercy and grace that changed my life and made me your child, making this all possible.

For the team at Lighthouse Publishing of the Carolinas: Eddie Jones, Ann Tatlock, Nancy Farrier and Brian Cross, I thank you so much for taking on this story and making it a much better one. You have been wonderful!

So much appreciation goes to my outstanding agent, Linda S. Glaz. She believed in my writing and always gave me such wholehearted support in finding a home for *Rumors and Promises*.

Kathryn Cushman and Susan Patricia Falck, you were there in the infancy stages of *Rumors and Promises*. With your guidance it became a full-fledged romance novel. Rohn Federbush also gave me much helpful input. And Jill Eileen Smith, thank you for your advice on my first few chapters and the encouragement to press on.

My dear friends, Toni Price and Carol Andronaco, you encouraged me to believe the Lord could use my writing to touch people's hearts. So many other friends have prayed for me and cheered me on in my writing endeavors. Though your name may not be mentioned here, thank you so much!

I also want to remember my mother-in-law, Frances Rouser, who has since passed away. She read the very first version of this manuscript. Her desire to keep turning pages made me believe it could become a story others might want to read. I only wish she could be here to see it in book form.

Most of all, I wish my mother, Lena Hensel, who taught me to love books, was here to see my dream become a reality.

Dedication

For Jack, my dear love and my best friend.
You've always believed in me.

&

In memory of my brother, John Hensel,
who early on nurtured my writing aspirations.

I am the Lord thy God, which have brought thee out of the land of Egypt, out of the house of bondage.

~ Exodus 20:2, KJV

CHAPTER 1

Stone Creek, Michigan
1900

Sophia Bidershem jerked awake as the train whistle blew. Her heart pounded a beat almost in cadence with the wheels upon the track. Prickles traveled up her arm so she wriggled her elbow into a different position around her two-year-old daughter, Caira, who had fallen asleep against her. Outside her passenger window, the pewter sky hung, cold and austere. Snowflakes glided downward, covering any dirt or tracks on the ground and blanketing the leafless trees with a pristine beauty. Could her new identity make her appear as clean?

A figure in a dark coat brushed against Sophia's seat, the scent of sweet tobacco smoke from a pipe causing her breath to catch. Her eyes swept up toward the tall, masculine figure. His gray derby sat low while the brim hid his eyes. The glove he attempted to put in his pocket fell to the floor. As he bent to pick it up, the train wound around a curve, and he bumped Sophia.

She gasped, covering her mouth and stilling the shivering which threatened to overtake her.

"So sorry, miss." The stranger tipped his hat, looking apologetic.

Sophia exhaled, leaning as far away as possible from the aisle. No scar slanted across his right cheek. She gave the stranger a slight nod and averted her gaze. Other passengers read, stared out the windows, or spoke to one another in low tones. Her daughter slept, oblivious to her mother's fear. Sophia sat against the high-backed seat and closed her eyes, trying to reclaim the blissful peace of a catnap.

But the passing figure had reopened a scab on Sophia's soul. Darkness surrounded her again in her mind's eye. *He* appeared, and there was no place to run. She blinked; daylight flooded in. Sophia held Caira tighter and focused outside the window.

Feeling a sheet of paper crinkle in the reticule on her lap, Sophia freed her other hand to fish it out. Unfolding the paper, she searched the information in the body of the letter sent to her by Mrs. Fairgrave.

The conductor strolled by her seat. "Next stop, Stone Creek, Michigan!"

Sophia scooped Caira up, gathering the carpetbag and sack with their belongings. Shuffling toward the door, she avoided eye contact with other disembarking passengers.

"May I help you, miss?" A grandfatherly gentleman offered his arm with a smile.

Sophia stiffened but nodded her assent, not wanting the embarrassment of tumbling onto the platform. "Thank you." She lifted her chin, hoping she gave an impression of assurance, at least until she had her bearings. The older man took his leave of them once she was firmly planted on the boardwalk below.

Taking one look back at the train, she again left Sophia Bidershem behind and became plain Sophie Biddle. Not much of a change in identity, but it was something. The snowfall grew heavier as well as Caira and their few possessions. They trudged past the icy millpond, down Main Street. Sophie spotted the local mercantile, a good place to ask directions, no doubt.

The bell jangled over the door at Neuberger's General Store. Homey scents wafted on the warmed air. Smells of spices, tobacco, new fabric, and coffee all blended, luring her farther in.

"May I help you . . ."

Embarrassed, Sophie curled up her work-worn, ungloved fingers as the proprietor seemed to inspect her hands, probably looking for a wedding ring.

"Miss?" A broad smile crossed the proprietor's face as he leaned his bulky frame against the counter.

"I'm looking for notions." Sophie placed Caira on the floor next to her and then peered into the glass casement to peruse the items of her trade. "And needles." Sophie pointed toward an economical book of them. That and some thread would do nicely. She made the exchange of coins for her purchases, and the clerk wrapped them.

"Candy?" Caira pounded on the glass with the palm of her hand.

Sophie sighed. "No, no. Come over here with me." Sophie took her package from the counter. "Thank you. Would you mind if we warmed up by the stove a bit?"

"Of course you can, miss. Have a seat in my chair while I'm not usin' it." He motioned toward a battered old wooden chair missing a spoke in the back. "Don't believe I've seen you in town before."

"You haven't. I'm Miss Sophie Biddle and this, by the way, is Caira. I'll be working for Mrs. Fairgrave."

"Isaac Neuberger here. Welcome to Stone Creek, Miss Biddle."

Sophie absorbed the warmth of the potbelly stove, preparing to brave winter's harsh winds. She took her daughter's bonnet and feed sack coat from her to put it over the back of the chair. The humble garment was all she could afford. Caira ran and patted the front of the glass display case again with her pudgy little hands. "Buttons!"

"No, no, sweetheart." Sophie shook her head and grasped at a chubby arm before she had a chance to sit.

"No, Soffie!" Caira giggled and scampered out of her reach.

Hearing Caira call her by her Christian name broke her heart, but what else could be done? The bell over the door rang, interrupting her melancholy thoughts.

"'Mornin', Reverend McCormick. That sheet music you ordered came in yesterday." Mr. Neuburger placed his pencil behind his ear.

"Just the good news I was hoping for." A tall man with wavy black hair strode toward the counter. His black wool overcoat fit across his broad shoulders, the rest cut rather narrow, fitting his wiry frame. Caira tumbled over an uneven floorboard and clutched the leg of his trousers to break her fall. The toddler stepped on his shoe in her clumsy attempt to right herself.

"Oh no," Sophie moaned. "I'm so sorry, Mister . . . er . . . Reverend." She sprang toward her child but not before the stranger had a chance to bend down to help Caira up as she let out a sob.

"Are you all right, little one?" The man got down on one knee as he examined the hand Caira held up. He brushed it off.

"Just a bit of dirt, no scrape." He gave the child a tender smile.

Sophie couldn't help but be impressed at this stranger showing such gentleness to Caira. Of course, it didn't hurt that he was handsome, too.

Reverend McCormick glanced up at her. Time slowed for a moment. "I take it she's your . . . "

She scooped Caira up into her arms. "She's my . . . sister." She bit her lip and looked away. "Come on, sweetie, you must stay by me." Her child's bottom lip quivered, and she buried her face in Sophie's shoulder. "You'll be all right. The nice man said so." She bounced the toddler a bit.

Reverend McCormick stood and seemed to study them both. "An adorable child. You can certainly tell you're related to one another."

Mr. Neuberger cleared his throat. "Reverend Ian McCormick, let me have the pleasure of introducing our latest addition to Stone Creek. This here is Miss Sophie Biddle and her little sister, Caira."

"Practically twins if there wasn't such an age difference." The minister chuckled at his own humor.

"That's a fact." The storekeeper grinned, propping his large frame with his elbows, square on the counter.

Sophie looked down at the chestnut curls that were so much like her own and the pink, freckled cheeks. Fiery warmth crept over her face. Sophie knew that despite the sixteen-year difference between their ages, she looked younger than her eighteen years, but it didn't help her feel any better about the deception. It wasn't how she'd been brought up to behave. "Excuse me, I best get my package and go. Thank you for letting us warm up a bit, Mr. Neuberger."

"No problem, Miss Biddle." The name she'd assumed on leaving her home still sounded strange to her ear.

"Could you please point us in the direction of Fairgrave's Boardinghouse?" Sophie turned to pick up the feed sack coat from the back of a chair and put it around Caira's shoulders. She pulled her own tattered shawl to cover the top of her head and tied a knitted bonnet onto the squirming toddler.

"Don't you have a bit of a walk?" The minister stood between her and the door. "It's getting worse out there."

Sophie glanced over her shoulder, catching the worried look in Reverend McCormick's eyes.

She felt her lips curl into half a grin. "I'm used to it." She raised her chin toward him.

"But what about the baby? Please, let me give you a ride in my buggy. There's not much protection from harsh weather, but I have a quilt. You both look tired." He beckoned them toward the door.

Sophie stiffened. What was she to this minister? She'd never even visited his church. She didn't need to be fathered or made to feel like some lost sheep. She'd already said enough and couldn't afford anyone poking around—even with the best of intentions.

She took a deep breath as she stepped toward the door but met his glance one more time before she pushed past him. Did she detect genuine concern in his plaintive expression? Maybe she was being a bit hard on the stranger. After all, how long had it been since Sophie had seen such sincerity in a man . . . in anybody? The store owner had been kind, but she was a customer.

Sophie glanced down at the child in her arms and then out the window at the swirling snow. Caira had been a bit feverish the other day. And bone-wearying tiredness dragged Sophie down after hours of travel. Perhaps they should take him up on his offer. "Well then, for Caira's sake."

••●)———————— ● ————————(●••

Ian McCormick saw the work-worn redness of the young woman's hand as he helped her into the buggy. He tucked the package at her feet, lifted her bags into the conveyance and wrapped an old quilt his grandma had made around the pair. The young woman shivered, although something in her widening eyes told Ian that it wasn't all from the cold. After all, he was still a virtual stranger to her.

"I must apologize for my rudeness." He tipped his hat. "We've been properly introduced, but I neglected to mention my pleasure at making yours and Caira's acquaintance, Miss Biddle."

"We are . . ." She cleared her throat when she paused. "We are pleased to meet you, as well." Miss Biddle gave him that slight, crooked grin Ian had noticed in the store. The frightened look in her large, amber eyes let up for just a moment. A wayward strand of chestnut hair blew free in a gust of wind. She tucked it back under the shawl.

The child snuggled against her big sister, popping a thumb in her mouth. She yawned.

"Now I think it would be proper for me to drive you home, don't you?" He went around to the other side and climbed to his seat. "To Fairgrave's Boardinghouse, then?" He waited in the silence.

Miss Biddle nodded. "Please."

"Have you been in town long? I don't believe I've seen you before." Another frigid blast of wind stung his face.

"I just arrived on the train today." Miss Biddle pulled the quilt tighter around herself and the child as though to shut out more than the cold, turning slightly toward the opposite side of the buggy.

"In that case, I'm sure you haven't visited Stone Creek Community Church yet." Silence ensued, broken only by the soft clomping of horse hooves in the fresh snowfall.

Cringing, the young woman finally answered, her voice was as frigid as the air. "No, Reverend, I've never been to Stone Creek before."

He looked sideways at her, but she turned her head farther away. Like a morning glory closing in the evening, Ian sensed her spirit closing to him. In his line of work, he'd seen the signs before. Whatever her hurt, he was sure it ran deep. "We'll have to fix that then. You're welcome to visit us any Sunday. Consider that a personal invitation."

There. He'd done his minister's job. He hoped he'd sounded more like a friend inviting her to supper than a condemning judge.

He cared to know the condition of her soul, but with someone like Sophie, Ian could tell he needed to tread softly.

"Anything special that brought you here? Do you have any kin?"

"Caira and I are the only family we have left. Mrs. Fairgrave and I will see if I work out as a maid at her boardinghouse. Sometimes I bring in sewing." She set her jaw. "It's honest work."

"Honest work it is," he said. Shivering, he thought the air must have dropped ten degrees in temperature, but then her weary expression seemed to soften.

The wheels strained through the snow and over the slick, frozen ground. Soon he'd have to get the sleigh out again. The February weather couldn't seem to decide what to do.

Glittering flakes landed on the young woman and her sister. Despite their tattered clothing, the pair was blanketed with diamond-like finery. He thought of Jesus teaching about the flowers of the field being better dressed than the wealthy Solomon. God's exquisite handiwork couldn't have shone better on two lovelier girls.

"Reverend McCormick." She bit her lip. "I was wondering what kind of music you bought today." She glanced up, and then her eyelids fluttered down with a shy look.

"Chopin—"

"Really?" Enthusiasm punctuated the question.

"And Beethoven. You enjoy music?" He noticed a sparkle kindling in her eyes.

"Enjoy it? Why, I love to play. Or I used to." Sophie grimaced, averting her gaze for a moment.

"Oh." What else could he say? She didn't look like she came from any affluence. Her declaration surprised him. How far had she fallen from her original circumstances?

"Beethoven, Chopin, Bach, I played them all." She stared as though looking into another world. "It's been awhile since I've been around a piano. A good one, anyway."

Their ride of several blocks length went too fast for Ian, despite the snow and wind slowing them.

"Here we are. Whoa." He pulled up on the reins.

"Oh . . . I see." The young woman sounded disappointed.

Could he blame her? He found the boardinghouse quite unattractive, but at least it was spotless inside and the proud Esther Fairgrave had a sterling reputation. The poor widow did what she could, but the paint was peeling, shingles lifted in the wind, and one of the shutters hung at an odd angle. He could send a crew of young men over from the church to fix things up . . . if only the widow would allow it.

"Wan get dow! Wan get dow!" Caira wiggled and strained toward the ground.

Ian stepped out of the buggy and took her from the young woman's arms. "There you go." He reached to assist Miss Biddle as well.

"I'm fine." Holding up the edges of her dress with one hand and grasping the side of the vehicle with the other, she all but recoiled from his extended hand. Her obvious distrust took Ian aback.

"Say thank you to Reverend McCormick." She patted her on the head as though nothing had happened.

"Tank oo 'Cowmick! Bye-bye." Caira waved, then hid in her sister's skirt.

"Feeling a bit shy, I see." He squatted to the child's level. "Good-bye, Caira. Be good for your big sister." He glanced up. The young woman averted her gaze.

When Ian took Sophie's carpetbag and sack from the buggy, she pulled the luggage from his hands. "I can handle them. Thank you for your kindness." Sophie's appreciation seemed genuine, despite her guarded manner. She took the hand of the little one with her free one. "Come along, Caira."

"You're welcome, Miss Biddle." He tipped his hat. "Let me know if you need any help at all." Ian watched them walk toward the front door before he could pull himself away.

Miss Biddle was obviously an educated girl, winsome regardless of her circumstances, which seemed to have been reduced to not much more than a beggar . . . a conundrum if there ever was one.

• • •)———————— ● ————————(• • •

The door creaked open before Sophie could even knock. "You must be the Biddle girls!" A plump matron with a fringe of gray curls and warm chocolate eyes took her bags. "I'm sure you'll need to freshen up a bit and then I'll show you the lay of the land. I'm just so pleased to find help this time of year."

"I was so grateful to find your ad, Mrs.—"

"Call me Esther, please! We are family here." She took Sophie by the arm. "Come along to the kitchen and then I'll show you to your room."

Caira stomped the snow from her shoes like she had been taught.

"Good girl." Sophie stamped her own feet on the worn mat.

Esther led them to the cozy kitchen. "Go ahead. Take your wraps off and hang them on those hooks over there." She pointed to the wall, next to the outside door on the back of the house. "You can leave your shoes here," she said, gesturing toward a braided rug.

After unbuttoning their shoes and slipping them off, Sophie placed them on the mat by the coal stove. Taking a look around, she surveyed the tidy room, painted a peeling, faded yellow. Pots and pans were stacked on open shelves. The smooth butcher-block counter was wiped clean. Peeking out from under a faded towel, a white and blue stoneware bowl sat on a corner table, holding bread dough, the yeasty scent wafting on the air. Judging from the pine floorboards, which had been worn smooth through the years, the house had truly been a well-used home.

Sophie enjoyed the warmth pouring from the cast iron stove. Esther had busied herself with replenishing fuel as she shoveled some of the black chunks from the bucket into the flickering fire.

If this was going to be Sophie's "home" and place of employment, she thought she might as well start acting useful. "May I help you stoke the fire?"

"No, no. You just warm your hands up here, and I'll be back in a few minutes." Esther grinned before she turned to waddle through the kitchen doorway.

"Thank you." Sophie held them toward the stove. Funny thing, did she imagine the hand Reverend McCormick had taken when helping her into the buggy needed no warming like its companion? Indeed, the image of his gaze, green-blue as a lake in summer, banished winter's chill. It somehow had breached the wall she had carefully built to protect herself and Caira.

Tall and lean, his strong frame was intimidating at first sight. Then he bent to care for the little one, and Sophie's heart had begun to melt. If she had a weakness, it was her daughter.

Sophie hung up their wraps, busying herself so that she could forget the handsome man. Maybe the minister had slipped so easily past her defenses because of her longing for acceptance. But what if he could see the ugliness that had caused her pain, though a sin not of her choosing? Would he so readily have invited her to the church without condemnation?

Perhaps he was just a good pastor looking for another member for his congregation. And when he locked gazes with her in the general store, he was looking for the condition of her soul, not the heart that nearly stilled within her chest. Besides, he was probably ten years her senior. He couldn't possibly view her as more than a child. Not that she really wanted him to. Did she? Of course not!

Caira's clothing, wet and cold from the snow, pressed against her as her daughter clung to Sophie's skirt and whimpered, drawing Sophie from her puzzling thoughts. She had to think of the baby first and foremost. Caira was the reason Sophie plodded forward through the icy winds of life.

"Don't fuss, Caira. We'll have you dry in no time." She peeled the damp dress from the child and then hung the garment on the line over the stove. The child's name, mistakenly given, again evoked sorrow in Sophie.

She wrapped a blanket around Caira, in her simple wool slip, pulled her onto her lap, and placed a kiss on her head.

The child clapped. "B! B!" she said.

"You want to play patty-cake, sweetheart? Alright." She recited the rhyme, much to Caira's pleasure, until her daughter began yawning.

Esther burst back into the kitchen. "Time for a nap, isn't it?" Not waiting for an answer, the older woman bustled toward the staircase. "Let's get you and the little one settled in your room." Sophie carried her daughter up the creaking stairs while following Esther Fairgrave.

"I'll be calling you for dinner in a bit, dearie," Esther said, all matter-of-fact.

"Thank you." Sophie entered the chamber with Caira in her arms, sat on the bed, and rocked her until she heard the even breathing of sleep. She eased the little girl down onto the threadbare sheets after peeling back the faded quilt, then covered her.

The toddler's eyes flickered open. For a moment, Sophie saw the deep gray of them, the one thing Caira had gotten from her scoundrel of a father.

Sophie shut the door, leaning back against this barrier between her and the world. At the memories, the usual reaction caught up with her in the quiet of the moment. Her heart still pounded at the very thought of being touched by a man, even a kind one like the reverend. Yet, a part of her had not found it as disgusting as usual. Raw fear clashed with an entirely different sensation until she felt dizzy and faint. She closed her eyes, forcing long, even breaths until the turmoil stopped. In the quietness, Sophie realized that she and the baby had some protection in the weather-beaten old house.

She watched Caira's chest rise and fall with each drawn breath. She brushed back the curls falling across her child's forehead. How peaceful she looked. They did not have much, the two of them, but she could not bear the thought of giving her up.

The peacefulness of that dingy room was far from how the little one had come into being. Sophie had sworn never to become vulnerable enough to trust a man again. Granted, Ian McCormick was a minister, but he was still a man.

She trembled with a chill, not from her damp skirt alone. No, indeed, she didn't need such attention. Undoubtedly, Reverend McCormick was motivated by brotherly pity when it came to someone like herself. Schoolgirl crushes were a thing of her past. She'd matured. Sophie knew the difference between the hollow warmth and embarrassment a girl might feel on seeing a handsome, charming man and the truth of being in love. At least, she hoped that the emptiness and betrayal that had come from allowing infatuation to blossom had taught her a lesson.

To Sophie, the true love of a man and a woman had to be the stuff of novels. She sighed. Although Nana and Grandpa Morton had that kind of love once, too. She saw it every time Grandpa had hobbled into their parlor, supported by his cane. His and Nana's eyes still sparkled when their gazes met. She smiled at the thought . . . until she remembered that she had been ruined for the possibility of ever having it herself.

No, Sophie would feel safer within the walls of Fairgrave's Boardinghouse, going about her business and not letting any man get too close. Finding and opening her carpetbag, she looked for her everyday brown skirt.

"Yoo-hoo! Sophie!" Esther's voice floated up the stairs. "Would you like to warm up with some tea?"

Caira stirred. Sophie patted her daughter, hoping the child's nap wouldn't be interrupted. Quickly changing her clothes, slipping through the door, and closing it, Sophie flinched at the squeak of the hinges.

"You'll find we've got lots of work to do here." Mrs. Fairgrave puffed as she trudged up the stairs with a pail of water for the large pitcher on the washstand in the hall.

"Let me help you." Sophie put a finger to her mouth, hoping her employer would take the hint. She steadied the pitcher for the heavyset woman.

"I'll peel the taters to go with the stew meat. Then I'll set some water on to boil so you can have a cup of tea and tell me all about yourself while our little gal is sleeping."

"There's not much to tell, but the tea sounds lovely, and I would be happy to peel the potatoes for you." Sophie nodded and then descended the stairway to the first floor.

In the kitchen, at the back of the house, she searched for a paring knife so she could set to working while Mrs. Fairgrave hummed and pumped water into a kettle.

"Looking for a knife? Here you go, dear. I set the potatoes out on the countertop."

Sophie nodded her thanks and smiled, taking the utensil. Outside the window, in the backyard, the blanket of snow thickened, glimmering in the slanting rays of sunlight.

Snowflakes drifted with sparkling perfection onto the white covering below. They appeared clean and pure, but Sophie felt defiled—and unworthy. Each time she told someone Caira was her sister, unworthiness flooded her soul anew, but she would do anything to preserve her daughter's reputation. How could it be that such a precious gift had come from such a vile act?

Yet, they had to keep going. Sophie bit her lower lip and blinked against the clouding of her eyes. Having just arrived, she couldn't let Mrs. Fairgrave find her like this. There would be lots to do before the day ended, but Sophie didn't really mind. At least Caira and she would be warm and fed.

Sophie heard her new employer's lumbering gait as Esther made her way down the stairs and entered the kitchen. "Well, now, perhaps you'd like to know something about us here at the boardinghouse." Esther grabbed a pot from a lower shelf and placed it on the table. "Mr. Graemer is our eldest resident. You'll often find him napping in his favorite rocking chair.

"Mr. Edwin Spitzer is a traveling salesman. He stays here a few days a month. As long as I have extra room it will be fine. He prefers my home cooking to that of the hotel in town." Esther beamed as she told of Mr. Spitzer's comment. "Not everyone thinks that fancy cooking is better.

"Albert and Chet Johnson are newer around these parts. You won't see them much. They're gone dawn 'til after dark trying to start up a printing business. And then we have one other young man . . ."

As if on cue, a fellow not much older or taller than herself, Sophie judged, entered through the back door.

"Well, well, who is this?" He swept his derby off and bowed, raining clumps of snow on the kitchen floor. "James Cooper at your service."

"I'll have none of your flirting with my staff." Esther had one hand on her hip and brandished a wooden meat-tenderizing mallet in the other. "I'll have you out on your backside, I will."

James' mock pout seemed to irritate Esther all the more. "Furthermore, I'll have a letter off to your aunt, in no time, telling her why. There'll be no such nonsense here. I run a respectable establishment. Now clean up after yourself."

"Yes, ma'am, of course." James took off his gray topcoat and hung it on a peg.

"This one," Esther continued as though she'd not been interrupted and James were invisible, "fancies himself a journalist. He's a copywriter at our local newspaper, the Stone Creek Daily Herald."

Sophie turned and nodded toward him. "I'm Sophie Biddle. Pleased to meet you."

"Likewise, Miss Biddle." James took a towel from the sideboard and began to wipe up his mess from the floor, looking rather contrite.

Sophie returned to peeling potatoes but stole a glance at him over her shoulder. James smiled. She reciprocated with half a grin. His laughing brown eyes reminded her of Paul, her brother. Something about James gave her that same co-conspiratorial camaraderie she once had with Paul. She missed him more than she'd realized. Then again, she didn't have time to indulge the emotions that fought within her regarding her family. She pressed on for her daughter's sake.

"Not my new towel!" Esther's hands went up in defeat.

Sophie tried harder to suppress a giggle.

"I'm very sorry, ma'am." James held the dirt-streaked towel out to her.

"The damage is done now." Esther sighed deeply. "Go wash your hands, so you're ready for supper." The corners of Esther's mouth twitched upward as James left the kitchen. "He's my best friend's nephew. She raised him from a tadpole. And when the job opened up at our little paper, I told her I'd watch out for him if he got hired." Esther pounded the tenderizing mallet into the stew meat. "He needs to grow up a bit. Then hopefully he'll meet a nice girl."

Sophie's neck itched. She scrunched up her shoulder, not liking where the conversation headed. "Well, what a good thing he has you to look out for him."

•••)——————— • ———————(•••

Ian came in through the back door of the parsonage, glancing at the two packages he carried under his arm. In her hurry to escape his company, Miss Biddle had left her purchases in his buggy. He'd been so taken with his new acquaintance, he hadn't noticed until he'd arrived home.

"What's in the extra package? I didn't ask you to shop for anything. I thought you were just picking up sheet music today." His sister, Maggie, sniffed, standing with hands on her hips.

Ian took no offense at her scolding tone. Maggie usually said what was on her mind, but had a heart of pure gold.

"No, I took Esther Fairgrave's new employee home. She happened to leave her bundle in the buggy."

"You shouldn't have been traipsing around in weather like this. Let them walk. I can't stand the thought of your getting a deep cough again—or heaven forbid, losing you to pneumonia, like . . ." She paused. "Like I lost Robert."

Maggie's protectiveness touched Ian when he wasn't annoyed by it.

"I thought, dear sister, that when we decided to move you here, we agreed that I didn't need another mother. God rest her soul."

"That's right. You need a wife."

"In due time. I've woman enough to deal with at the moment." Still very much the younger brother, Ian enjoyed teasing her.

Maggie's anger dissipated. "I guess I have been rather shrewish lately. I'm sorry." Her expression grew melancholy. "I know I haven't been the same since I don't have Robert to nag anymore. And at six, Philip doesn't listen to me, anyway."

"Maybe you shouldn't nag either of us." He grinned, raising one eyebrow at her. "Hmm?"

Maggie crossed her arms, frowning at Ian's gentle jibe. The sad, faraway look disappeared. "I suppose if you put it that way, I ought to have already learned my lesson living with nothing but stubborn men."

He brushed the snow off his hat and coat before Maggie hung them up.

"I do need to get these back to the young lady." He held up Sophie's package.

"You can't go out again in this weather. Stay home and have some soup with Philip and me until the snow subsides."

He rubbed the side of his face thoughtfully. His stomach rumbled at the tempting aroma of onions and potatoes. It sounded much more practical than hitching up the horses to the sleigh and losing his way in a near blizzard.

"All right, then," said Ian.

"I'm eager to think Philip will be home in time to eat with us. In this weather, I'm expecting his teacher will dismiss early."

"Let's hope so."

Ian made his way to the upright piano in the parlor. He pulled the music from its wrapping and placed the sheets of Chopin on the rack.

The piece was new to him, but he attempted to bring the notes on the page to life. Ian liked to joke that God had made him a rather poor musician so that he would hear the call to preach. He loved music and had a bit of talent, but he would never have graced the concert halls of Europe or New York City.

The melancholy melody brought up the image of Sophie Biddle in his mind with her ivory complexion, tinged with pink. Dark circles gave her amber eyes a haunted look, as though sad stories were buried in her heart.

And what of the girl's sister? Such a heavy burden for a young woman to bear alone! Where were their parents? Had there been other brothers and sisters?

His fingers crossing in a clumsy tangle, Ian began again in frustration, trying to pour all his concentration into the music. He didn't need to get involved in the life of a young woman who wasn't interested in his help. The job of preacher came with enough complications already. Plus, he had plans, important things to accomplish for the Lord.

Maybe he should tell the Stone Creek Ladies' Aid Society about the bedraggled pair. Yet, even as he considered this, Ian knew within that Miss Biddle wouldn't be dismissed so easily. The silent plea in her eyes dredged up emotions he thought he'd long buried. With a groan, Ian banged on the ivory keys and then laid his head on his arms. *Annie.* He'd seen the same look on her face before.

"What's wrong?" Maggie placed a hand on his shoulder.

Ian looked up at his older sister, not wanting to speak of the plaguing thoughts of failure. He could barely swallow. She had enough to worry about as a widow raising a son. Besides, even if he wanted to vent his anguish, the stinging, sharp blade in his throat would not allow it.

Where would he begin, anyway? He hadn't told Maggie the whole story. "I'll be fine, Maggie, really." He managed to croak out that much anyway.

"Very well, then. How about if I make you something warm to drink. Tea? Cocoa? Besides, I want to hear about the kind of gal Esther managed to rope into helping take care of that bunch of fellows in her house."

"I suppose we could both use some lighter conversation." He forced a smile. No reason to dwell on the past when the present held a more pleasant subject.

CHAPTER 2

The snow-cushioned clip-clop of the horse's hooves and the tinkling of sleigh bells created a winter melody as Ian drove the sleigh toward the boardinghouse the following morning. He'd thought he felt a spool or two of thread through the brown paper wrapping of Miss Biddle's package and wanted to get them to her as soon as he could. Since she was a seamstress, they were surely vital to her livelihood.

Besides, returning the package gave him an excuse to see what else he could find out about the two sisters. The cold air stung like eucalyptus oil vapors Maggie made sure he inhaled when he'd had a cough, yet the wind opened his lungs and refreshed him. Even Maggie's scolding would not keep him inside. He wrapped the scarf closer around his chin. Snow blanketed the ground and adorned the trees. Sun strained through the dull, gray clouds, sending thin shafts of golden light onto the glistening snow like God raining down His blessings.

•••)——————— ● ———————(•••

Sophie cleaned the cast iron bacon skillet while Caira sat on the kitchen floor banging a wooden spoon on a dented pot. "Shush.

Not so loud, honey, Mrs. Fairgrave has a headache." Sophie bent, placing a finger over her mouth.

"Sh." The little one repeated and put her finger to her lips.

"Here, let's stir instead." Sophie pulled a wooden bowl off the shelf. "We'll mix up batter for pancakes." She poured in an imaginary cup of flour, stirred and pretended to taste the concoction. "Mm." She handed her daughter the bowl.

"Mm." Caira imitated her mother again and giggled.

"There you go." Sophie couldn't hide a smile or even pretend to be cross when her daughter played joyfully on the floor next to her. They would clean up the strewn utensils later. Her mother had always commented on how she had grown up "in the blinking of an eye." Sophie had begun to understand her mother's lament. Though their life wasn't easy, she determined that she would enjoy Caira's childhood, especially since she would likely be an only child.

A few chips of paint scattered the sideboard. Sophie glanced up. Paint peeled from the ceiling as well as the walls. She would have to make sure none got into the food. Shaking her head, she swept the paint pieces from the sideboard into her hand and disposed of them in the wastebasket.

"You must have our little gal stop jingling bells or whatever she's doing!" Mrs. Fairgrave said from where she lay on the chaise. "And bring me some headache powder in a glass of water, please." She groaned.

"What?" Then Sophie heard it, a soft jingling that brought up memories of Christmases past, back home. She closed her eyes for a moment, savoring the cheerful sound.

"Sophie!"

"It's not Caira, ma'am. Someone's coming down the street in a sleigh." Sophie measured the powder and stirred it into a glass of water she'd poured from a full pitcher.

"What's next, an army coming through? I am going to rest in my room. I only hope you can handle everything."

"I'll be fine." Sophie assured her employer as she stepped into the parlor to hand her the remedy. She was amazed Mr. Graemer slept through the commotion in the midst of the parlor.

"Well, I'm already learning to rely on you since yesterday, my dear." The widow lumbered toward the stairs with the glass in her hand.

Sophie hurried to peek out from behind the yellowed lace parlor curtain. Reverend McCormick? His sleigh was gliding toward the boardinghouse. Unprepared for an unannounced caller, she sighed. Her neck and face warmed. Her silly nerves!

Reaching for stray strands of hair, she adjusted her hairpins to catch them, hung up her apron, and smoothed her dress. After all, he was an important person in the town. Of course, she would want to look presentable. "A justifiable reason," Sophie whispered in argument with herself.

More important, Esther would want her to make sure the parlor looked presentable. Sophie pulled a sock she'd been mending from the walnut end table cornered between the horsehair sofa and chair, plopping it in the basket under the table. She straightened the faded quilts covering the backs of the furniture.

She stole a glance at ancient Mr. Graemer, who snored through his morning nap in the rocking chair. At least she and the minister would not be alone. The thought soothed the less savory reactions that reared to counter the uncharacteristic flutter in Sophie's stomach.

Caira came toddling after her mama, dusted with white specks.

"Oh, how did you get into the flour? I took my eyes off you for just a moment!" Sophie tried to brush her off while the child had the pleasure of placing a white handprint on her skirt.

When a brisk knock sounded on the front door, Mr. Graemer jumped. "Look out for Stonewall Jackson!" After he yelled out, he slumped back into the rocking chair, which creaked with the movement. The cry startled Sophie though Esther had warned her.

Mr. Graemer's sharing of his dreams about the War Between the States was legendary.

Sophie opened the door, her gaze meeting the summer-warm one of her visitor. A gust of wind blew the door from her grasp, yet she barely felt it. "Reverend McCormick, what brings you here?"

He stared at her, his eyebrows furrowed with seeming bewilderment. "You look busy. I don't mean to interrupt."

"'Cowmick!" Caira dropped the ladle she had filled with flour and ran toward them.

"So that's how you got so messy!" Sophie picked her up, and the baby flirted with the minister from the safety of her mother's shoulder. "I'm so sorry about this mess. Would you like a cup of coffee, Reverend?" She forced a tight-lipped smile despite her irritation. Could he have stopped by at a more inconvenient time?

"Though I'd like to take you up on the offer, I'm not sure that this is the opportune time. But I did want to bring you your package."

Sophie received the parcel in brown paper wrapping from him with her free hand.

"You shouldn't have gone to all this trouble. I figured that I would pick my sewing things up next time I went to that end of town." With arms full, Sophie twitched her nose, hoping to prevent a sneeze. "I'm afraid I'm twice obliged to you, now. Thank you."

Reverend McCormick didn't smile, yet his eyes brightened with merriment. "Think nothing of it."

"How can we repay you?"

"Well, actually." He rubbed the side of his face. "I have some mending to be done." He held out a waistcoat that hung over his arm. "I'm afraid I have some buttons missing and a rip here." He showed her where the seam had come apart. "If I ask Maggie to fix it again, there'll be no end to her tongue-lashing for being so hard on my clothes. She mended this very waistcoat not that long ago."

Maggie? Why had she assumed that the minister was a bachelor? Of course, that should mean nothing to her, so why did her stomach feel heavy at the thought? "But if your wife found out someone else was doing your mending, Reverend, she might not approve." Sophie didn't need rumors of her and Reverend McCormick carrying on. No, nothing should draw that kind of attention to her and Caira.

"What? Nothing like that." He put his hand up. Was he trying not to laugh? "Maggie's my sister. She came to keep house for me after her husband passed away a year ago."

"I think I can help you then." Sophie reached for the garment. That strange, merciless flutter returned. "Are you quite positive you wouldn't like to warm up with a cup of coffee?" She knew Esther would expect her to show hospitality.

"Thank you, but I should take my leave. Your hands seem quite full right now."

Mr. Graemer let out a loud snore, and Reverend McCormick whispered, "I guess I don't need to invite you to hear that during the church service."

"He falls asleep during church?"

The minister fished out his pocket watch. "Perhaps it's his usual naptime." He grinned. "Of course, someone usually wakes him up when he starts fighting the whole lot of the Confederate army."

Sophie failed to contain her chuckle.

"He keeps the rest of the congregation awake during some of my longer sermons."

"Oh, I can't imagine you'd be that boring." Her candid thought slipped out before she could keep from saying it. Sophie bit her lip. She couldn't afford to get involved with a group of people who might pry into her past. The last thing Sophie intended was to sound interested in attending his church. However, she didn't want to offend him, either. Perhaps there was a better way she could have said it, but the Reverend's presence unnerved her. He was well groomed, refined, and highly educated, the kind of young man who used to be in her social circle. Her lower status no longer warranted being courted by such company.

"Perhaps you should visit one Sunday and see for yourself."

"We'll see." Sophie averted her gaze for a moment, not wanting to hurt the kind minister's feelings, but she had no intention of opening herself to the scrutiny a congregation always seemed to invite. "I'll get this back to you as soon as I can." She held out his waistcoat, draped over one arm.

"All right. Good day, Miss Biddle." His eyes twinkled as he tipped his hat and left.

She would have to see him again when she returned his mending. How long could she avoid a visit to the church?

••●)———————— ● ————————(●••

Two weeks later on a Sunday morning, Sophie had hoped to send the mended waistcoat to Reverend McCormick with Esther, but she had yet to find some matching buttons for the garment. Becoming familiarized with the routine of how the boardinghouse ran consumed most of her time.

She claimed not to feel well, which was partially true. Her headache pounded harder each moment she thought of the inevitable. Attending church would lend to a picture of good character, but only if she could keep everyone at a distance. Yet, to avoid attendance at the services indefinitely would impede her from developing a sterling reputation.

Sophie's list of excuses grew more pathetic each week. The previous Sunday, Caira had seemed a bit feverish. Esther Fairgrave protested with concern and offered help. How long would it be before she suspected that Sophie might be less than a good Christian?

"Come, Caira, it's time for our Bible story." Sophie read Psalm 23 aloud. The six verses were short enough for her daughter's attention span. "You're like one of his little lambs, you know."

"Baa."

"That's right, that's what the little lambs say."

Being raised in a Christian home had left an indelible mark on Sophie's soul. She intended that Caira would be instructed in the ways of the Bible. She also realized that her resources were limited. Eventually, her daughter would need more in-depth instruction, from people who could provide a better example. If she could just raise her right, perhaps someday God would bless Caira with what Sophie had missed out on. Then maybe He would forgive Sophie for this ruse that hurt her down to the heart.

"Let's sing now." She attempted to teach Caira, "Jesus Loves Me, This I Know." Then the tune of "Jesu, Joy of Man's Desiring" came to mind. She hummed a few bars and sang the words she remembered.

"You know what? We're going to bring that old pianoforte to life with some music. Come over here."

"Pano!" The little one shared her love for hearing the piano played.

Sophie sat Caira next to her on the creaking, scratched bench. She picked out the tune from memory, but each time she hit a chipped ivory key, a tinny sound emanated from the damaged keyboard or, worse yet, silence. The musical instrument was as worn out and forsaken as the rest of the parlor. With one look around she took in the faded Persian rug and flowered wallpaper. Quilts had been arranged over the horsehair chair and couch to cover their threadbare spots. Twenty years ago the room had probably been at the height of elegance.

"We'll make our own music then." Sophie took the toddler into her arms and spun around the room, humming the grand hymn. She closed her eyes for a moment to imagine she stood in the midst of a lovely, large church, where the congregants smiled, welcomed them, and asked no questions.

Sitting down as dizziness overtook her, Sophie clasped Caira in a hug and placed her cheek on her baby's soft hair. She shut her eyes again. Tears squeezed out, rolling down her cheeks. Once Sophie had been part of a church family where she'd been loved and accepted, but that was before the incident. Since then, church had been a place of shunning of her soul, which they assumed was leprous. Sophie longed to be able to go to church again but did God want her and her falsehoods, no matter how necessary they seemed?

••◉)─────── ● ───────(◉••

Ian's hopes had thudded when the small group from the boardinghouse had entered the sanctuary, just before the service started. They sat near the back, but he didn't see Sophie and her young charge among them.

At the end of the service, he hoped to get Mrs. Fairgrave's attention. He caught a glimpse of her waddling toward him as he stood by the door, with Mr. Graemer holding fast to her arm. Ian would have to be patient as he shook hands with everyone coming through.

Ian had a different view from the entrance than from the pulpit, upon the raised platform. He could survey the congregation from the front, where some looked at him with expectant eyes as though he spoke the very words of God to them, though he were a fallible vehicle. Others looked distant, checking their pocket watches, enduring until they could move to the next task that day. And others, like dear Mr. Graemer, simply had trouble keeping their eyes open that long. There was such responsibility in getting to know his current flock! Leaving his last situation behind, he planned to make the best of his fresh start. Even after a year, much still seemed new to him.

As he waited to receive those who stopped to shake his hand and comment, Ian liked blending in on their level and seeing them face-to-face, individually. He wondered if, up close, they found him ordinary. After all, he really was a servant sent there by the Lord, to help, to teach, and to guide. If anything, he was beholden to God and to them.

"Fine sermon this morning." Mrs. Myles put out a dainty, gloved hand.

"Why, thank you. And how is your husband feeling?"

"Oh, gout has him down. I'm hoping he's well enough to come with me next week."

"Tell Asa I continue praying for him and that he's missed." Ian held onto her hand tightly for a moment. "I hope he'll be well enough for the next elder meeting."

"Thank you, I pray so, too." She gave him a slight smile. "Come visit us soon." She left looking burdened.

Ian thought of the best time to visit them over the next week. He suspected that more than gout kept Asa Myles away, since the couple greatly mourned the accidental deaths of their daughter and son-in-law, when their carriage had overturned alongside a road coming back from the city. What a blessing that their granddaughter had been staying with her grandparents at the time! The little girl would receive no greater love and would be cared for with the best resources, which the Myles family could afford. Though the wounds of their grief remained deep, Elise's presence was very healing for them.

Several other families, couples, a few widows and widowers stopped to greet him. When expressions of joy replaced the usual exhaustion and grief in their faces, he was glad to have been a comfort. In the year since Ian had become their pastor, his love had grown for his small-town flock. He felt for each one in their hardships and trials.

Only the Good Shepherd possessed limitless power to heal the brokenhearted, ready to care for their needs. As their earthly shepherd, Ian offered what he could. He pondered on the probable needs of his congregation and the earthly resources he could find to help and comfort.

"Yoo-hoo! Pastor! I brought you one of my pies—made with dried apples and plenty of cinnamon. Thought you would enjoy it with Sunday dinner. I know how your nephew loves my pie, too." Esther Fairgrave held a covered basket toward him.

"Yes, he does. I'll probably have to wrestle Philip down for the last piece."

Only Esther's pies rivaled Maggie's. Though he had to give much, as a pastor, Ian received much in return. Even those who had little, like Esther, found ways to make him feel more at home, part of the church's family.

"I must confess that Sophie actually used my recipe to make this pie, and she is learning quickly."

"Ah, yes." Ian took the basket from her and then gave her hand a squeeze. "And how are Sophie and her little sister doing?"

"I urged them to come with us, but last week Caira was feverish. Today, the older one didn't feel well enough. I think maybe Sophie is a bit shy." She shook her head. "You'd think a pretty young lady like that would want to get out and socialize. Oh well, I'll keep trying."

"I understand. Please give her my regards."

Ian turned to the elderly gentleman with Esther. "It's good to see you, Mr. Graemer. How are you today?" he shouted toward his good ear.

"Just fine, young man. These ears don't work the way they used to. Being anywhere near the cannons at Gettysburg didn't help."

"I'm sure it didn't, but we appreciate the contribution you made to the war effort."

Mr. Graemer nodded back, but Ian was pretty sure he didn't hear a thing.

He watched as the last of his congregation left him in the quietness of the sanctuary. Lifting the napkin covering the basket, Ian inhaled the scent of cinnamon and spied the flaky brown crust. To think that Sophie's small, work-worn hands had fashioned the delectable pastry. Something about the fact pleased him. He couldn't wait to taste a piece of the pie.

"Quiet today, wasn't it?" Maggie interrupted his thoughts.

Ian stroked his chin. "Come to think of it, yes it was."

"I'll tell you why." His sister adjusted her gloves. "Gertrude Wringer wasn't here."

The thought of the busybody with the shrill voice caused his neck muscles to contract in aching tightness. "But who else would run the Ladies' Aid Society or be more respected by the women?" Ian tried his best to find something good in each one of his parishioners.

"You mean feared." His sister's eyes narrowed.

"Now, Maggie, that's not very charitable."

"But it is true." His sister wore a smug grin. She turned on her heels. "Come along, Philip," she called to her son, "it's time to go home for dinner."

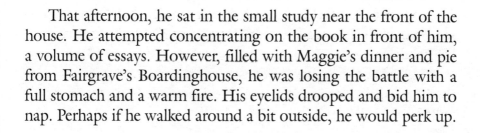

That afternoon, he sat in the small study near the front of the house. He attempted concentrating on the book in front of him, a volume of essays. However, filled with Maggie's dinner and pie from Fairgrave's Boardinghouse, he was losing the battle with a full stomach and a warm fire. His eyelids drooped and bid him to nap. Perhaps if he walked around a bit outside, he would perk up.

Ian shrugged into his waistcoat and opened the door to a blast of frigid air. He paced the length of the front porch, exhaling wisps of steam. The white coating the ground lacked the luster and sparkle of a fresh snowfall.

The squeak of the opening door got his attention. Maggie poked her head out. "Come, have a cup of tea with me. And I've got some snicker doodles I baked yesterday."

"You don't have to bribe me, you know."

"Well, I never knew a man who didn't like cookies." His sister stood with the door cracked open, looking rather hurt. She shrugged and put her hands in the air. "Besides, it's lonely in here. Philip's looking at books in his room."

"That's all you had to tell me." Ian took Maggie's arm and strolled into the dining room with her.

"Didn't want to be a burden." Her eyebrows furrowed.

"We may not see eye to eye on everything, but you're more help to me than you could possibly know. I need someone trustworthy to keep house for me. And having my sister here keeps the gossipers at bay."

"It doesn't keep them from trying to match you up." She brightened. "By the way, who were you looking for today?"

"What?" He looked straight into her eyes and lifted an eyebrow, purposely.

"Don't be coy with me, little brother." She looked down as she poured tea into the china cup in front of him. "I saw you searching that sanctuary and looking as forlorn as though you'd lost your best friend."

Maggie held out the plate of fragrant golden cookies like it was some kind of peace offering. "Now, 'fess up."

"No thank you." He glanced at the sugar bowl as he took out a single cube. "To both."

His sister sat there pouting.

"If you must know—"

"Yes?" She leaned toward the table and grinned.

He took a sip of the sweetened tea. "Young Sophie Biddle from the boardinghouse." The hot liquid slid over his tongue and warmed his throat.

"Oh," said Maggie, but it was a knowing, "oh."

"That's all? Have you heard anything more about her?" He pictured Sophie huddled by Neuburger's stove and then covered in flour with Caira in her arms.

"Not much. Just heard that she and her sister appeared in town recently, poor as church mice. Sophie responded to Esther's 'help wanted' ad. She had to be desperate to take what Esther could pay." Maggie stirred her own tea and then took a dainty bite from a snicker doodle.

"I guess you don't know any more than I do." Ian sighed.

She swallowed. "The child looks so much like her. Everyone's first guess is that Sophie is the baby's mother."

"My first assumption as well, but we have no reason to disbelieve her. Something unfortunate must have overcome her family. Miss Biddle seems well educated and genteel." Ian tapped his fingers on the table. "We have an obligation to help such people. She's trying to do her best, I'm sure."

"Yes." Maggie took her cup with both hands and blew into it before taking a sip. "You're right. The gossips of the town always want to make more out of everything than is there." The china cup clinked against its saucer. "You know I'll do what I can to help her. She's always welcome here."

He nodded. "I knew I could count on you."

••●)————— ● —————(●••

After the evening service, when it had long since grown dark, Ian stood by the study window. Weariness pressed on his shoulders as he leaned against the sill and stared at the front yard. Clouds blew overhead, and a sliver of moonlight shone on the blanket of crisp snow. Underneath, the world lay dormant and cold, as cold as the young Annie's skin had become when they had pulled her from the depths of the swirling river.

Ian had tried to tell others that the young girl needed more help weeks before, but it had been too late. He shivered at the horrific memory. He swallowed the bile down like the day they had found her.

"You look tired." Maggie turned the gaslight down and then touched his sleeve.

"I'm cold." He rubbed his chin. "And exhausted."

"Is that all? What are you thinking about?"

He looked her square in the eye and sighed. He couldn't even form the words as distasteful as they were.

"Not that again, Ian. You've got to let it go." She linked her hand with the crook of his arm.

"I could have done something about it, but I listened to people instead of God. And a young woman died because of it." He patted the hand on his arm. "I don't really expect you to understand." He closed his eyes for a moment, but that only served to make the chilling image clearer—the bluish-white skin, so void of life.

"You shouldn't blame yourself so much. Do you want to talk about it?"

"No!" He spun around and gripped her elbows until he saw fear in her eyes. "Don't you understand? You can't help." The haunting thoughts wouldn't let go.

"Ian, I-I only wanted to comfort you."

Did he see pity in Maggie's eyes? How little of a man must she think he was becoming?

"I'm so sorry. You didn't do anything wrong." He hugged Maggie tight and swallowed a sob, desperate to contain his emotions.

"I just hate to see you suffer like this," she said, sniffling.

There could be little comfort when Ian knew he had failed God and a member of his flock, a precious lamb entrusted to his care. Was he even worthy of such a task?

"I guess I never really told you why I left that church to come here. I wanted to be in a smaller town like Stone Creek, to start over." He paused. "And forget." It wasn't just another call. Ian also wanted to prove to himself that somehow he was truly capable of his charge.

"He that is in you is greater than he that is in the world." Maggie pulled away but held each of his hands firmly in hers. "Little brother . . ." She stared up at him with tears rolling down her cheeks. "You're already forgiven. Remember that."

Ian's jaw tightened. He could only force himself to nod. He knew in his heart that she spoke the truth, not chastising him as she often did, but with tenderness. When he managed to speak, all he could utter was, "Thank you."

Perhaps he had let Annie down, but never again. Maybe it was why God had sent Sophie and Caira Biddle to Ian. After all, God had proven throughout scripture to be the God of second chances.

CHAPTER 3

When Esther learned Sophie needed buttons a few days later, she gave her some from an old waistcoat of her dear departed husband. Sophie was grateful for a fine set of brass buttons to use, especially since they were for the Reverend McCormick. Now she could repay him more fully for his support. She polished the buttons until they shone and mended the rip with tiny even stitches, barely detectable to the naked eye. She was thankful that Esther had given her the afternoon off.

When finished, she pressed, folded, and then wrapped the garment in brown paper. Sophie's fingers shook, frustrating her attempt to tie a string around the package. The thought of speaking with tall, handsome gentlemen, several years her senior, seemed to affect her that way. . . but Reverend McCormick seemed kind. He didn't look or behave like the one who betrayed her. Was he truly worthy of her trust?

"Going somewhere?" James interrupted Sophie's thoughts.

"Oh! Good afternoon, Mr. Cooper. I'm getting ready to deliver a package to the parsonage."

"I'm going in that general direction. I'd be happy to walk with you as far as the corner of Bradford, near the parsonage."

"Why not?" At least she would be sure of where she was going with James to ask for specific directions.

After Sophie donned her shawl and helped Caira with her feed sack coat, they headed out the door. James lifted Caira into his arms.

"No, no. I'm quite capable of carrying her myself," Sophie insisted.

"At least let me be a gentleman and carry your package."

"Very well, then."

The two exchanged bundles, but not before Caira had made a grab at James' mustache. "What dat?"

"My mustache." The young man ran a thumb and forefinger over his thin, poorly grown whiskers as though he were quite proud of them.

"Sorry about that. Caira hasn't had an opportunity to be around men much without . . . a father around." Sophie shook her head. No doubt the sparse growth was James' attempt at appearing older and more businesslike. So much like her brother, Paul.

"No offense taken." He chuckled.

They continued their walk in silence for several minutes.

"Penny for your thoughts."

"I was just thinking of how much you remind me of . . . someone . . . I once knew." Sophie pressed her cheek against Caira's pink knitted bonnet. How sad that her daughter wouldn't have memories of a brother to have snowball fights with or race up and down the stairs. Half of her mother's headaches must have been caused by Sophie's confounding behavior, when all Mama wanted to do was make a young lady out of her.

"Hope it's a good person I remind you of. I can't tell by the sad look on your face, though." James didn't dawdle before he cut to the chase. Perhaps he would make an excellent journalist if he were given half a chance.

"Nothing to worry about."

The cloying, sweet, and woodsy aroma of pipe smoke wafted toward them. A man standing in front of Neuberger's puffed on a pipe stem. Caira wrinkled her nose, sniffing the air. He wore a dark overcoat and hat to match. Smoke clouded his face. Could it be *him*? *Caira's father*? The wind cut through Sophie's shawl. She shivered, closing her eyes, and held Caira as closely as possible.

Sophie opened her eyes. The cloud of smoke dissipated to reveal a man with a white beard. Exhaling with relief, Sophie realized she had stopped in her tracks, unable to move for a minute.

"Are you quite all right?" James stopped alongside her.

Caira pushed away. Sophie put her down, ignoring James for the moment as she started her journey again. The toddler took quick little steps to keep up with Sophie's stride as their feet crunched into the fresh icy snow. Flustered, she changed her mind. She grabbed her daughter into her arms, wanting to carry her and hold her close again though the little one pressed her arms against Sophie and fussed. "You don't have boots. Your feet will be soaked when we get there."

"Miss Biddle?" James frowned and kept up with her. He offered his elbow, but she sidestepped him.

"I'll be fine. I thought . . ." Sophie stopped. What could she tell him? Besides, if she never voiced her fears of Caira's father looking for them, perhaps they would go away. "Never mind." She picked up her pace and thought about how to change the subject. "Do you enjoy working at the newspaper?"

"A good investigative reporter would believe he's being diverted."

"Reporter? I thought you were just a copywriter!"

James puffed out his chest and stiffened his shoulders, no doubt attempting to repair his damaged pride. "I am a copywriter with aspirations. One has to start somewhere. Why, one of these days, I'll find a story that will make the front page of our town's Daily Herald. Don't you have dreams, Miss Biddle?"

"I'm afraid dreams are a luxury when you have a little sister to raise." Her voice cracked and she avoided looking directly into his face. "I have too many worries."

"What a pity. You're too young to stop dreaming." James halted, turning to face her.

Sophie hadn't been prepared for the pain caused by the reopening of her wound. Like a scab had been picked off to reveal an unhealed sore, memories long pushed down flooded into her mind. What had she wanted to do before Charles' actions had irrevocably changed her life? "I suppose I have one dream." She slanted a glance sideways at her walking companion. The fantasy came out of the necessity she felt for independence, for a living she could pass on to her daughter. "I'd like to have a dress shop."

"So you do have a few ambitions?" James raised an eyebrow at her.

"I suppose." But they were a far cry from her original dreams of husband, home, hearth, family, and continuing with her music.

James stopped walking. "You're quite fascinating, Miss Biddle. I almost missed your street."

"Perhaps you could point me in the right direction, then. I've never been to the parsonage."

"Certainly. Take Bradford Street left, here, and walk past the second corner. The house is on the left, as well. White picket fence. You can't miss the parsonage. It's just a couple down from the corner. Good day." James handed her the brown paper package and tipped his derby.

"Thank you. Same to you." Sophie turned onto Bradford, making her way down the quiet street. Was he kidding her? Several homes boasted white picket fences.

Funny how comfortably she conversed with James. Like Paul, he had much growing up to do. Talking about the weather or silly wishes was one thing, confiding in him was another thing altogether. Besides, if James aspired to become an investigative reporter, she needed to tread with care. He probably couldn't be completely trusted not to pry where he didn't belong. But while James' company was rather easygoing, Reverend McCormick's presence unnerved her altogether.

The wind picked up, howling through the tree branches above long enough to remind her that the world was a cold and lonely place without friends. Sophie shifted Caira's weight, attempting to balance the child and the package. Caira nodded off, laying her head on Sophie's shoulder and adding what felt like an extra five pounds to the burden. Her arms ached.

Sophie believed God existed, but would He help her when she kept up this deception? She carried her obligations alone. Continuing an acquaintance with Reverend McCormick, when she didn't know if he could be trusted, was stepping out in her dwindling faith.

Her heart palpitated as quickly as a hummingbird beats its wings. The thought of seeing the minister once more made her feel unsettled. Yet, how could she not look forward to his easy smile, as she recalled his kind way with her daughter?

More than ever, she needed a friend, but nothing more. Besides, Sophie must remember her place in society. She was no longer the privileged daughter of a wealthy family, but she didn't intend to hold her hand out for charity either. This was another reason to keep Reverend McCormick at arm's length. With Caira carried on one side and the package on her other, she made her way to the parsonage, following James' directions. No, she wouldn't take his charity.

"Soffie, wan' down!" Caira awoke, pounded on her mother's shoulder and pushed away.

"What did I say now?" Sophie scolded. "No." She held Caira all the tighter.

She sighed and looked at her little daughter. The child's brows knit together in a frown. Hearing Caira call her by her name, rather than Mama, once again squeezed her heart with grief, knowing she had no other choice.

The sin that had brought Caira into the world had not been her fault, yet it could mark her for life like the sore on a leper. If anyone thought that Sophie was actually her mother, how long would it be before they found out the whole truth? The deception cut into Sophie's heart. She had been brought up to be honest. She sighed, feeling more alone. Where was the Lord in all this? Why had He allowed Charles to hurt her that way? If the purpose was to bring the child into the world, couldn't there have been a better way? Her throat dried as she contemplated her loss and embarrassment.

In Greenville, the last town they had lived in, Sophie had confided in someone who turned out to be the town gossip. The woman had played an evil game, gaining her trust before she turned on her. Soon, everyone had spurned them both. Sophie blocked from her mind the names they had hurled at them.

Clouds parted for a few minutes, allowing a patch of blue to peek through like a promise of spring and with it, hope. Maybe, just maybe, Sophie's plan would work, and they could be part of a community this time.

The house two down from the second corner stood before them. The neat white clapboard sides of the cozy home shone brightly in comparison to the boardinghouse she had left behind. She spied the white picket fence and dormant rose bushes. Oh, what a lovely flower garden she could picture in bloom during the summer!

Sophie stopped at the end of the flagstone path. At that moment, her legs felt rubbery and heavy. Perhaps this wasn't such a good idea. She swallowed. Even in the cold, her palms began to sweat.

Maybe she could just set the package on the front porch by the door. Then they could leave quietly. Reverend McCormick would find his waistcoat and that would be the end of it. He could pay her later.

Sophie steeled her weak legs while the brisk wind pushed her farther up the walk. She really needed to brace herself against these silly feelings when she was only visiting the parsonage.

Treading as lightly a step as possible on the ice-covered wooden stoop, Sophie placed the bundle on the porch and turned to go.

Caira let out a scream at the worst moment. "Wan' it!" She reached for a sparkling icicle, pointing down from the overhang.

"No, Caira. It will freeze your little hands. After I knit you some new mittens, we'll find you one from the maple tree. It will be sweet like sugar. This one won't taste good."

Caira wiggled and reached again, making even more noise.

"Quiet down, you can't have everything you want." Sophie's voice rose above a whisper.

Hinges squeaked open behind her.

"What a fine set of lungs she has!"

Sophie swung around to find a pleasant-looking woman filled with mirth.

"I'm Maggie Galloway." The woman wiped her hands on her apron and held one out in dignified greeting.

Sophie supposed it was like shaking the hand of royalty; Maggie had done it so delicately.

"I'm Sophie Biddle and this is m-my sister, Caira." She coughed. "We're pleased to meet you."

Maggie captured her gaze with almost the same blue eyes that the reverend had, only a bit lighter and more playful. The woman had the loveliest deep auburn hair pulled back into a knot, with small curls framing her face. The emerald stripes in her cream shirtwaist and matching evergreen skirt flattered her coloring.

"And I'm most pleased to meet you, too. I see you have done some work for my brother." Maggie had already spotted the package.

"I, well, I—"

"Oh, don't worry, not much gets by me. Ian thinks he's getting away with something, but he's not."

Speechless, Sophie shrugged.

Maggie scooped up the brown paper bundle. "Won't you please come in? We're just about ready to have some dinner."

Caira squirmed in her arms and poked a thumb into her mouth.

"I really don't want to impose." Sophie shook her head.

"Not at all. Please come in and warm up. Your little one looks quite tired. I'll bet she's hungry too."

Would it be ruder to refuse? "Well, all right, if you insist."

"Of course, she insists!" Reverend McCormick appeared behind his sister. "And well she ought to. We don't make it a practice to leave anyone out in the cold."

Those lake-blue eyes twinkled, and Sophie's legs returned to their rubbery state, against her will.

She entered the modest kitchen, suddenly realizing what a heavy load Caira was. Relief came when she put her down on the dry floor.

With much fussing about, Maggie took Sophie's shawl and shoes, had her wrapped in a blanket and led her to sit near the parlor fire. "Let's get the chill out of your bones, and I'll find some blocks for Caira. Philip will be home soon and he'll play with your little sister. You look awfully tired."

Caira, oblivious to Maggie's plans, clapped her hands while she marched after "'Cowmick."

Sophie thawed by the fire, amused by Caira's antics. "Who is Philip?"

Reverend McCormick sat on the floor next to Caira piling wooden blocks to form a shaky structure. He looked up at Sophie for a moment. "Maggie's son." The little girl knocked the stack down with one swipe of her hand.

"You knocked my tower down," the minister said with mock surprise in his voice.

Caira giggled and they repeated the game until he could persuade her to help him build with the blocks.

"Won't Philip be bored with Caira?" Sophie thought she should try to make polite conversation with the pastor.

"He'll like having someone smaller around."

"Oh." She cleared her throat and smoothed her skirt.

Sophie lost track of time as she rocked with much contentedness by the fire. Maybe fifteen minutes had passed, or an hour, for all she knew by the magic of it. The sage green walls added to the calmness of the room. A lovely pastoral landscape with roaming sheep and a cottage down the road a distance hung above the clock on the mantelpiece. Enticing spices scented the air. Did she recognize cloves? Maggie sang in the dining room while she placed gleaming china plates on the table.

Realizing how busy Maggie was, Sophie jumped from the chair. "Maggie, don't you need some help?"

"You're my guest, and I'm guessing you have plenty to do at the boardinghouse."

"But—"

"Sophie, my brother should have gone to pick up his package from you. I won't have you and little Caira contracting pneumonia. The hem of your skirt and your shoes were soaked."

"Really, I am quite dry and warm now."

"Well, you may come fold these napkins and place the silverware, but then back to the fireside with you." Maggie smiled and beckoned her.

Maggie's table impressed her. Each white plate, covered with a blue oriental design, was smooth, without cracks. And each polished piece of silver matched the others. This contrasted greatly with Mrs. Fairgrave's hodge-podge collection. "Such beautiful dishes." They reminded Sophie of her childhood home.

"Thank you. I just love the Blue Willow pattern. They were given to me by my parents, for a wedding gift. Not a day goes by in which I don't remember them, may they rest in peace." Maggie sniffed.

After Sophie finished her little job, she returned to the rocking chair as her daughter seemed quite content. To be among such kind people was more than she deserved. She did feel like they were almost friends. The minister and his sister hadn't seemed to look suspiciously upon her but instead showed such graciousness. At the doorway, she had been apprehensive, but now she felt more relaxed.

Sophie wiped the fresh tears trickling down her cheeks with the back of her hand.

"Miss Biddle, are you quite well?" Reverend McCormick's brow furrowed with concern.

"I'll be fine." She could barely manage a whisper for the sobs she choked back. She swallowed hard. "I just miss our family sometimes." There was the truth. In this happy place, she missed the security of a loving family.

How many evenings had Sophie, her parents, and Paul sat by the fire reading aloud or singing together with their happy laughter ringing out at times? At the boardinghouse, people would come and go. Esther Fairgrave was very caring, but Sophie was nobody's daughter or sister, only hired help.

"I'm so sorry. How long have you been without them?"

A sob escaped with more tears. How had she allowed this display of emotions to happen? She shook her head.

"How careless of me, of course you don't want to talk of it now." Reverend McCormick placed a clean, folded handkerchief in her palm.

Sophie felt the warmth of his hand melt into hers from his gentle touch as though it were reaching for her heart.

"I'll leave you alone for as long as you need." He led Caira away by the hand. "Let's see what kind of help Maggie needs in the kitchen."

Sophie squeezed her eyes shut against the image while a thousand emotions vied for her attention. How sad. Reverend McCormick thought her family all dead and gone when she was the one all but dead to them. To see him cradle Caira's hand in his own was too much. Her child would never have a papa to love her in such a tender way.

Alone in the parlor, she heard that still small voice speak to her heart, something she had learned in childhood, a verse from the Psalms. *"He is a father to the fatherless."* Yes! That was it! Perhaps, even though she could never be good enough to marry someone like Ian McCormick, God was providing a father figure for her daughter.

For a long time, God had seemed so far away, but in this humble pastor's home, Sophie thought that the breath of the Lord's presence came a little nearer. She dried her tears. The commotion in the kitchen pulled her out of her reverie as she heard Maggie greet her son, Philip.

A few minutes later, everyone made their way toward the dining room table. Once grace had been said, Sophie nibbled at a warm biscuit spread with honey. "Delicious biscuits. Would you mind giving me your recipe?"

"I'd be happy to give it to you though Esther may have it in her box of recipes . . . somewhere." Maggie chuckled.

"Do I have to eat the peas?" Philip's face crinkled with disgust.

"If you want to grow tall and strong, yes. Besides, I didn't give you much. Eat them up." She tsked at her son.

"Yes, Mama." Philip's bottom lip went out, and he pushed the peas around in his potatoes as though hoping to hide them.

"Once again, you've outdone yourself with this tasty dinner, Maggie." A forkful of the smoky ham nearly hid Ian's grin.

Sophie had to smile as the creamy mashed potatoes almost melted on her tongue. Being with the pastor's little family nourished not just her body, but also her soul as the meal continued.

Once Caira had half eaten the food on her plate and squashed the rest, she rubbed her eyes and yawned. Sophie let her daughter down from her lap and untied the napkin from around the toddler's neck.

"May I be excused?" Philip wiped his mouth with a crisp linen napkin. "I'll play with Caira and show her some of my toys."

"That's a good boy now, but mind you don't be too rough. Remember, she's a lot smaller than you are." Maggie's stern look was a warning in itself. "And keep the marbles away from her. I don't want her to swallow anything."

"Yes, Mama." The little red-haired boy grinned and revealed a space missing a baby tooth.

"He's only six, but he thinks he's older. He's grown up more than a little boy should, since my husband died." Maggie sighed as she watched after her son.

"I'm so sorry." Sophie spoke barely above a whisper. She longed to say that she understood somewhat how such a loss might feel, yet the words wouldn't form.

"Well, it's been a whole year now. Nothing we can do about it, but accept it as the good Lord's will."

It grew quiet enough to hear the ticking of the mantel clock.

Reverend McCormick leaned back into his chair with both hands behind his neck. "How about some music?"

"Would you play something for us, Reverend McCormick?" Her heart did a little pitter-patter at the thought of hearing music once again. "That is, after I help Maggie clean up."

"Actually, I was hoping that you would do us the honor."

"Me?"

He sat up and folded his hands on the table. "I remember hearing someone say how they used to play the piano. I daresay that your landlady's pianoforte is hardly fit for Beethoven or Chopin. Sadly enough, that instrument has already seen better days."

Sophie couldn't contain the joy that bubbled up. Her fingers almost throbbed with the desire to touch a fine instrument again. She reached for the empty plates near her place and stacked them.

"You really don't have to, Miss Biddle. You're our special guest." Ian tugged at the back of her chair and pulled it away from the table when she allowed him.

"But the sooner Maggie's done, she can join us. I won't take 'no' for an answer." She raised an eyebrow at him.

"All right then." He lent a hand as well. A little while later, the last dish was dried and put back in place.

"Come, Miss Biddle, let me show you the piano I've been blessed with." Ian offered his arm. Sophie placed her hand in the crook of his elbow ever so lightly.

"I inherited it along with my sister."

"I think he only let Philip and me move in because we were bringing the piano." Maggie grinned.

"Well, I must say, it sweetened the deal."

The dark polished wood gleamed in the daylight that streamed through the parlor window. He pulled the seat out for her. She sat down and lifted the lid from ivory keys. Sophie had to touch them to see if they were real.

"It's a Bidershem piano, one of *the* best in the country." Reverend McCormick gestured toward it.

"Why yes." She nodded. "So it is." Her voice caught in her throat, and she looked away. Heat crept up her neck and spread to her cheeks. She wanted to hide, to fold up like sheet music and slip underneath the cumbersome instrument.

The piano loomed before her. The shining mahogany finish made her want to cry for the desire of having one of these beautiful pianos again. Its clean ivory keys begged her to touch them, and yet they mocked her. Weren't they so much like the ones she had learned on?

Sophie gripped its edge and swallowed against the burning sensation at the back of her throat. She tried not to shake visibly, yet her whole being trembled inside until a shiver coursed down her spine. She blinked and then focused on arranging the music in front of her, anything that would make the reverend and Maggie believe that nothing was amiss.

Sophie brushed her fingertips across several keys. Two expectant people watched her. She wondered if she could muster the strength to play the splendid instrument before her, one that was so deeply entwined with her past.

CHAPTER 4

The clean smell of soap and a spicy, citrus scent made Sophie more aware of Ian McCormick's presence as he leaned casually against the side of the piano. "Is something wrong, Sophie?"

"I'm a little warm." *For one thing.* The heat of turmoil, fear, and embarrassment worked its way from inside to out.

With a shaky hand, Sophie opened the sheet music before her and set her fingers to performing. She had played this brand of piano over a thousand times before. Once she steadied her fingers, they flew over the keys and Chopin's composition filled the room, drowning out even the childish laughter of Caira and Philip. For several minutes, the world's cares ceased to exist. Sophie took solace in the music, transported to another time and place in her mind.

How old had she been at her first recital? Eight? Nine? She remembered looking down and clasping her hands together until Papa prompted her to greet each guest at the entrance to their large parlor. She walked across deep burgundy and hunter green Persian rugs and sat down on the stool provided. Paul stood next to her, nodding and smiling. Her brother readied himself to turn the pages as she scaled the keyboard. Papa, Mama, and all the audience clapped after the last chord had been pounded out. Sophie had adored the feeling of such approval.

Maggie's piano transported Sophie far away from the others in the parlor. With passion, she poured the aches of heart and soul, betrayal and love lost out through the music she played. Relieved, she finished, looking up to find the reverend staring at her with his mouth open. He tapped his forefinger on his chin for a moment.

"Ian, this young woman deserves applause!" Maggie clapped and her brother joined in. Soon Caira left Philip with a pile of blocks and climbed up next to Sophie so she could bang on the keys. Then the little one smiled and clapped as though hoping to gain the same approval her mama had.

"That's an incredible gift you have!" Did the depth of expression in his lake-colored eyes reveal admiration? Was it possible?

Sophie bowed her head. The emotional energy she'd given to her playing left her spent. Sadness returned. The real world surrounded her again. "Thank you." She caressed the ivory keys once more before she stood from the bench to face the present.

"Would you play something else for us?" Reverend McCormick placed his elbow on the piano.

"No, we should take our leave. Caira is sleepy, and I'm afraid I've already taken enough of your time." She forced her mouth to shape a slight smile.

"At least have some pie with us first." Maggie's insistence broke her down.

"My sister really does make the best apple pie—rivals Esther's, or should I say, your pie?" The reverend's voice lowered, along with his chin.

Sophie regarded his shy compliment. "I'm afraid I could use more practice at baking pies." Perhaps he only flattered her.

"You're not far behind. The crust on that pie of yours that Esther gave Ian last Sunday was nearly as perfect as my mother's." Maggie nodded.

"Well then, Maggie, at least yours is better than our mother's."
He winked at Sophie and then whispered, "If I don't tell her that,
I'll never get her to bake again."

"Shame on you, Ian. Nobody's pie was better than our saintly
mother's!" She put her hands up in the air in what seemed a gesture
of defeat.

Sophie couldn't help herself smiling at the teasing way between
the brother and sister. She enjoyed one more hour of that warm
family circle before Maggie had her and Caira wrapped in blankets
and on the sleigh, seated next to the Reverend McCormick.

Ian glanced over at his passengers. First, Caira yawned, and
then her sister. The little bundle could hardly keep her eyes open.
Miss Biddle tucked the blanket tighter around her younger sister
with such love and devotion!

As the sleigh pulled up in front of the boardinghouse, Ian felt
relief that the young woman seemed more relaxed than the day
they had met. "Well, here we are already." He pulled up on the
reins.

"Thank you, Reverend." Her amber eyes glowed with
appreciation as she flashed him a shy smile.

"You are welcome to visit any time." Ian cleared his throat.
He hoped he wasn't being forward, but he sensed that she needed
friends she could trust and a place of refuge, in the absence of her
real family. Why couldn't he, Maggie and Philip provide that for
her and Caira? "Maggie would enjoy having your company again,
I'm sure. She's tired of being the only lady around us men."

Miss Biddle looked surprised. "I'm sure she must keep busy
socially."

"Being my sister, she often has to keep her guard up." He
studied the young woman before him. Even though they'd shared

a meal, and she'd spent time in his parlor, she looked nearly as shy as the day they'd first met.

"I think I understand how that is." She chewed her lip and glanced down.

"But you and Caira seemed very comfortable." Ian paused. "I hope I won't seem too forward by mentioning what a lovely first name you have. Did you know in Greek it means 'wisdom'?"

"It's too bad I can't claim that virtuous meaning for myself." Her eyes seemed clouded with sadness.

How he would love to know the thoughts behind them! Ian sighed. It would take a long while for anyone to gain Sophie's confidence. But there he was in territory where he didn't belong again. His concern should be for her spiritual condition and physical safety, nothing more.

"I'm afraid it often comes with time. Though I'm sure with the large responsibility you've had placed on your shoulders, you have more wisdom than you realize." Ian climbed down from the sleigh, intent on helping Sophie, but by the time he got to the other side, she was making her precarious way to the ground.

"At least let me take Caira from you." He reached up for the sleeping toddler.

"All right."

Ian carried Caira toward the door alongside Sophie. She stepped sideways after her elbow bumped his arm. When they reached the entrance, Ian cleared his throat. "I hope you'll not think me impertinent, but we are in great need of a pianist at the church. I haven't heard anyone play like you in a long time. Would you be willing to take the job?"

Her face turned crimson at his praise. "I-I don't know what to say."

"Say that you'll at least consider it. Please? I'm sure we could pay for skill such as yours though it may not be much."

Sophie appeared to be pondering the offer. "I'll think about it, then."

As Ian pulled the sleigh away from the boardinghouse, he chuckled. Wouldn't the elder board be surprised when he asked for a small stipend for a new pianist? And wouldn't they be more astonished when the old sanctuary piano produced beautiful music by means of her amazing gift?

•••)━━━━━━━━ ● ━━━━━━━(•••

Sophie paced in front of Stone Creek Community Church. What had possessed her to further consider the position of church pianist? Wisps of steam curled into the frosty air as she breathed more quickly.

A week after he had asked, she had sent a note to Reverend McCormick telling him that she wanted to get the feel of the piano, to practice before she committed. She left Caira behind to nap with Esther Fairgrave close at hand. Now she stood on the path to the church. How long had it been since she had entered such a sanctuary?

Her view swept from the thick oak doors to the steeple pointing heavenward. Oh, Sophie desired to go to church again, but people always started asking questions. If only she could bring up Caira in peace!

Well, she owed the minister something for his kindness, she was positive of that. It would be a simple thing to do for him, and she could again practice and perhaps improve her ability. Besides, they needed the money, no matter how small an amount the pay might be.

Caira's needs were paramount. If the congregation were as caring as their pastor, everything would be fine. Her daughter could be raised among decent folk, above reproach. Sophie's life may have come to naught, but she couldn't let Caira's turn out the same way. Maybe Sophie could finally earn the acceptance she craved for them both.

She swallowed and inhaled deeply. On the other side of the door in front of her stood a man who incurred her admiration as much as his seemingly ideal ways got under her skin in the short time since they had met.

Loud creaking pierced the cold, quiet air as she pulled the heavy door open. Her eyes adjusted to the darker inside of the building.

Sophie's breath caught in her throat. Reverend McCormick sat in the middle of the sanctuary with head bowed as though he were praying. She didn't see anyone else. Then her memories of a different place dragged her where she didn't want to go. The shining brass light fixtures sparkled like those in the large and elegant high-ceilinged Warner parlor had on that fateful day. Sophie stiffened as a pungent whiff of lemon oil on the polished wooden pews transported her back in time to a room where thick mahogany tables had been rubbed to a high gloss.

She stumbled forward and grasped the back of a bench as though she could anchor herself into the present. Her sweaty hands stuck to the finish. Instead of Reverend McCormick's wavy black hair, Sophie saw straight brown hair. When he turned his head, she saw a face with a slanted scar. The man stood and strode toward her. *No! It couldn't be.* He came closer. She let go of the pew—or was it a chair? And backed away, gasping for air with her heart thudding so loudly she was sure he could hear her fear. The light dimmed, and the room grew darker. The tall man clutched both her arms, but she was too weak to twist away.

CHAPTER 5

"Sophie." Was that Ian McCormick's voice? "Sophie, are you ill?"

She opened her eyes. Where was she? Oh yes, the sanctuary. The hard wood of a pew pressed against her back. That was better than falling on the floor. Then she remembered what had made her faint—the memories of the day she'd been trying to forget. But what of such ugliness could she tell this godly man who must have lived a spotless life?

"Have you eaten anything today?"

Her tongue stuck like peanut butter to the roof of her mouth. She nodded. His warm hands engulfed her clammy one. She closed her eyes for a moment, waiting for the lightheadedness to pass. Finally, her tongue loosened. "I-I'm not sure what happened." That, at least, was the truth. The thought of being alone with a man in any building put Sophie out of sorts . . . but not usually quite that much. "Perhaps I just need some water. Where's Maggie? I assumed she would be here."

"She should be here shortly. You are a little early." Her eyes focused to take in the reverend kneeling next to her. His furrowed brow revealed his obvious concern.

Sophie blinked and tried to sit up. "I'll be fine, really."

"You gave me quite a scare. Let me help you." Reverend McCormick held one hand and supported her back with his other. "Stay right there, and I'll get you a glass of water."

"Thank you." She gazed around the sanctuary. Beams slanting high above the eggshell-colored room supported the cathedral ceiling. Even the grayish light of winter highlighted the spectrum of color that came through the stained glass windows. Though far different from the room she'd been catapulted into by her mind's eye, she still found its appearance lofty. The wind howled outside. "Are we alone?"

•••)━━━━━━ ● ━━━━━━(•••

"No." Ian wondered at Sophie's fainting spell. His heart had sped up as she fell into his arms and continued a drumbeat as he went to get her water. She'd acted comfortable at his house a week ago, but her eyes had widened and an almost imperceptible shake coursed through her as though she had seen a ghost before she'd blacked out. Her fingers had clung to the front of her shawl as though they were frozen there. A cold sweat of fear had swept over Ian.

"Uncle Ian!" Philip bounded down the center aisle behind him when Ian returned. "I've found the broom. Where would you like me to sweep first?"

He turned to the energetic boy for a moment. "Be a gentleman. Miss Biddle isn't feeling well."

"Yes, sir. Is she going to be all right?" Philip stood close behind him, waiting for further direction.

Sophie took in a breath and let it out. All at once, she seemed more relaxed. Could she be so nervous about performing? She'd played like a professional the other night. Why would the presence of a child ease her fears? Perhaps she was only cold from being outside.

Her long slender fingers curved around the glass he handed her and brushed his hand. How chilly! "Would you like to warm up by the stove before you practice? Maggie will be bringing a pot of tea."

"That's very thoughtful of you both. Will Maggie stay for awhile?"

Warmth thawed into the once terrified look in her amber eyes. He somehow felt relief as he took in her gaze. The tenderness he discerned there both captivated and alarmed him. He cleared his throat and glanced away.

"I'm sure she would enjoy hearing you play again so soon." Ian rubbed his idle hands together to generate heat as the cold sweat abated.

He turned to his young nephew. "Philip, start at the front and work your way to the back. There's usually more dirt in the vestibule. And then you can sweep it right out the door."

"Yes, sir." The boy nodded.

"But sweep as quietly as possible when Miss Biddle plays."

Philip nodded again and chuckled. "I'll try."

Ian held Sophie's elbow and helped her up before leading her toward the front of the church. They sat near the stove in the corner, and Sophie held out her reddened hands. Ian had felt their roughness just a few minutes before. How hard she must work helping Esther and washing laundry. It seemed unfair that those hands that made beautiful music had to take such abuse from lye soap.

She gave him that crooked smile, but an uneasy quiet hung between them. Only the swish of Philip's broom across the floor interrupted the silence.

Funny, as they walked up the aisle together, Ian realized that he'd never done this with a woman at his side before. Maggie certainly didn't count. He'd stood apart as he'd watched many a bride come forward and join her groom's side for Ian to perform their marriage ceremony. *Why on earth was he thinking this way?* He shook himself from his odd reverie. They needed to get to work.

"Warmed up a bit?" he asked.

"I think so." Sophie sighed and pushed a wayward curl back from her pretty face. "It's probably time for me to familiarize myself with the church piano and the hymns you've chosen."

"Let me take your shawl." Ian reached to take it from her.

Sophie pulled the seat away from the instrument. With grace, she sat up straight and arranged the folds of her patched gray skirt like an aristocratic lady. He saw class in her, yet not a bit of haughtiness or arrogance.

"It's not a Bidershem, but it's decent." He probably sounded more apologetic than he needed.

Her cheeks tinged with pink, and she looked as though she was concentrating on the hymnal in her hands, frowning for a moment. "I'm sure it's a fine piano."

When Ian handed Sophie a list of hymns, her fingers brushed his. She pulled her hand back rather quickly. It was all he could do to not hold the roughened appendage in his own, transferring a message that he wanted to protect her from whatever fear held her captive.

Why did this accidental touch catch him off guard? Somehow, when he grasped her hand between both of his own a few minutes earlier, his concentration was spent on making her feel comfortable. Yet now, Ian could barely focus on the list in front of him.

"Do you mind if I play a few familiar pieces first?"

"Take your time. I'll be right here in the building if you have any questions. I need to give my nephew a bit of direction."

Ian turned and walked toward Philip. Her masterful use of the chords in each hymn filled his ears. His heart swelled with worship.

"Let's find a bucket and clean these windows to a shine." He loved the colorful stained glass, especially when the sun shone through in all its glory. When spring arrived, they would be ready to receive back the winter shut-ins.

After they pumped water into the bucket and he found a piece of chamois in the closet, they returned to the sanctuary. Ian had to stop for a moment, inhaling sharply at a beautiful sight. A rare bit of winter sun poured through the window behind Sophie and bathed her in a brilliant glow, transforming her from a helpless girl to an ethereal angel. Why hadn't he noticed this before? Or maybe he had but wasn't willing to admit it to himself. She wasn't just a second chance to do justice to someone like Annie but someone he wanted to watch over.

Ian couldn't pull his gaze from her freckled face, framed by chestnut curls. Her hair hung loose around her shoulders. A small cleft in her chin sat below the full pink lips that she pushed together as she seemed absorbed by her task. Her hands moved with such gracefulness upon the keyboard.

The yearning in his heart had grown beyond compassion. He blinked and swallowed. Why, this had to be the desire to protect her—that was all—and an appreciation for the beauty that God had created in her. Wasn't it? He had to get control of such feelings. He knew so little about her, and his duty was to care for her soul, first and foremost, to earn the right to shepherd her.

The question was how best to help her and the child. One moment, she projected an independent spirit. Yet, when she'd fainted in his arms, he'd observed a vulnerable young woman. Independence he could deal with by helping her find ways to supplement the pittance she earned from Esther, but beauty and vulnerability were dangerous territories. Ian had a calling to fulfill before he got entangled in any woman's life, or more likely, his heart became ensnared by hers.

She stopped playing and looked up. Their gazes locked. "I'll start on your list now, Reverend."

When Sophie caught Ian's expression, she saw an intensity that hadn't been there before. Her heart palpitated as she became lost in the pools of his aqua eyes. His Adam's apple bobbed, and he cleared his throat.

"Of course." He dropped the chamois into the bucket. "I thought that we would start with a Fanny Crosby hymn, "Rescue the Perishing." Ian raked his hand through his wavy, black hair.

Sophie searched the pages of the worn music book. "Ah, here it is." She perused the words as she began playing. "One of my favorites." She couldn't keep from forming a slight smile.

"Rescue the perishing, care for the dying, snatch them in pity from sin and the grave . . ."

Were they only dying souls the hymn spoke of? Or perishing hearts, as well? The pain twisted deep inside her—the hurt of betrayal and sting of rejection. Weren't these things murdering her slowly? Was there hope for healing? God still seemed so far away.

However, the music was a balm to her, purging her sadness. Sophie's cheeks felt wet. When she finished the song, she found Ian pressing a clean handkerchief into her hand.

"That was truly moving. I can see you feel the message of the lyrics, Sophie, assuming there's nothing else troubling you."

His closeness and the warmth of his touch had made her want to stay right there at the piano in the sanctuary, to play for him the whole afternoon. What was wrong with her? Her emotions were like a sailboat bobbing on the Detroit River during a storm.

"Well, I think I understand how it feels to be perishing, in a way." *How can I let him see me cry like this again?* "It doesn't seem to take much to move me to tears these days." She tried to deny the comfort his closeness brought. She smoothed her skirt and sat up straighter. Perhaps if she appeared more poised and matter-of-fact, they could get back to the business of making music for the next Sunday service.

"What's the next piece on the list?" She spoke more abruptly than she intended. "I can't be interrupted continually when I'm practicing." The way he said just the right thing in such a perfectly soothing way annoyed her. She could get through this by herself, even if God felt far away. Sophie didn't need a patronizing pastor always rescuing her, but for the time being she needed the job he offered.

Ian nodded. "I'll leave you to your work then." The tension in his voice told her that even ministers could be hurt by sharp words.

The door flew open. "Here we are! Hot tea and cookies for a hardworking musician!" Maggie carried a tray and bared a glowing smile as she looked from Sophie to Ian.

Did she notice the hint of a knowing gleam in Maggie's eyes? She was being sensitive, of course, probably her imagination.

"What about me?" Philip piped up.

"And I suppose for custodians, too." She winked at her son.

She set the tray on a front row pew.

"Thank you, Maggie." Sophie took a deep breath filled with relief.

"You're welcome. Are you sure Esther is feeding you enough? You're positively too thin. Or is rationing a part of the conditions of working for her?"

Sophie chuckled. "Oh no, there's enough to eat for all of us." She thought of the plump widow who employed her. "I'm just so busy that I forget to stop and eat sometimes."

"Well, I don't think she ate enough this morning, Maggie. She positively fainted away at the thought of performing in the church."

"You don't say?"

How aggravating that the brother and sister spoke to each other as though she wasn't even there!

Maggie grabbed her hand. "Then let me get some bread and cheese for you, too!"

But Sophie was feeling much better with another adult present. "No, thank you, these cookies will do the trick, I'm sure. I really am quite well now."

After she nibbled on Maggie's spicy snicker doodles, and the strong, black tea warmed her suddenly parched throat, she returned to practicing each hymn a few times.

Maggie listened while sitting nearby and knitting. She occasionally tapped her foot in time to the hymn or hummed a bit.

As Sophie put the music away and wrapped up in her shawl, Ian spoke to her. "I don't think it will be a problem, but you will be on a sort of probation this Sunday."

She nodded. "I think I understand."

Ian's face broke into a wide grin. "I'm sure once the board hears you play, they will approve."

Maggie sat with her arms crossed. "I agree that the board will support you, but not everyone in the church is so kind."

"We don't have to talk about this now." Ian's mouth set in a grim line as he stared at his sister.

"Hopefully all will go well." Squaring her shoulders and pushing her mouth to form a smile, Sophie looked from Maggie to Ian. She didn't feel so confident on the inside, but she wasn't going to let the reverend know that. He shouldn't be looking at her as some helpless child.

"I'm sure that's true, dear." Maggie came over to hug her.

Ian looked worried as she prepared to leave. "You need gloves to protect those talented hands."

"I'm knitting mittens with some yarn that Mrs. Fairgrave gave me. I'll be fine until then." Sophie jutted her chin forward and waved his concern away.

"But it's so cold out." Ian sighed. "I suppose I'm stating the obvious." Looking bewildered, he thrust his hands into his pockets.

"Here, take mine for now." Maggie held out a lovely pair of dove gray leather gloves, finer than any she had seen in a long time. The last decent pair she'd owned, she'd pawned in Greenville, just to buy food.

"No, no, I couldn't take them." Sophie shook her head at the offer. "I have pockets in my skirt, anyway."

"Please, at least until you have mittens ready. I have another pair at home." Maggie grabbed Sophie's hands, pressing the fine gloves into them. "I will worry about you getting frostbite. Goodness, where has my head been? I should have noticed you needed gloves when you were at the house the other day!" Her cheeks flushed a bit.

"All right then, you may loan them to me, but only until I finish my mittens." Sophie couldn't keep herself from smiling. These two were cut from the same cloth. "See you tomorrow, then. Thank you, Maggie."

"Until tomorrow." Ian nodded.

Sophie turned and walked out the door of the church, hinges creaking behind her. A gust of wind caused her to shudder. She pulled the shawl tighter and braced herself as she walked into the blustery weather. The walk home didn't seem as long with gloves to keep her hands warm.

Ian and Maggie had been more than kind. *Ian!* When had she started thinking of him by his given name and not as Reverend McCormick? She had broken every rule she'd set out for herself.

The first rule was to not trust any man, and Sophie had trusted Reverend McCormick to take her home twice. She'd even eaten at his table.

The second rule was to not get physically close to a man or be alone with him. She had been relieved to see that Philip was in the building with them, but she should have taken precautions ahead of time. And how could she work with him on the music without talking to him regularly? Would people understand they were communicating about church music or think her a flirt, spending so much time with the bachelor pastor?

And third, she was never to let herself have feelings toward a man. The first day that he'd taken her to the boardinghouse, his presence had caused a spark of emotion. When he played on the floor with Caira at the parsonage, she felt such deep longing for a father for her child that she had to push out any thought of him being that kind of man.

Perhaps the fact that Reverend McCormick was a minister made him seem safer. The very fact of his vocation made it impossible for him to be anything more than a friend to her and Caira . . . especially if he knew she was blemished.

Sophie clenched her fists. She would not give in to these childhood fantasies. She must stay away from him at all costs. There had to be a way to come in contact with him as little as possible while still taking the position. Then again, maybe she shouldn't even take the job he offered.

She marched up the front walk of the boardinghouse. One more gust stung her face before she reached safety inside the front door.

Mrs. Fairgrave paced from the kitchen to the parlor and back again. She frowned and grew pale when she looked upon Sophie. "Oh, dear. Oh, dear." The widow wrung her hands and spoke only a bit above a whisper.

"What is it?" Sophie pulled the shawl from her back and hung it on a peg by the door.

"Oh Sophie, I'm so sorry."

"What's wrong?" She grasped the older woman's arm.

Mrs. Fairgrave put her other hand to her cheek. "I-I put Caira down for a nap. Then one of those cursed headaches started to come on." She rubbed her temple and shook her head.

Fear's cold tendrils sent a shiver down Sophie's spine. "Yes?"

"I just mixed up some headache powder and lay down for a bit." It came out more like a moan. "But when I awoke to check on her, she was gone!"

CHAPTER 6

"What?" Sophie's mouth dropped open. "Where did you look for her? Caira!" Her feet followed her heart as she ran upstairs to search the room they shared.

"But I've looked everywhere I can think of in the house." Mrs. Fairgrave stayed close behind Sophie, wringing her hands. The older lady's brow creased.

"Caira!" Sophie didn't want to frighten her daughter, but she yelled out her name as she ran back down the stairs and searched the kitchen cupboards and anywhere she could think.

"Did you look outside?" She grabbed Mrs. Fairgrave by the shoulders and looked her square in the face.

"Not yet." Her landlady shook. "I'm so sorry, child."

Sophie grabbed her shawl from the peg. *What if I can't find her? Who can help me?*

She flew out the back door with her heart thudding like a drum corp. Her glance darted from one side of the yard to another. "Caira! Caira! Where are you?" Clouds hid the winter sun that had peeked out earlier. It hung lower. There couldn't be more than a couple hours of sunlight left.

The little boy who lived next door looked up from the pile of snow at his feet. Sophie's footsteps crunched as she walked toward him. When she could focus on him, she realized he was building a snowman.

"Tommy, have you seen Caira?"

"No, miss."

"You're sure?"

Tommy nodded.

Another thought gnawed at her insides. Was Caira's father following them? Would he take the child? She wouldn't put it past him to hold her daughter hostage for some financial gain.

And what about the times she thought she'd seen him? Had she imagined such things?

"Did you see anyone you didn't know come to our front door? A tall man, with a scar on his face."

The boy shook his head, giving her a measure of relief.

Sophie hugged her arms to herself and paced the side yard. She headed for the front of the house. The quiet street revealed nothing. Where could she go for help? How many people did she know other than Esther? Perhaps Ian. She chewed on her lower lip. After the way she had talked to him when she left, Sophie felt embarrassed. What other choice did she have? He was the only man in town she knew who might care. She ran back toward the front.

Tommy's mother came out onto her porch. "I heard a commotion. Is everything all right, Miss Biddle?"

"Caira's gone missing." Sophie waved both hands.

"How can we help?"

"Do you know where the Reverend McCormick lives? I need someone to get him for me, to tell him Caira's missing."

"You heard her, Tommy. You know where the parsonage is. Go get the reverend and be quick about it!"

"Yes, Mama!"

"Thank you, Mrs. Richards."

"Much obliged. Let us know if we can do anything else and keep us posted." The boy's mother nodded before she went back inside her house.

She searched for signs of little footprints in the snow. Seeing none, she became frantic, turning one way and then the other.

Would Caira have even put her shoes on? Or just run outside? She shivered at the thought of those pudgy little feet traipsing through the frigid snow. The door to the storm cellar was still secure, which left the shed to check.

She hurried to the other end of the yard. The door stood slightly ajar. She flung it open. Daylight poured in, and she searched the area. "Caira?" All she could see were overturned pots, rusty tools, and a few small pieces of discarded furniture.

Still, Sophie moved things aside in hopes of finding her daughter, despite the lack of evidence she had wandered outside. "Caira, please be in here," she whispered to no one but herself.

"Oh Caira, where are you?" She dropped to her knees on the dirt floor in the sanctuary of the shed and buried her face in her hands.

Maybe she wasn't fit to be a mother. Perhaps that was the real reason Papa and Mama wanted her to give Caira up. Echoes whispered in her mind . . . *"You have growing up to do . . . you have no business caring for a child without a husband."* Though they had said those things, Sophie couldn't believe their rejection of Caira came from the fear of social stigma or the assault that brought on the pregnancy, as they had claimed. She'd heard the whispered stories of girls like Ariel Carruthers, who'd been sent away for a visit with an aunt in the spring, then returned the following winter with a haunted look in her eyes. All the same, Ariel attended Christmas festivities in the city, but Sophie knew her smiles were forced. How Ariel's heart must have ached, doing what society expected of her—of them.

She wished her family could be different. The baby had stolen her heart. Why not her parents'? The child's conception hadn't been her fault.

"Please, God." Her breath hitched. "Don't let anything happen to Caira because of me. Mama was right. She needs a father, too. You're a Father to the fatherless. Oh please, we need You now!" Alone and shivering in the confines of the dusty shed, she pleaded aloud with Him.

She looked up at the wooden roof. Did a liar's prayers travel beyond the ceiling? She pressed a fist onto her closed mouth, stifling a sob. Losing her composure would be no help. Sophie could only hope the Good Shepherd was merciful enough to hear prayers said for the protection of little children despite the unsavory lips from which they were uttered.

Sophie pulled herself from the solace of her thoughts and exited the shed. Circling the property again, she called out the little one's name over and over. She knocked on a couple of neighbors' doors, but neither one answered. Finally hoarse from calling for her daughter, Sophie walked back toward the boardinghouse.

Sleigh bells sounded down the street. Turning, she spied Ian, Tommy, and Maggie waving from the sleigh. Cold and weary, Sophie waited.

"Sophie! I made my way here as fast as I could!" Getting down from the sleigh, Ian took her by the arms. "Are you all right?"

All she could do was nod.

Ian let go, stepping back, but covered her hands with his and patted them. She felt his strength and gentleness at the same time, his reluctance to release her.

"Caira's not out here." She shrugged. Sophie bit her quivering bottom lip, determined not to break down in his presence once again.

"Have you found footprints anywhere?" He still held her hands. She gently pulled them away.

"No, but Mrs. Fairgrave said she looked everywhere in the house." Sophie furrowed her brow, tense with worry.

"Esther's probably rather overwhelmed." Ian turned and headed for the house. "If I know Esther, bless her heart, she may have missed some place. I put the word out to some of the townspeople. Hopefully, they will search the woods before it gets dark, just in case something's been missed." Ian nodded toward a row of trees a short distance from the back of the house.

"Oh." Sophie groaned and hung her head. "I hadn't thought of that." At times over the past couple of years, she wished to disappear into a forest where nobody would bother them. But the woods became a tangled cluster of large trees able to swallow her daughter in the gloom of their shadows. *No.* Caira mustn't have disappeared there.

"We'll have some folks check." A frown hooded Ian's eyes. He placed his hand on her back to urge her toward the house.

Sophie crossed her arms tightly, sidestepping the minister's touch. Weariness and cold overtook her like she was bearing blocks of ice on her back. She shuddered, wishing she had someone to lean on, maybe even Ian. Where could her child be?

Sophie trudged in through the back door, through the kitchen and into the parlor with Ian at her side.

Maggie, who had hurried into the house ahead of them, rushed to engulf her in her arms. "You poor dear! You must be worried sick about your sister."

Sophie peered over the other woman's shoulder. Mr. Graemer looked agitated and leaned on his cane. He hobbled toward them. Not much usually stirred him from his rocking chair. He clasped his Union Army cap in one hand. "What is the trouble here?" he boomed.

Esther Fairgrave put her hands on her hips. "Well, it's about time you woke up from your nap with all the commotion going on. We can't find Caira!"

"That sweet little child? Why didn't you tell me?" He tottered forward a bit. A brass star, clenched by an eagle, dangled from the faded red, white, and blue ribbon pinned to his waistcoat.

"He's reliving the glory days, no doubt. Humph." Mrs. Fairgrave rolled her eyes.

Sophie sighed, rubbing her hands together. Why were they all standing around when her daughter was missing? She shifted her weight from one foot to the other.

"I'd like to hear how you earned that Medal of Honor later Mr. Graemer, but we need to return to the task at hand."

The old man's expression brightened at Ian's interest. He stood up a little straighter. "Well, I don't take this old thing out very often." The old man thumped his chest. "Just when I think about losing one of the old boys those many years ago." Mr. Graemer's eyes grew misty. He leaned closer to the reverend as though he were going to whisper. "I hid my war relics up in the attic for awhile. Used to share a room with Crazy Louie. He wasn't insane, but he was a thief." He pointed an accusatory finger into the air.

"We don't call each other by those kinds of names here. This is a Christian establishment." The older widow's face flushed.

Maggie broke in. "Esther, I'm sure this is a fine boardinghouse, but we don't have time for your scolding—"

"Yes! We have to find Caira!" Sophie clasped her hands together, wringing them as though in desperate prayer.

The others stared at their feet for a moment until Ian cleared his throat. He walked across the parlor and took Esther by the hand. "Have you looked *everywhere* in the house for her?"

Esther sat down on the worn chaise. "Every place a little child could possibly hide. I'm sure."

"I think we should look again, Sophie. You know the house and where your sister might have hidden." Maggie grasped her hand.

Your sister. The words nicked at her heart. If only Maggie knew the depth of responsibility she felt as a mother. Yet, the young widow held Sophie's hand with such compassion.

Sophie led the renewed search effort while Ian and Maggie followed behind her. She'd already looked into the lower kitchen cabinet and the pantry, half expecting to find Caira playing with a bowl and a ladle. She headed upstairs instead. "Caira?"

They separated, even checking in the boarders' rooms. No closet door stood unopened. Boxes that had sat dormant in those dark places were moved and overturned. Dust and cobwebs flew as they moved small pieces of furniture. Everyone checked under the beds in their assigned room.

The searchers trudged back down the stairs. "Come into the kitchen. I have hot coffee for you." Esther, despite her flustered state, had managed to brew a fresh pot.

Numbly, Sophie went into the kitchen and reached for the cup her employer handed her, in time to see Chet and Albert trudge in through the back door. "No luck," Albert announced, shaking his head. "We closed up shop as soon as we heard you couldn't find the little gal."

•••)———————— ● ————————(•••

"Looked for her high and low in the woods," Chet said. "But there's no sign of her anywhere," the other man said, holding his hat in his hand.

Ian rubbed the side of his face. He also took a cup of the hot brew offered. "Thank you, gentlemen, for your efforts." They exchanged mumbled "good-byes" and shuffled back out the door. Ian turned to go toward the parlor, where he heard the tap of a cane. His eyes followed Mr. Graemer while he shuffled back and forth across the threadbare Persian rug, as though he could worry Caira back into sight.

The mantel clock ticked in the quietness of the room. Ian sipped the brown liquid. Esther usually made weak coffee, but the numbness inside made him care little about the bitter blandness. Caira disappearing? Unbelievable!

Sophie sighed. Her face paled compared to the rosy glow of a couple of hours before. Her forehead crinkled with worry lines worthy of motherhood. He noticed Sophie's rumpled hair and dark circles. To have lost one's parents and then to worry over your only other family member must be a burden beyond bearing. Did instinct give him the desire to want to enfold the girl into his embrace? Or had he been enchanted by her innocent loveliness?

Ian desired to take her aside, to ask what thoughts lay behind her amber eyes and know how best to comfort her. However, her independent spirit had given him a clue to the boundaries she set. He blinked, attempting to concentrate on the task at hand. They needed to find Caira.

Ian closed his eyes for a moment, mentally recalling each room of the boardinghouse. Why hadn't they thought of the attic? He supposed it seemed an unlikely and scary place for Caira to venture by herself. "Mr. Graemer, were you by any chance up in the attic today?"

The old man blinked. Then he opened his pocket watch. "Why yes, I'd say it was about three hours ago at 1500 hours." He snapped the gold cover shut. "I might not seem very useful, but I am praying, you know."

"Sophie." Ian turned toward the lovely young woman. "I have an idea." He sensed a measure of relief in her as she sighed when he smiled and placed a hand on her arm for a moment. He hoped she would trust him enough to hear his idea. "Does anyone else go into the attic?"

"No, it's usually locked." Sophie shook her head.

"I never even thought to look up there. Couldn't imagine the little gal going up there by herself." Esther stood.

Ian's slight touch seemed to infuse her with determination. Why hadn't she thought of that earlier herself? "Let's go." Sophie headed toward the stairs, lifting her skirt slightly as she reached the bottom step.

"I'll get the key!" Esther hastened to the secretary where she kept such things, returning to the staircase, breathless.

Sophie hurried up the stairs to a door that led to another flight with the brother and sister behind her. Her heart pounded at the thought of her daughter being alone in such a cold, dark place. Sophie snatched the ring of keys from Esther, jiggling the key in the lock until the door opened.

"I'll bet that she followed Mr. Graemer up, and he didn't hear her. She may have been playing up here all this time," Ian commented with a hopeful note in his voice.

Let's hope so. Sophie couldn't bring herself to speak the words, but Ian's confidence gave her a reason to hope. He held a lantern for her. A gust of cool air curled around her ankles. Maggie stayed close behind them. Wisps of steam appeared as they exhaled.

"Brr." Maggie hugged her arms to herself.

"A-shoo!" Sophie sneezed as the musty smell of dusty, antiquated objects and aged rough-hewn wood met her nose. The scents tugged at her memory. Their attic back home had been a place of wonder where old books, paintings, and furniture had been piled. Trunks had been filled with old clothes to dress up in.

However, an attic's darkness and shadows could also be most frightening. If Caira had been up here alone, had she been scared? They hadn't heard her crying or calling out to them. And what if they didn't find her here? What next? Sophie clenched a handful of her skirt and took quick, shallow breaths. She braced herself for the worst.

Ian lifted the lantern, dispelling any darkness.

"Over there." Maggie pointed.

The pink glow of the sun slipping into the horizon shone through the small round attic window, where lacy patterns of frost clung. The shimmering rays bathed a curly-headed child. Caira slept soundly on a ragbag. Her arm curled around the little rag doll Sophie had made her.

She covered her mouth. Gasping with relief, she hurried to kneel alongside her precious daughter. Sophie pushed the curls from her child's forehead, where cold sweat clung. She shivered, realizing her baby must be freezing. Caira's lips were a bluish hue. As though he understood Sophie's needs immediately, Ian handed her an old quilt that he'd pulled from atop a crate. She wrapped it around the baby, not caring about how dusty or worn out the item appeared.

Caira sneezed at the light cloud of dust then yawned as her mother scooped her into her arms. Her eyes rolled open for a moment and she smiled with contentment before she nestled into Sophie's shoulder.

The little one seemed a bit listless from her nap in the frigid attic, but otherwise none the worse for wear. Likely, she'd soon be awake and looking for something to eat. "Don't ever scare me like that again," Sophie crooned into her daughter's ear.

"Such a little darling. What a relief to find her. Let me get the doll for her." Maggie patted the little one's head and then bent to pick up the toy.

Ian smiled, looking quite pleased. Sophie, aware of the warming presence by her side, was comforted by the minister's nearness. What would she have done without him and Maggie?

When they reached the parlor again, Sophie saw a tired Mr. Graemer rocking as though he would wear a hole in the rug. As soon as he noticed them, he cried out, "My prayers have been answered! That precious child is safe." He wiped a moistened eye and pulled out a crumpled hanky to blow his nose.

Esther Fairgrave hovered and fanned herself. "If you hadn't gone up to the attic today, Caira wouldn't have found her way up there!"

Sophie touched the woman's arm. "It's all right. She's safe and sound now. We've locked the door again."

Next, she went to the elderly gentleman and squeezed one of his hands. "Thank you for praying, Mr. Graemer." Perhaps God didn't always hear *her* prayers, but He still must listen on behalf of little children. "And, Reverend, thank you so much for organizing everyone, for being clearheaded enough to think of the attic."

"You're welcome."

Sophie hoped the warmth of her words and a smile meant for him truly conveyed her gratitude.

"Reverend McCormick, would you and your sister care to stay for some stew?" Esther looked expectant.

"Thank you, Esther, but I must get ready for tomorrow."

"Oh yes, it'll be Sunday, won't it?" She shook her head and shuffled toward the kitchen. "How can the days go by so quickly?"

Maggie fastened her boots up and took her coat off the hook. She tugged on Sophie's sleeve and nudged her toward the front door. She pursed her lips for a moment and took a deep breath. "That was just ridiculous. I will not have you worrying about Caira every time you leave the house to rehearse." She leaned close and whispered, then clucked her tongue. "I insist that you bring the little one to the parsonage and practice there while I keep an eye on her. What do you say? Philip will love having Caira around."

"I wouldn't want to hurt Mrs. Fairgrave's feelings."

Ian nodded. "I'll talk to her."

"And you could have her come along to visit me some of the time." Maggie's face brightened.

For the second time since Ian had arrived, relief settled on Sophie like the warmth of being wrapped in a cozy blanket. There was one less thing to worry about.

"And no need to thank us." She was surprised to feel his gentle grasp on her elbow. How could he know what she was thinking? Though perhaps he seemed a bit pompous. "Think of it as our appreciation to you for playing tomorrow. Now get some rest. You look exhausted."

He patted her elbow before he reached for her hand and squeezed it for a moment. Her breath hitched, and she pulled her hand away. An unusual, uncomfortable spark of warmth had been transferred between them. But the sunny sparkle in his eyes was just friendly concern, wasn't it?

"Goodnight, Sophie."

She nodded toward him, speechless.

The back door opened and closed with a bang. James Cooper practically flew from the kitchen to the parlor in the front of the house, hat in hand. "I got here as soon as I could. Are you all right, Sophie?" The young man pushed his way toward her until Ian and Maggie backed away. "I heard that Caira was missing! Oh, there she is." He patted the child on the back. The worry in his brown eyes disappeared.

Esther reappeared in the doorway. "Humph. Some hero you turned out to be."

James had been looking straight at Mrs. Fairgrave. He turned and his eyebrows rose when he seemed to discover the silent Ian and Maggie. "Um, hello, Reverend." He nodded. "Mrs. Galloway."

Ian cleared his throat. "We were just leaving. See you tomorrow morning, James?"

"Well . . ."

"He'll be there if I have something to say about it," Esther piped up. "Besides, Sophie will have her debut playing the piano for the church. You wouldn't want to miss that now, would you?"

"In that case, I'll be there, Reverend."

A pelt of winter air, sailing in when Ian swung the door open for Maggie, reminded Sophie to be thankful for the boardinghouse, even with its shortcomings.

"When are we going to get some supper around here?" Mr. Graemer's grouchiness made Sophie smile. Things were getting back to normal.

She glanced down at the sleepy head on her shoulder. Caira had barely stirred with all the commotion. She yawned. "You surely will be cranky, too, if I don't get you something to eat, before putting you down for the night. And if I wake you up now, I wonder if you'll go back to sleep."

Caira's eyelids fluttered open. "I hungry."

"All right then. How do you ask for food?"

"Pease."

Sophie sighed. Tomorrow would be a big day for them. She hoped they would be able to get some rest.

••❯)———— ● ————(❮••

Pearly gray light peeked through the gap between the curtains. Sophie stretched. Though Caira had lain awake a bit later than usual, she had slept through the night. Well, it was a blessed respite between bouts of fussiness with her molars yet to come in.

Sophie pushed away the covers and crossed her arms against the cold. She shivered as she placed the soles of her feet on the frigid floor. How she looked forward to the end of another Michigan winter.

Opening the door to the armoire, she pulled aside her work clothes. The only decent dress she had managed to hold onto, an evening dress that her mother and she had sewn together, hung there. The burgundy silk jacquard held such a lovely sheen. She touched a sumptuous puffed sleeve. The heart-shaped neckline was so feminine compared to many of the tailored skirt and jacket outfits of the day.

Sophie supposed she could get away with wearing something a little less eye-catching, but how could she perform at church in a worn out calico shirtwaist and a patched skirt? She hoped such an elegant gown wouldn't seem too unfitting.

Before Caira could wake up, she dressed and fixed her hair more carefully than usual, pinning it up. She glanced in the mirror over the old, scratched vanity table and smiled. At least the church and their handsome minister wouldn't see a girl who looked like a housemaid for once. She pinched her cheeks to a deeper pink and shrugged. It never lasted anyway.

She felt a jolt of surprise at her thoughts. What did she care what anyone thought, especially Ian? *Well, I can't embarrass him, can I now? He asked me to play piano for the church. Shall I go looking bedraggled?*

She squared her shoulders and turned away from the mirror.

CHAPTER 7

Ian stood near the back of the sanctuary. He wanted to concentrate on each person as they stopped to shake his hand, but his gaze wandered back to Sophie as she finished the postlude, looking absolutely lovely.

When she had come through the door earlier in the morning, Ian stared at the transformed young woman. The tattered shawl had slid from Sophie's shoulders, revealing a shimmering burgundy dress. With her hair swept up and tendrils framing her face, she looked older. He blinked. Was this Sophie, the servant girl and seamstress he left the night before?

"Elisha, good to see you this morning. Are you ready for spring?" The gentleman nodded and replied, but Ian only half heard him as his glance trained back on Sophie closing the piano lid.

"How is your mother?" He tried in vain to concentrate on Leona Packer's round face.

"Much better, now, thank you." The gloved hand didn't let his go. "Reverend, are you quite all right?" Leona spoke a bit louder.

"I'm sorry. What is it?" He moved his hand to pat the arm of his concerned parishioner.

"You don't seem quite like yourself this morning."

"I'm fine, just have a few things on my mind." He cleared his throat and stood up a bit straighter. "So, what did you think of the music during the service?" But then heavenly visions of Sophie were replaced with the sight of Gertrude Wringer pushing her way forward. An unwelcome chill slid down Ian's spine.

Leona's eyes brightened. "It was just wonderful. I—"

"Excuse me, Reverend." Gertrude's pinched and sour face appeared directly in front of him as she shouldered the other woman out of the way. Ian sighed. He knew she wouldn't leave until she said her piece. And once she did, no one would want to add their praise of Sophie's work.

Gertrude didn't accept the hand he offered her, but only nodded.

"How are you this morning?" Ian tried to maintain his pleasant smile though his cheeks strained at the effort.

The thin woman made a noise like she was sucking on her teeth, a sort of "Tsk, tsk." Her small eyes, an indescribable color, mostly because it was difficult to gaze into them for more than a few seconds, pierced him with an accusing stare over the bridge of her pointed nose. "Quite a spectacle that young woman made of herself this morning, parading around in an evening gown . . . at church. And whose child does she have with her, hmm? They're both from an unknown upbringing. Where do you think she got such a dress? Some ill-gotten gain, no doubt! I'm surprised you'd allow such people in a prominent position here."

Ian clasped his hands together in front of him. He might as well get to the point with the malevolent woman. "How did you find Miss Biddle offensive, Gertrude?" He hoped his inquiry sounded kinder than he felt. This was one of the many difficulties of pastoral duties.

"First of all, you never mentioned her credentials. Who recommended her to you?" She pulled in the already shallow hollows of her face like she had just tasted a spoonful of cider vinegar.

"No one, but Miss Biddle will be presented to the board. I'm sure they'll speak to her of these issues."

"I'm rather disappointed. I thought you were waiting for my niece, Nora, here, to come for a visit." The thin girl standing next to her, wispy as field grass, had pale blonde hair. She stared at the floor. "She's graduated from Miss Melton's Finishing School, a fine academy with excellent musical training. She's not some riff-raff off the street." Gertrude's eye twitched. She gave her niece a backhanded whack on the arm. "Say 'hello' to Reverend McCormick, dearie."

Nora, turning the lightest shade of pink, looked up at him with light blue eyes, and smiled. She rubbed her arm. "How do you do, Reverend?"

"I'm pleased to meet you, Miss . . . ?"

"Armstrong, Nora Armstrong. I'm pleased to meet you as well."

Ian reached out a hand in greeting. "I assumed that your coming here was purely conjecture. I thought that a girl with so many talents wouldn't want to come to such a quiet place as Stone Creek."

"Humph. "Why, Nora's the kind of girl that a pastor needs to stand alongside and be a helpmeet to him." Gertrude sniffed.

He swallowed. So that's what Gertrude was up to. Nora turned a shade closer to crimson than Ian thought possible for her fair complexion.

"We would still welcome her as a musical guest." Ian smiled sympathetically toward the girl, who seemed equally uncomfortable with Gertrude revealing such intentions outright.

"I would be honored. You have a fine musician in Miss Biddle—"

"So that's how it is." Gertrude's voice rose as she put a hand up to silence her niece. "I thought we had an agreement." Her thin frame leaned toward him.

Ian hoped to reason with her. "But I never—"

"You'll be sorry, mark my words. You'll be sorry you didn't listen to Gertrude Wringer. Let's go, Nora." She pushed past him, toward the door, and mumbled as she stomped through the foyer.

Nora looked back, shaking her head as if in apology, but followed her aunt like a lamb to the slaughter.

Leona stood as though frozen, her mouth agape in her blanched face with her hand at her throat.

"Are you all right?" Ian took the chubby woman by her other hand. "What were you saying about Sophie?"

"I-I don't know, Reverend." She swallowed and lowered her voice, looking around. "Perhaps it's too soon to judge. I best get home now and check on Mother."

The usual line of greeters dissipated, many sending Ian apologetic looks, but seeming anxious to go about their own business. True to form, Etta Stout and Millie Wilson, Gertrude's closest cohorts, frowned at him, shaking their heads and passing him by.

Elisha Whitworth edged his way back through the stragglers toward Ian. "I wanted to tell you that Miss Biddle's playing was delightful, but you weren't listening." A grin filled the elder's face. "She's something else. I'll talk to the board. Hopefully, they'll listen to me instead of any troublesome woman." He pumped Ian's hand again. "Don't you worry, we'll see about a stipend for her, too."

Ian's cheeks creased with a smile he could not contain. "That's good news. I was anxious to hear your verdict."

Thankfully, Sophie and Caira were happily visiting with Maggie and Philip, alongside the piano. The little one clapped her hands and climbed up onto the bench, only to throw back her head with laughter each time her sister pulled her off. Ian hoped they hadn't heard much of what Gertrude had said. He rubbed the side of his face. When had his head begun to hurt so much?

* * *

Sophie arranged the music neatly on the rack and took what she thought she needed for practice. When finished, she had strained to see Ian's face over the heads of the church members that crowded around him. No wonder. His kindness, the gentle truthfulness of his sermon, and his cheerful ways must make him beloved by his congregation. There didn't seem to be one crack in the surface of his character. Stone Creek was a small town, but this church seemed to thrive.

Her palms had gone a bit sweaty at the realization of the size of her audience when the service began. How silly of her. It hadn't been the first time she played for this many people. The pews were comfortably full. She had performed for much larger audiences before, but it had been awhile. Somehow, she had never pictured herself playing in this venue again.

Quite frankly, Sophie wasn't sure she deserved to be there. But for the sake of Caira, she would take chances. She needed the money, but was it right to take it from a church, when she knew her ruse wasn't pleasing to the God worshipped there? Would that He would have mercy on her for her daughter's sake!

Caira toddled after Philip and Maggie. She hoped that the little one wasn't too much trouble for them. It was a blessed relief to have a break from the energetic child occasionally.

Sophie bit her lip. What had the people thought of her musical abilities? More importantly, what did Ian think? She needed the money, but most of all, she realized she didn't want to disappoint him.

Who was that pushy woman in line with the ugliest brown hat she'd ever seen? It looked as though she'd been berating Ian.

Should she find out what was wrong? Or stay out of it? Before Sophie had a chance to decide, her thoughts were interrupted.

"Your playing is really something, Miss Biddle. You belong in a concert hall. How did you wind up working for Mrs. Fairgrave?" James stood before her in a brown wool suit.

"What kind of question is that?" Sophie examined his expression. After all, he might remind her of her brother, but who knew what James was attempting to dig up.

"Whatever can you mean?"

"You sound more like you're looking for a newspaper story than starting a polite conversation." Sophie gripped several sheets of music in front of her.

"Well, I suppose I do let my curiosity and concern for friends get the better of me."

Sophie attempted a smile. "Don't forget that such care will use all of a cat's nine lives up. Or so it has been said. You needn't worry over my situation. Now, if you'll excuse me, James, I think someone wants to speak with me." Being in public made her more uncomfortable than usual as his gaze trained on her. She really shouldn't take out her worries of being discovered on James, but his questions about her past unnerved her. She made her way toward a woman standing patiently nearby.

"I'm Gloria Myles." A petite thing, she glided in Sophie's direction wearing an elegant black silk gown trimmed with what was likely French lace. "We are so delighted to have you here today." Blonde hair, just starting to fade to white, framed her youthful face. As the lines around her eyes crinkled when she smiled, Sophie guessed the woman to be in her forties.

"Sophie Biddle." The two shook hands in ladylike fashion.

"And this is my husband, Asa." She gestured toward him with a hand gloved in fine soft leather.

A few strides behind Gloria, a portly man limped along with the help of his cane. The lines on his bearded face had dug their troughs. As he drew closer, Sophie could see he probably was a few years older than his wife.

"Pleased to meet you, sir."

"The pleasure is mine, Miss Biddle. I wasn't sure if I could make it to church this morning—the gout, you know, but I'm elated that I did." His smile seemed pained, but sincere.

A child who she guessed wasn't more than five or six clung to Asa's pant leg. "This is our granddaughter, Elise Barrington." The gentleman patted the little girl's head.

"I'm so glad to meet you, Elise." Sophie bent and reached out for the small child's hand.

Two luminous gray-blue eyes stared from the expressionless void of her face, then blinked. She snuggled closer to her grandpa's side.

"I must apologize. She's been through a lot, and she doesn't talk much to anyone since the accident." Gloria lowered her voice to a whisper and leaned closer. "W-we lost my daughter and her husband, Elise's parents, nine months ago."

"I'm so sorry." Sophie touched Elise's shoulder for a moment. She felt kinship with a child who had lost so much.

Gloria Myles moved closer to Sophie. "Sometimes she whispers, 'Mama' and watches forlornly out the window. She's terribly shy and doesn't talk much to anyone besides us, but she loves to sing. Don't you?"

Silence claimed the next few moments while Elise nodded. The sad expressions on the Myles' faces spoke far more than their words could have.

"I could tell that she loved listening to you playing the piano today, though." Gloria breached the quietness.

"How could you tell?" Sophie wondered at how much they could understand a child who didn't communicate very much to them.

"She smiled." Gloria paused and her eyes glistened with moisture. "She hardly ever does that."

Mr. Myles drew himself up to his full stature. "We were wondering if Elise could come and listen to you practice sometime?"

"That depends on Maggie's approval. You see, I'll be practicing at the parsonage."

"If what's all right with me?" Ian's sister returned from placing the hymnbooks back in their holders with Philip's help. "Caira was trying to help us, putting the books upside-down in the holders and dropping some of the hymnals, so I didn't hear everything you said." Maggie chuckled. "Took a minute for me to correct the little one's help."

"The Myleses were just asking if Elise could listen to me practice."

"Only when it's convenient, of course. We wouldn't want to impose on you in any way." Gloria's eyebrows rose. She looked mortified at such a suggestion.

"We'd love to have her, if it's all right with you, dear." Maggie waited for Sophie's reply.

"Of course. How about Wednesday afternoon around three? That was the time that you and I discussed."

Maggie nodded her confirmation.

"I believe we are free that day. We'll bring her then." Gloria clasped her hands together like an overjoyed child. "It will be like attending a private concert. I have a feeling this will be just what our Elise needs."

Sophie glanced from one face to another. Elise's eyes brightened at the news. If nothing else, perhaps she could share the soothing touch of music with this bereft little girl. Maybe helping the Myles family would bring her acceptance into the community without drawing too much attention to her and Caira.

"All right, then. Thank you, Miss Biddle." Mr. Myles snapped his pocket watch open. "I'll go see if George has brought the carriage around yet, my dear." He gave his wife a congenial smile.

"Elise and I will be right behind you." Gloria took Elise's hand and nodded toward Sophie. A black hat trimmed with crepe and one black silk rose tilted fashionably atop the elegant lady's head.

Hopefully, the Myleses were as quiet and private as they seemed. Weren't they? How many more surprises awaited her in a sleepy little town that wouldn't allow her to remain anonymous? Just what was Ian McCormick getting her into?

CHAPTER 8

After the harshness of winter, the promising February thaw refreshed her with new hope. Sophie could still see wisps of her breath in the cool air as she and Caira puffed along Main Street, toward the street where the parsonage stood. Her eyes were drawn to brightly colored calico dresses in the window of Millie's, the only dress shop in town.

Green prints like the budding leaves of spring and pink prints that were as glorious as hyacinth and perfect for making an Easter outfit were displayed. They caused Sophie to stand still as though her feet were nailed to the boardwalk while she examined them. *How lovely.* Sophie sighed, recalling the days when she had a new wardrobe for each season as she had grown up, made to her mother's specifications. Back then sewing had been a hobby, something to be enjoyed with her mama, not a requirement.

Caira fussed and pulled at her hand. Sophie looked down at her daughter, wearing a well-worn dress from a charity. Staring at both of their reflections in the glass made her think of pictures of immigrant refugees from Ellis Island. How she wished she could provide better for the two of them. No. She must sacrifice to give the best she could to Caira and not worry about herself. Perhaps if Esther continued to be happy with her work and she picked up more mending jobs, she could stay long enough to save a nest egg and start her own business. Yet the true detriment to her would be the impractical nature of settling permanently anywhere. *Well, at least I can dream.*

Caira pulled her back to reality with a tug. "We'll be on our way soon, sweetheart."

The toddler stomped and whined.

"Sh! Stop that Caira, right now." Sophie tugged back.

The door of the shop swung open.

"Hmm." A woman with a pinched, bird-like countenance gazed upon Sophie and crossed her arms.

Where had she seen her before? Atop the stranger's head sat the ugliest brown hat she'd ever seen. It looked like a pile of crinkled brown paper with equally dull feathers sticking out every which way.

Ah yes, perhaps that was the woman she'd seen scolding Ian after the service last Sunday. She didn't look like someone you'd want to make an enemy of, though Sophie wasn't inclined to extend herself much toward the woman. However, there was no time like the present to attempt to melt the icy hardness in those eyes.

"Excuse me, I believe I've seen you at the Community Church. I'm Sophie Biddle." She extended her hand gently and did her best to put a generous smile on her face.

"Humph. I'm Gertrude Wringer, not that it's any of your business." Her arms remained crossed against an emaciated frame. One eye narrowed and the other bulged with seeming scrutiny toward both of them.

Caira took one look at the hawkish stare and hid in her mother's skirt, howling at the sight of the frightful woman.

"Well, it's nice to meet you, I'm sure." Sophie swallowed and picked up her daughter, holding her close to her shoulder. She hated these lies in her life, even the "white" ones. Would she ever be able to live honestly again?

Truthfully, she did hope that it would be good to meet the woman, that her kindness would have softened the tough exterior.

"What an absolutely horrid child. I can see you do nothing but spoil her. And that get-up you wore last Sunday, well, I hate to say where I would think that came from—"

"Whatever can you mean?" Fury rose with the bile in Sophie's throat and she attempted to swallow it down. She pulled the end of her shawl closer.

"You might be able to perform a bit of music and have the wool pulled over the pastor's eyes, but not mine. Mark my words, he'll be sorry. I can see you're just a pretender. How did *you* come by such a nice dress? And wearing something that fancy in church? You're trying to call attention to yourself, no doubt! Rather tawdry, don't you think? You're not the decent sort of girl my niece, Nora, is, for example . . ." Frantically, the woman looked around, opened the door and called back into the store, "Nora, come here this minute!"

A wan-looking young woman probably around Sophie's age, shuffled out. "Yes, Aunt Gertie." Head bowed, Nora barely made eye contact.

The aunt's chin went up, and her hand moved in a flourish toward her niece. "Now this is an example of a modest, accomplished young woman. Furthermore, she's academy educated."

Heat pushed its way over Sophie's cheeks. Her eyebrow went up as she bit her lower lip. The venomous reply on her tongue melted into sorrow when she saw the other girl's sad, pale blue eyes for just a moment.

"And another thing . . ."

Sophie wouldn't watch that awful woman wag her finger and her tongue any longer. She couldn't wait to be out of earshot.

Instead, she grasped Nora's hand. "I'm so happy to meet you, Nora. It seems your aunt thinks very highly of you."

Nora's eyes brightened. Her lips parted, but nothing came out, as though she disbelieved what she was hearing. Clearing her throat, she said, "I am pleased to meet you, too, Miss . . ."

"Sophie Biddle. Please call me Sophie. This is my . . . little sister . . . Caira." As usual, Sophie pushed the words out, unwillingly.

"Care-uh," the little one added, pointing to herself.

Nora smiled. "She's adorable." The young woman patted Caira's back.

Gertrude stood there, fuming. She grabbed her niece's arm. "Come, Nora. We have better things to do. And she is Miss Armstrong to you," the Wringer woman snapped at Sophie as she dragged Nora away.

Sophie wouldn't give in to her temper—for Ian's sake—after he'd given her a chance to be hired as the church pianist. *And for Caira.* She would not draw additional attention to herself for her daughter's sake.

Before she could turn to walk away with the little one in her arms, Sophie noticed that a haughty-looking woman with a measuring tape draped around her neck stood, crossing her arms, next to a shorter woman, wearing a hat too big for her stature. Both glared at her through the store window. Feeling somehow exposed, Sophie turned on her heel, gulping the cool air, yet her chest felt as though it burned with the fury she sought to keep inside. When all Sophie wanted to do was take care of her child, to give her daughter a life among good people, to protect her from evil men, how could that awful woman insinuate such terrible things?

Her footing became slippery along the slushy street and the faster she walked, each step became more of a struggle. *The nerve of that woman!*

Sophie's wet skirts whipped about her lower legs like the cool blade of a knife. Images of the people back in Detroit, where she grew up, paraded through her mind. They hadn't been much different from the Wringer woman. How many had insinuated that she had seduced the handsome and ingratiating Charles? Somehow, in the few months that he had spent in their social circles, he had won their hearts in a way that a native daughter had not been able. Then again, her own father had wanted to force her into a marriage with the cad. Truly, the children of darkness were more cunning in the ways of the world than the children of light!

The sting on her calves moved to her heart, where the cold steel of pain and rejection cut deeply into it. She thought that maybe Stone Creek would be different. Ian had seemed to become a protector to them, but it would be wrong for her to expect. Such assistance could come at too great a cost to him. But what had she done to incite such accusations from Gertrude Wringer?

Her vision blurred as she made her way through the thick slush. She took a deep breath and freed one hand from carrying her daughter to wipe the tears from her cheek with the back of her borrowed glove and stumbled.

Sophie put her hand out and hit a tall but warm solid wall of wiry frame and muscle in a black wool overcoat. *Ian!* She gazed up into the compassion of those lake-blue eyes.

"Sophie, are you all right? You look positively ruffled."

He braced both of her arms with his strong grip.

"'Cowmick!" Caira reached out to the kind minister. This was the first time in hours she wasn't whining.

Someone gasped. Sophie turned to find one of the women she'd seen in the dress shop window a few yards behind her, eyes wide open and hand covering her mouth. Pulling from the reverend's grasp, Sophie regained her balance.

"Well, I never!" Mrs. Wringer's cohort pointed at them. "Wait until Gertrude hears about this." Her voice hinted at a smirk.

"Reverend McCormick only sought to keep me from falling."

"Better he should keep you from falling into sin than into the mud." The woman wearing an oversized hat placed gloved hands on her ample hips.

Sophie, her heart feeling like shredded fabric that couldn't be mended by human hands, opened her mouth, yet nothing would come out. Ian took Caira into his arms. This relieved Sophie, who hugged her arms to herself and then placed a hand on her forehead. She blinked back tears, determined this woman wouldn't get the better of her.

"What's the meaning of this, Etta?" Though at least a decade younger than the other woman, Maggie appeared and placed her arm around Sophie, ready to defend her.

<hr />

Sophie shivered. Ian's heart wrenched at the situation before him. Chestnut curls blew in wisps around her face and she appeared practically as vulnerable as little Caira.

"Now, Mrs. Stout, aren't you being a bit unreasonable here?" He wasn't sure what else to say.

"I'm being unreasonable?" Etta turned to Maggie. "Your younger brother needs some lessons in how to become a true gentleman."

"Pardon me? Etta Stout, you take that back right this instant. I heard what Sophie said. My brother is a man of God, and he deserves your respect." Maggie set her mouth in a straight line, her eyes lit with fury.

"Hmm . . . we'll see about that." Etta backed down and turned on her heel, no doubt he could guess where she headed.

Ian sighed. "Maggie, you didn't have to take her on, but thank you for your loyalty."

His sister shook her head. "I kind of did, since you couldn't seem to find your voice."

He cringed. "A soft answer turns away wrath. I was trying the diplomatic approach."

"I see." Maggie rolled her eyes and hugged Sophie closer. "Whatever happened?"

"Before Etta supposedly caught me in Ian's arms? That woman . . ." Sophie swallowed her sobs and her face flamed with anger. "The one whom I saw scolding you last Sunday. You know, I think she said Wringer is her name?"

He waited for the rest of what she had to say. Inwardly, any bit of hope sunk. Already, Gertrude's crusade had begun, and with Etta's tongue to add to the fury, this could turn purely disastrous. Ian nodded.

"She said awful things to me—right out in public." Sophie stopped to swallow before she went on. "What have I done to her? I just don't understand it. Or her niece—what have I done to *Miss Armstrong*? Who is she to you? To the church?"

Caira contented herself with laying her head on his shoulder, playing with his collar and popping a thumb in her mouth. Oh, the blessed naiveté of children.

"The girl is nothing to me. I've only just met her myself. Gertrude is trying to wield her power as head of the Stone Creek Ladies' Aid Society." But he wouldn't let anyone hurt Sophie the way they had hurt Annie. His jaw tightened. The thought of the poor girl still caused a wrenching grief in his soul.

"She's an unwitting pawn in Gertrude's ploy to marry her off to—"

"Maggie, let me finish. The woman had hopes that her musically inclined niece could have a more permanent place using her talents for the church." Ian's gaze connected with Sophie's.

Her amber eyes searched his countenance while her pink lips parted a bit. Her freckles were close enough to count one by one. "And?"

Was she probing to see if he was really someone she could rely on? Yet she was no Annie. The warmth of her slight form against his coat, as the winter wind had whipped around them, had attested that her presence clearly meant more to him than the tormented girl he had once known.

Ian stiffened but continued to hold Caira. Was that what it had come to? He was attracted to this young woman so he would do whatever it took to protect her? He'd been more worried about his reputation than Annie's safety. When would he ever get it right?

"That's all." Ian exhaled.

But Sophie looked down as though she were disappointed in him. "There has to be more to it than that. That awful Mrs. Wringer said that *you* would be *sorry*. What did she mean?"

Ian pondered. What did Gertrude have on her mind now? He rubbed his neck with a gloved hand. "Nothing for you to worry about, Sophie." Likely dealing with the bully was his problem, instead. No doubt Gertrude would try to block his plans for building a charity home for unwed mothers or a school for orphans.

Clearing his throat, he motioned back toward the parsonage. "Let's head to the house. Maggie would be happy to prepare tea for you and hot cocoa for the little one."

"Co-co, co-co." Caira nodded her head in rhythm to the syllables she repeated.

"Gladly. Come away from all that gossip and discord." Maggie threaded her arm through the crook in Sophie's arm as though the girl were the sister she'd never had. "There's nothing a hot cup of tea and a bit of fellowship can't soothe away."

Silent, Sophie pulled her shawl tighter around her shoulders. Whatever his role was in her life, Ian was still a pastor. "Is there anything else you want to tell me?"

"No."

But for the swishing of the slushy snow around their feet, they trudged in silence. Even Maggie was uncharacteristically quiet. The same kind of discomfort of their first buggy ride together pervaded the atmosphere.

Ian's glance met Sophie's. His heart wanted to reach hers, to keep the wall from being rebuilt between them, yet there must be an honorable purpose. It could not be for his gratification, not because her flushed countenance and dimpled chin melted the very inside of him.

Sophie looked away.

"Are you sure there's nothing else you need to tell me?" With God's help, he would care for her as a sister, but nothing else.

She slouched forward a bit. "There's nothing worth telling you, believe me."

"Ian, Sophie's just had not one, but two awful encounters. Let her be for now."

"Very well." He trudged alongside the women.

Before they reached the house, a spicy scent beckoned him. He closed his eyes and inhaled the comforting smells of cinnamon and ginger. "Come on, Caira, why don't you ride on my shoulders?" The toddler giggled as Ian swung her up into the right position. "It smells like Maggie has been baking snicker doodles again."

"Indeed I have, but I'm not sure you deserve any, little brother." Maggie winked at Sophie and a hint of a smile played on the girl's lips.

CHAPTER 9

As Sophie and Ian walked through the gate of the white picket fence and up the pathway, the Myles' buggy came around the corner.

"Why, we're back just in time." Maggie smiled and let Sophie walk ahead of her when she reached the doorway.

When Sophie stepped inside, she momentarily forgot the stinging words of Gertrude Wringer and the sudden discomfort she'd experienced with Ian. Maggie had defended her as though she were a sister.

"Come on with you now, take off your wraps and warm up. Surely you'll need a chance to do that before you start playing the piano."

"I suppose a cup of tea wouldn't hurt." Sophie nodded.

"It's so good to see you." Gloria reached her hand out in greeting with such gracefulness once she and Elise had entered the parlor. She stood so straight and even in a simple black wool jacket and skirt looked like the epitome of elegance.

Elise gave a slight smile and stood with her hands behind her back.

"Say 'hello'." Her grandmother pushed her forward with a pat on the back.

Immediately the tiny smile disappeared and her blue eyes were hidden as her eyelids swept downward. Only her long golden lashes were barely noticeable.

Sophie watched as the child closed off like the shriveled bloom of a flower. She felt that way on the inside sometimes, but couldn't afford to totally close herself off. Adults didn't understand if other grownups felt like that, but they would indulge a child. Was she wishing that she were a child again? Life certainly had been simpler then.

Though it seemed Mama had to practically tie her to the piano bench, and she'd spent much of her childhood playing endless scales, it had been worth it. *Mama.* How she longed for the comfort of her mother's hugs. But Papa's controlling ways had come between them. She shook herself from her reverie.

Sophie curved up one side of her mouth and touched Elise's shoulder. "After we have a little tea or hot cocoa, you can sit next to me at the piano. How would that be?"

Elise nodded.

Gloria gave a nervous laugh. "Well, at least we are making a bit of progress."

"I'll be happy to amuse Caira. I can finish my sermon later." Ian didn't look directly at Sophie. He sounded a bit terse.

What was wrong? Had she upset him by implying that one of his church members had insulted her? After all, Gertrude wasn't the newcomer, she was. Perhaps Sophie was assuming she held too much importance in his life. The sudden withdrawal of the annoyingly honest, prying gaze that had breached her defenses and had stilled her heart, puzzled her.

Sophie already knew that she couldn't entertain any truly romantic thoughts about Ian, but she'd already come to depend on his kindness. Did it seem that she had thrown herself at him? Flirted with him? Just the thought made her flush.

"Sophie, dear, are you quite all right?" Maggie handed her a cup filled with tea.

"I-I'm fine," she stammered. "I'm just a little warm today, that's all."

"With this wonderful promise of spring amidst the winter, I can understand." Gloria sighed.

"Yes, of course." Sophie sat down at the table.

Ian talked to Caira much of the time but barely looked Sophie's way during the serving of refreshments.

"No more cookies for you, young lady." Ian shook his head.

"Mo' pease!" Caira stuck out her bottom lip and put out her hand.

Ian looked Sophie's way. Their gazes locked for a moment and then he looked toward the little one. "She's already had two. I didn't think you'd want her to have any more."

"No, I don't think that she should. That's enough, dear." She leaned toward Caira to wipe her sticky hands.

Her daughter whined and kicked her feet against the chair.

"That's quite enough. Do you want to go home or stay and visit 'Cowmick?" Sophie kept her tone firm and didn't dare look at Ian.

"'Cowmick!" Caira grabbed onto his lapel with fierce dedication.

"Then you must be well behaved." Sophie took Caira's chin in her hand and turned the child's face toward her. "What do you say?"

Leaning that way, with the child between them, Sophie caught the scent of Ian. Crisp citrus, like a warm breeze. Whether it was the residue of shaving soap or cologne, she could not tell. She wondered how it would feel to touch his shaven cheek, causing a pleasant shiver to course down her spine. Such a musing shocked and frightened her. She turned her thoughts back to the child.

"Yes, Soffie. Pease?"

"All right, then." Sophie felt warmth creep over her cheeks yet again that day. She met the sympathetic glances that Maggie and Gloria sent her way, shyly. "I'm afraid she is a rather spirited child."

"My dear, be glad your little sister still has some spirit. I'm hoping that someday my granddaughter will have hers back." Gloria lowered her voice and patted her mouth with a napkin, as though she hoped Elise wouldn't hear her.

"Well, I best get to practicing while Caira is slightly subdued."

Sophie once again sat at the mahogany Bidershem piano. Its beauty hadn't ceased to amaze her. *God, give me strength*. Emotion swept over her as she moved her hand across the lid of the piano and felt its smoothness.

Memories of Miss McGillicutty tapping the end of her cane on the floor, to keep the beats even during her music lesson, took over her thoughts. The old maid's wrinkled cheeks had been almost as hollow as Gertrude Wringer's. But the piano teacher, who tried not to smile her approval too often, had a sparkle in her eye. When Sophie had approached near perfection in a piece, Miss McGillicutty had always exclaimed, "Fine, fine! You're coming along now, child." Remembering such times eased her thoughts of the encounter with Gertrude, cheering her considerably for a time.

Shouldn't she choose to think of the happy times of her childhood? Yet the events that led her to take Caira and leave her home crowded their way in. How bittersweet! To wish to be home again, yet believe it beyond possibility. All this twisted in her heart. Between Ian's sudden aloofness, Mrs. Wringer's verbal attack, and her memories, Sophie desired to bolt to the comfort of the boardinghouse and hide from the world.

However, Gloria stood smiling nearby, with her arm around her granddaughter, waiting with such patience.

"Oh dear, I'm afraid I haven't dusted this lovely instrument often enough, have I?" Maggie worried over the top of the piano, running a clean hanky on its already highly polished surface.

"Oh no, it's fine. I was just thinking . . . of the first Bidershem I ever played." Sophie stiffened, sitting straight and resolved to lift the lid, which covered the keys.

Maggie opened her mouth, a question forming in her expression. It was time for Sophie to change the subject. "Come sit by me, Elise. You can watch me play now."

The child's eyes widened. The hint of a smile played on her lips.

Sophie picked out a few children's tunes to warm up and caught Elise grinning more than once. Then, opening the hymnal, Sophie played each piece Ian had suggested for her in his list.

When the little blonde girl reached for the keys, Gloria spoke up. "That's not a toy. I don't want you banging around on it."

"What if I teach her how to play?" Surely the warm memory of Sophie's piano teacher caused the words to slip out of her mouth before she realized. "I mean, only if it's all right with you, Maggie, and you give me permission to teach your granddaughter, Gloria."

"Would you like that, darling?"

Elise nodded toward her grandma and smiled, looking as though she would burst without talking.

"Are you sure you wouldn't mind?" Gloria's eyebrows furrowed.

Would she mind? Sophie wondered at her impetuous offer. Yet she remembered her own enthusiasm and curiosity over how to play the piano when she was a little girl. Maybe Elise would have the same natural ability. If nothing else, perhaps being able to express herself through music would bring healing.

How many times had Sophie buried her woes in playing tempestuous or worshipful pieces on the piano, or singing out to God? As a young girl asking questions of life, it had brought great comfort. After the attack, Mama had often cried when she'd play, saying her music ministry was ruined. Causing her mother hurt hadn't brought much succor. Yet using Maggie's piano felt like the comfort of a family hearth.

The Myles family's hurts were different, but she understood something about such profound losses. They were kindred spirits. Perhaps God had a further purpose to use her broken life to help heal another's and maybe eventually her own.

Sophie gave Gloria a genuine smile. "Of course not. If Maggie doesn't mind my being here a little longer, then perhaps we could begin by giving her a lesson before I practice each week."

"I would be happy with the company." Maggie clasped her hands together like a tot just given the promise of candy.

"I'd be happy to teach Philip too. You're so generous in letting me use your piano and welcoming us all into your home. What an interruption we all must be!"

"Hmm . . . I guess I thought perhaps Master Philip would take lessons from his uncle, when he's ready, that is." Maggie gazed toward Ian.

He looked up from the book he read to Caira. "I'm sure Miss Biddle would be my superior in teaching." His glance brushed off Sophie as he returned to his task.

"Perhaps we shall take you up on that offer, then, Sophie." Maggie beamed.

"Well then, we'll begin in earnest next Wednesday, with at least one student." Sophie patted Elise on the back. She wondered at Ian's comment about her being the superior teacher, finding it hard to believe he had that much confidence in her.

As she straightened up the books on the piano rack, she was more than aware of Ian reading to Caira by the fire. The glow of the hearth upon her daughter's face made her look perfectly cherubic. Ian's tender smiles and patience made him look like a prime candidate for fatherhood.

Why hadn't he found a wife yet? He was kind, handsome, and a good pastor. Perfect for someone else—probably too perfect. Sophie bristled. If he ever found out the truth about both of them, would he even want her as an acquaintance?

Gloria and Elise said their "good-byes" and left bundled in their wraps.

Maggie scurried around, setting the table with her gleaming Blue Willow plates. "Would you like to stay for dinner?"

The smells of chicken frying and, perhaps, sweet potatoes lingered in the air. Warmth emanated from the coal stove. Sophie's stomach rumbled. Her heartstrings sought to tie her to a chair. Remembering her earlier exchange with Ian, she squared her shoulders. "No thank you, Maggie, I have chores at the boardinghouse." That was the truth. "Caira, come, let's put your coat on." Sophie went to the coat tree near the front door for the garment.

Caira whined, rubbing her eyes. Clearly her nap hadn't been long enough. Ian scooped her into his arms. "Now, now, Caira, you must listen to Sophie. Did you like our story time?" The toddler nodded. "We'll do this again when your sister comes to practice, but you must be well behaved."

He helped Sophie put the coat on the little one, who insisted on emphasizing her goodness by saying, "Sh," and putting her finger to her mouth.

Sophie concentrated on her daughter's face, anxious to pull her away from the minister. "Thank you for amusing Caira, Ian. I'm sorry she's a bit fussy with her molars coming in."

"She's never a problem."

Their hands brushed and he stepped back. Ian pulled her shawl from the coat rack and held it out to help Sophie. She grasped the shawl away from him. "I'll take that." Setting Caira down, she wrapped herself up and took her daughter's hand.

Ian cleared his throat. "Let me take you home."

"No, thank you. It's quite nice out actually. We could use the brisk walk."

Maggie rushed to hug her. "I'm sorry to see you go so soon. I hope you won't catch a chill."

"We'll be fine." Sophie hugged Maggie back, trying not to glance over her shoulder at Ian, but there he was, running a nervous hand through his dark, wavy hair and looking anywhere but at her. What was happening between them?

<hr />

If silence could speak louder than words after dinner, then the quiet shouted at Ian, especially considering his sister's usual chattiness. The stale odor of frying grease from the chicken hung in the air.

"May I be excused?" Philip wiped his mouth with a white linen napkin.

"You may." Maggie nodded at her son.

Then she looked toward Ian with such coldness that he thought he might feel warmer if he stepped outside.

"Out with it, Maggie."

"Hmm. Like you would listen to me anyway, little brother."

Ian stirred a bit of sugar into his tea and leaned back in his chair, stretching his legs. He sipped the hot liquid, savoring its warmth as it glided over his tongue.

"What was going on between you and Sophie today?" Maggie asked.

The tea went the wrong way. Ian's windpipe closed, and he choked. When he recovered he mumbled, "Nothing."

"That's just it. I don't understand it." She spoke in low tones through her teeth. Ian counted two spoonfuls of sugar that were mercilessly dumped into her tea. The noise of the spoon clanking against the side of her cup rang out in the dining room. The sip his perfectly elegant sister took sounded more like a slurp.

Ian leaned forward and placed his elbow on the table. He rested his chin in his hand and attempted not to spew tea when he coughed.

"What? Oh, go ahead and laugh at me. You always have found some incongruous humor at my fury."

He measured her expression—the brows furrowed together, the mouth set defiantly. Ian knew he needed to tread with utmost care. "I'm not laughing this time, but I know your bark is worse than your bite, and I'm sure that whatever you have to say is in my best interest." Well, at least she would think so.

Maggie's expression softened. "I was positive that you two were smitten with one another." She stirred her tea again and tapped the spoon on the lip of the cup then made a circle above it with the utensil. "There seemed to be something in the air. Though, how Caira and she could be so smitten with you, I don't know."

"Smitten?" He shifted in the hardback dining room chair.

"You're either as hot as a flame in a coal stove or as cold as an icicle outside the window, Ian. It's not the first time you've acted like that, but those two girls are different." She paused, slurping her tea again, and banged the fragile cup on its saucer so that Ian feared it would shatter. "One minute, you're trying to have her installed as the church pianist and next thing I know, hardly a word passes between you."

"Well, it's good to know I'm being watched like an errant toddler." His sarcasm came out with a meaner edge than he had intended.

The hardness returned to Maggie's face. "How dare you, Ian! You're still my younger brother, and I'm concerned about you. You need a wife and a family—not an older sister nagging you. Do you think I enjoy this role?"

Ian sighed. "Are you trying to find a replacement to nag me?" He tried to soften his question with a grin and a softer tone this time.

Silence again enveloped the dining room for several minutes. Maggie folded the edges of her napkin. "Ian, let me try once more. What happened this afternoon?"

Ian rubbed the side of his face. What was his sister looking for? "I want to help them, but what kind of a pastor would I be to take advantage of a young girl romantically? We hardly . . . know her."

"What's that supposed to mean?"

"I want the congregation to trust me, Maggie. I need to keep everyone's best interest at heart. Sophie and Caira need friends to lean on right now, without feeling we're interfering. You've seen how independent she can be. Sophie's not looking for a courtship right now."

"Sophie would be good for you, Ian. She's hard-working, responsible, obviously she'd be an asset to the ministry with her musical talent."

"The Lord sent me here for a reason, Maggie. There are unwed mothers and orphans who need tending to. We can take care of them in this town. Once I have that in place, I can think about other things."

Her eyes sparked as though ignited by a gaslight. "I saw Gertrude Wringer scolding you last weekend. If you're truly worried about rumors, then get yourself a wife. You're going to need someone to at least support you in your vision, if not share it. Don't you think a houseful of girls they consider fallen women would make fodder for gossip for the entire ladies' missionary society?"

Ian didn't deny the accusations but stared at the amber liquid in his cup, almost the color of Sophie's eyes. He didn't usually have cream in his tea, but tonight he would try some. He poured a bit in and swirled whiteness into the brown liquid. He would do anything to avoid Maggie's gaze at this moment. "I'm protecting Sophie. Gertrude will make sure that nothing nice is said about her."

"I see." When Ian looked up, Maggie's eyes narrowed. "You're still doing some kind of penance, aren't you?"

"Penance? I don't do penance."

"Annie."

That one name sliced through his heart and soul again. A pale, lifeless face rose in his mind. Would he ever be rid of this haunting memory?

"You would avoid the affections of a perfectly lovely young woman because of having to make up for some supposed failing?" Maggie sat a little straighter and pointed her spoon at him. "I haven't seen her do anything unseemly. There's quality there. You heard her play today, saw her patience with Elise. You've seen how she is trying to raise her little sister without any help. And she wouldn't have asked for a thing from us."

Ian sat with his chin resting on clasped hands. What could he say to a one-person judge and jury like his sister? All she said was true. But she couldn't fully understand. In fact, Ian wasn't sure he understood. He only knew that he felt there was something he needed to make right and there were people depending on him to lead the way.

His sister stood and began piling dirty dishes on a tray. She grabbed his unfinished tea. "What's wrong with you? How can you risk losing her? I guarantee you. Someone will come along and snatch her up, and then how will you feel? Are you going to wait until you're old and gray to take a bride? When you are too blind and feeble to enjoy the love of a good woman and dandling children on your knee?"

"That's quite enough." Ian rose to his feet and pushed the chair away from the table so that its legs squeaked across the floor. He tossed his napkin onto the tablecloth and stomped toward the back door. He slammed it behind him as he went out onto the stoop. He could bang things around, too, and see how she liked it.

Ian shoved his hands in his pockets and stood breathing hard with steam curling from his nostrils as though he were an angry stallion. Then he rubbed his hand along the side of his face.

How could Maggie understand his predicament? When Sophie had stood so near earlier in the day, he'd nearly forgotten propriety.

She'd obviously been upset, and he desired to comfort her, to hold her in his arms and plant a loving kiss on her lips. Yet he had no business, especially as a man of God, thinking those things about a girl he hardly knew.

How had this happened? Did he truly want to make up for his travesty of failing Annie? Had attraction always played a part? Was he capable of pure motives? A sweet young woman like Sophie deserved so much more. But when all was said and done, Ian was still very much a man.

He let the chilled air sweep over him, stinging his face and hands. When would he truly realize the forgiveness of Christ, who had borne all of his sins away already? Why did he try to punish himself when he knew the punishment had been taken for him?

CHAPTER 10

When the church elders congregated early the following Thursday evening, the sun was heading downward toward the horizon. Its beams cast a strange glow through the colored glass windows. Ian had said it would be best for her to make an appearance, and Sophie found herself drawn to the meeting, she mused, like a "moth to a flame." She clenched and unclenched her gloved hands, smoothing her skirt again and again. Having felt self-conscious with the lovely evening gown she had worn on Sunday morning, she had donned her other least threadbare outfit, attempting to look more businesslike and hoping the jacket didn't seem too mismatched with the skirt. Sophie stood stiffly between Ian and the head elder, near the pulpit, wishing the meeting was already over. Only a few of the elders welcomed her with a smile. A couple of them refused to look her way and the other two frowned. Had they heard Mrs. Wringer's lecture in the back of the church the other day?

The head of the board, Elisha Whitworth, opened with prayer, and then the board secretary read the minutes of the previous meeting. "As long as you're here, Miss Biddle," Elder Whitworth added, "we'd like to ask you a few questions."

He introduced the other elders to her, which included a man by the name of Edmund Wringer. She assumed he was Gertrude's husband. He attempted a superficial smile, covering a sad, weary expression. "Miss Biddle, what kind of training do you have?" He fiddled with his tie.

"Your wife put you up to that question, no doubt. Hearing Miss Biddle play was proof enough for me." Dr. Moore, the town physician and the board secretary, crossed his arms and leaned back against the second-row pew.

"It's all right." Sophie clasped her gloved hands together, intertwining her fingers. "I began receiving private lessons at quite a young age, from a Miss McGillicutty. She's gone now." What could it hurt to tell the name of her teacher who had passed on?

A few eyebrows went up at the declaration of receiving "private lessons."

"Well, that's just fine, young lady," Mr. Whitworth piped up, looking pleased.

Sophie only nodded. "It's a shame that your family must have fallen on hard times," another elder said.

Should she say anything? The truth was that they hadn't fallen on hard times, but she had, on account of leaving them. The Bidershems had fractured and fallen away from one another.

"And you've played in other churches?" Mr. Wringer's quiet voice interrupted her thoughts.

"Yes, sir."

"Do you have references?"

"Just what are you implying about her past, Edmund?" Mr. Whitworth sounded very annoyed.

"I haven't any with me, sir." Sophie bowed her head. Disappointment caused a lump to lodge in her throat. Surely her time was almost complete in Stone Creek. She'd leave rather than be thrown out. It wouldn't be long before they'd figure out the whole truth.

"Reverend, we've had enough interrogation. This wasn't what I'd had in mind as far as asking questions. Her playing so far has been simply heavenly. I haven't heard the congregation sing like that in a long time." Elder Whitworth extended an arm in her direction.

"I second that." Dr. Moore stood. "We couldn't do better if an angel came to play the piano for us. Maybe we could get the choir back together now."

"My thoughts exactly. If anything, I would like to hear your testimony, young lady." Elder Whitworth's smile invited her without censure.

"Well, I, um . . ." What could Sophie say truthfully without giving away too much?

She stood straighter and cleared her throat. "I grew up in a Protestant church and accepted Christ as my Savior when I was around six years old. There was an altar call one Sunday . . . the pastor had preached about how Jesus said that the little children should come to Him."

"How much did you understand about sin? Did you repent?" Elder Wringer tapped his walking stick on the floor at the end of each question.

"Sir, of course, I understood what sin was, but I only needed to be sorry for such things as disobeying my mother or lying about whether I'd kicked my brother or stolen a cookie from the jar." Sophie tried not to smile in spite of herself. Faith had been simple as a child, but the fact that she wasn't forthcoming about her recent struggles made her stomach churn with guilt.

After they asked several doctrinal questions, Dr. Moore stood. "I think she's answered our questions to satisfaction, which are far more important than references."

All but Elder Wringer nodded in agreement and mumbled assent. He kept his glance cast down, not making eye contact.

"We can't offer much, but we know you could use the job, Miss Biddle. However, we'll need you to step out while we take a vote."

"Of course." Sophie nodded at Mr. Whitworth and pulled her shawl tighter around her shoulders before making her way toward the entrance.

Gertrude Wringer burst in, flanked by the two women Sophie had seen through the dress shop window. Fury flamed in her eyes as she marched forward like the general at the head of her own miniature army.

———————————————————

"Gertie?" Edmund stood.

Ian shook his head. This time Gertrude brought reinforcements. The tall, angular Millie Wilson, owner of the dress shop, and Etta Stout, a short woman, swathed in clothes too large for her frame, followed close behind her. His jaw tightened. This wasn't the first time she'd manipulated Edmund to influence a vote of the elder board since Ian had been there. And he'd heard plenty about the fiasco where she'd wanted the name of the church changed to Armstrong Community Church in her father's "loving memory."

Though having no personal experience, Ian knew scripture set the standard for marriage. He liked to refer to the book of Ephesians for advice to couples, where it said, "Nevertheless let every one of you in particular so love his wife even as himself; and the wife see that she reverence her husband." Poor mild-mannered Edmund had the greater task in loving such a woman, but the way Gertrude disrespected her husband infuriated Ian.

Gertrude sniffed. "I told you if this process took too long, I would come in to find out just what's going on."

"I'm bringing up the questions you asked me to . . . " Her husband's face reddened as his voice trailed off.

"My issue is with everyone else here." Gertrude stared Ian right in the eye.

The Reverend steeled himself so as not to flinch under her glaring scrutiny.

Elisha spoke up first. "Gertrude, Millie, Etta, this is an elder board meeting. You're welcome to bring your complaints to us before or after, but you are interrupting right now."

The obstinate ringleader pointed toward Sophie, who stood at the back of the sanctuary. "The respectable women of this congregation should have something to say about allowing this tawdry woman in our midst."

Sophie's mouth hung open. Her eyes widened. Was she hoping to say something?

Ian put up a hand in warning and shook his head, wishing he could tell her he'd handle the confrontation. As if Sophie understood his intentions, she nodded and exited the sanctuary.

"Gertrude is right." Millie spoke more quietly than Gertrude.

"Absolutely." Etta pointed her nose in the air, not looking at Ian.

"Speak your piece, and then you'll need to leave." Ian stayed behind the pulpit. Elisha stood alongside, shoulder to shoulder.

"Young man—" Gertrude pointed a finger at Ian.

"You will address our pastor as Reverend or be invited to leave!" Elisha's meaty, work-worn hand struck the pulpit.

"Very well, then." The haughty woman sniffed. "*Young* Reverend, I will remind you that my father, Hiram Armstrong, was one of the founders of this town. Edmund and I were two of this church's founding members . . . " Her eyes narrowed as she continued her usual litany.

Ian bit his tongue. *Lord, give me compassion for this merciless woman.* He realized she'd fallen from more grandiose circumstances, but didn't want to let go of her last shred of influence. Still, she was a woman of some means. She had no understanding of Sophie's situation.

"Furthermore, we need fine upstanding examples for our young people, not someone like that seductress, Sophie Biddle. You saw her flaunting herself in that evening gown, rather than a plain, modest church outfit. And where did a *humble* creature like herself procure such a fancy item?"

"Perhaps if she had better wages she could afford what you believe is a suitable outfit." Ian gripped the sides of the pulpit with both hands. When Gertrude had walked toward him, he had to resist the impulse to grasp her by the arm and march her out to the street. "Last Sunday, I saw a young lady who wore the nicest clothes she owned and she shared her musical gift to the best of her ability. It's probably been awhile since she's lived in as comfortable circumstances as you or I."

Maybe lumping Gertrude into the social strata of a lowly parson had been the wrong thing to say. Anger flashed in her—what would you call them—mud-brown eyes? She flushed crimson and stood with arms akimbo.

"Unlikely she ever did! I think we all know why, too. Do you really believe that child is that trash's sister? We haven't even approved the plans you've suggested to the elders for homes for immoral women and illegitimate children, but the lowlife are already infiltrating the town!"

Etta nodded demurely, but Millie spoke up. "And she won't be allowed to darken the doorway of my fine establishment."

"Not only that, but I was shocked at the news I heard from Etta, here, that she saw the temptress in Reverend McCormick's arms, on the street, no less." Gertrude lifted her head and sniffed again, glancing down on everyone.

"With all due respect, Mrs. Stout knows very well I only kept Miss Biddle from falling into the slush and catching pneumonia. Sophie never meant for that to happen."

"We've heard quite enough. There's no reason to reject what the young lady or our esteemed pastor said. You can leave now."

When Elisha became angry, he resembled a wolf, with teeth bared, a whisker-covered chin, and a wild look in his eyes. Ian thanked God for sending the congregation their very own avenging angel.

Gertrude backed down from this formidable figure. "Very well, then. Come along, ladies. Edmund, you know how to vote on this matter. And I'll be waiting for you at home, so don't dawdle."

"Yes, dear." His head went down like a chastised dog's.

The elder board discussed the matter awhile longer before they took a vote. Three voted for hiring Miss Biddle permanently and four against.

Elisha leaned forward in his chair. "Gentlemen, I must say that I'm disappointed with this outcome. What goes on in this room should not be influenced by anything but prayer, the leading of the Lord, and a bit of common sense." Ian saw how the head elder looked straight at Edmund.

"Absolutely," Dr. Moore said. "We should not allow ourselves to be influenced by idle gossip."

Edmund Wringer fiddled with his tie and seemed more interested in his shoes. Lawrence Stout tapped his foot on the floor and averted his gaze. Ira Blanding folded his arms across his ample middle while Burt Wilson was the first one to speak up. "Elisha, remember who we have to go home to."

Lawrence cleared his throat. "Don't you believe that peace at home is God's will too?"

The other three naysayers nodded in agreement.

"And helping a talented, but impoverished young woman isn't?" Elisha shook his head.

They sat in silence a few minutes longer before Ian prayed and they adjourned. He always knew he could count on Elisha and the doctor, but he was truly disillusioned that the elder board he depended on wasn't made of sterner stuff.

"Is the meeting over, Miss Biddle?" Nora paced outside the front of the church.

Sophie, flustered by Mrs. Wringer's declaration, felt like a house with a broken window and cold air seeping in. Caira and she hadn't been in Stone Creek very long, and already someone had attempted to shatter her dreams of a stable life in town. Though the stipend would have been small, she would have been able to buy supplies more easily for her sewing business. Surely she was being punished for her ruse.

"Miss Biddle, are you all right?" Nora's pale eyes exuded compassion, the opposite of Mrs. Wringer's feelings toward her.

"I will be." Could she tell Nora that her aunt was the cause of the misery that threatened to overtake her? "The meeting took a turn I didn't expect. Please, call me Sophie, Miss Armstrong." Sophie remembered the Wringer woman's admonition.

"Only if you call me Nora." The young woman gave her a genuine smile. "Aunt Gertie can be rather harsh. I-I'm sorry she's trying to ruin things for you. Perhaps the elders will hold their ground this time."

Somehow Sophie didn't feel so hopeful, but her heart warmed toward Nora for trying to make her feel better. The girl wasn't her enemy, but perhaps a victim of her enemy as well. She wondered about Nora's dependence on her miserable relatives. "I never meant to take a potential position from you, Nora. I'm sorry for any trouble I've caused." In fact, Sophie didn't want to fuel any discord in the small town congregation either.

"There's nothing to be sorry about." Nora took a step closer. "Aunt Gertie gets her ideas, but I wasn't promised a thing. Besides, I could learn from you. Your musical talent and ability are beyond mine."

Once again, Sophie found herself speechless.

The church doors opened. Nora stepped away from Sophie. Three dour-faced women marched out. Gertrude glared at Nora. "Come along, now."

"Yes, Aunt Gertie." The subservient tone had returned to her voice. While walking away, Nora looked back and gave a discreet wave over her shoulder as if wanting to say "good-bye." Still, the woeful look had returned to her eyes.

Sophie pondered what Nora's life must be like. She had a family and likely a complete education. She probably lived in a comfortable home. But was there any real love or friendship in her life? Sophie felt richer despite her hardships. She wanted to befriend this poor soul, imprisoned by a cross aunt.

Twenty minutes later the church doors squeaked open. Four somber men filed out. None of them looked her way as they passed. Ian stood at the entrance beckoning to her. "Come inside," he said.

The head elder and Doctor Moore gave her sad smiles.

"Sit down." Mr. Whitworth motioned toward a pew. He sat down next to her. "I'm afraid we won't be able to offer you that position right now. Perhaps another time."

"I'm very sorry about all this, but I would still like you to play for us sometimes." Ian averted his gaze. She noticed a tick in his jaw.

Could he be annoyed with her? Was there something she'd done? "I see." Sophie looked away. Though she'd been frightened by their curiosity, she'd been hopeful of this boost to her income . . . and a chance to play the piano again on a regular basis. She remembered her manners. "Thank you for your time, for at least giving me the chance. If you'll excuse me, I have evening chores to tend to."

Her chin went up. She put on the fullest smile she could brave and left the church as quickly as was polite.

CHAPTER 11

Though Sophie realized not being employed as church pianist would keep unwanted attention away from her, the disappointment stung. That Wringer woman had no business influencing the elder board to decide her fate. Yet, there were some who stood behind her. Maggie and Gloria brought their dresses to be altered. A shy Leona Packer brought her fabric and asked her to make a dress, one evening after dark. Sophie hoped they would be happy enough with her work to become repeat customers. Though a small start, she needed to build a customer base and had to begin somewhere.

Nora had been hired to provide music for the congregation each week. Though Sophie no longer needed to practice on a regular basis, she still visited Maggie weekly so that she could give Elise a piano lesson. Besides, Maggie insisted Sophie play her Bidershem piano just so she could hear it make beautiful music. Since the pastor's sister had been so kind and the piano was in the parsonage, she felt obligated to attend the Sunday service. She sat in the back with Caira unless coaxed to move up farther by her acquaintances.

Sophie reasoned with herself if Caira must grow up as part of a church, Stone Creek Community Church might as well be the one. And seeing Ian was a bonus though she often ran into him at the parsonage. Yet every Sunday morning her stomach knotted as they dressed for service and she pleaded with God for forgiveness every time she entered the sanctuary. Occasionally she begged off with her stomach symptoms, and they stayed home.

The snowy weeks of March passed into the rainy days of April. Sophie's student flourished. Most Tuesday afternoons, she only caught glimpses of Ian as he ducked in and out of his study, but she enjoyed Maggie and Gloria's company.

In the evening, after Caira slept, snuggled down in their bed, Sophie sewed new clothing for them both. With her earnings from the music lessons and sewing for others, she'd bought fabric and thread. With much effort, she'd foregone the temptation to buy brightly colored calicos, settling for dull browns and grays for herself. After she hemmed a skirt, she tried it on with the jacket.

Sophie stood in front of the mirror over the washstand, combed her hair straight back, and twisted it into a knot. She wetted it down a bit, trying to straighten out her curls. "There, that should do it," she commented to her reflection. She looked just like the old maids she'd seen, with their "Psyche knot" hairstyles. Sophie remembered Miss McGillicutty's white hair, pulled severely back into a tight bun and the plain, somber attire she wore. With her former piano teacher as an example, Sophie would not fail to make herself look more businesslike. This would perhaps also help her be taken more seriously and attract new customers as a seamstress. Women like Mrs. Wringer probably preferred going to a no-nonsense woman who wore modest clothing rather than a fashion plate.

Sophie had never cared for the dent in her chin, her freckles or her unruly curly hair, so she didn't think of herself as very attractive, but she needed to look as plain as possible. Ian shouldn't think that she was attempting to flirt with him or anybody else. Maybe this would keep his eyes away from her and slow down the looks of disgusted appraisal from Mrs. Wringer and her followers. No man would consider her fair game for courtship or think her an improper woman this way.

One Tuesday afternoon, she sat directing Elise at the piano. "You need to curve your fingers a little more like this." Sophie held the little girl's hands with her own and helped form them into the right position.

Elise scaled the keyboard with concentration.

"There, that's much better now, isn't it?"

Her question elicited a nod and a smile from her shy student.

Sophie felt as though someone was watching them both, as though a strong presence waited nearby. She glanced up to find Ian's eyes twinkling with a pleased look. Their eyes met and his flitted to the list in his hand.

"These are the hymns I'm suggesting for this week. I'm not completely happy with them." He paused. "I'm open to any suggestions you might have. What do you think?"

"Oh." Sophie wasn't sure quite how to respond, surprised Ian had asked her opinion at all. She'd been disappointed that he almost never looked directly at her anymore and then angry with herself she would feel that way. Perhaps her plan of making herself less attractive was working a little too well? But she mustn't think that way! She perused the list. "They look fine to me." Sophie shrugged. "What does Nora think?"

The front door flew open. "Yoo hoo!" Esther Fairgrave's sing-song greeting pierced the air with off-key notes. The chill breeze that blew over the threshold made the remnants of late winter known, sending a shiver down Sophie's spine.

Maggie went to greet her newest guest. "What brings you out on such a blustery March day, Esther?" She reached to take the heavy woman's woolen coat. "Would you care to warm up with a cup of tea?"

Mrs. Fairgrave huffed and puffed as she waved a piece of paper at them. "No time for tea today." Yet she collapsed into the nearest chair as her wet boots dripped upon the floor.

"My daughter sent me a telegram. She's in dire need of help. She's in the family way and all four children have the measles. Who knows how long I'll have to be there to help take care of them. I'll be taking a train to Marshall tomorrow."

"Oh, Esther, how awful!" Sophie stood up from the piano bench. "I'm so sorry about your daughter's predicament."

"The only thing is, Sophie, you shouldn't be left alone with all the men in that house. And Mr. Spitzer will be returning soon."

"'Tis true." Maggie stood nearby, smoothing her skirt.

"Wait a minute." Sophie gestured with her hand out. "But who will cook and clean for the men? And Caira and I truly depend on the wages you kindly pay." *As meager as they are.* Could they hear the hint of a whine in her voice?

"But it wouldn't be proper, dear." Maggie patted her arm.

"You're right, it wouldn't be for the best." Sophie worried her lip, intent on stilling the trembling within. The whole thing would be rather unsavory for her, but did she have a choice? "But what will you do with your guests, Esther?" Poor Mr. Graemer certainly needed someone to check on him at least.

"You will stay here with us at night, and I will stay there with you during the day." Maggie's tone held insistence.

"But I couldn't possibly ask you—"

"Nonsense. You are like family to us. Isn't she, Ian?"

Sophie's gaze flitted to the tall, handsome man who often stopped his work to play with Caira. His brow usually darkened with a brooding expression around Sophie lately. He stood in the doorway of the study, and rubbed the side of his face. "Well I . . ."

"Of course he agrees." Maggie crossed her arms.

Ian looked rather sheepish. "I suppose we have no other choice." He put his hands in his pockets.

Maggie came alongside Sophie and linked arms with her. "You can help me with chores here, and I will help you with chores at the boardinghouse." She wore a grin that made her look very pleased with herself. "You'll see, dear. It will all work out."

"And you must share some meals with us," Gloria piped up.

Sophie felt overwhelmed by the love these new friends had so quickly imparted to her, but she wished she knew why Ian had become so strangely distant. "Well, thank you, then. I will certainly do all that I can to not be a burden." How much she appreciated their care!

"It's settled then. Oh, what a relief. I can go to my Daisy now without a worry." Esther inhaled a deep breath. "You know, Maggie, perhaps I will take you up on that cup of tea. It's quite blustery out. And I'll have some of your delightful spice cookies."

***

One evening almost a week later, Caira stared up at Ian with large, gray eyes, pleading. "Read to me, 'Cowmick."

"Caira, how do you ask?" Sophie sat across from them near the hearth, darning one of the child's small woolen socks, but didn't look up from her mending. She hadn't meant to sound so terse, but exhausted from her work at the boardinghouse and traipsing back and forth with the new routine, she felt more irritable than usual.

"Pease 'Cowmick?" Now the child gave him one of her most endearing smiles.

"Of course, little one." Ian tousled her curly head and pulled Caira onto his lap. She snuggled against his chest until she seemed comfortable and clasped her hands together with giggling delight as she waited for him to open the book.

He read the colorful pages aloud, pointing to the different pictures while Caira's childish laughter filled the room. How soft the child's hair felt. He imagined that's how Sophie's was as a child. Her round cheeks and sprinkle of freckles resembled her older sister's so much.

"Kitty." She pointed at one of the pictures with a chubby finger.

"What does the kitty say?" Ian asked, much like his father had asked him when he was little.

"Me-ow, me-ow!" She wriggled with the effort and curled up like the little kitten.

Ian caught a fleeting sad glance, combined with a wistful smile on Sophie's face. What was she thinking? Perhaps she was remembering her own childhood. Were the memories more painful since their parents had passed on? Surely Sophie must wish that her little sister could have had a more normal childhood, like her own.

It was difficult for Ian to believe the patience and love with which he'd seen her care for the child and her work with Elise, for that matter. Sophie seemed so motherly, so mature for the age he assumed she was. He admired such depth of character.

Caira yawned and stretched.

"It's time for you to go to bed." Sophie stood and held out her arms to her sister.

"No, no." The toddler's widened eyes begged Ian for mercy.

"You must do what Sophie says." He hugged Caira before turning her over to the supposed enemy.

"Thank you," Sophie whispered. She leaned toward Ian to scoop up the child. A whiff of lavender, or was it roses? filled his senses. An errant lock of curls escaped from her new, severe hairstyle and tickled his chin. He was positive she didn't realize her hair had brushed against him. He felt the tenderness of the flesh on her arms as he passed Caira over to her. The warmth and sadness in her amber eyes, as their gazes locked for a moment, begged for Ian to touch the roundness of her cheek. He did not, but her look infused a desire to comfort her, to break into the loneliness she must feel in her world.

How solitary his own world had become. He'd dwelled in the parsonage with Maggie and Philip this last year, but he still felt so keenly alone.

If the truth were told, Maggie probably still felt very alone in her own grief. He swallowed against the dry, pasty feeling that thickened in his throat. They existed together in one house like islands in the same sea.

How wonderful it might be to become a husband and a father. He supposed that it was a ministry in its own right. Ian had performed weddings before, spoken of how man could not put asunder what God had joined together, but never before had he glimpsed what such oneness might entail for himself. To share a meal and then sit pleasantly by the fire while your wife performed ministrations as simple as mending, took on new implications. To hold a precious child on one's lap, a child that would be part of each of you, how wondrous that could be! Or even to care for your wife's little sister. Oh dear, had he really thought that?

Ian had taken his parents' marriage for granted. He remembered how Mama had proffered her cheek for a "hello" kiss while she stood at the stove and Father had come in from a long day at the office. He'd scoop little Ian in his arms and give Maggie a pat on the head. Mama's eyes always sparkled at this. Now he realized how the family had somehow been a culmination of his parents' love for one another—a fact and a mystery to Ian at the same time.

"Good night, Caira."

The whining began. "Nooo!"

"Shhhh, be good for Sophie." He stood and placed his hand on the child's back while her sister held her. The little one quieted to a whimper. "Would you like to ride up the stairs on my shoulders?"

Sophie didn't look up. "You must ask the Reverend nicely, Caira."

"Pease 'Cowmick?" She thrust out her bottom lip.

"No pouting then." He took her from Sophie's arms for what was becoming a routine. Caira giggled.

Sophie smiled in silent appreciation.

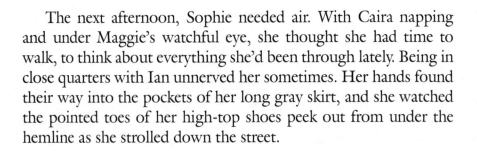

Sophie had gone up to bed to tuck Caira in but never came back down. Ian rubbed his sweaty palms together and then on the legs of his trousers. How could he maintain his ability to care for her out of charity if her presence continued to unnerve him the way it did? Ian raked his hand through his hair and stared into the flames of the hearth.

"A penny for your thoughts." Maggie interrupted his musings as she bit a thread off from her mending.

"I was just wondering how soon Esther would be back. I ought to be praying more for her grandchildren." *For healing, in earnest.* The sooner Sophie returned to the boardinghouse full-time, the better. He had known having the two girls in his home every night would make his life difficult. If only Maggie had allowed him to beg off and find another place for Sophie and Caira to stay.

Maggie raised an eyebrow. "I certainly thought you've been enjoying the company. I surely am."

The next afternoon, Sophie needed air. With Caira napping and under Maggie's watchful eye, she thought she had time to walk, to think about everything she'd been through lately. Being in close quarters with Ian unnerved her sometimes. Her hands found their way into the pockets of her long gray skirt, and she watched the pointed toes of her high-top shoes peek out from under the hemline as she strolled down the street.

The sweet fragrance of blooming hyacinth wafted on the early spring afternoon air. How long it had seemed in coming. Birds chirped, celebrating the budding trees even as white clouds like puffs of cotton scudded across the sky, sometimes blocking the sun. Sophie felt divided in the core of her being. She wanted so much to embrace the newness of spring, to feel hope in her new beginnings, the love she'd received from Esther and Maggie. Ian and his sister had become like a makeshift family for her and Caira.

But something was missing. While Ian acted like a big brother, she was afraid she was attracted to him like she would never be to her own brother. They'd been avoiding each other while Maggie tried to bridge the gap, and Caira and Philip's chatter filled in the silence. Sophie wished she could stop thinking about her dilemma, so she kept walking toward the center of town. Maybe she would watch the ducks and geese that had returned to the millpond.

A sad, forlorn sound emanated from behind some shrubs. Sophie stopped to listen. The voice somehow sounded familiar. Sobbing and sniffling gave way to a low wailing. Whoever it was must have one deeply broken heart. Her own melted in kinship. She closed her eyes. *What can I do to help? Or should I just leave them alone?* But what if it was a hurt child? She should make sure they weren't injured at least.

Tiptoeing toward the sound, Sophie parted some thick branches that sported budding leaves and peeked through. A lone figure sat on a bench in a gazebo. Nora Armstrong? What did she have to be sad about? Then again, what did she have to be happy about, living with a sour old woman like her aunt?

"Nora?" Sophie lifted her voice barely above a whisper. "Are you all right?"

The blonde girl sniffled and looked around, wiping a handkerchief across her face. "Who is that?" Her thin frame hunched over and she drew her knees up to her chin to hug them as though she could hide.

"Sophie." She felt compelled to find a path through the shrubs and not sneak up on the poor girl. Her glance flitted to the other end of the property, where a large house, built of brick and stone, stood. Standing on the edge of the yard, once she broke through, Sophie waited to be invited further. "Is there something I could do to help you?"

"You must hate me for taking your job away . . . and I'm no good at it anyway." A deep sob wracked the poor girl's body again.

"Whatever can you mean?" Sophie fingered a curled leaf pushing forth at the end of one branch. "You're doing a fine job."

"You wouldn't understand. Everyone thinks you're pretty and talented. Aunt Gertie tells me I must eat more, plump up and gain color. She says I don't practice enough, and I'm as clumsy as an oaf at the piano." With this declaration, Nora peeked up at Sophie with red-rimmed, swollen eyes.

Sophie averted her gaze, not wanting to embarrass Nora by staring at her. What a different story she had to tell compared to what had been observed in public! Taking tentative steps toward Nora, she moved closer.

"You can sit down." The other girl shrugged and patted the bench next to her. "Aunt Gert's taking a nap and Uncle Ed won't mind."

"If you're sure . . ." Sophie waited until she nodded. "Perhaps your aunt is not feeling well and doesn't mean what she says." Sophie tried to sound hopeful. Gertrude must truly care for her niece. Why would she otherwise have Nora living with them?

"She says she's just being honest with me for my own good. She thinks I should know more about music after they paid my way at Miss Melton's. It is an excellent finishing school." Nora sat up straight and swung her legs down, then pulled a dry lacy white hankie from her apron pocket and dabbed her eyes. "I'm afraid you caught me acting like such a child."

"We all have times we need to shed some tears. You sounded so wounded, I wanted to make sure that you were going to be all right." Sophie paused and bit her lower lip, not sure what to say next. "I was concerned someone might be hurt."

Nora sniffled. "Only my pride, I'm afraid." She twisted the wet handkerchief she held. "Did you hear the mistake I made during the service last Sunday?" She turned a watchful gaze on Sophie.

Should she tell a fib to comfort the disheartened girl? Or be completely honest? Under the girl's examination, she could hardly tell a white lie. Sophie looked away again.

"You can tell me the truth." Nora sighed.

"Nora, if you're not used to performing in front of a crowd it can be unnerving. I've made plenty of mistakes in front of people."

"You can't mean that." Nora shook her head.

"I started as a young child." Sophie glanced up at the clouds. Her childhood seemed as far away as they were.

"Really? Was your family musical? Or were you just wealthy enough to afford lessons?" Nora's eyes brightened with her curiosity. Surely she wasn't fishing for information that her aunt wanted? No. The look in her eyes was as transparent as a squeaky-clean window, but her questions were getting a bit too close to the truth about Sophie's past for her comfort.

She smoothed her gray wool flannel skirt, careful to choose her words. "My parents thought very highly of musical training. It was kind of . . . an investment . . . for them."

Swallowing against the constriction of her throat, Sophie stared down at the toes of their shoes. "Don't be so hard on yourself. You're doing perfectly fine and you look lovely the way you are." She truly felt the other girl was lovely and possessed a sweet innocent spirit about her. As thin as she was, Nora walked gracefully and sat straight at the piano. How could Mrs. Wringer be so heartless toward her niece?

"There you are with all your responsibility and you can't be much older than I am, but I sit here and complain. Please forgive me. I can't do anything right!" With that Nora swiped away a fresh outpouring.

"You mustn't say that about yourself. It won't do you a bit of good." Sophie patted the other girl's knee, clad with the finest royal blue wool skirt. The tortoise shell combs that held her string-straight blonde hair in place, were encrusted with shiny stones. Her aunt and uncle saw well to her needs. And though the paint peeled on the gazebo, their fairly large home boasted a wraparound porch and sat on a rather generous piece of property.

Sophie once had these entrapments of wealth and more. Perhaps her life with Caira was rough, but she didn't envy Nora, whose ease came at a cost. Sophie wouldn't have been willing to pay the price of giving up her daughter. Without the hugs, kisses, and giggles of her little Caira, her life would be much poorer indeed. The temptation to envy Nora was fleeting.

"Then what am I good at?" Twisting the wet hanky again in her hands, Nora gave her an imploring look. "I truly don't know."

"You are a very good pianist and getting better each time you perform. Don't worry about what people think. You're playing for God, aren't you?" Mama had often encouraged her with those words years ago.

"Well, yes, of course."

"And you are kind rather than letting your aunt make you cranky and mean. That's a choice you make every day, and I admire you for it." Sophie gave her an encouraging smile, not sure she could do as well with Gertrude.

"Really?" Nora's eyes held the tiniest spark of hope.

She nodded. "Please believe me . . . and if your aunt would allow it, I would be happy to help you when you practice, though I don't think she'd be very agreeable to the idea." Sophie looked toward the towering brick structure with black shutters. "In fact, I should probably go. I don't want to get you in any trouble."

"Thank you, Sophie. Maybe Aunt Gert would let me visit if it's to help with my music. I'll pray that she will." Nora stood when Sophie did. "And I best get back to the house and face her like a grown-up." She chuckled. "I appreciate your friendship. Nobody wants to spend time getting to know me, because . . . well . . . they're scared of you-know-who."

Sophie, on impulse, gave her a quick hug. When Nora drew back, she blinked, looking surprised. "I'll see you at church."

CHAPTER 12

Ian knew he needed time away from Sophie and Caira. To think. Their lives and hearts were becoming as intertwined with his as threads in a tapestry. Seeing Sophie each day laid bare emotions he once thought he could control. He needed something else to focus on and had been relieved Elisha could meet with him early the following week.

Though not as lovely and feminine as the burgundy evening gown she once wore, the new clothes Sophie had made for herself fit her nicely. The simple but smartly tailored garments accentuated her talent and her petite waistline. The wispy curls escaping from her severe hairstyle only served to make him wish that the rest of her thick tresses would fall free, as well. What was he thinking?

He sat behind his desk. Elisha, perched on a chair across from him, interrupted his thoughts. "I'm only saying that perhaps we should take a day to make a trip to the new rescue home in Detroit, to see how they run things there. I believe it is one of the newer Florence Crittenton Homes. What do you think?"

"I'm sorry, Elisha." Ian closed his eyes, rubbing his thumb and forefinger over the bridge of his nose.

"You do seem to have other things on your mind, Ian. Perhaps this isn't a good time."

"I'm afraid I'm not doing a good job casting all my cares on the Lord is all." Yes, more time in prayer would help, along with meditating on God's word. That was it. Once he received the spiritual help he thought he was obviously lacking, he could deal with everything logically.

"Oh, now, don't let that Wringer woman get to you, son. She's like a wounded lion. Her roar's kind of loud, but sooner or later people will figure out she's a gossip. I pray God will show us how to guide her to her proper place." The head elder shook his head.

Ian's eyes popped open. Elisha thought that he was afraid of Gertrude. At least this dear friend and mentor didn't realize who truly made him want to run. "You're right, Elisha, on both accounts. When would you care to embark on our journey?"

⋯•●)————— ● —————(●•⋯

Two days later, Ian stepped off the train behind Elisha and onto the platform of the Fort Street Union Station in Detroit.

"There he is!" Elisha hailed a rather short, paunchy man with a gray handlebar mustache hiding half of his broad smile. "Dr. Conrad! Good to see you again." The two men shared a hearty handshake.

"This is my pastor, the Reverend Ian McCormick."

"I'm honored to meet you, Reverend."

"Call me Ian, please." He was touched by the pride his head elder took in him and in the ministry of the church. The awareness of the fact that these were older, wiser men made him feel like an inexperienced boy in their presence. Hopefully, he would learn something from being with them.

"Well, then you must call me Robert. Come along now. With this spring weather, our walk to the home shall be a short, invigorating stroll. Follow me." Dr. Conrad gestured toward Fort Street.

The impressive red brick structure that they left behind was matched in grandeur by the Presbyterian church on the corner. Its beautiful spire would dwarf Stone Creek's humble steeple.

"I understand from my friend, here, that you're interested in establishing something similar in Stone Creek." The doctor took long strides for a short man, but they kept up with his quickened pace. They turned left onto Washington Boulevard.

"Yes, well," Ian said, pausing to clear his throat, "but perhaps something on a smaller scale than you would have here in the city." In his mind and heart, he had imagined a small homelike atmosphere for residents so that they felt more like part of a family.

"Our ability to join forces with Charles Crittenton's work is most fortuitous, or should I say, blessed." The man paused as though reverent. "He began to spread these homes across the country in memory of his daughter. Poor little gal passed away when she was only four. But the conversion that took root during his bout of despair has borne much fruit. While he was heartbroken over his daughter's passing, Mr. Crittenton has certainly moved his affections to the worthy cause to which God led him."

"So I've read. As sad as the situation was, surely much good has come of it." Elisha always seemed to have a positive comment for each situation. You couldn't feel glum around him for long.

"The women should just have finished their dinner. They have a quiet time in the afternoon, during which I could give you the tour. That should work out nicely."

They arrived in front of a three-story structure on Miami Avenue. As they strode toward the front door, Ian took in the large sturdy house with its ruddy brick face. Not knowing what to expect, an ominous feeling overshadowed him. But perhaps it was his nerves, not the building; for inside would be housed many fallen young ladies, living on charity while they waited out their confinement.

A lump grew in his throat as he remembered the awful discovery made when Annie's body had been found. The swollen belly she'd hidden under her baggy clothing gave away the undeniable fact that she had been with child.

How would Annie have felt climbing the steps to the front door of such a mission home? In fact, how had she felt when she had knocked on the door of the parsonage? It troubled him greatly that he could have been instrumental in saving both lives. That thought alone drove him to the desire to give young women who'd made a mistake a place where they would be accepted and loved. A place where they would have the opportunity to bear their babies in peace. A place of healing. If they couldn't take care of the infants, he wanted them to have a loving place to leave them so the mothers could start a new life. But in his grand scheme, they would be encouraged to keep those children.

A trim young lady opened the front door, wearing a white cap with an apron to match. She bid them enter.

"Please kindly let the matron know I have arrived with our guests." Dr. Conrad removed his hat.

"Yes, sir." She took their hats and coats before she led them to a reception room and gave them a shy smile. Not unlike Sophie, when she began working at Fairgrave's, Ian noted. *Sophie.* What was he doing thinking about her again? Wasn't he there to distance himself from the young lady whose endearing ways had begun to entangle his heart?

Ian nodded and turned away from the servant, taking in the clean and simply appointed room. He was there because he had a job to do. Brisk, light footsteps in the hallway interrupted his reverie.

"Good afternoon, Dr. Conrad, I see our guests have arrived." A woman who could not be yet forty years old greeted them. The crisp white outfit she wore accentuated the gray creeping over her temples. While her dark eyes were bright with kindness and hope, dark circles belied her tireless efforts at the mission.

"I am Mary Heartwell, the superintendent of this facility, which I hope you will find pleasing."

"Miss Heartwell, let me introduce Reverend McCormick and Elder Whitworth."

"Of course!" She extended a work-worn hand, motioning and added, "I am the nurse, the matron, and confidante of these dear young souls. We are pleased to have Dr. Conrad here, as well as the other generous doctors who take their turns in rotation, a month at a time."

Miss Heartwell exuded warmth while still maintaining her sense of decorum, a rare quality for a woman in charge.

"Carrie Smith needs to see you, Doctor. Perhaps you would allow me to take these gentlemen around the home and you can catch up with us later." Miss Heartwell opened the watch dangling from the fob pinned to her shirtwaist and snapped it shut.

The doctor nodded. "Of course. Gentlemen, I'll rejoin you later."

"Let's begin upstairs since the women are away from their rooms at the moment." Miss Heartwell headed into a rather long hallway, toward the stairs.

Ian heard the low hum of conversation, along with an occasional giggle from the back of the house. He supposed the chatter came from the dining room. They passed an empty parlor on their right.

"We are very fortunate to have a rather large sitting room. Our young ladies are able to read their Bibles or other books in there while there is also room to take out the sewing machines in the morning for them to do their work. Sometimes in the evening there is needlework and knitting to do. We keep their hands busy. If they're fortunate enough to have family supporting them, we encourage them to keep up a correspondence."

Ian noticed the cleared tables around the perimeter of the room while there were also plenty of chairs and a sofa where they could sit comfortably.

"You understand this dwelling place is likely temporary." Miss Heartwell nodded toward Ian and Elisha. "As we are now affiliated with the Florence Crittenton Mission, we are hoping to soon have an even more suitable abode. We hate to turn anyone away." Her smile warmed Ian, making him feel quite at ease.

He and Elisha followed the kindly Miss Heartwell up a steep flight of stairs. Once they reached the second floor, doors on either side of the hall stood open to good-sized rooms with three sturdy white beds apiece. Though ready to accommodate more than one resident at a time, the room they entered felt lonely as their shoes echoed on the polished wooden floor.

"Here's where the young ladies sleep or come to rest when they're not feeling well. As you can see, they all seem to be up and about today." Her arm swept toward the perimeter of the room.

This begged a question. "The room is very tidy. Who does all the work?" Ian noticed sheets and blankets tucked neatly and any of the girls' possessions must have been hidden from sight.

"Why, the residents take care of their rooms. They need to learn skills to take with them. Whether they are from a poor, uneducated lot and never learned habits of cleanliness or they were from wealth and never had to lift a finger, they must know how to care for a home."

"Important skills to have. Naturally." Elisha nodded.

"Speaking of skills, what do they do when they leave here? And what happens with the children?" Ian again could not suppress his curiosity.

Miss Heartwell tied a section of the airy muslin curtain back so that more daylight entered through a tall window. "Most often we train these fallen girls in useful skills, so they can go on to become domestics. Some, with understanding families, will return home.

We encourage them to love their children and keep them. We do our best to make sure they have secured a reputable position when they leave here." She paused.

Floorboards squeaked under an uneven gait in the hallway. A young lady carried a stack of linens into the room. When she saw the men, she halted.

"Put them down on that bed for now, Julia," the nurse said.

"Yes, Miss Heartwell." Placing the pile onto the bed revealed folds of clothing barely hiding a growing belly. She blushed. Ian thought the girl must be nearing her time.

"It's all right, you are excused to go back to your work." Miss Heartwell's sympathetic gaze told of her affection for the residents. She then turned toward Ian and Elisha to whisper, "They are used to feeling safe in their own world. I'm afraid they're a bit shy to outsiders."

Julia smiled at the matron before she looked toward the floor and exited the room. The nurse's voice took on a hushed, matter-of-fact tone. "Not all of these dear girls are simply 'fallen women.' Some are victims of deceit, seduced into what they believed was an act of love, rather than sin." She grew even quieter. "Others are victims of force. It may not seem ladylike to divulge such information, but these are the facts, gentlemen, as sad as they may be. But we don't allow them to wallow in the past either." Miss Heartwell averted her gaze and turned rather pink. "Perhaps I should write up a pamphlet addressing these travesties more delicately. Please excuse . . . my rather forthright manner. Someone must speak for these hurting women."

Elisha shook his head. Ian attempted to take it in. Miss Heartwell had a difficult job. Brotherly feelings filled him. The desire to go to fisticuffs with the brutes who'd taken advantage of naïve girls made his jaw tighten. His fists clenched. Violent thoughts usually repulsed him. Perhaps this was what the Bible meant by "righteous indignation."

"Poor girls." Miss Heartwell shook her head, then stopped and raised her chin. "We do not cater merely to brazen women or prostitutes though we try to help them, too. All are welcome. Sadly, they are the ones likely to give up their children rather than turn over a new leaf. Then there are some girls who want a fresh start. Their children usually go to a childless relative or to the foundlings' home. But we always encourage our young ladies to allow the natural love for their babies to flourish. Which brings us to the nursery." She beckoned them to follow her to another room.

Four young women, wearing white aprons, rocked the babies, cooing to them. One changed a diaper. The sight did Ian's heart good. It reminded him of something. In fact, it was Sophie's care for Caira, so loving and maternal. But he shook the thoughts from his mind. Sophie had said they were sisters and that settled it for him, Maggie, and he hoped the rest of the congregation, besides Gertrude and a few others.

After they were allowed a peek into the other rooms on that floor, the superintendent led them up a second flight of stairs. Pointing to one of the smallest rooms in the house, she said, "These are my quarters. And we have another small room, as well, in case someone needs to be quarantined.

"As fine a medical care as you could expect in this kind of institution. Dr. Conrad and his colleagues make sure of that." Miss Heartwell's encyclopedic description continued. "However, we don't yet have the facilities to handle the birthing of the babies. They are welcomed at the Women's Hospital, where I was once employed, thankfully. And then they return here. We try to keep them with us for at least six months after the babies are born, making sure they have a solid foundation."

By the time they journeyed back down both flights of stairs, the residents were removing their plates from the table in the spacious dining room. The easy chatter stopped when the men came into their sight.

"And here, of course, is our dining room. The kitchen is in the basement." Miss Heartwell halted and smiled.

Ian looked over the collection of young ladies. Some were tall, some short, some were pretty, others only possessed that glow of youth that lent to their attractiveness. Their current states were hidden well by clothing and sometimes the addition of a long apron.

He felt the warmth creep into his face and looked away, pretending to stare out a window. To stand there and study them would be no better than to treat them as caged animals in a zoo. He cleared his throat. "Thank you, Miss Heartwell, for the tour. I'm sure Elisha and I don't care to disrupt the day's activities any longer."

"Absolutely not. We do appreciate your time, Miss Heartwell." The head elder nodded in agreement.

"We so appreciate your interest. Anybody who wants to have a mission for girls such as these touches my heart. It has been my passion for quite a long time. We're a long way from what Dr. Kate Waller Barrett, our national General Superintendent, envisions for the mission homes, but we are making progress."

"I believe Dr. Conrad mentioned in his letter that you will soon be incorporated with their name?" Elisha asked.

"Yes, we will soon officially be called the Florence Crittenton Mission. And we hope to eliminate the burden of rent by purchasing a house for its use. Please keep us in your prayers!"

Dr. Conrad strode in from the main hallway. "Ah, there you are! Sorry I was detained for so long."

"We were just finishing up, Doctor," Miss Heartwell informed him.

"Is there anything else we can do for you?" Ian offered, wishing to be of some help to the worthy mission.

"Well, actually, you could. I'm afraid I received word that the speaker for this evening's evangelistic service—we have them on

Monday and Thursday—took suddenly ill. I'm always willing to fill in, but I think our young ladies would enjoy someone with a fresh perspective."

Ian had started to observe one of the young ladies. Her braid sat cockeyed on her shoulder, her clothing seemed a bit disheveled. She looked away, reminding him of a frightened animal. He supposed they didn't have the means to allow the mentally unstable to stay in the facility, but how like Annie she seemed.

"Reverend?" Elisha again caught him unawares.

"Yes? I'm sorry." Ian looked around at the other men and the matron.

"Miss Heartwell would like you to preach to the women this evening." Elisha nodded.

"Of course, but we need to catch the train before dark, Elisha."

"I won't hear of it. You'll come home for supper with me." Dr. Conrad waited, smiling. "And, of course, stay the night."

"Well, I suppose. Maggie and I did discuss the possibility that I wouldn't make it back this evening, and I left her a note to remind her." Ian shrugged. "I guess I should have listened and packed a bag."

"I'm sure the missus will be able to come up with an extra pair of night clothes our son left behind," Robert said.

"My wife suspected as much, too. I'm sure Lila will understand. The boys will see to what needs to be done on the farm. I think she'll be fine."

"Excellent! I'll let my wife know we'll be having guests."

CHAPTER 13

Early that evening, Ian entered the large parlor. Dark paneling adorned the bottom half of the walls while the upper half had been whitewashed. A simple wooden cross was fastened to the wall opposite him. Just then, he also noticed a print depicting Christ and the woman at the well. He wondered how many times they'd heard a message about this fallen woman, later redeemed. Did they also hear about Gomer? Delilah? The woman caught in adultery?

He sat in a plain oak chair. *What do you want me to tell them, Lord? What is Your message for them?* He thought how scared and lost some of the girls appeared. Sheep. That's what they made Ian think of. Lost, bleating sheep looking for help. And how many of them had been deceived by wolves in sheep's clothing? He set his jaw.

"We require them to attend worship, but sadly, some of them don't take the mercy of our Savior to heart." Miss Heartwell interrupted his reverie. "They'll be here soon."

When the young ladies filed into the sitting room a few minutes later, most carried Bibles, but a few crossed their arms and looked down. Their chatter hushed as they entered. Did they wonder where God was . . . having to navigate an unexpected route placed on the map of their lives? Ian admitted to himself that he'd spent more time analyzing the probable thoughts of ruined girls like these than he needed. He'd carried this burden since he'd turned from a chance to help Annie on that cold autumn evening. He shivered.

Ian hadn't remembered meeting the woman sitting in the back row. She kept her head bent over some knitting, but when she looked up, the warmth of her brown eyes smiled a blessing on him. Gray streaked her chestnut hair and she wore a black dress, reminiscent of widow's weeds.

He cleared his throat. "Let's open our Bibles to Matthew, Chapter 18." Eyes alight with expectancy met with his. Others, hardened and void of spiritual life, averted their gazes. Ian read the passage, speaking of God's love for the one sheep who had wandered away. "There is one path to following our Lord and Shepherd, Jesus, but sometimes a lamb loses its way . . ."

Speaking to the young ladies in a gentle but firm voice, he explained how everyone goes astray with the choices they make at one time or another, but that the good news was about the Father's compassion and mercy toward those who He was calling back. Ian ended with the comment, "Yes, the Good Shepherd will truly rejoice when He's found the one sheep who went astray. He only wants you to hear His voice, to accept the forgiveness and peace He offers you." He paused.

The older woman in the back dabbed her eyes with a handkerchief before she touched a simple locket hanging at her neck. Something about her heart-shaped face haunted him.

One of the girls shook her head while crossing her arms in front of her. "It's easy for you to say! What have you ever done wrong? You're a minister. You could never understand!"

"Muriel, calm down! Act like a lady." Miss Heartwell stood. "I'm so sorry, Reverend."

Ian studied the young woman with golden hair and cornflower blue eyes, raising her chin. She would have seemed lovely but for the hard glint beneath her lashes.

"No," he said, "it's a fair question. I am a sinner, too, and yet God has called me to the ministry. I have let Him down. Believe me. It's only because of His grace and mercy that I stand here today. I am no better or different than you, Muriel. As St. Paul said, 'I am the chiefest of sinners.'" *No better than a murderer.* He might as well have tossed Annie right into the river with his own two hands. His throat felt dry. How could he preach when he didn't always act on what he believed?

You're forgiven, Ian. Your sins are as far as the east is from the west. Ian's heart pounded as he perceived the Holy Spirit's quiet voice within. Why could he only receive it as a dry fact for himself, instead of the Father's love for his child? He closed his eyes and began praying aloud. When he opened them, he noticed Muriel's expression had softened. Were her eyes bright with tears? Or hope?

After he'd finished, one of the girls waited by the door while he spoke with the doctor, Miss Heartwell, and Elisha.

"What is it, my dear? Shouldn't you be getting ready for bed now?" Miss Heartwell sounded a bit anxious.

"May I please speak with Reverend McCormick for a moment?" The matron looked at him for his answer.

"Of course." Ian went forward toward the young lady. Something about her seemed different.

"I'm afraid when you saw me earlier, I was quite a mess. I'd been helping out in the kitchen." She paused. "And I'm usually rather shy."

Then Ian remembered the disheveled girl reminding him of Annie.

"But I had to tell you how much I appreciate your message and your truthfulness, Reverend. I've been praying for Muriel to come to the Lord since she arrived a month ago. And praying she will stay here through her time of confinement."

"What is your name?" He wanted to remember this girl with the bright eyes and dark hair, neatly combed. She wore a clean shirtwaist.

"Hope."

How appropriate. He couldn't help but smile at her.

"I heard you're trying to start a home . . . for girls like me." From behind the Bible Hope clutched in one arm, she brought out a white handkerchief with the corners tied together. He heard a couple of coins clanking inside. "It's not much, but I'd like you to have it."

Her grin widened as she untied the cloth and emptied the treasure into his hand.

"What about you and your baby?"

"The Lord will look out for us. Please take these."

"Thank you, Hope. I will pray for Muriel, too." A lump grew in his throat as he finally understood the parable of the widow's mite. Feeling chastised about what he'd thought of Hope earlier, Ian was learning how often things weren't what they seemed.

The mysterious older woman stood a few paces away, waiting patiently as Ian spoke with Hope. "Excuse me, Reverend," she said in almost a whisper when they had finished.

"Is there something I can do for you?" Ian was surprised to see her moved by the message, when he had targeted the residents of the home.

She nodded. "I am Olivia Bidershem."

"Bidershem?"

"Yes." Her slight smile seemed pained, her sigh ragged. "Of the Bidershem Piano Company family. Being wealthy and well-known doesn't keep us from having problems. Sometimes I think it creates more havoc. May I speak with you . . . about something important?"

"Of course. Let's sit down." He pulled a chair so that they sat perpendicular to one another. "What's wrong, Mrs. Bidershem?"

"My child. I fear she is a lost sheep . . . lost to us anyway." Weeping, she dabbed her eyes.

Ian waited, praying silently.

"It's all our fault. A young man we trusted . . . he forced himself . . . on her." Mrs. Bidershem reddened at the revelation. "She was with child." She hesitated. "After the baby was born my daughter ran away." She wept again. "D-do you think there's hope for her, like the lost sheep? I come here to assist once a week, just hoping to help some poor young woman, someone like my little girl. And I knit these little things for their babies, since I can't give anything to my granddaughter." Mrs. Bidershem held tiny white booties out to him, almost as though she were looking for approval for her little offering.

Ian leaned toward her. "Of course there's hope. There always is with our Savior. He loves your daughter more than you do."

"Will you pray for her? For our family?" Her eyes shone with fresh tears, pleading for someone to understand the brokenness of her heart.

He nodded.

"Her name is Sophia." Then the soft-spoken woman lifted the delicate gold locket and opened it to show Ian her picture.

A heart-shaped face, with a dimpled chin below a slightly crooked grin looked out at him with eyes full of innocence and trust. Ian blinked. He swallowed hard and cleared his throat. "How long ago was that?" His voice came out in a rasp.

"It's been two long years without Sophia and the little one. Caira's what we named her. I wonder how big my granddaughter is now. We've done everything we can to find them. All we can do now is pray."

Ian nodded again. *Sophie Biddle was actually Sophia Bidershem? Caira was her daughter, not her little sister?* And this lovely, sad woman in front of him was looking for answers that he didn't feel free to give until his suspicions were confirmed. Surely there was some reason Sophie had not told him the truth. He wasn't sure whether the knife in his soul was from seeing the poignant heartbrokenness of her mother or from knowing that Sophie had held a secret back from him. How could he reassure one without betraying the trust of the other?

He patted her hand. "Praying is the best thing to do. Remember that. God will hear you. You don't know that there isn't a miracle waiting for you around the corner, Mrs. Bidershem." In fact, Ian was sure this meeting was no accident. He wished he could assure her that all would be well, but first he would have to gain Sophie's confidence.

"Thank you, Reverend. I just had to talk to someone . . . to have someone share our burden in prayer. I had a little son who died from a fever when he was just a tyke. The grief of not knowing what has become of my daughter and granddaughter is almost as deep . . . other than to believe I will see them again someday."

"Of course. Your burdens have been great, Mrs. Bidershem."

"You've been so kind."

A rotten feeling set in for not telling her about Sophie and Caira, but he had to be sure it was the correct thing to do at the right time.

⋅•⋅)⸺⸺⸺ ● ⸺⸺⸺(⋅•⋅

Sophie and Maggie went around the parsonage to turn up the gaslights as darkness descended. Stopping, Sophie stood up straight, rolled her shoulders back and rubbed her sides.

"Monday is a busy day at the boardinghouse . . . all those linens needing to be washed. I'm afraid I feel it, too." Maggie rubbed her neck. "And it doesn't sound like Esther will be back anytime too soon in her letter. It's a shame the children are having such a rough time with their mother being sent to bed in her condition."

"I'm sorry, Maggie. It will be a good thing for you, too, when Esther gets back."

"Don't you worry, now. I wouldn't have it any other way. I only hope that I didn't mix up my brother's things with any of the boarders'." Maggie chuckled. "I might get fired."

"Hardly." Sophie joined her laughter. She looked around. How quiet the house seemed. No light gleamed from under the study door. The woodsy citrus scent that always followed Ian was absent. Disappointment weighed on Sophie's heart. "Where is Ian?"

"Ian!" Maggie called out. No answer. "That's odd. Oh yes, he was going into Detroit with Elder Whitworth today. I remember now."

"Look, did you see this?" Sophie pointed to an envelope on the table, addressed to Maggie.

"How could I have missed this?" She unwrapped and read the note. "Ian says here though he hopes to return on the evening train, there's always a possibility they will have to stay the night, so not to worry if he doesn't come home. I suppose he was kind to leave a reminder, knowing how I fuss over him."

"What are they doing in Detroit?" Why didn't she know what was going on? Sophie remembered Maggie speaking in hushed tones with Ian in his study the night before, but she figured they discussed family business. Yet somehow she felt badly she'd been left out.

Caira started to whine. "Where 'Cowmick?"

"It sounds like you need to have some warm cocoa with us, little one. Sophie, would you like some, too?" Maggie smiled, her eyes filled with concern and tenderness toward Caira.

"Reverend McCormick went out of town, dear." Sophie sat in a rocking chair and pulled Caira onto her lap.

Her daughter stiffened in Sophie's grip. "Wan' 'Cowmick!"

"He's not here. If you want warm cocoa and a story tonight, you need to calm down, sweetie." Sophie rocked her while Maggie disappeared into the kitchen.

Maggie came back and reached for Caira. "There, there. Let Mrs. Galloway help you put your nightgown on." The little girl wailed.

"Sophie, why don't you stir the milk until it's hot. I'll take care of your little sister. You need a break, my dear," Maggie said as she carried her up the stairs.

"Can I help you, Mama?" Philip met Maggie as he was coming back downstairs.

"If you're done with your homework, then put away your playthings and you can have cocoa before you go to bed." Maggie's voice trailed up the stairs.

Sophie went to the yarn basket to find the mittens she was knitting for Caira. She'd already made one small pair and was delighted to find that she had enough yarn for a larger pair to be prepared for next winter. Taking them into the kitchen with her, she sat in a chair by the stove. Her hands warmed as the needles clicked together, but her heart lacked the spark to be warmed, as well. After all the time she'd spent trying to prove to Ian that she wasn't a flirt, she had to admit his absence left a void. Steam rose from the pan of milk. She went to stir it.

Ian hadn't even said "good-bye" to her. Then again, he probably left while she and Maggie were at the boardinghouse. Sophie sighed. She shouldn't feel so hurt. Ian had no obligation to her beyond that of a pastor and a host.

She reached to the shelf above the stove for the cocoa powder, a little sugar, and a pinch of salt and then mixed them in. *Just the way Ian likes it.* Maggie had shown her. As she stirred the ingredients into the warm milk, Sophie thought about how delectable the cocoa smelled. Yet, without the sugar, one could only taste the bitterness. Perhaps life held the same quality; without some trouble in life it was hard to appreciate the good.

When life had been pleasant, without a care in the world, she hadn't been as grateful as she should be. This time of being at the parsonage was definitely precious to her. While she missed Ian that night, she would do her best to appreciate the warmth and safety of staying in Ian's home for a short time, but his absence brought the thought of the bitter times of loneliness in her past and likely in her future.

Maggie and Caira's giggling caught her attention. She heard the sound of their tromping feet as they descended the stairs while they sang "London Bridge."

Sophie poured the steaming hot cocoa into Blue Willow teacups and carried them into the dining room on a tray.

"Oh my dear Sophie, you do enough waiting on people. Working at the boardinghouse with you, I can surely attest to that! Sit down, right this very minute."

"But Maggie, your magic banished Caira's crabbiness. I don't mind waiting on you." Sophie exchanged a smile with her friend. She'd always wanted a sister. The way Maggie had taken her under her wing and helped her in many ways made Sophie think of her as the closest thing to a sister she had. Ian was blessed.

Maggie sipped on her cocoa. "It's perfect."

"Thank you, Miss Biddle." Philip smiled and blew on the liquid in the cup in front of him.

"Mm. Co-co, co-co." Caira took sips from the spoonful that Sophie blew on to cool the hot drink.

"I guess I owe you an explanation," Maggie confessed. "As you know, Ian has a heart for the less privileged." She looked off as though thinking of something far away or perhaps long in the past. "Once the children go upstairs, what do you say we'll have a little talk and finish up what's left of the cocoa?"

"Of course." Sophie kept her face straight, hoping to hide her strange unease though her stomach knotted while she waited to hear what Maggie had to say.

Twenty minutes passed before Philip excused himself. "I'm done with my hot cocoa. Can I play with Caira?" The little boy looked up at Maggie.

"Why don't you read to her now. It's almost bedtime."

"Yes, Mama." Philip smiled.

Sophie watched her baby eagerly take Philip's hand, her big gray eyes shining with the anticipation of hearing a story and with trust for someone she looked up to. Philip had been very kind to Caira. Sophie supposed that not having any younger siblings, the toddler provided a novelty for the little redheaded boy, though she could be naughty sometimes. She marveled that he'd not grown sick of her yet, supposing she was the only one who loved Caira enough to not get tired of her antics.

Sophie had made enough cocoa to include Ian without thinking, so she reheated it and peeled the skin off the top after the children were tucked into bed, pouring the serving into two china cups. The two young women settled themselves on the chaise. Maggie began again in hushed tones. "Ian has seen some very sad situations as a minister. He takes on responsibility for things that aren't really his to worry about."

"Like what?" Sophie continued to enjoy the bittersweet cocoa drink.

"Suffice to say, he saw a young woman, shunned from good society. The poor thing had been abused by relatives and had nowhere to go. There were rumors of insanity. They found her dead, with child, in a river. Ian's never gotten over the awful sight." Maggie paused to take another swallow. "My little brother is bound and determined to start a home for wayward young ladies and even a small orphanage."

Sophie blinked. The pretty earthenware cup almost slipped from her hand. She felt the blood drain from her face. Putting the cup down haphazardly on the saucer, she could feel the warm liquid slosh over the top, onto her hand.

"Sophie? Are you all right?" Maggie reached over to pat her arm. "As I was saying, he went to visit the Florence Crittenton Home to see how they run things. He should be back tomorrow."

Sophie shook herself from dizzying thoughts and took a deep breath. The implications flooded her mind. Home for unwed mothers? An orphanage? Girls would enter the home before their pregnancy showed. Likely the neighbors they left behind would have been told that they were visiting a distant relative. After they gave birth, the babies would be plucked from their arms and sent to the orphanage, so the girls could go home and pretend nothing happened. Then each one could be available for the next eligible suitor . . . like Ariel had been.

Her fate would have been the same, but for the fact her father had hoped she would marry Charles. In nightmares, how many times had Caira had been yanked from her arms? Sophie had often awoken to look for Caira, afraid she would never see her again. Her heart would only calm from its wild beating when she could see and feel her daughter in the bed, next to her.

A shiver traveled Sophie's spine at the thought of being separated from her precious daughter. She hugged herself, attempting to control the shaking.

"Sophie, are you all right? Or are you getting sick? You're positively pale, dear." Maggie had lifted the teacup and saucer from her hands and set them on the round table near the end of the chaise. "Let's get you to bed."

Sophie nodded. "I'm sure I'll be all right. I'm just tired." But she couldn't find the strength to stand. What kind of disease made you feel as though your very heart and soul were being pulled apart?

"Honestly, Esther leaving you like this—not that she had much of a choice. This going back and forth is just too much for you. I can see you're more delicate than I am and probably need to stay inside more this time of year, when everybody is catching cold."

Sophie's throat burned as she swallowed. Perhaps her heart alone wasn't becoming sick, but her whole body. She didn't have time for such a thing!

Later, as she lay awake in their moonlit room, Sophie watched the rise and fall of Caira's chest with each peaceful breath. Long eyelashes rested on the baby's chubby pink cheeks. Hot tears streamed down Sophie's face like a summer rainstorm. She tried so hard to keep her mournful cries quiet, so as not to wake anyone.

Shivering under the blankets, Sophie's cheeks warmed with humiliation. Ian must have realized her secret and taken pity. Why else would he have shown an interest in her and Caira? On the one hand, he would be helping girls who might be victims, like herself. But to think of their babies being ripped from each young mother's arms hurt her. Then again, the children would have a chance to go to a good family with a mother and father. Isn't that what she often lamented Caira would never have? Perhaps she'd been selfish. Oh, the shame of it all. How would she face Ian ever again?

The wind blew under the eves of the doctor's house. The low moaning brought no comfort to Ian as he tried to sleep. He tossed and turned on the luxurious feather bed, thinking he should have been exhausted from his full day. Ian couldn't stop thinking about Olivia Bidershem's unexpected revelations.

Along with the grandchild's name, the picture in the locket confirmed her identity. Though showing a younger, innocent Sophia, he recognized her just the same. He so wanted to tell her mother that she was safe, she was loved, and Caira was healthy. But even more than that, Ian would have liked Sophie to feel as though she could confide in him. He recalled her discomfort in saying Caira was her sister when they'd met. There had to be a reason she carefully guarded her secret, even around her friends.

An image of the pained expression on Sophie's face as she readied herself to play Maggie's Bidershem piano came to mind. The way she showed such gentleness with the child rather than be annoyed with a little sister . . . the whole situation made sense now.

Her ruse troubled and disappointed Ian. After all, she'd lied to him and the whole town. Yet he of all people could afford to show mercy. Was he any better in his failings? He didn't consider himself any better than a murderer for letting Annie down.

And yes, Sophie was a wonderful mother to Caira and a hard worker. But just how did he feel about Sophie? His heart had ached as they'd sat in the Conrads' parlor drinking Earl Grey tea after dinner. Their comfortably appointed home had lacked something . . . no . . . someone.

He had missed watching Sophie knit those little woolen mittens, her pretty head bent over her work while she chatted away with Maggie. And then there was Caira. How he loved reading to her and looking at Philip's old picture books through the little one's eyes. At the end of every evening, Caira rode upstairs on his shoulders, giggling with delight. Often he caught the appreciative glance of Sophie with her smile appearing so sweet in the soft amber glow of the gaslight. Who had taken

Caira up the stairs tonight? And who would take her up in the future, helping Sophie tuck her in each night over the next several years? Who, indeed?

Yet he had to be more careful than ever with Sophie. If Gertrude and her cohorts knew the truth and how his affections were growing for Sophie, the gossips would happily run them both out of town. Instead of answers, he had only questions.

CHAPTER 14

"I insist that you stay here and rest today, Sophie." Maggie clucked about like a mother hen the next morning, fluffing a pillow behind her and pulling a blanket up over her on the settee. "Philip is off to school, so the house should be pretty quiet until I'm able to come back."

"Really, Maggie, I'll be fine. A-achoo!" She covered her mouth just in time, then sniffled. She swallowed. Her throat was raw and she shivered with chills. She had to admit, it was nice being mothered a bit.

"About all you're fit for is making yourself a pot of tea, but the first one is already brewing. After I bring you some, I should probably get over to the boardinghouse. I just need to get Caira up and dressed. I'll feed her over there."

"No, no, I insist you leave her here." Sophie spoke with the little forcefulness her sore throat would allow. "You'll have your hands full enough."

Maggie sighed. "Very well. We'll let her sleep in case she's fighting what you have. But you must promise to take some white willow extract in your tea to take care of that fever."

Sophie knew she'd made the face of a child who didn't want to take disgusting medicine, but it was too late.

"We'll even add some extra sugar for the invalid." Maggie rolled her eyes. "You're as bad as my little brother."

Ian. Sophie had just stopped thinking about him for a few minutes. She closed her eyes, pretending she didn't want to talk anymore.

"When you're somewhat better, I'm sure you can find something to read in Ian's study if you're bored."

If nothing else good came of being sick, she would at least have time to enjoy reading a book. Sophie drank the concoction her friend had put together for her, taking a sip at a time. Then she lay back on the pillow and drifted off to sleep.

••◦)━━━━━ ● ━━━━━(◦••

"Soffie." She heard a little voice chirrup. "Soffie." A pudgy hand patted her through the blanket.

Weary, Sophie opened her eyes one at a time to see her daughter with matted hair, standing there in her nightgown. Caira carried her ragdoll in one arm while a blanket trailed on the floor behind her. It was a miracle that she hadn't tripped and fallen down the stairs. Sophie's heart pounded at the awful thought.

She pulled her hands out from under the blanket and hugged her baby. "Sophie's sick today, so we're staying . . . here." She'd almost said "home." And how she wished she could call herself Mama. She hated this whole charade, pretending to be someone she wasn't! Not feeling well had made Sophie all the more cross about her situation. Was she doing what was right for Caira? Perhaps she would have been better off pretending she was a widow. At least then she could own up to Caira being hers though she would still be lying any way you looked at the situation.

"I hungry, Soffie."

"Let's see what Maggie left for us this morning." When she sat up, she realized she wasn't quite as feverish or achy. Even her throat felt a little better. Perhaps the white willow extract had been what she needed. But Sophie was still careful not to get up too fast. She'd passed out before when she'd been feverish.

Caira left the doll behind and took her mother's hand. She almost galloped to the kitchen, pulling on Sophie's arm.

"Slow down." Sophie was hoarse, and it was painful to speak above a whisper.

When they reached the kitchen, Sophie found biscuits on a napkin-covered plate and a jar of strawberry jam next to it. This would probably be a good time to make another pot of tea.

Sophie split a large, flaky biscuit with Caira, slathering it with the gooey jam to help it go down more easily. She really wasn't any hungrier than her daughter that morning. Then she set up a little tea party for her and Caira on the oak table near the settee. She wished she could talk more, but it hurt too much.

The little one clapped her hands together, giggling at their game. After Sophie brought out the blocks and a number of books for Caira, putting them on the floor nearby, she went to search Ian's well-equipped study for herself.

Sophie loved having time with Caira alone. These occasions were rare and fortunately they had this time in such a lovely home. She could almost pretend that she was a mother with a husband and her own home. When she opened the door to the study, the scent of leather-bound books and the leather upholstery of the desk chair awoke her senses. Spring sunshine streamed through the filmy curtains on the window, lighting Ian's private world to her. She read familiar author's names: Yeats, Dr. Johnson, Milton, Dante, Dickens. She slowed down, noticing titles, too. James Fennimore Cooper's *The Last of the Mohicans* and George Eliot's *Silas Marner* stood on the shelf among other titles. His hand must have held each of them at some time. She could almost sense his presence as her fingertips brushed each spine. Biblical commentaries and dictionaries graced the shelves, as well. His eclectic library reminded her of her family's.

Ian wasn't just some dull country preacher, reading only theological tomes. He understood people's character. She sighed. If she could have married him, these would be her books, too. The forbidden study would be a place where they could spend time and laugh together. She'd missed him the night before, missed the even tones of his quiet voice as he read to his nephew and then to Caira. He was a good man.

What was she thinking? What kind of spell had she been under? Ian was off limits and neither of them needed people getting the wrong idea about their friendship. She shook herself from her reverie and pulled a couple of books from the shelf.

Surprisingly, Caira played quite well on the floor by herself. Sophie was worried that she would grow bored and lonely for Philip and the commotion of Fairgrave's. But the little girl looked up lovingly at her several times, bringing her dolly to Sophie for hugs and kisses on imaginary boo-boos. Did Caira know the truth deep in her heart? That they shared the mother and daughter bond in their souls? Sophie smoothed the child's hair back, delving into the dark gray eyes. *Do you know?*

· · ●)━━━━━━ ● ━━━━━━(●· ·

Sophie had managed to help Caira wash up and dress later in the morning. Early afternoon arrived. Her stomach rumbled. Returning aches and pains sent her back to the settee, when a knock sounded at the front door.

Who could it be? Ian or Maggie wouldn't knock. Perhaps a package had come for one of them. She stood up, seeing stars. She gripped the arm of the settee and sat back down until the dizziness subsided.

"What dat?" Caira sucked her finger and looked up from the pile of blocks she was playing with.

Rap! Rap! Rap! The visitor grew more insistent. Sophie stood slowly and took her time moving toward the door. She moved the curtain away from the window. "James?"

Sophie pulled her borrowed robe tighter around her middle before she opened the door. "What are you doing here?" she whispered.

"I brought you dinner. Are you all right? I was afraid something had happened to you." His brow furrowed.

"I'm just kind of weak."

"This should give you some strength. Maggie made chicken soup this morning and asked me to bring it to you." James smiled.

"Thank you. Go around back, and I'll let you into the kitchen." He held quite a large pot and Sophie would have hated to drop it and waste it all because of her weakness.

She hurried through the house with her heart pounding. Her skin had begun hurting again. No doubt her fever spiked.

She tried to wait as Caira's quick little footsteps padded behind.

Sophie reached the back door and opened it since his hands were full. James was looking for a place to put the steaming pot and left the door open behind him. She rushed to get a trivet, but changed her mind. "Just put it on the stove." Sophie had turned too quickly to give directions and saw stars again. "James—help!"

Sophie heard James plunk the pan onto the cast iron surface. Then she felt him grip her by the arms.

"Easy now." He helped her into a chair by the kitchen table.

Sophie closed her eyes, taking deep breaths, sensing that James knelt down in front of her. She surrendered her head to the support of James' shoulder. "Steady now. Take as long as you need."

Caira's tiny frame barreled into James.

"Hi, Cooper!" Her little voice gave away her happiness of seeing a familiar face from the boardinghouse.

"Be careful, you don't want to hurt Sophie, do you?"

Sophie opened her eyes. James put an arm around Caira. "How's my little friend today?"

The stars began to clear from Sophie's vision. She picked up her head off James' shoulder in time to see Ian standing as though frozen in the doorway while a chill breeze swept in, matched only in intensity by Ian's icy gaze.

CHAPTER 15

Ian closed his mouth as soon as he sensed it had fallen open. He blinked, not believing what he was seeing. Was he dreaming?

A pale Sophie sat by a kneeling James Cooper. In fact, he was almost sure that he'd seen her head resting on his shoulder. And James held the beloved little Caira. Her shining smile beamed up at him.

How had this happened? Ian hadn't been gone yet two full days. Or perhaps Sophie and James had always been sweet on each other, and he had been too daft to see it. Was there even more she hid from him? Although, Ian noticed, James knelt rather precariously, supported Sophie's elbows, and moved back. The young man's eyebrows knit together.

"Reverend, Sophie is terribly weak. Could you help me take her back to the settee?" James pointed at the pot on the stove. "I was just dropping off some soup that Maggie made for Sophie and Caira." He scratched his head.

Ian swept off his hat, leaving it on the table. "I'll take her up to bed, where she belongs."

"No, no, I'll be fine. I just haven't eaten much today," Sophie whispered.

He felt her forehead. "You're burning up." Almost before he realized it, Ian had scooped her into his arms and pushed the kitchen door open with his elbow as he stepped through sideways, careful not to bump Sophie's head.

"But, but . . . I'm not a child. Put me down." Sophie pushed her hands against him until their gazes locked. The amber fire in her eyes abated to reveal fright.

No, you're *a beautiful woman who needs to trust your friends and let them care for you.* And she was a mother, who needed to recover so she could care for her child. But knowing how she'd been hurt, he could now guess what caused the wide-eyed frightened deer look that often possessed her. Her eyelids flitted downward. His sense of hurt made room for compassion.

"Please, take me to the parlor." Shaking, Sophie turned away.

"'Cowmick, where you going?" Caira pulled on his pant leg.

Ian stopped and looked down. "Sophie's sick, so I'm taking her . . . to the settee." Realizing he would overstep proper boundaries by going upstairs, Ian strode to the parlor. He wished he could hold Caira, too, when he saw the crestfallen little face. She whimpered. He softened his tone. "We have to take good care of your . . . sister, don't we?" How easy it would have been to reveal the secret he possessed and refer to her as Caira's mother. He knew he needed to watch himself.

"Wan' Soffie. Wan' 'Cowmick," Caira wailed, holding tighter to his pant leg and hiding her face in the scratchy woolen fabric.

"Now, now. Mr. Cooper will gladly watch you."

"I suppose." James stood in the kitchen doorway with hat in hand and shrugged.

For all the talent he claimed as a journalist, the boy could be clueless about the simplest things. Somebody needed to educate the young man about real life. "Well, come take her by the hand."

"Of course, Reverend." James smiled. "Come along, Caira, you can help me get some soup for your big sister." He reached his hand out to take the little girl's.

She looked up at James and then Ian. He could tell she was hesitant. Her lip quivered. "'Cowmick?"

"Go on, Caira." Ian's voice grew sterner. His heart squeezed a bit with grief as he thought about how he might have to get used to seeing Caira walk away with James.

More than ever aware that Sophie's head rested against his shoulder, the scent of lavender wafted up from her soft, curly hair, tickling his cheek. Grasping the front of her robe, she crossed her forearms against her chest.

"I hope you don't think I'd ever drop you." Ian was immediately sorry for his attempt at humor, knowing Sophie had been overtaken by deep fear.

Concern for her well-being buoyed him up with strength as though he carried a mere hummingbird instead of a young woman. Having his arms under her, surrounding her petite frame felt right, protective, like she was meant to fit there. He clutched her harder as limpness overtook Sophie's body. Had she blacked out as she had in the church when she thought she was alone with him? Or had sickness overtaken her?

Fear infused him with a fire of energy. He set her down, placing her head on a pillow as though she were a little bird. "Sophie." Ian patted her hand. No response. He reached to pat her porcelain white cheek. "Sophie. Can you hear me? Wake up!"

She looked pale, even against the white pillowcase. What if she became sick . . . unto death? The thought pierced Ian's heart, as if only the thought of her dying took a large chunk of his heart with it.

"Cooper! Look in the cabinet to the right of the stove for smelling salts!"

"Whatever you need, Reverend." James' whistling annoyed Ian.

"Hurry, would you please!" Ian smoothed the hair back from her forehead, which beaded with sweat. Perhaps she'd fainted.

James had found them and brought the small bottle to Ian. Caira sniffled, chewing her fingers, and clinging to the younger man's hand.

Ian moved the smelling salts back and forth below Sophie's nose until her eyelids fluttered open and she inhaled deeper.

With terror returning to her eyes, she grabbed his wrist as though to push him away.

"Nobody is going to hurt you." Ian mustered the most soothing tone he could. "You need rest. Maggie will be home soon."

Sophie nodded as recognition lit her face. Her forehead smoothed. Her lips relaxed in parting. "Thank you."

"I'm going to get Doctor Moore."

"But I can't afford—"

"Nonsense. You're a guest in my home. And we treat our guests like family. I'll take care of it." What had Maggie been thinking? Why hadn't she called the doctor for her sooner?

James ambled into the parlor. "I've got a bowl of soup for our patient. Would you like to feed it to her?" James stepped into the room with a napkin over one arm and a steaming bowl of hot soup. The rich scent of thyme and onion in the chicken noodle soup filled the room. Caira traipsed behind like a chick behind a mother hen.

Ian took a deep breath. His stomach rumbled though eating had been farthest from his thoughts. Maggie's soups tasted as delicious as they smelled. James offered him the bowl.

"Don't let Caira get too close." Ian felt a need to take control. "We don't want her to get sick, as well. You go ahead and see if Sophie will eat some of this. I'm going to call Doctor Moore, but if I can't get through, I'll go get him myself, once Maggie returns." He rubbed the side of his face, wanting to flee Sophie's presence, the closeness overtaking him.

The back door slammed. "James? Where are you? Sophie?" Maggie called out. A few moments later her firm footsteps echoed in the kitchen.

Caira danced in the dining room between the parlor and the kitchen, waving a cracker around. "Cooper, 'Cowmick, Cooper, 'Cowmick." The spirited toddler sang the two names over and over as though she were weighing which one sounded better.

"What are you doing running around with a cracker in here?" Maggie took it away, brushing the crumbs from Caira's hand into her own. She looked from Ian to James. "And just what are you two doing here with Sophie?"

"I was bringing her lunch to help her eat." James showed her the bowl.

Ian smoothed his hair back. "I'm afraid this is my fault. She was feeling faint, and I thought it best to bring her in here to rest."

"She was perfectly fine with Caira. This is most improper. I sent James to do a simple errand and told him I would be coming home to help Sophie shortly." Maggie snatched the bowl from James' hand. "Off with you now. Get back to the boardinghouse. I left your lunch on the sideboard. You men may be on your own making sandwiches for supper tonight."

"Yes, ma'am, thank you."

"Ian—"

"I'm on my way to see about Dr. Moore." He put up his hand, wanting to halt his sister's tirade.

"See that you do!" Maggie turned to Sophie. "Let me get some nourishment into you, my dear. I'm so sorry about those two. They're supposed to behave like gentlemen."

Ian made his way toward the back door, and James followed, looking as sheepish as a scolded puppy. Their shoulders bumped as they hurried through the doorway.

Ian changed his mind and didn't bother to telephone the doctor first. He needed some time by himself to think. The March wind blasted his face as he set out in the direction of Dr. Moore's house. How ignorant could he have been? He had wanted to get away from Sophie to stop his growing feelings. But perhaps he shouldn't have fancied himself the object of Sophie's return affection.

James Cooper must have had plenty of time to charm both the older and the younger girl while living at the boardinghouse. He sighed, walking with head down and hands behind his back for the distance of two blocks. Would Cooper be so cozy with Sophie if he knew her secret? Taking on a woman raising a sibling was one thing, but if he knew Caira was her very own daughter? And what had he been thinking by almost leaving her alone with the boy after what she'd been through in her past? In his moment of panic and jealousy, Ian had wanted to be away from both of them, from witnessing any affection held between them. As usual, he'd acted selfishly.

Ian knew one thing for sure. As hurt and disappointed as he had felt with Sophie, he didn't like to think James had any special claim on the girl's heart. She could do better than that immature, self-important newspaperman. Sophie needed a godly man to share God's love with her and help her heal, not a backslidden fellow who barely attended church, and then as not much more than an afterthought.

The red brick front of the two-story home stood like a sentinel on one of Main Street's corners. When he reached the porch, Ian hammered the ornate brass knocker into the thick front door.

The muted yellow glow of spring sunshine slanted from the west through the lone window in the bedroom. Maggie had helped her move upstairs earlier. Sophie since figured the afternoon had slipped away. Maggie's delicious soup had been soothing but hard to swallow. Wrapped in a blanket, each touch sent pinpricks of pain through her skin and made her shiver. It was so difficult to get warm. She tried to read the book she'd asked Maggie to fetch, but dozed off several times, awakening to Caira's tinkling laughter while her friend kept her amused. What her daughter really needed was a nap.

Hearing heavy steps and deep voices travel up the stairs, Sophie opened her eyes once again to find Ian with a tall, older man close at his heels and Maggie leading the way.

She recognized Dr. Moore from the disastrous elder board meeting. He looked out through his spectacles with kind brown eyes. "Let's see what we can do for this young lady."

Sophie dug the heels of her hands into the sheets underneath, pushing herself to a sitting position. "The white willow extract Maggie gave me this morning helped," she rasped.

"I'm sure it did." Maggie patted her hand on the side of the bed opposite the doctor.

"Hmm." Dr. Moore touched her forehead with a large cool palm. "Fever's likely up again." He found a thermometer in his bag, which he promptly unsheathed from its case and shook down. "Open up." After placing the glass object under her tongue, he took out his stethoscope and listened to her chest. Once finished with that he snapped open his pocket watch.

Tick, tick, tick. Sophie could hear the timepiece in the silence of the room. The feeling of someone else watching came upon her and she looked up, behind the doctor. Ian stood with arms crossed, leaning against the doorframe and searching for something in her eyes. She felt it, like a penetrating question. But what was he asking of her? She pulled the sheets up a bit farther, gripping the edge. One of Ian's hands went up to rub his chin. His gaze flitted to the back of the doctor's head. "Well, Thad, what do you think?"

"Let me have that, my dear." Dr. Moore pulled the thermometer from Sophie's mouth and studied it for a minute. "A hundred and three. Let's see your throat now."

Sophie opened up.

"A little wider please. Ahh. That's good." He turned round toward Ian. "The quinsy, Reverend. Her tonsils are quite swollen, and I see some pus back there. Nothing a few good days of rest and a bit of medicine can't fix."

Dr. Moore turned back to Sophie, gently feeling her neck. "You need to sleep and to drink lots of fluids. White willow extract should bring that fever down, as you mentioned. You'll need a bit of this tincture applied to your throat twice a day." He pulled out a small bottle and a brush. "And a bit of laudanum will help you sleep these next couple of nights, but just a small amount. We want you to get better or I may have to lance those abscesses."

Sophie put her hand to the base of her throat. The thought of a brush or lancet touching her painful tonsils made her nearly gag, but she nodded her assent.

Ian loomed over them with a sudden hawk-like gaze. "How can I help?" Ian held fast to the back of the doctor's chair.

"Ian, really, back up and give Dr. Moore a little elbow room." Maggie sent her little brother a cross look.

"Make sure she follows my instructions. And don't hesitate to let me know if she gets any worse. I'll make up some poultices if that's the case."

"Of course. We'll take excellent care of her, won't we, little brother?"

Ian crossed his arms and grimaced at Maggie's bossiness. "Of course."

Sophie sank back against the pillow. Who was going to watch after Caira? Or take over her duties at the boardinghouse? Maggie couldn't keep up both houses without getting sick herself.

"Don't worry. You just follow the good doctor's instructions. Maggie and I will make sure that Caira and the boardinghouse are looked after." It seemed like Ian knew exactly what she'd been thinking. "Thank you, Doctor Moore."

"Only doing my job, young man." The medical man winked and turned to hand Maggie a small glass bottle and a larger one, giving her instructions on dosing the patient before they left the room.

While once cheery, the walls of the little guest room grayed with the dull late afternoon light, encroaching on the space around the bed. Sophie hated the weakness enveloping her. Used to being healthy, she had taken care of things for them both, but illness crumbled further the fortress she sought to fortify around her and Caira. If anyone learned her secrets, she had no strength to run.

⸺ ● ⸺

On Sophie's sixth day trapped in the parsonage guest room, she awoke drenched in sweat, and groggy from the laudanum, no doubt. But with her fever broken, Maggie helped her freshen up and move to the settee in the parlor. Grateful not to feel cooped up any longer, Sophie was anxious to soak up the fledgling spring sunshine.

Maggie plumped a pillow behind her. "You'll have a new visitor today while I check on things at Fairgrave's."

"Gloria and her friends have been so kind to help." Sophie felt relieved to be able to speak again without her throat hurting too much.

"They see how kind you've been to Esther, the Myleses, and the difference you've made in little Elise's life. That means something, especially to the few that don't kowtow to Gertrude Wringer." Maggie smiled.

Sophie shrugged. She knew that Gloria Myles had been behind the effort. Gloria's friends had brought meals and helped Maggie at the boardinghouse. Gloria had even come to watch over Sophie and Caira the day before and sent a servant to work at Fairgrave's.

"You'll be surprised who is coming today."

CHAPTER 16

"Who?" Sophie wondered at Maggie's smug expression.

"Nora Armstrong." Maggie stepped back and crossed her arms.

"No!" Sophie couldn't imagine Gertrude allowing Nora within a mile of her presence.

"Oh, yes. Gertrude was as sweet as pie and insisted that Nora show neighborly kindness. And undoubtedly she was happy to send her to spy on you."

"But Maggie, you know as well as I that poor girl is an unwitting pawn at best." Sophie remembered the sadness in the girl's eyes. As cruel as Gertrude could be, Nora had acted kindly to her.

A knock at the door diverted her attention. "Looks like she's here. I hope you can bear it." Maggie rolled her eyes before she went to answer the door.

"Good morning, Nora. Thank you for coming." Maggie greeted her with grace, as usual.

"Good morning, Mrs. Galloway. How is your patient doing? And where is the little one?" Sophie heard Nora return the greeting.

"Caira is in the dining room, finishing her breakfast with Philip. I'll be taking her with me today, though, after I walk Philip to school. She's been quite rambunctious."

"I'm sorry to hear that. I miss my younger brothers and sisters. It would have been a joy to watch her for you."

Sophie pondered how Nora could sound so cheerful after having to deal with Gertrude Wringer every day. Perhaps being out from under the awful woman's thumb for a while was enough freedom to console her for the moment.

"Our patient is just over here in the parlor resting." Maggie appeared in the doorway from the hall with Nora behind her.

"How are you feeling?" Nora's eyes held sympathy.

"Much better this morning, actually."

"I almost forgot—Mrs. Galloway!" Nora called after the retreating Maggie, "Is the Reverend McCormick here this morning? I wanted to make sure I went over next Sunday's music with him."

"Ian!" Maggie called. "He's in the study. If he doesn't hear me, you're welcome to knock on the door." She pointed at the door across the hallway before she looked at Sophie and raised an eyebrow. She cleared her throat. "I'm sure Sophie can help you as well."

Nora's mouth bowed into a shy smile. "I was looking forward to that." Her eyes shone. "I was hoping if you were well enough, you could give me some advice."

"How can I help you?" Sophie shrugged.

"I think everyone knows you're the one with more talent, that you should have my job." Nora looked down.

"You shouldn't say that. The elder board wouldn't have offered you the job if they didn't think you could do it." The other girl's modesty astounded Sophie.

"Well, I might be capable, but that's a far cry from being the best qualified." Nora smoothed her azure sateen skirt.

A doorknob squeaked as it turned. The man behind it poked his head out from the study. "Did you call me, Maggie?"

"Yes, you have company."

Ian exchanged pleasantries with Nora while Maggie readied herself, Philip, and Caira to leave for the day.

"I believe I left the hymnal in the study. We can go over the music I thought appropriate. We'll see what you think." He smiled at the stick-thin girl before him. Raking his hand through his hair, he glanced at Sophie.

Nora gave Ian rapt attention as he spoke. She followed close at his heels as he returned to the doorway to his study. "Oh, what a lovely library. You have so many books! And the walnut paneling is so well polished."

"Maggie keeps the house very well for me."

"If you ever marry, Reverend, your wife will have a time keeping things as beautifully." Just then, Nora turned to the side. Sophie saw a blush come to her face as she bowed her head and stepped back. "Oh dear. I probably shouldn't have said something that familiar, but I do think your sister is a wonderful example. And she is all kindness."

Ian came back out into the hallway with a hymnal in hand. "That is, if you're not her little brother." He chuckled.

Her cringe turned to a slight smile as she lifted her face toward Ian. Although Gertrude claimed that Nora was the perfect example of morals and deportment, she must not treat her as such at home. Why else would she seem to shrink from someone as gentle as Ian?

••●)———————— ● ————————(●••

Before she left, Maggie had parted the hunter green velvet drapes, so that the rays of early spring sunshine, mellowed by intermittent clouds, shone over the tops of the creamy madras curtains, hung halfway down the window. The mahogany of the Bidershem upright sparkled under its subdued glow. Nora sat on the piano bench, facing Sophie rather than the piano.

Sophie wanted to know more about Nora. Something about the other girl's pale blue eyes and the seriousness of her expression told her that they must have deep hurt in common. Ever since that day she'd comforted her in the gazebo, she could see Nora didn't live an easy life. "You mentioned missing younger brothers and sisters. Would you care to talk about them?" Sophie took a sip of the tea with honey that Nora had insisted on making for her. The hot liquid soothed her healing throat as it slid down.

"Very much." Nora gazed off into the distance. "I haven't been away long, but I miss them already. I'm the oldest of seven." She paused. "I have a sister, two years younger. Her name is Evelyn. She sings and embroiders beautifully. She calms the most nervous of cows so that they give us milk. My brother, Nicholas, is twelve. He has a way with plants. Papa said he never had such remarkable harvests until Nick was old enough to make quite a contribution. But I'm talking too much."

"No." Sophie shook her head. "Please go on." She swung her feet over toward the floor, pushed herself to a sitting position and leaned forward.

"There's also David, ten, the twins, John and Mark, who are eight. Those three are full of mischief, and Charity is six. She's spoiled." But even as she stated the fact, she laughed.

"Do you mind if I ask how you came to live with your aunt and uncle?"

"My parents don't have much. My grandparents didn't approve of Papa marrying my mother. They thought she lacked social status and money. But Papa took what savings he had and put it down on a small farm. Of course, once Mama and Papa started having a family, Grandma and Grandpa broke down and wanted to see their grandchildren. Grandpa would have helped my father find a more acceptable position in Detroit, but by then Papa was determined to stand on his own two feet. In the end, my grandparents left the small remains of their fortune to Aunt Gertrude." Nora set down the cup of tea she'd been holding. She smoothed the skirt of her dress and folded her hands together. Her knuckles whitened.

"When Aunt Gertrude found out that the good Lord had gifted me somewhat with musical ability, she insisted that I have a proper education. She paid for that and for a modest but acceptable wardrobe. Since she has no children, my family felt obligated to send me to be a help to her and Uncle Edmund." Nora paused before she added, "I graduated not quite a year ago, but after several months at home, my parents felt it was time for me to take my place here."

Sophie could only nod. Nora was honoring her obligation, but it was a shame that she was stuck with such miserable relatives. She picked up her cooled tea and stared into the dark brew. Nora had complied with what her parents expected. She was a kind person. What had the girl done to deserve her current situation? Surely God had nothing to punish her for.

Sophie looked up. "You must miss them very much."

Nora met her gaze with misty eyes. "Of a certainty. What about you? You must miss your parents."

"There's not much to tell. I no longer have my parents . . . or my brothers." Information she hadn't shared with anyone else slipped out. What was she thinking? "Caira and I do our best. We must move on."

"You're crying."

"Am I?" Sophie touched the tears that poured down her cheeks like a leak had sprung in a pipe.

Nora pulled a lacy white handkerchief from a skirt pocket. "I'm so sorry, Sophie. I should have known that it was too painful for you to talk about."

Sophie took the square of cloth Nora offered and wiped her blurry eyes. "Thank you. It's not just my family, but I was thinking how lonely you must feel sometimes."

"You are so kind." Nora's eyes were downcast. "I must confess . . ."

"What?" Sophie worried at Nora's tone of voice.

"My aunt sent me not only to work on music." She looked up, silent for a moment. "She wanted me to spy on you, to come back with information." The thin girl's cold hands captured Sophie's and held them. "But I think you are a good person. Only God could gift you to play the piano so beautifully or take as good care of your little sister as though she were your own child. And I see how patient you are with people like Mr. Graemer . . . and Aunt Gertie."

Sophie pulled her hands away and stiffened as though afraid their touching would somehow reveal her secrets.

"I especially was hoping you could help me with my music. I have no intention for your harm. I can't obey such a command." She stood and went to look out the side window. "If anything, I am ashamed that I didn't stand up to Aunt Gertrude, but agreed to come here under false pretenses. It was the only way I would be allowed to help you, though. I was worried when I heard you were so ill."

Sophie's throat grew tighter. She swallowed, wishing she could tell Nora that she lived a ruse and that her aunt wasn't far from the truth. How she hated the lie she lived and wished she could confess right there! Had God sent Nora as an example? Sophie's heart pounded. "I understand," she choked out. "We all have our downfalls, but we all need friends. If we waited to meet perfect people, we'd always be lonely, wouldn't we?" Sophie forced a smile through the anxiety. "Would you like to play for me now?"

"Are you sure you're not too tired?" Nora turned to her with eyes wide and brighter than usual. "May I play 'Jesu Joy of Man's Desiring?'"

"It's one of my favorites." Didn't this prove to Sophie that they were meant to be friends? "Of course."

She listened from the settee, directing where Nora should pick up the tempo or give more emphasis.

"This piece is sounding much better!" Nora declared. "Your ear is amazing."

"What is this?" The piano music must have called Ian from his study.

"I'm just helping her a bit." Sophie nodded toward Nora.

"Most excellent!" Ian sat in the overstuffed armchair and leaned forward, with elbows on knees and hands folded. He listened, making comments when appropriate. "I think you're quite ready for this Sunday."

"I'm so thankful for this job. Sometimes I'm able to send some of my stipend to my parents to help with all my little brothers and sisters on the farm."

Sophie's heart squeezed with guilt at any thoughts of envy toward Nora she'd ever had. The kindness and generosity of her friend's soul flourished, even under the most difficult of circumstances. And somehow, with her sewing business, Sophie had been able to put a little by here and there to help grow her nest egg, despite not becoming the church musician.

"This is one of the nicest pianos I've ever played. I see it's a Bidershem."

"So you appreciate my sister's fine piano, too. Sophie became quite emotional the first time she played this amazing instrument. Didn't you?"

Both Ian and Nora turned to look at her as though expecting an answer. Heat spread over her cheeks. She cleared her throat and whispered, "It is indeed a fine instrument." She pulled her feet up, lying back on the pillow.

Ian stood and walked toward her. "You look flushed again. Is the fever back?"

She closed her eyes as he touched her forehead. The warmth it sent tingling through her rivaled her recent fever. "I'll be fine."

If I don't open my eyes and look into yours. "Please, go help Nora. I promise I will rest now."

He pulled his hand away. "All right, then, I suppose we should get to work."

Ian leaned against the piano. He pointed out any changes he wanted, whether to skip a verse or play the chorus an extra time. Sophie watched them through half-closed eyes, pretending to sleep. Their chattering sounded comfortable. Ian chuckled.

Other than the day he came home from Detroit, swept her up in his arms, and brought Dr. Moore to her, he'd seemed strangely quiet when they were in a room together. When she caught Ian watching her, she read something in his eyes before his glance darted away . . . perhaps hurt and curiosity. The same unease didn't accompany his and Nora's conversation.

Like a horse bolting free from a pen, an idea struck her. Nora needed the gentle kindness of someone like an Ian McCormick, and Ian needed a girl with a spotless reputation, who could contribute to his ministry. Besides, how could Mrs. Wringer manipulate the elder board or Ian, for that matter, with a gentle buffer like Nora? Perhaps she just needed to stay out of the way so that her kind friend and the man she cared for would discover their need for each other. Though she knew someone like her would never be fit to marry Ian, Sophie's heart stung at the thought of someone else married to him. But Sophie was growing used to loss and grief. She would survive this, too.

CHAPTER 17

A few days later, Mr. Neuberger's daughter wrapped some of the order for the boardinghouse. "Have you had any news from Mrs. Fairgrave lately?"

"Yes, she's fine, but now that the children are doing better, Esther is waiting for the baby to arrive." Sophie nodded, thinking how thankful she was Esther had thought to leave behind just enough funds to restock the essentials.

Cecilia Neuberger, all corkscrew curls and ribbons, couldn't have been more than a year or two younger than she. "I heard that you've been ill. Now that you're better, are you going to Helena Blanding's Welcome Spring Social? It's the young people's social event of the year." The girl giggled. "Besides, some of the town's handsomest young gentlemen will be there," she whispered, leaning forward. "Perhaps even Reverend McCormick will be there, but I suppose you see quite enough of him. My mother heard he was *awfully* worried about your being sick."

Sophie's throat dried, and she gave a little cough. "N-no, I haven't heard anything about the social." She hardly expected she'd be included in any young people's get together. She felt ten years their senior with her responsibilities, but she still had a heart and feelings. Averting her gaze for a moment, she willed herself not to let the girl's snub, or insinuation, bother her. "I've no doubt Reverend McCormick and Mrs. Galloway have been equally concerned. They are such kind people."

"I'm sure." Cecilia rolled her eyes. "But I did think *all* the young gentleman and *ladies* at church had been invited." She clapped a hand over her mouth, looking all innocence.

"Cecilia! Get into the storeroom. I need your help back there. Your father can take care of the customers." Mrs. Neuberger stood with arms crossed, staring at Sophie through narrowed eyes.

Mr. Neuberger stood at the other end of the counter, scratching his head and looking apologetic over his wife's less than friendly attitude.

Maggie came to Sophie's side. "Let me help you with your packages, *dear friend,*" she spoke louder than necessary.

A few minutes later, the bells over the entrance of Neuberger's General Store jingled as the door closed behind Sophie and Maggie. The heady perfume of spring air mixed with the scent of coffee and spices clung to her clothing. Sophie inhaled. How good it was to be outside of the stuffy store and away from the house. Over a week stuck inside the parsonage was enough.

"I think I have everything to restock the boardinghouse. Thank you so much for your help . . . in more than one way." Sophie held onto the handle of a wicker basket with one hand and lifted her skirt with the other as she stepped down into the road and toward the wagon. Ian lugged a large sack of flour to the wagon for them.

"We don't mind." Maggie smiled. "Don't worry about what Cecilia said. She's a silly child." She put a hand on Sophie's arm.

Sophie nodded, not willing to look at Maggie and risk revealing the hurt deep within. "Thank you for standing by me."

"I wouldn't think of doing anything else." Maggie gave her arm a pat.

Sophie didn't add that she wouldn't mind being part of the carefree socials occasionally, but knew that with Gertrude Wringer's influence in town, that wouldn't happen. Other than the unusual, rather secret friendship she and Nora had struck up, the other young ladies close to Sophie's age wouldn't bother to endanger their reputations by getting to know her.

"Really, Sophie, the likes of Cecelia and Helena aren't worth your time." Maggie patted her back. She seemed to understand Sophie so well.

Caira pattered along the boardwalk, sucking on a stick of candy. Mr. Neuberger had offered it to her, and Sophie couldn't refuse the gesture of kindness toward her child. He had always been kind to them both, despite his sour wife and snooty daughter. Sophie could tell Caira heartily enjoyed the sugary lemon treat.

"I'm glad I only gave her half. Come back here, little one!" Sophie tucked away the hurtful comments made in the store and observed the child's widening eyes and her busyness. She hoped the sugar wouldn't make her sick.

Caira turned and toddled in the other direction. Too late, Sophie saw the self-assured form of Gertrude Wringer striding along the boardwalk flanked by Millie and Etta. Busy talking to her friends, Gertrude cackled and didn't watch where she was going.

A sick feeling hit Sophie's mid-section. A moment too late she called, "Look out, Caira!"

The glaring Wringer woman knocked the child backward. As Caira fell backwards on her bottom and hit the boardwalk, the lemon candy stick flew from her hand and landed plunk into a crack between the boards. She let out a wail.

"What a rude child! I told you she was ill-behaved."

Sophie ran to rescue her with clenched fists glued to her sides. No polite smile could be beckoned forth at this meeting. "I beg your pardon. I'm sure it won't happen again. Caira was excited about the candy she'd just gotten. She didn't see you." Sophie helped her daughter up, swiping at the dirt on her backside. Caira clung to her skirt.

"No wonder she's rude and excitable. You allow this child sweetmeats rather than soundly nutritious food. You obviously do nothing but indulge her." Gertrude wagged her bony finger in Sophie's face. A thin brown reticule hung from her arm like a turkey's wattle.

Anger and embarrassment overtook Sophie as she endured the stares of all three women. She shook and heat suffused her neck while flames consumed her face. "Excuse me?" She managed to pipe up. "Caira—"

The firm squeeze of Ian's large hand on her upper arm stopped her short. "Gertrude, I know you haven't been blessed with children. Perhaps you don't understand what it's like to have little ones around, to be a child yourself, or how much patience they require."

Sophie turned her head. Ian put up a gloved hand, signaling her to wait until he was finished. "I can vouch for Sophie here. I've observed her while they've been staying with us at the parsonage. She has a big task in raising a spirited child. And it's a task I believe she's up for."

Sophie's mouth dropped open as she stared into his sympathetic gaze, as deep as the aqua blue of Lake Huron. He must care something for her to take her side like this.

She looked back to see the shocked expression in Gertrude's beady eyes. "Is that so? You're defending this common flirt instead of taking my side?" Her arms crossed against her thin frame. Millie and Etta stood behind her, looking just as sour.

"It's as simple as that; I am standing up for this fine young woman." Ian scooped Caira into his arms and patted the whimpering child on the back.

"Well, what insolence! I'd like a sincere apology from Miss Biddle for her obnoxious so-called sister running into me." Gertrude lifted her chin.

She was given more of an apology than she deserved. Oh! How Sophie wanted to say that. For Ian's sake she wouldn't.

"For what, Gertrude? The child didn't mean to run into you. That kind of thing happens all the time. Perhaps you're having a bad day. Are you feeling poorly?" Ian attempted a smile.

The nasty woman's face broke out in red splotches. "I have not been chairwoman of the Stone Creek Ladies' Aid Society for nothing all of these years. I will not be patronized in this way! Wait until the truth about those two comes out!"

As the three women turned to walk away, Sophie heard Gertrude's louder than necessary comment. "How cozy, the two of them staying at the parsonage *every night.*" Her cohorts' gasps followed.

"Yes, I'm surprised by our saintly pastor," Millie added.

"How scandalous!" Etta put in her two cents.

Sophie's heart pounded in her ears. Her very insides shook. She whirled around. Pedestrians, frozen in the street momentarily, walked quickly away. Men tied their horses to hitching posts in a hurry. Passersby were all too quiet. Faces that had peered out from the storefronts disappeared away from the windows. How much of the town had observed the humiliating confrontation?

And Ian had defended her. Sophie sensed that she couldn't be the first victim of the Wringer woman's cruelty.

As he lifted Caira into the wagon, she grabbed his sleeve. "She was absolutely horrible. How can you let her go on like that? She's insinuating the worst and how many people heard her? Never mind that's the second time she frightened Caira." Sophie's voice rose, and she didn't care.

He lifted his hand again. "A soft answer turns away wrath."

"Does it with someone like that?" She wanted to cry and to scream that justice needed to be done—that Gertrude Wringer was filled with nothing but hateful venom, which would never be softened by anyone's kindness.

"Sophie, don't let her get to you. That's what she wants. If you give her evidence, she'll build her case," Maggie implored.

"What evidence? What case? What have I done?" How did you defend yourself against someone who was bent on hating you? This wasn't the first time she'd been wrongly accused. But this time Ian was considered her accomplice. She didn't want to see these kindhearted people get hurt on her account. She groaned. Her muddled, torn heart lay heavy in her chest.

⸻ ● ⸻

Sophie filled a water bottle with hot liquid and placed a cork in the opening. "Here you go, Mr. Graemer." She handed it to the elderly gentleman and tucked a blanket around him. "I worry about you not having someone here if you need anything during the night." Esther's absence seemed to drag on. Two days before she'd encountered Gertrude's spitefulness on the boardwalk, but it seemed a week ago.

"What? You don't need to strike up a light. It's daytime!" He boomed at her.

"Of course." Sophie smiled.

She stepped back to watch him rock contentedly in the ancient chair for a moment. She hoped the creaky piece of furniture wouldn't ever fall apart under the delightful elderly resident.

The squeak of the front door caught her attention. Mr. Spitzer, the traveling salesman, entered. "Long time, no see, Miss Sophie. Has Esther held my room for me?"

"Yes, sir. I'll make up the bed for you this afternoon. Will you be in town long?"

"I never know quite how many days, but it's good to be back. Say, are those your buttermilk biscuits I smell?" His black handlebar mustache twitched under his nose as he sniffed the air.

"Yes, they'll be out of the oven soon." Sophie had to smile. Mrs. Fairgrave's boardinghouse may never be quite full, but it didn't lack for characters. The thought lightened her spirits for a few minutes.

She walked through the doorway into the kitchen. After she'd taken the biscuits from the oven, she lifted each flaky, golden morsel off the pan and onto a platter. The buttery smell caused Sophie's taste buds to water. Her stomach growled in anticipation of lunch. At least she and Caira had not gone hungry. Maybe God really wasn't punishing her after all.

She sighed and tried to push dark thoughts away. Father's grim face still forced its way in. He had sat there and shook his head as her pregnancy became obvious. *"There's only one solution to this. Marry Charles."*

"Please, Papa, no."

"I thought you cared for him. Otherwise, I wouldn't have let him court you." His tone was impatient.

"Lemuel, please. I told you she was too young, that a man like Charles was too worldly for her. And now it seems he's shown her the 'ways of the world' and you're blaming our girl." Mama stood behind Sophie, with hands placed on her shoulders. *"I told you there was something that I didn't like about him."*

"But it would be for the best, Olivia. He came to me with honorable intentions. Sophia would want for nothing." Papa stood with hands behind his back and began to pace.

"And neither would the family company. Is that it, Lemuel?" Mother surprised Sophia with the way she spoke up for her.

"Papa, he scares me." She bowed her head.

"Well, he didn't frighten you enough, when you went into that parlor with him . . . alone."

"He tricked me." Then Sophia lowered her voice to a whisper. *"He forced me."*

"We've been over this all before. I believe she's telling the truth."
Mama's voice rose in pitch. "Paul should never have left her there. He
should have waited until he knew Charles' parents were there."

"How could you ruin our good name like this? God will punish such
sin!" Her father spat out the angry words.

Sophia's anguish washed over her with an ill feeling. "But I didn't
lead him on. I tell you the truth—there was no sin on my part. I cried
out. I couldn't get away." She knelt in front of the family patriarch.
"Please, Papa, please believe me." Her vision had blurred with a flood
of tears. "Please."

She shook herself as she scraped the biscuit pan with a spatula.
Ever since that day, she questioned her heart. Had she given Charles
the wrong idea? He'd been handsome, charming, and attentive.
He'd even gone to church with them occasionally. In her girlhood
fancies, she dreamed someone like that would come along and take
her for a wife.

Charles had told enchanting stories, listened to her hopes and
dreams as they sat on the back porch, in full view of everyone. He
seemed to seek her friendship because he enjoyed her company,
not because of her family or their fortune. Charles even told her
a tale of heroic proportions—one that caused Sophie to want to
touch the scar slanted across his cheek, which he said he'd earned
defending an innocent woman's honor. When she had placed her
fingertips ever so lightly on the raised spot, she hoped to connect
with him in sympathy.

But there was one evening as twilight arrived when he had
put his arm around her and held her more tightly than she liked.
Something about his closeness made her feel trapped, and his
hungry kisses aroused fear in her. Something was wrong. She
pulled away and went into the house. She wasn't trying to be
coy, but a flicker of anger in his eyes that night frightened her.
Sophie had tried to keep her distance until that wretched day he
had deceived her. She continued to scrape away at the metal sheet

and shivered. Truly, Charles had been a master at manipulating her emotions. She shivered at the thought of ever being in his grip again. During her short stay in the Lansing area when Caira was but a few months old, Sophie left as soon as she'd heard that a man of his description had been asking about them.

Maggie came in. "You're going to scrape a hole right through the bottom of that pan." She stirred the stew in the large saucepot.

Sophie glanced at her friend, so glad to be pulled back into the present. She met the mirth in Maggie's eyes, much like Ian's. "I suppose you're right. I best get this dinner on the table." She wiped her hands on her white cotton apron and looked around for the soup tureen. White paint on the ceiling, as well as sunny yellow on the walls, had been peeling for some time.

She almost tripped on the buckled edge of the threadbare rug when she carried a tray of food into the dining room.

Maggie clucked behind her. "You know, the more time I spend here, helping you, I realize how much this place has deteriorated."

Sophie spooned the hearty brown stew into a bowl for Mr. Graemer. "The thing is, Mrs. Fairgrave has a heart of gold. She took Caira and me in though we were strangers." She placed the bowl on a tray with a soupspoon and a biscuit, so she could take it to him. "People like Mr. Graemer need a place to stay, and she would never turn them out though they can hardly pay a thing."

"I can see that for sure." Her friend set out some butter she had taken from the icebox. "And she's never taken charity, I understand."

"No." Sophie shook her head and paused. "But if she's not here right now, why can't we do something? She'll have to accept it if it's already done."

"Why didn't I think of that myself?" Maggie's eyes brightened. "I'll talk to Ian about it tonight."

Sophie placed a hand on her arm. "No, Maggie. Please let me do this for Esther." Besides, it wouldn't hurt to have an excuse to talk to Ian, to thank him for sticking up for her earlier that day.

———•———

Ian paced outside that evening. He had read Caira a bedtime story and then he had turned his thoughts toward Sunday morning's sermon. The black sky hung as the backdrop of countless sparkling yellow gems. "The heavens declare the glory of God, and the firmament showeth his handiwork," he whispered into the nighttime quiet as he faced the stars.

"Ian."

"Oh, Sophie, I didn't hear you come out." In the glowing moonlight, he could make out her creamy complexion as she stood before him in one of his sister's altered cloaks. Maggie had insisted that she replace her tattered shawl.

"What can I do for you?"

"It's not so much what you can do for me though Caira and I would also benefit." She sounded rather breathy, nervous.

"Go on."

"Though Esther considers the boardinghouse a business, you and I know that much charity goes on there." She spoke up now. Her tone was firm. "With her gone, do you think that we could get some folks from the church to fix it up?"

Ian wasn't sure what he had expected her to say, but he felt disappointed. He'd hoped Sophie would finally confide her deepest secret to him. He exhaled, longing to understand the gulf that remained between them, affecting their friendship.

Her amber eyes shone in the moonlight like two beacons in the darkness surrounding them. She moved a bit closer.

"Ah, well." He couldn't take the brightness of those eyes anymore unless he claimed the privilege of a beloved one in looking upon them. He wasn't ready for that, especially with a woman who couldn't fully trust him. He turned away, his face again toward the stars, toward heaven, seeking help to overcome temptation.

"Ian?" Her gentle voice touched his heart.

He took a deep breath and faced her once more with his hands clasped behind his back. "Yes, I agree something needs to be done. Maggie chatters about it every time she has visited Esther. I notice the outside every time I go by. I'll bring it before the elder board, and I'm sure that we'll be able to get a committee together."

"Thank you."

"For what?" A soft breeze wisped around them. It seemed that Sophie stood closer than a moment before, and he could hear her breathing. It was almost as though he could listen to her heart, but then, perhaps he heard his own.

"For being willing to help Esther." Now he could feel her breath. "And for sticking up for me a couple of days ago. I'm sorry for accusing you of letting Gertrude off the hook when she was acting so spiteful in front of the mercantile. After all, she was part of your congregation before I was. I—"

"No! There is no excuse for the way she behaved. She is a troubled woman, I'm sure. She's bitter, no doubt, about past misfortunes, but she should not be taking things out on you."

Before Ian realized it, he had put a hand on her shoulder in sort of a brotherly gesture. How long had it been since he was close enough to smell the fragrance of her hair? He had when she was sick and he'd carried her. He had felt the warmth of her closeness then. Yet the longing to had compelled him to stay away while she abided under his roof.

"Is . . . is there anything else you want to tell me?" Ian gazed again into those eyes, wanting to somehow will her to tell him everything, draw every hidden piece of truth from the depth of her heart.

Sophie stepped back. Her arms crossed in front of her as she shivered. "It's just that Caira and I needed friends. You . . . and Maggie . . . have been so good to us. It's more than I deserve, more than I expected."

How could he not defend her against that awful woman? "We need to be your friends as much as you may need our friendship. It's not about deserving, it's about God's grace." He deserved the friendship of this beautiful young woman less than anyone. But for the secrets of her true identity and relationship to Caira, she was guileless.

"I guess I should have expected you to say that." Her airy, evasive laughter followed. "Good night, Ian."

"Have a good rest, Sophie." She had pulled out from under his gentle grasp and strode toward the house. All that she left behind was that flowery scent and the warmth of her shoulder under his hand. She might not be running like a frightened animal, but still she didn't seem to quite trust him. Why? Because he was a man? Surely all the time they'd spent together under the parsonage roof would've shown her he was more than trustworthy. He'd never treated her differently—beyond friendship. He compared their relationship to family. That was all.

But a faceless, nameless man divided them by his evil attack on Sophie. Ian's jaw tightened along with his fists. Anger fueled the hatred in his heart, yet such feelings were counterproductive. Praying for Sophie's healing would be more profitable. He would master this, forgive the man, and wait patiently to earn the right to become Sophie's confidant.

Sophie hung the cloak on a peg and ran up the stairs to the small guest room. Her heart pounded faster than the rhythm of her feet on the stairs. She closed the door behind her and leaned against it inside her dark room. "Oh, yes," she whispered into the dark and clasped her hands together. Esther would have the improvements she needed. While she was overjoyed for her friend, other feelings vied for her attention.

Sophie touched her shoulder for a moment. Did she imagine the encompassing heat coursing clear through? She sighed. One moment she closed her eyes and savored the feeling. The next, her stomach wrenched with nervousness. She knew, as though by instinct, Ian was trustworthy. He'd never given her cause to believe he was anything else.

Did she fear becoming too close to him and having to tell the truth? If she did, the relationship would end anyway. They could never be more than dear friends. Yet somehow she also realized the fact in her heart; her feelings went much deeper than that.

Sophie put her head in her hand and sat on the edge of the bed. A shaft of moonlight pushed through the opening between the two blousy muslin curtains. Ian still stood outside in the yard, under the same moon. The kindness in his voice, the touch on her shoulder, and the tilt of his head all seemed to speak of his concern for her when they talked.

A part of her wanted so much to have his admiration, to believe that he could care. He had been charmed by Caira's antics and showed true affection for her little girl. Yet if he knew Sophie was a defiled imposter, would he care for either of them? Perhaps Ian would pity her and continue to be concerned about Caira, but as pastor of Stone Creek Community Church, he couldn't be closely associated with her romantically. How many people in Detroit, Pontiac, or Greenville, who'd learned her story, had called her a tramp or worse?

She worked at redeeming her reputation from the horrible crime that had been committed upon her. How Sophie wanted to believe that God wasn't going to punish her or Caira. Had the assault been her fault? Had she somehow tempted Charles? Many people had made her feel so cheap and looked upon her with suspicion. She wanted to live an honorable life. Was this enough in God's eyes?

As a child, she had asked Jesus to be her Savior from her sins, accepting God's forgiveness. With her mother and brother, she had ministered her gift of music in many churches. Sophie had utilized her talent to her fullest ability. Why had God let such awful things happen to her? Why had most Christian people in her social circle turned against her in her time of need? Caira had done nothing to deserve such rejection.

The child's even breathing caught her attention. How peaceful she looked with her eyes closed and curls framing her face. She popped a thumb in her mouth.

Sophie had to smile. Her beautiful little angel slept, unaware of the hatred and cruelty in the world for the moment. She would do her best to protect her daughter as long as she could. Sophie tucked the blanket tighter around Caira.

This life of hiding was bondage, but the burden of caring for the child was sometimes forgotten when generous hugs were placed around Sophie's neck, when the child said, "Love 'ou," and blew her kisses.

Sophie would make the best of it. As much as her heart ached to be closer to Reverend Ian McCormick, friendship would have to be enough, especially with the eyes of Mrs. Wringer on them both. He would be better left to the shy, unassuming girl, Nora, anyway.

Sophie and Maggie strolled along the boardwalk. "It was good to hear from Mrs. Fairgrave. I'm writing back, telling her everything is fine and not to rush home." Sophie held an envelope, ready to mail, in one hand.

"The board approved the fix-up day not a moment too soon." Maggie sighed.

"I only hope she won't suspect anything since I'm hinting that she take her time."

"Just a few more things to get." Maggie held a list for the upcoming workday at the boardinghouse as they strode toward the mercantile.

Main Street bustled with traffic. Horses clomped without care along the muddy road and women lifted the edges of their skirts with daintiness as they crossed the street. More than once, a wagon wheel made a revolution through a puddle and splashed pedestrians with dirty water.

"Disgusting!" Maggie took a handkerchief from her reticule and wiped a muddy spot from her skirt.

The sky hung overhead with a sickly gray pallor, and Sophie held her hat onto her head when the wind lifted it.

The letter slipped from her other hand, and she bent to retrieve it. As she looked up, she noticed a young man swaggering along, farther up the street. He wore a fancy dark suit and a hat to match. He had the same build as Charles, the same confident strut. How many women would he deceive with his insincere charm in this town, given a chance? Sophie gasped.

Her mouth grew dry, and she fell to her knees, unable to move. Her heart hammered inside her chest so that it was the only thing she heard. When he turned around and strode toward them, Sophie muted the scream she felt rising in her throat and attempted an escape. The letter again fell to the boardwalk and she covered her mouth and the squeak that sounded from it.

The slick hair that peeked out from under his hat and the trimmed mustache were so much like Charles', but she could see that his coloring was different as he walked closer.

"What is it?" Maggie bent toward her and offered a hand. "Are you all right?"

"Good afternoon, ladies." The gentleman, probably several years older than her child's father, tipped his hat. "May I help you?" He bent to retrieve the envelope for her.

Sophie realized her unabated stare must appear very rude to him and Maggie. She inhaled. How long had it been since she'd taken a breath? "Th-thank you," she stammered.

She took the offered white envelope and observed his questioning gaze. "I'm sorry, you just remind me of someone . . . someone I haven't seen for a long time."

"That's all right." The stranger nodded and gave her a kind smile, one filled with sincerity—so unlike Charles. He tipped his hat before he went on to pass them.

Maggie took her arm. "What was that all about?"

"It's nothing, Maggie, really. It's all in the past."

Maggie clucked her tongue. "I can see you don't want to talk about it." There was hurt in the tone of her voice.

Sophie patted the hand that grasped her arm. "Some things aren't worth talking about. They're better left unsaid." She forced a smile toward her dear friend. She would not, in fact, she could not, burden Maggie with her secrets. Besides, as lovely and kind as she was, Ian's sister was decent folk, and Sophie reminded herself that she would not be considered decent anymore, if the truth were known.

"Sophie, dear, sometimes I positively wonder about you."

She stiffened and took in another deep breath. "How so?"

"You've never told us where you were from or what happened to your loved ones."

"It's still too painful to talk about." Now that was the plain truth. Rejection's sting didn't seem to lessen much over time. Sophie held her head high and turned away so that Maggie couldn't see the tears clouding her eyes.

CHAPTER 18

The following Friday, the yeasty scent of baking bread and the warmth of Esther's stove surrounded Sophie with the comfort of a mother's hug. Caira sat on the floor, banging a wooden spoon on a dented pan and chattering to her rag doll, which was propped against the cupboard door. Sophie's return to the boardinghouse had been a relief. Being at the parsonage day and night, when she was sick, had pushed her into a melancholy state. Ian's nearness interfered with her attempt to bring an end to her growing feelings for him.

Sophie stirred the golden batter with vigor, wanting her yellow cake to be light and fluffy for the coming church workday at the boardinghouse. Maggie hummed as she dusted in the other room. A knock sounded at the back door.

Sophie pushed aside the curtain to find Nora standing on the stoop. She squinted in the bright sunlight. Pulling open the door, Sophie greeted her friend. "Nora! What brings you here? Come in."

The girl stepped over the threshold. She wore a muted green plaid suit and held an apron over one arm while she carried a basket in the same hand. "I've brought quince jelly, compliments of Aunt Gertie. And I've come to help."

"Truly?"

"Well, Aunt Gertie won't be here for the work bee, neither will she allow me." Nora paused. "It's her contribution. She doesn't want to seem completely against Esther, especially as head of the Ladies' Aid Society." Nora set the basket on the kitchen table. "But she didn't say I couldn't help you get ready."

Sophie shivered when she took hold of the jars—as cold as the woman who'd produced their contents—and placed them on the sideboard.

"Won't they be upset if they find out you stayed very long?" Confusion clouded Sophie's thoughts. As much as she disliked Mrs. Wringer, she didn't want to encourage Nora to act disrespectfully or dishonestly to her aunt and uncle. However, as lonely as the other young woman seemed for friendship, Sophie couldn't bear to send her away.

Nora squeezed Sophie's flour-covered hand. "Aunt Gertie and Uncle Edmund will be gone all day." She paused, looking a bit guilty. "I'll only stay for a couple of hours, but you and Mrs. Galloway have shown kindness to me. I truly desire to repay you both. Besides, how can Aunt Gertie fault me for ingratiating myself with the reverend's sister?" The sincerity of the look in her blue eyes brightened with a bit of mischief. "After all, my usual chores are done, and I'll have plenty of time to practice on Aunt Gertie's piano later. I'll tell her that I felt the Ladies' Aid Society needed to be represented in some small way at least."

"What would you like to help with?" Sophie asked her while she wiped her hands on a clean cotton towel.

"I was hoping you needed help with baking. I figured you'll need to feed the workers this weekend. I keep some of my mother's best cookie recipes right up here." Nora patted her head.

"What's this I hear about cookies?" Maggie had opened the kitchen door and peeked in.

"You might have some competition with Maggie's snicker doodles." Sophie had Nora giggling, along with herself.

Maggie came all the way into the kitchen. Her hands went up as if in defeat. "I'm sure the town has had enough of my old snicker doodles."

"Never!" Sophie put an arm around her, thinking of all the times the spicy scent of cookies in the parsonage oven had made her feel at home. "But Nora would like to help us bake this morning."

"Really? Well, we're glad to have you." Maggie hugged Nora, whose eyes widened at the gesture of affection. The young widow stepped back and reached for her apron. "We better set to helping Sophie. There's a lot to do."

•••)———————— • ————————(•••

Though baking was one of Sophie's favorite chores, having help made things go much more quickly. In fact, cooking took little effort with her friends.

She stopped, dipping a ladle into the stewed chicken she'd put together for the midday meal and then tasted a seasoned carrot and bit of potato. The men would traipse through the door and search for something edible soon enough.

"Before I go, I wanted to ask your opinion on some music I'm working on for Sunday." Nora swept a washcloth across the table while Maggie swished a broom over the floor.

"Oh?" The bite of vegetables stuck in the back of her throat as she attempted to swallow. She tried not to think of the friendship that must be developing between Nora and Ian. He'd taken her for her individual value, rather than show prejudice against Nora, despite her aunt's machinations. Though it was for the best, sadness intruded on her musings, along with reality.

"I hope I can play the piano as well as you some day. Then maybe I could teach eventually." Nora squeezed the washcloth over the sink basin, looking like she was a hundred miles away in her thoughts.

"Nora, you're doing very well. As I've said before, I had a lot of practice when I was younger. It will come with time." Sophie reached for bowls and placed them on the sideboard. "By the time my sewing business is in full swing, you'll be ready to teach and can have my students."

"I'm so thankful for the extra bit of money for my family." She neatly folded the rag and draped it over the edge of the basin. "But you know, Sophie, I'm sure you need it more than I do. Would you consider sharing the position with me if the elder board goes along?" She untied her apron and pulled it up over her head. "I should shake this out."

Sophie opened her eyes wider. "Wouldn't your aunt make a fuss? And what about your family?"

"I'll tell her I want more time to work on my painting and drawing, which is partly true. She takes stock in having such genteel abilities. And I can make up the difference for my family with part of my allowance. Please think about my offer." Her friend looked over her shoulder bearing a smile and mischief in her eyes. As Nora opened the door with her apron in her hand, James Cooper barreled through.

"Ow!" she squeaked as she fell backward, hitting the floor.

James looked up, obviously shaken. He glanced down. "My apologies. Let me help you up."

"Nora, are you all right?" Sophie rushed to her.

Her friend stared up at James, her eyes barely blinking. "I'm most certainly fine."

James grasped Nora's arms and pulled her to her feet. His eyes didn't leave hers either. "That was absolutely clumsy of me. I was so concentrated on an assignment from the paper, I didn't even see you." He steadied her before he let go and pushed a hand through his hair.

Sophie took Nora's elbow while James picked up the apron, and his hat, from the threshold. "This is James Cooper, budding, sometimes absentminded, journalist. May I introduce you to Nora Armstrong? She's quite new in town." Sophie knew she'd shot James a scolding look, just as she would have to her brother, Paul. "If you went to church more often, you'd know who she was."

Nora's pale face turned sunset pink. "Pleased to meet you, Mr. Cooper."

"The pleasure is all mine, Miss Armstrong." Sophie rolled her eyes at James' flourished bow.

"Nora is the principal church pianist, living with her aunt and uncle, the Wringers."

"Please consider taking me up on my offer." Nora hugged her. "I so want to be a help to you."

Sophie's heart positively expanded with affection for her friend. This could be an opportunity to see Ian once she'd moved out of the parsonage, but the thought scared her as much as it gave her a sense of pleasure. "Nora, you are too generous. Don't worry about me. I am still glad to help you and to be backup if you need it."

Nora's mouth drooped.

"I'll think about it." Sophie closed the door after her dear friend turned to leave. Afterward, she realized with all the commotion, Nora had never asked her music question.

·•●)———— ● ————(●•·

Rhythmic pounding of hammers rang out in the crisp afternoon air. After working inside for several hours, Sophie went outside to check on the men.

"Anyone thirsty?" She grasped a rung of the ladder and climbed the first several with care while carrying a bucket of water.

"Yes, thank you." One of the workers reached down and Sophie handed him a ladle full.

Her foot caught in the hem of her skirt as she moved back down the ladder, pushing her leg against the rungs. Sophie dropped the bucket, but not in time to prevent her from losing her balance and tumbling backward. She closed her eyes. *Help!* Her silent plea went up to God, even while she opened her mouth to scream. Everything was happening so quickly, yet it seemed to take one hundred years. Just as she thought that she wasn't far from hitting the ground, Sophie felt the warmth of two strong arms supporting her weight. She opened her eyes and gasped.

She could feel Ian's heart pounding in cadence with hers as he held her close. "Sophie, are you hurt?" His Adam's apple bobbed. Sweat glistened on his furrowed brow above his aqua eyes.

Her voice came out barely above a whisper. "I don't believe so." Sophie closed her eyelids for but a moment, wondering if this could be a dream. No, she could still feel the strength of his arms underneath, the muscles of his chest taut against her. She opened her eyes again. Yes, Ian had caught her and still held her. She remembered the afternoon he had carried her against her will when she was sick. Like the proverbial knight in shining armor, he had rescued her again. How could her reserve melt so quickly? She was surprised with the awareness of how right it felt for him to hold her, much like it had that afternoon at the parsonage. What was this man doing to her?

"Let me take you inside." The grin on his face replaced the worried expression he had worn moments before.

Sophie nodded though she'd rather continue to melt into his arms.

"Good work, Reverend!" Mr. Graemer's exclamation boomed from the doorway.

Ian placed her on the ground as delicately as though she were a porcelain doll. Taking her elbow, he guided her into the house and waited for her to settle on the chaise in the parlor. She wished the moments in his arms had taken longer.

"Are you sure you're quite well?" He bent over her. "May I get you something to drink?"

A nervous giggle bubbled up inside of Sophie. "I'm fine, really. I was just a bit scared, is all. It's you who are probably worse for the wear. You did all the work. I hope I didn't hurt you."

Gloria Myles rushed to Sophie's side and held her hand. "Let me fix you a cup of tea, dear. You've been working hard all day."

"Thank you, but I'll be fine." Sophie waved a hand.

"How frightful that you fell. I heard all about it. Thank the Lord our dear Pastor McCormick was here to catch you." Gloria patted Sophie's hand.

"Well, I'll be back to work then." Ian nodded and headed back outside.

"Quite a young man there, isn't he?" Mr. Graemer toddled off to his rocking chair and lowered himself into it. "I just happened to open the door for a bit of air, when I saw what happened. Wore me out, it did, watching him run to catch you like that. You're one lucky lady." He mopped his brow with a handkerchief.

"I—" Sophie was interrupted.

"Providence, Mr. Graemer, providence. Our pastor would tell you that there is no such thing as luck." Gloria wagged a finger at the elderly gentleman, but she did it with a smile.

"Ah, yes." He agreed. "Providential for both of them, indeed." Mr. Graemer grinned in such a way that he looked quite pleased with himself.

Did his statement hold more meaning than he let on? Sophie shifted her position on the settee. Warmth crept into her cheeks. She noticed that her shin smarted. After rubbing her leg, she bent her head and rubbed her cool hands on her burning face, hoping no one would notice.

Ian swung the hammer onto the head of a nail, fastening one more loose board. He sighed. They had accomplished much though it was only early afternoon, but they would have to come back to whitewash the clapboard and paint several rooms inside. He stood up straight and rubbed the small of his back for a moment.

A cloud blew across the blue sky along with a sharp breeze, warning that nobody should get too used to spring's presence. He tried to concentrate on his thankfulness for the industriousness of those helping that day rather than the disappointment he felt in the absence of several families. Though most of the elder board approved of a workday to assist the kindly Esther, the Wilsons, the Stouts, the Blandings, and a few others whom Gertrude possessed influence over in the church found excuses for not being present. No doubt Gertrude couldn't stomach the thought of publicly helping someone who'd given Sophie a chance.

He'd heard that Helena Blanding said they were much too busy with preparing for the Welcome Spring Social they held annually for the young people of the town. You'd think with her father being an elder, charity toward a widow would be considered more important, but Stone Creek's social calendar seemed to take precedence for the family.

He thought he'd check on Sophie one more time. He walked through the back door. "I see the invalid is up." She was scurrying around the kitchen, clad with a white apron over her navy blue dress. Strands of chestnut hair had fallen loose from her bun. How he would like to loosen all of her shining tresses and see them frame her pretty face.

"Thanks to you I only have a bruised shin to contend with. Your timing was perfect." That endearing crooked grin caused her to look even more fetching. "Besides, I had so many people fussing over me that even if I had been hurt, I would have been mended in no time."

How true! More than once, Ian had poked his head in to see how she fared. Not only Gloria, but several other women had brought her a pillow or recommended a tonic for her nerves and various other remedies. Many of the people of his congregation cared about her.

Sophie sniffed the air. "Oh no, I hope the beans aren't burning now." Armed with a potholder and a serving spoon, she took the lid from a large pan and stirred the contents as a steamy molasses scent rose from the pot. "Somehow, I need to get these people fed. We have a small army here."

"The turnout has been quite heartening indeed." Ian nodded. He crossed his arms and leaned against the wall. He spied a vase of golden daffodils. "Where did those come from?"

"Oh, a dear friend brought them." She moved the pan to the table by the wall. "I believe these are done."

Sophie wore a mischievous smile. What kind of "dear friend" would bring her such a lovely floral offering? Perhaps she had an admirer. He scratched his head, thinking of the men and boys who had inquired about her. Most of them were married, too old, or too young. Then again, what did it matter to him? Ian knew that any hint of a relationship with him could be ruinous if certain people had wind of it, especially while she was still under his roof . . . and protection. Caira's out-of-wedlock birth wouldn't be received lightly.

A vision of James Cooper kneeling before Sophie in the parsonage kitchen nagged him. Thoughts of the immature young man attempting to court her gnawed at him like a wolf at a bone. Though he tried for the next few minutes to shake off such jealous feelings, they pained him.

Maggie burst through the door, startling him from his confused state. "Ian, what are you doing just standing there? And you look perfectly cross."

Sophie's forehead creased as her brows went up, a question forming in her eyes.

His sister put her hands on her hips. "The men need you to help set up the tables, so we can eat. And our darling Sophie here," Maggie said as she moved to link arms with the younger woman, "has worked so hard despite her mishap."

Ian had to keep himself from rolling his eyes. How quickly his older sister had forgotten the role he played in Sophie's tumble from the ladder.

"Maggie, don't forget your brother did save me from injury."

"Yes, yes, of course. Ian's a good soul. Such a gallant act is the least he could do." She waved her other hand about as though shooing a fly.

He noticed then that Elise had entered the kitchen. With all her shyness, she attempted to hide behind Sophie. She tapped Maggie on the arm.

"What is it, dear?" Maggie spoke with a kinder tone toward the little girl. Elise pointed to the daffodils.

"Where did that lovely sign of spring come from?" Maggie bent closer toward Elise.

"Tell her." Sophie put her arm around the child's shoulder.

"From me," she whispered, smiling up at Sophie.

"She brought them to me from her grandma's garden."

"They are just beautiful." Maggie clapped her hands together. "How thoughtful."

The blooms seemed even more beautiful to Ian at that moment. His heart warmed to think of how Sophie's music had touched Elise's heart, causing the child to come out of her shell, but even more, he felt relief that the flowers hadn't been from a gentleman. He slipped silently back outside, at peace.

Ian grasped one end of a large wooden plank while Elisha Whitworth picked up the other. Ian contrasted the rough hardness of the lifeless wood to the warm softness of Sophie in his arms earlier that day. For a second, he had felt complete. It was as though he had been lost in the pools of her amber eyes and had to draw himself out before he drowned in them. At moments like that, he could forget the secret wedged between them and her lack of trust in him. He took a deep breath and exhaled.

"You're awfully quiet, there, Reverend." Elisha's gruff voice ended Ian's reverie. "If it weren't for Maggie and her boy, I would say that you're alone too much. Though you're at just the right age to find yourself a wife." The large, bearded man grinned and mopped his forehead. A small amount of activity set Elisha to sweating.

"Indeed? I have plenty of company with my family around. Not to mention Sophie and Caira. Although they won't be around much longer." *Thank the Lord.* Once Esther returned, he could be freed from what Sophie's alluring presence did to him. He would miss them, certainly, but there was nothing else to be done.

The two men worked together as the planks clanked on top of the sawhorses to form makeshift tables.

"Aw, you'll miss them both. Won't it be a lot quieter without them?" Elisha was used to having five strapping sons around the house. Philip probably didn't seem like he would be of much consequence.

"Easier to study." Ian grinned.

The larger man moved alongside him and clapped a hand on Ian's back. "Well, there's more to life than sermon writing. I think she's sweet on you," he attempted to whisper, "and I heartily approve." Elisha winked.

"Be assured, you can stop thinking on that, Elisha." Ian bent over to hoist up another board. "God will bring me the right wife in time, so please don't get any ideas." An edge of gruffness tinged his voice.

"Well, all right." The elder scratched his head and looked confused before he stooped to pick up his end.

How many more people had an idea that Sophie was sweet on him? He could only imagine the rumors that might be afloat. How was he going to protect Sophie's reputation, let alone his own? And if any of them got wind of Sophie's secret, Gertrude's following would grow. Would Sophie run away again before she had a chance to confide in him?

Light laughter rang through the air. As the women carried out plates, along with heaping platters of chicken, bowls of beans, and other side dishes to the hungry workers, Ian feasted on the sight of Sophie. Her lips bowed into a complete smile. She had the most endearing upturned, freckled nose and dimpled chin. Then the warm gaze of her amber eyes met his and time ceased for a minute until she turned away, looking embarrassed.

His heart tripped in an odd way as it only had since he met Sophie. Ian could not deny, as he watched her work with the others, that this young woman was special to him. What else could explain why he would be jealous over a vase full of flowers? He swallowed and turned back to the work of setting up tables.

Elisha Whitworth chuckled and winked again. "Looks like a match to me."

"But, I—"

"No need to explain, Reverend. It's only the natural course God intended." Which was a piece of wisdom Ian wasn't sure he was ready to hear.

••●)━━━━━━ ● ━━━━━━(●••

When Sophie turned away, her heart hammered at the awareness of Ian's gaze on her. A napkin slipped from her hand, and she bent to retrieve the square of white linen. "How clumsy of me."

"Perhaps you're feeling a bit self-conscious today." Gloria placed a gentle hand on Sophie's back. Her eyes were bright with a knowing look.

Sophie shook her head with dismay and put a free hand to her hip. "Self-conscious of what?"

"Of *whom?* Would be a more appropriate question." Gloria giggled like a schoolgirl.

Sophie busied herself setting out napkins and plates, trying to ignore what had been implied by her friend's statement. Yet she knew the truth of it. The moment she and Ian gazed upon one another, she recalled the warmth she'd experienced while his arms supported her weight. How good it felt to fall into his embrace, though it had been an accident. In their closeness they had been almost one, but not quite. No, they never could be.

She loved Ian, she knew it for sure, and there could be no man to take his place. Sophie's heart was heavy with the realization that she would treasure the secret of this unrequited love to her grave. Both his reputation as a minister of God and the reality of her hidden truth dictated this.

CHAPTER 19

"Whoa!" Ian pulled on the reins as they drove up in front of the boardinghouse, which shone like a pearl in the sunshine with its fresh coat of white paint. Esther stood in the doorway with arms open wide. "Welcome home, dears."

Sophie allowed Ian to help her down from the buggy. He lowered Caira to the ground.

"Farfy!" Caira's shrill cry of happiness showed that she had not forgotten their kind landlady as she tore up the path and into Esther's skirts. No matter how many times Sophie tried to teach her to call Esther "Mrs. Fairgrave," Caira's enduring term for her had stuck, much as "'Cowmick" had become Ian's name.

"Slow down!" Sophie commanded to no avail. Though her daughter was still not much more than a baby, she was determined to steer her into the path of becoming a lady.

Sophie saw the tears in Esther's eyes. She hoped they were tears of joy. Her employer clutched Sophie to her ample bosom. "I'm so happy to be home and have both of you here." Esther wiped her cheek with a handkerchief. "And look at how big our little gal is." She patted Caira on the head.

"It is good to be back." *Though things won't be the same without Ian around.* How Sophie had loved watching Caira's delight over the books Ian read aloud to her. And at bedtime she took joy in how he willingly let Caira ride up the stairs on his shoulders. They had been given a sweet taste of what could never be, and she would always cherish the memory.

Esther stepped away but held tight to both of Sophie's hands. She frowned. "We have to do something about that hair. I hate Psyche knots." Once the older woman released Sophie and exchanged greetings with Maggie, they went inside the house.

"Good to see you, Mrs. Fairgrave." Ian inclined his head as he carried a crate of items Maggie insisted Sophie could use.

Esther exclaimed as she swept a plump arm through the air, "You orchestrated all of this, Sophie?"

"Of a certainty, it was the love of the people of Stone Creek in response to your years of kindness and service to them. I could never have done all the repairs and painting, inside and outside, on my own."

The older widow's eyes watered again. "This must be the nicest thing anyone's ever done for me."

Sophie sighed with relief at Esther's proclamation and listened to her chatter about the vivid green of the parlor walls, the loveliness of the new lace curtains and comfort of the reupholstered settee.

Sophie turned toward Maggie. "Thank you again, Maggie, for everything. And you really didn't need to have Ian bring all this. I don't expect such charity." She pointed to the crate of gently used clothing and various other household things.

"When you're part of a family, it isn't plain charity, but the kind of love God wants us to show one another. And you've spent enough time under our roof to qualify for that."

"I hope I can be that much of a blessing to you someday." Sophie glanced over her shoulder.

"You don't realize how much of a blessing you already are."

Fearing the catch in her throat would betray her, Sophie only nodded. While relieved she was returning to Fairgrave's, she would miss the sort of family they'd become each evening.

"Your help has been invaluable to us, Maggie, Reverend. I don't know what my daughter would have done without me!" Esther paused. "And would you believe of all things, the new rocking chair doesn't bode well with Mr. Graemer? He missed the rickety old chair so much, I had to ask Mr. Spitzer to bring it out of the attic and put it in his room. The only thing is that darling old man spends too much time up there, where it's draftier. Perhaps you can help me find a way to entice him downstairs, short of bringing that chair back with him."

Sophie smiled and patted Esther's arm. "I'll bet a batch of gingersnaps would do the trick. I'll start them as soon as I can."

"That's a wonderful idea. Oh my, I almost forgot." Esther sauntered to the secretary in the corner of the parlor and retrieved an envelope from the top. "I have something for you from the Myleses. It came in the mail today."

Sophie took it from her. "Hmm, what could it be?"

"Wan' see it!" Caira jumped and pulled on the corner of the piece of mail.

"Hold on, Caira." She sat on the settee and took the child in her lap. "Let's see. It says: *You're invited to a luncheon picnic at Apple Blossom House. 2 p.m. on Saturday, May 19.*' It's just a few weeks away. And, what do you know? She wants me to bring all of you, as well."

"Oh, my. I come back to a new home and a party. How lovely." A look of panic swept away the blissful expression on Esther's face. "I must think of something extraordinary to bake. I can't go empty-handed to Apple Blossom House."

"I'm afraid you'll have to." Maggie had made herself at home next to Sophie on the chaise and read over her shoulder. Caira moved from Sophie's lap to hers. "It says here that they only request the pleasure of your company. They'll provide refreshments and beverages."

"You'll have other chances to bake something for the Myles family. It's not something worth fussing over." Sophie smiled while she reached over and tousled her daughter's hair.

"Oh dear, Apple Blossom House. What will I wear?" Esther smoothed her skirt over her plump hips.

"It's just a picnic." Sophie shook her head and chuckled. She couldn't understand what all this trouble was. Though Gloria was an elegant woman, she never snubbed those who had less. She saw them for the good souls they were.

"You don't understand. Even a picnic at Apple Blossom House is an event." Worry lined Esther's brow. May 19th couldn't come soon enough.

With all the talk of the upcoming picnic luncheon at Apple Blossom House, one would think Helena's soiree might be forgotten. Or perhaps Sophie wished it had been. While she realized she belonged with her true friends, who were several years older than she, sometimes she found herself feeling like an outcast. The last thing she wanted to hear about was how the spring social had gone without her. For once, Sophie decided to mail in her Sears and Roebuck catalog order for more sewing patterns, rather than order them through Neuberger's. She could at least avoid Cecilia's smugness for one day.

When she walked from the cool spring air outside into the stuffy little post office, she nearly ran right smack into Helena Blanding, with Cecilia close behind. Sophie sighed. There would be no escaping them, so she lifted her chin and nodded at them. "Good afternoon, Miss Neuberger, Miss Blanding."

"Why, look who's here, it's Miss Biddle. How delightful to see you." Helena wore a stylish mauve hat, perched atop her medium brown hair. Her mouth curved into a smile, a gesture that accentuated her large, slightly protruding teeth. The girl did have pretty blue eyes, though. She must give her that.

"I didn't mean to slight you, by the way, not inviting you to our usual Welcome Spring event. I always think you have so much on your plate, taking care of your little *sister* and being employed as a maid at the boardinghouse. Why, you wouldn't have time for such frivolity, would you?" Helena glanced at her sleeve and picked some imaginary form of lint from her elegant lace cuff.

"No offense taken. I am quite busy." Sophie attempted to step around them, but Cecilia blocked her path.

"It was the most beautiful party ever. We had a lovely, delicious punch and sandwiches made with the flakiest croissants, besides appetizers and the desserts. I wish you could have seen them." Cecilia tittered like an annoying little bird, bent on stealing the attention.

"And my brother, Malcolm, brought home a couple of his friends from the University of Michigan. One of them, Peter Morgan—"

"Is so handsome," Cecilia interrupted her friend. "Why, his father is president of a bank and Peter has eyes only for Helena."

"Don't be silly. He hasn't even asked whether he can court me yet." Helena waved away the comment.

"I'm sure the whole affair was elegant indeed." Sophie smiled in spite of herself. They didn't know of her past, how many social events she'd attended, where the guests were waited on by maids and ate off fine bone china plates and drank lemonade from crystal goblets. She hadn't given them the crestfallen reaction they had hoped for.

"Of course, there's always next year." Helena patted Sophie on the arm like she was some bedraggled mutt looking for a handout.

"Yes, next year. I'm sure it would be lovely." Sophie squeezed the girl's hand as though her social equal. Helena's eyebrows rose as she moved away, seeming uncomfortable.

"Good day, Miss Biddle." She and Cecilia finally let Sophie pass as they headed toward the door, whispering to one another.

Sophie was relieved to see Nora was finishing up at the counter as she turned to greet her with a smile. "Don't pay them any mind." So she'd heard the whole miserable conversation.

"Hello, Nora. It's good to see you." Yet Sophie was a bit embarrassed, knowing the other two girls thought of her as nothing more than a disreputable maid.

"I was there. The party wasn't as lovely as they like to make it sound. Aunt Gert made me go, said I needed to get out and socialize with decent folk. But they're not really my type. I'm just a poor farmer's daughter, remember." Nora grinned. "I sat in the corner with my cup of punch. The girls all had their noses in the air, and the college boys were positively boring. And the croissants tasted stale." She scrunched her nose and stuck out her tongue.

"I'm sorry you didn't have a good time. Really, it's all right they didn't invite me. I've had enough of that kind of thing." Then Sophie became concerned Nora might realize she was referring to her past. "I mean, I've had enough of their snubbing me. Thanks for helping me feel better. If you wait for me to post my mail order, perhaps we can talk a little more."

"Of course." Nora nodded.

They would have to be discreet and walk down a side street, rather than Main, but Sophie knew she had the best qualities of a friend in Nora, not to mention Maggie, Gloria, and Esther. Now she would feel out of place at such a young person's event like the Welcome Spring Social. With the responsibility of being a mother and her past courtship turning disastrous, Sophie couldn't relate to the other young women. There was more to life than dressing up and sipping lemonade while she batted her eyelashes at prospective suitors. She was happy to welcome spring in her heart.

* * *

The following Sunday evening Sophie played the piano at Nora's urging. She finished the postlude before Ian stood to make an announcement. He cleared his throat. "As I reminded all of you earlier, there will be a congregational meeting following the service. If anyone would like to stay and hear my plans of hope for a future ministry of the church, you are welcome. There will be a light meal to follow."

As the congregation stood and mingled after he gave the blessing to dismiss them, Ian strode toward her. His eyes shone with mischief as he grinned. "You were my first choice for the position. Nora's done a fine job, but don't ever forget that you're irreplaceable, Sophie." Ian's expression softened and grew more serious. His gaze sought to connect with hers, his eyes probing.

It seemed he knew the very thoughts of her heart. The warming of her face betrayed her. Sophie found she couldn't look away. The reassurance soothed the insecurities that sometimes overwhelmed her. "Thank you." To know that she would have the hope of serving and being near Ian for a while was enough for the present.

Elder Whitworth cleared his throat as he stood near Ian's side. "Perhaps I should call the meeting to order now, Reverend."

"There are a few more details I wanted to go over with you, Elisha." Ian turned to Sophie for a moment. "Excuse me," he said, his tone apologetic, before he left her.

Sophie nodded. Standing by herself, she held her breath and searched for the busy Caira. Her daughter traipsed after Philip. Maggie watched them both. Sophie exhaled. She had nothing to worry about. Gratefulness for the support filled her until an ill wind interrupted her thoughts.

Gertrude Wringer marched toward her with Nora in tow. "I hope you're happy now that my niece has allowed you to help her shoulder the music ministry. Not that she needs any assistance, but she has better things to do with her time." The woman sniffed, lifting her nose in the air as if offended by a putrid odor. An egret plume, the newest addition to the ugly brown hat, flopped forward in front of her face.

Sophie pressed her lips together, looking at Nora, whom she could tell by the sparkle in her eyes, also tried not to laugh. Mrs. Wringer grasped at the feather, attempting to tuck it back into place. Her eyebrows knitted together in consternation. "Don't expect such good fortune to last forever. Come along, Nora."

Sophie bristled. That woman would stop at nothing, even though sharing the job had been Nora's idea.

Nora put a hand on her aunt's arm. "Aunt Gertie, I need to speak with Sophie . . . a-about music." She looked down as if in deference.

"She doesn't deserve your help, but very well. Headstrong girl. I have business to take care of myself. Edmund!" she screeched after her husband.

"Your music was so lovely. I've never heard anyone play hymns so beautifully," Nora said, once her aunt was out of earshot.

"Thank you." Sophie reached out, wanting to take one of her friend's hands in her own, but thought better of it around Gertrude and clasped her fingers behind her back.

"I get so nervous being in front of this many people. I make so many mistakes and could learn so much from you." Nora wrung her hands.

"You've always covered them nicely. Don't be so hard on yourself."

"So did you inherit your talent?" Nora grinned and tilted her head.

Sophie motioned her to follow as she walked back toward her pew. "It's not important." She shrugged. "Let's just say practice makes perfect, and God gifted me with a love for music, which helped." Bittersweet memories of singing with her mother and brother, taking turns at accompanying on the piano, the smiles they shared and the joy, which had welled up in her at those times, warmed her. Even when she'd been tired and she asked her parents if they had to perform at a church, by the end of the service her heart had filled with happiness from the worship.

"There's something else I would like to talk to you about." Nora bit her bottom lip, glancing sideways at Sophie.

"Go on."

"Tell me something about James Cooper." Her pale face deepened to the sunset pink Sophie had observed a couple of weeks before in the boardinghouse kitchen.

"James?" The thought of someone being interested in James as more than a friend made her chuckle. "He does remind me of my brother."

"Surely there must be more to him than that," Nora commented as they walked together and she drew closer. "He seems like such a gentleman. His mustache is adorable."

Sophie resisted the temptation to roll her eyes. "He's a copywriter and part-time reporter at the local paper, with aspirations to become a full-fledged journalist."

"How exciting! Is he here today? I haven't seen him."

"If he's gotten wind of the Reverend's announcement, James will show up for it. He's always looking for a story to prove himself." Sophie paused. "He is a kind fellow." *Though a bit immature.* However, there was no reason to portray him as anything less than thoughtful, so she kept the extra thought to herself.

"I hope I see him." Nora patted her blonde hair as though she were trying to make sure every strand was in place.

"Either way, I'll tell him Miss Armstrong sends her regards when I see him at the house." Sophie grinned at her friend.

Nora's eyebrows went up as she stepped back. "You're positively scandalous."

Elder Whitworth's voice boomed over the hum of conversation in the sanctuary. "Those of you who are staying for the congregational meeting, please be seated now." He took his place on the platform, a few paces to the side of the pulpit.

"I suppose I should return to my seat next to Aunt Gert." Nora patted Sophie's arm. "Thank you for the information about you-know-who. Maybe I'll see you later this week." She gave Sophie a hopeful smile before going to seek out her aunt and uncle.

Sophie scooted into the pew, sitting next to Maggie, who held Caira on her lap. The toddler rubbed her eyes and yawned, reaching out to her mother. "Soffie."

"Sh." Sophie took Caira into her arms, holding her close so that she rested her head on Sophie's shoulder. She stroked Caira's baby-soft hair and rocked her a bit.

James Cooper slid into the seat beside her. He took his hat off, fussing with its brim. "Did I miss anything important?"

"Only the entire church service." Maggie peeked around Sophie to give James an accusatory look.

"I was in the back, Mrs. Galloway."

"And I assume quite late." Maggie's eyebrow went up.

"Ah, yes. I . . . I had some work to do this morning." James smoothed the pencil-thin line of facial hair he called a mustache. "What about the announcement Reverend McCormick said he was going to make?"

"You didn't miss that." Sophie rolled her eyes in disgust, but then she saw that Nora stole a glance at the young boarder. The sunset pink hadn't left her face.

Could Nora be truly smitten with the copywriter? Although she had thought Nora would have been a better choice for the minister to court, it comforted her that neither seemed too interested in the other. Yet she felt badly that the sweet young woman would be infatuated with such a silly, immature boy as James, especially with his lack of devotion to God. Nora deserved someone far superior in character.

Sophie wondered where she stood in the game of romance with Ian. Somehow, the impossible was beginning to seem possible. No. She shook her head. She must be stronger for all of their sakes. *God, I love Ian, but I know he deserves better. Please help me to think of him as a brother. Please bring him a truly good woman and help me to let go of any other thoughts of him.* The heaviness in her chest made her think that her prayer wasn't as sincere as it needed to be.

Ian took the pulpit once again and a hush fell over those in attendance. "I want to thank you for staying a bit longer this evening.

"Elder Whitworth and I have visited a . . . maternity home, the Florence Crittenton Mission in Detroit. We are impressed with their work and as such would like to propose something on a smaller scale in Stone Creek." As Ian continued, he quoted several scriptures, which described the need to care for those less fortunate, and particularly the command to care for widows and orphans in the book of James. "And so we are hoping to raise funds to start a ministry to house a few young fallen women who find themselves in a compromising situation." He paused. Was Ian averting his gaze from her? "We want to give them a chance to begin life anew, knowing that Jesus loves them and has died for them. Or perhaps some need to renew faith in their Savior. After all, He is the God of second chances." Ian mentioned the woman at the well and the lost sheep. "And for those who can't care for their babies for whatever reason, we would like to begin a home for foundlings, as well."

People whispered. Questions of "What?" "Where?" and "How?" echoed around the sanctuary.

"I'm asking you to please join me in prayer for the beginning of a new work . . . a work that will be committed to showing Christ's love to those who need it most." Their eyes met longer than necessary. She saw the question, the anxiety in Ian's eyes. Was he only seeking her support?

Sophie's shoulders slackened as she sat back in the pew. And so it began. Could he have realized the truth she hid and pitied her? He had seemed to understand the thoughts of her heart more than once before. How painful facing him again would be. The contents of her stomach swirled and her heart squeezed with grief and confusion.

Movement to the right caught her eye. Gertrude Wringer stood, pointing a finger at Ian. "How could you propose such a thing for this town? Am I the only one in this church who cares about Stone Creek? Why would we bring immoral ne'er-do-wells and their illegitimate children to sully the reputation of our blessed town? When my father, Hiram Armstrong, settled in this town a generation ago, he came for the fresh air and clean living away from the city! This would dishonor his vision!"

While Ian rubbed the back of his neck with one hand, pain was written across his face.

A vein stood out on Elder Whitworth's forehead. "I knew your father when I was a boy, Gertrude. When he started this church, he wanted to see the Body of Christ come together and love the unlovely—"

"I'm well aware of my father's philanthropy! And *whom* should be considered worthy to receive it," she hissed.

Elder Wringer stood next to his wife. "You shouldn't get yourself so worked up about this, dear." His voice sounded strained as he placed a hand in the crook of her elbow.

"Worked up? We already have one disreputable woman in this congregation influencing the pastor. Do we want more of them in this town, bent on showing our young men their evil ways?"

The congregation fell silent. Sophie wished she could dissolve into the puddle of tears that were forming in her eyes and slip underneath the pew. She grasped Caira close to her heart. What she'd feared all along was finally happening. Sophie felt frozen in time and stuck to her seat, reliving a scene played out in her life again and again—Caira and she were outcasts.

Gertrude's eyes trained on Sophie. "And furthermore, I'm sure we could find out the truth about Miss Biddle over there if we wanted to. Who really believes that child is her little sister anyway? And if that wicked girl is going to be at the Myleses' luncheon party, I don't care to darken their doorstep."

Gasps ascended from every corner.

"That's quite enough of your haranguing, Gertrude!" Elder Whitworth boomed.

Gertrude pulled away from her husband's grasp. "We're leaving now, Edmund. Nora, I simply will not allow you to associate with that deceitful girl any longer." Mrs. Wringer had Edmund and Nora well trained. Her niece stood, and they both followed her, bowing their heads. A chill draft followed behind the angry woman as she passed.

Gloria stepped into her path. "Sophie is our dear friend. She will be allowed to attend our party whether you like it or not."

The congregation broke into hushed conversation. Electricity charged the audience as murmurs broke into arguments.

"This will be quite the story," James mumbled.

"May I have your attention for another moment?" A bewildered Ian raised his voice. "It's God's desire for unity in our congregation. I had hoped we'd come together to build this ministry. Perhaps all of you need to pray about what God's will is in this and then we should continue this discussion at a better time. I believe we should adjourn now."

"I second that." Dr. Moore stood and waved his hand. "Of all things." He shook his head, looking disappointed as he frowned. The chaos in the congregation prevented a further vote.

Ian's eyes glazed. Were those unshed tears? Sophie had never seen him seem so dejected when he glanced at her as he walked toward the back of the church. "Maggie, please take Caira for me." While she should still feel rooted to her seat, something stronger than her will, a depth of compassion for the man she cared for above any other drew her out of herself.

"Certainly." Her dear friend took the sleeping child to her own lap.

As she made her way down the aisle, Cecelia, Helena, and their friends turned away, snickering and whispering to one another. Sophie's chin went up. This wasn't the first time she'd been shunned and hurt deeply, but she didn't have to let them know. "Excuse me, ladies." She sidled past them.

"Can you believe how brazen she is? Why, I heard she fell into the arms of the pastor on purpose when they were at the work bee at that awful boardinghouse." Helena's comment was spoken just loud enough for her to hear.

"You don't say?" One of the other girls dignified the gossip.

"And I heard she threw herself into his arms out on the street during the winter." Cecilia's stage whisper did nothing to hide her contempt.

Sophie followed Ian as he made his way through the crowd and out the door. His long strides took him outside the building and down the street much faster than she with her shorter legs. "Ian! Please wait." He kept walking.

She finally reached his side, a block away from the church. Feeling like a foolish child, she tugged at his sleeve. When Ian stopped and turned toward Sophie, her heart pounded.

"What is it?" Ian's lake-blue eyes had grown mercurial with emotion, perhaps sadness . . . and anger.

She'd grown to trust him, so the fear that crept in with his response surprised Sophie. "I . . . I wanted to make sure that you. . . are all right." Maybe she should tell him her whole story—that she understood he was trying to help people like herself, who had no place to go, but this didn't seem to be the time.

Ian raked a hand through his dark waves. "All is not right with me or the world. You of all people must understand. You've seen it for yourself. Look how they treated you. And I certainly never meant for you to take the brunt of it." He took her gloved hands into his. "I'm truly sorry for that. But as long as Gertrude Wringer has her way, the congregation will see me as no more than a boy manipulated by a board of cowering elders and unruly, spiteful women!"

"No. I wouldn't think that for a minute. You have Elder Whitworth, Dr. Moore, Asa and Gloria Myles who believe in you." *And me*, she lacked the courage to add. "You can't just give up." Sophie stared up at him, searching for his usual hope and cheerfulness.

"It's over." He shook his head. "If you'll excuse me, I have some thinking and praying to do. Alone." Ian pulled back and turned away.

Sophie wished she could tell him that she would pray for him with all her might, but she wasn't sure if God yet wanted to hear her prayers. She would try as she always did. *Please help Ian. He's a good man.* A slight breeze chilled the air as the sun ducked behind the clouds. Sophie hugged her arms to herself. She felt as empty as a teacup turned upside down on a drain board after being washed out.

CHAPTER 20

Ian handed over the reins and charge of his horse to the stable boy at Apple Blossom House after they alighted from his buggy.

"This way, sir, ma'am." Mr. Starks, the tall, straight-faced servant bowed.

"Thank you." Ian and Maggie followed him on the path around to the back of the house while Ian's nephew bounded ahead. "Philip! Don't run! You need to behave like a gentleman—the way your mother told you to."

The boy slowed to a jaunty walk. "Yes, Uncle Ian."

Maggie caught up and grabbed him by the collar. "I expect a much better demonstration of behavior in front of Elise and Caira." She straightened the collar beneath his red hair before he could barge ahead.

"Yes, Mother." His tone sounded deflated, if not disrespectful.

"There will be plenty of chances to run later. I'm sure the Myleses will have games for you to play." Ian patted the boy on the back. He felt sympathy for Philip. Ian's heart was alight with joy every time he pictured Sophie. How he would like to run ahead and embrace her as Philip wanted to embrace this beautiful Saturday in May with all of his youthful exuberance. Ian's conscience placed a heavy feeling on his heart, holding him back. He sometimes wanted to pull from its grasp and run ahead, but he knew what kind of risk the impetuousness might bring them ... both Sophie and himself.

They rounded the corner of the large Queen Anne style home, with its welcoming wraparound porch, scattered with arrangements of wicker furniture. Mr. Starks cleared his throat. "The Reverend Ian McCormick, Mrs. Margaret Galloway, and Master Philip, ma'am."

"Thank you, Starks." Gloria came toward them with arms outstretched. Her eyes shone with a brightness that Ian hadn't noticed since before the death of her daughter and son-in-law.

"I'm so happy you're all here. Philip, help yourself to some lemonade. Elise will be out to keep you company soon." The elegant woman was dressed in an outfit draped with a layer of silvery gray chiffon. She linked arms with Maggie and walked between her and Ian, guiding them toward the backyard. "I have a lovely surprise for all of you. I can't wait to share it after lunch." She chatted on about her English-style gardens before excusing herself to take care of some social detail.

Ian took in a sweeping view of the gardens and the fruit orchards beyond. Tulips had poked their head above the soil and stood in different stages of bloom while leaves unfurled in trees nearby. Harp music drifted across the lawn, soothing his anxious thoughts.

A young woman stood with curly chestnut hair flowing down the length of her back. She turned toward him. Sophie? He'd never seen all of her tresses cascading over her shoulders before. She wore a dark green gown with a sheen that contrasted with the spark in her amber eyes. A half smile dimpled her cheek. His heart quickened. Though no severe hairstyle or plain clothing could hide her beauty, this softer side of Sophie reflected the caring young mother he'd come to know.

He swallowed. Only a few weeks ago she had abided under his roof while he hid in the study. Yet he'd been able to converse with her every day. Why was it so difficult to think about greeting her now? Recalling his gruffness the last time they had spoken didn't help. He remembered the wounded look in her tawny eyes. Ian shoved his hands in his pockets, and like a schoolboy tried to find his voice.

She ambled toward him. Other people's voices faded into the background. "You're all here. I'm so glad." Sophie hugged his sister.

"We wouldn't miss the social event of the season, would we now, Ian?" Maggie poked an elbow into his ribs.

"Of course not." Now, what would he say next? Eloquent words escaped him. Somehow, not seeing Sophie every day caused him to observe her in a whole new light. Could she have grown more beautiful in just a couple of weeks? Or was it because he missed seeing her with a flour-splotched face, or patiently bent over Caira, teaching her some new skill?

The elbow dug into his side again. "We're equally pleased to see you, Sophie."

"Took you long enough," Maggie whispered.

A long table had been set with crisp white linens and gleaming china. Esther Fairgrave sat fanning herself while Mr. Graemer, seated next to her in a wicker chair, had a blanket wrapped around his shoulders. Ian smiled. You couldn't keep either of them comfortable with spring weather. A light breeze suffused the balmy air and the sun attempted to dodge the clouds.

"Looks like there will be quite a spread, doesn't it?" His stomach rumbled. Until then, he hadn't realized how hungry he was.

"If everyone would please be seated, I'll say the blessing." Asa Myles made his way to the head of the table and bowed his head. "For what we are about to receive, may we truly be thankful. And for the rich blessings of friends and family." His voice caught in his throat. "Amen."

Ian noticed the faithful group that Asa surveyed among quite a few chairs that sat empty. No doubt Gertrude's comments had influenced those who decided not to attend or associate with Sophie. When she had been concerned about being the cause of dissension, he was relieved Maggie and Gloria both insisted she attend.

<hr />

Sophie sat with Elise to her left and Caira to her right. Ian sat directly across, where she couldn't avoid meeting his stare. Name cards had been set by each place so there wasn't a convenient escape. Once Gloria began eating, Sophie picked up a polished silver fork and took a bite of savory chicken salad. The delicate ivory-hued china underneath sparkled in the spring sunshine. Delightful breads, biscuits, and cheeses graced the table, along with fruit compote.

A robin flew in on the light breeze and landed on a maple tree branch above. With the girls giggling on either side of her, the Myles family, Ian's family, the occupants of the boardinghouse seated around the table, and other kind townspeople, she felt safe for that moment. Sophie took a deep breath and thanked God for this substitute family surrounding her. No, it wasn't the ideal she would have imagined, but perhaps there was still a slight chance that Caira could grow up in Stone Creek being loved and accepted. For a change, some of the burden lifted from her heart.

The servants kept their crystal goblets filled with cold lemonade. When almost everyone had finished the last course before dessert, Gloria stood and tapped a spoon against her glass. "I'd like to make a toast to our dear friends who have helped us through our time of grief. To all who comforted and cared for us, may God bless you abundantly." She lifted a sparkling goblet, filled with the sweet and sour beverage, into the air. "Next, Asa and I have an announcement."

"Now, my dear, it's really more of an idea. But we hope all of you will approve." The quiet, unassuming Asa took his place by her side.

"Yes, my husband is right. As most of you know, since our daughter . . ." And here Gloria paused and lifted her chin as though trying to regain her composure. "Since our daughter and son-in-law passed away, our granddaughter has been much bereaved. Nothing seemed to bring her out of her shell. Then Sophie came along." Gloria reached out toward Sophie and smiled. "The time that Elise has spent with her at her piano lessons has been the most healing time of all."

Gloria leaned forward a little and gripped the edge of the table. "Asa and I believe that there is a wonderful healing of the soul in playing or listening to music. We want to spread that healing." Now her eyes brightened with promise, and she clasped her hands together. "We want to begin the Barrington Home for Orphans in memory of our daughter, Anna, and her husband, Jared. Of course, we would have a school attached."

Asa cleared his throat and piped up. "My wife is quite excited about what she has read about the work of George Mueller in England. Perhaps some of you have heard of it? He has made such a difference in the lives of orphans."

Some of the people nodded before Gloria continued. "And, of course, we want Sophie to teach the children music. The way you play the piano, dear, your credentials must be impeccable."

Expectant faces turned toward Sophie. "Well, I . . ." What would she say next? *By the way, I'm from the family of the famous Bidershems, manufacturer of fine pianos. And, of course, I was taught by the best teachers.* She was certainly well equipped for such a job, but what of the sewing business she sought to build?

"Don't worry, we'll discuss it all later, including your wages." Gloria's smile widened.

"Well, I wasn't expecting such an offer." A dizzy lightheadedness assailed Sophie.

Maggie stood. "Well, I for one think it's a marvelous idea." She raised her goblet to toast. "To the memory of Anna and Jared Barrington. May the home and the school be blessed with much joy and healing."

Mr. Graemer, though not likely to hear much of anything, raised his glass to clink it against his landlady's and piped in, "Huzzah!"

Ian remained speechless, but he grinned at her across the table as though pleased. Sophie looked down and smoothed her napkin, weaving the end of it through her fingers.

Then Gloria looked toward their minister. "Reverend McCormick, it's your heart for orphans that further inspired us."

"Yes." Asa nodded. "What Gloria and I would like to say is that we have plenty of property to donate and the funds to start building. But we'll need a director for our board. We couldn't do it without your vision and Elder Whitworth's support."

Ian folded his hands, bowing his head for a moment before he lifted his face toward them and began to speak. "I am truly humbled, and I would like to do anything I can to help."

"It's a start, Reverend," Gloria spoke with sincerity. "We haven't forgotten the rest of your vision."

Sophie swallowed. "What about Mrs. Wringer? Won't she try to thwart your plans?" She could feel her forehead involuntarily wrinkle with worry.

Ian's eyes met hers before she could avert her gaze. "Sophie has a point. Mrs. Wringer has almost as much influence over the town council as the church people."

"We'll deal with these things one at a time." Asa reached for Gloria's hand and held onto it. "Won't we, my dear? As George Mueller's orphanages began as a walk of faith, so will ours."

Gloria beamed at her husband. "Yes, with God's help we'll find a way around the obstacles. Surely, He's blessed us so that we can be a blessing to others. We've been cloistered in our mourning and ignoring the needs of others long enough."

Asa and Gloria's new lease on life touched Sophie. If they knew her secret, perhaps they wouldn't be so quick to include her in their plans. In fact, she was sure they would be deeply disappointed. Sophie could only see herself becoming the center of more controversy.

A server whisked away Sophie's entrée plate and soon placed trays of delicate petit fours and other desserts on the table. The pale pastel greens, pinks, yellows, and whites mimicked the flowers around them, but she possessed no appetite. Even the airy sponge cake with berries could not tempt her.

The sun hid behind a cloud, casting a silvery light. A breeze blew across the landscape. Sophie shivered in her sateen cotton dress.

Gloria hugged herself and rubbed her upper arms. "I do hope a storm isn't brewing." She furrowed her brow.

"If it does, we'll just take everything inside, my dear." Asa placed a shawl around his wife's shoulders.

How nice it would be to have someone care for you like that, whether you lived in a mansion or just a simple cottage. Sophie picked at a slice of sponge cake, hoping to appear polite. She still avoided eye contact with Ian.

Esther waddled over with labored breathing. "I'm so happy for you. Looks like I'll have to find new help. Perhaps you know of someone, Reverend."

"Well I don't think it will take me away full-time—"

"Isn't it wonderful, Reverend? Why, by giving Sophie the chance to play the piano, you've opened up a whole new opportunity for her." Esther swept her hand dramatically through the air, clutching a lace handkerchief.

"I'm glad you think so." Ian cleared his throat.

Sophie felt his gaze hard upon her. "It's still difficult to believe." She swallowed a crumb and took a sip of the sweetened lemonade. "I hope both of you will please excuse me. I think I need to take a little walk." She pushed her chair away from the table and stood, reaching for the shawl draped over the back.

The orchard, yes, she would head toward the orchard to think about her dilemma. She strolled first through the colorful garden and then walked more quickly to the shelter of row after row of budding fruit trees. Strains of harp music faded. The laughter of her friends grew more distant. Sophie stopped, looking around to the comforting green bushes and trees, the pastel shades of flowering plants. Birds chirped a melodious song in the branches above, seeming to beg her to gaze upward.

God, what do I do? They need me, but what if they find out my history? Perhaps I could teach the children, but I'm no Professor of Music. What if they find out I'm not who I say I am? And then the old guilt niggled at her. She was living a lie no matter how she rationalized, but she still couldn't see a way out.

Sophie pushed her hair away from her face and clutched the locks to her scalp. She took another step forward, but something tugged at her. What now?

"Sophie." Ian called out behind her. "Where are you going?"

"Not very far." She looked up from where her skirt had hooked itself on a fallen tree branch, and she fumbled to loosen it. Why had Ian followed her when she needed this time alone? Her thoughts swirled as he neared her, and she pulled harder at her hem.

Ian caught up, breathless. "Let me help you." His tone was tender, and she felt his presence more deeply than ever. A spark passed between them as their hands brushed.

"I hope it's not torn." Sophie worried over the fabric and did her best not to look at Ian. His being close, his scent, the dark hair that fell across his brow, and the muscles in the arm pressing against hers, made her senses reel. Again, she felt lightheaded.

"You look pale. Are you feeling quite all right?"

"Well enough." She changed the subject with a laugh. "It seems you are always coming to my rescue."

"It seems you are in much need of rescuing." Ian's smile reached his aqua eyes. "There. Good as new." He brushed off the hem of her dress. He held his arm out to her. "Please, let me walk with you. I would be a cad to leave a damsel in distress by herself."

"I guess you would." She smiled in spite of her reeling emotions, then wondered what excuse she could give him to leave her alone. Besides, didn't she truly want Ian by her side, if only as a friend to guide her?

An uncomfortable silence hung between them.

"Would you forgive me for how I spoke to you after the congregational meeting?"

"What's to forgive?" Yet, she had to admit his gruffness had hurt her, making her feel excluded from his world.

"I shouldn't have spoken to you the way I did. Or left your defense to Elisha. I was wrestling with my agenda versus the Lord's, but none of it was your fault." He paused. "And here He answered some of my prayers in a way I least expected."

"You don't seem too enthused about it." Sophie glanced sideways to see his reaction.

"Perhaps I don't." Ian's wry chuckle surprised her. "God has a way of humbling a man. I thought He wanted *me* to bring a foundlings' home about, but it seems that He had other plans."

"But the Myleses surely want your help. You're still part of it, and if it's God's will, He will make a way."

"We'll see about that. You seemed upset about Gloria's offer, though. Don't you like teaching? You're wonderful at it. Maggie would still like to have Philip take lessons if you could put up with a rambunctious boy."

Sophie smiled. If only Ian knew about how at one time she had to put up with an older and for a time, a younger brother. "I don't think that would be a problem."

Her gloved hand in the crook of his arm felt right. She looked up at Ian's handsome profile and a shiver went down her spine.

"Are you cold?" Ian took the shawl that had partially slid from her shoulders and pulled it up around them.

"Not really." But Sophie had felt a delectable chill of pleasure course through her because of his closeness. It seemed a hummingbird took flight in her chest. A sense of shame and guilt snuffed it out. Between that and Gloria's news, she felt positively faint.

"Maybe I'm not feeling so well after all."

"Why don't we sit down over here?" Ian's gentle hands guided her toward a bench under a cherry tree. "Please, rest against me." He supported her back with his arm in an almost brotherly way. She didn't have the strength to pull away.

What was it about him that brought her near fainting so easily? Sophie didn't consider herself a weakling. How frustrating!

Starry shapes filled her line of vision and she rested gently against his shoulder until they cleared away. His heart beat in accord with hers. Oh, this wasn't helping, but it felt so right to be held by Ian, to lean on him like she had leaned on no other. As they sat together, the calm growing within surprised her. After all, she was alone. With Ian.

The only other noises were various birds calling to their mates and a gentle breeze rustling the branches. Light clouds had skidded away across the sky, freeing warm beams of sunlight.

Sophie closed her eyes, pretending the moment would last forever. If only this were another time and place, where she had met Ian before she'd been expecting Caira. If only her family could have gone to his church to sing and perform. Their gazes would have caught one another's and fate would have taken over.

He would have sought her out, yes, surely. The situation would have been much better if she were still the well thought of Sophia Bidershem. Then she would have been an asset to his ministry and his church.

Caira's distant chattering broke Sophie's reverie. She opened her eyes and sighed. It was too late for her, but not for Caira to have a protected life. But where could she go? She was tired of running. If she could play a behind the scenes role at the school, perhaps they would be safe enough.

"What is it, dear Sophie?" Ian placed his fingers under her chin and lifted her face toward his. "Your heart seems so heavy. I wish you would allow me to share your burden . . . all of your burdens, truly."

Sophie felt the warmth of his breath brush her cheek. His quiet tone soothed her restless soul. The masculine scent of him filled her senses. Part of her knew that she should pull away, but she felt drawn to Ian. A peace overcame any fears she had formerly experienced, and she relaxed in his embrace.

She swallowed hard, forming a reply. "B-but some burdens cannot be shared."

"Then let me lighten them for you a bit." The intensity of his gaze drew Sophie closer. Their lips were only inches apart.

CHAPTER 21

"**T**here you are!"

Sophie and Ian simultaneously pulled apart and sat up straight, almost tumbling from the bench.

Maggie stood with one hand on her hip and the other holding one of Caira's. Her brows knit together with concern. "Caira was looking for you, Sophie."

"I'm sorry. I felt like I needed a walk and to think about things by myself. I-I shouldn't have run off like that."

Ian jumped to his feet, cheeks flaming with guilt. He cleared his throat. "Yes, and she wasn't feeling well. I thought she would quite faint. That's why we were sitting here together. I wanted to make sure—"

"I see. Why don't you get Sophie something cold to drink." Maggie stood with crossed arms. A smug smile replaced her look of worry. Caira scurried toward Sophie and climbed on her lap.

"An excellent idea." Ian strode away, head down, with his hands in his pockets like a child caught with his hand in the cookie jar.

"'Cowmick?" Caira whined.

If Sophie didn't know better, she would have thought Ian was avoiding her gaze. How could he leave her alone to face his sister?

Sophie smoothed Caira's hair and held her close. "I think I'll be fine now. Thank you for your concern, Maggie." She nodded toward Maggie without looking directly into her friend's eyes, then stood and took her daughter by the hand to return to the luncheon party.

She may have to be separated from Ian for the moment, but she didn't want to leave the people of Stone Creek. If people like Gloria and Maggie continued to believe in her, if Gertrude Wringer didn't find out the truth, Sophie could stay here for a time. This meant she would have a chance to see Ian. She cared for him though it would have to be from a distance. How foolish of her to allow their closeness in the orchard. She must be much more careful.

She marched with assurance toward Gloria and Asa. When Sophie reached the table again, she spoke, hoping that she wasn't making a mistake. "I accept your offer. I'm ready to help you in any way I can—as long as I can maintain my sewing business."

Gloria clasped her hands together like an excited child. "Oh, good. You disappeared, and I was afraid that somehow my offer had upset you." She hugged Sophie. "We'll begin as soon as possible and work out something that will suit us both. The girls will need to learn sewing, as well."

Sophie smiled and returned the embrace.

Mr. Graemer gasped, and Sophie turned in time to see him grab his chest. "Help." He choked out a strangled cry. He labored for each breath taken.

"Mr. Graemer! Oh dear!" Esther Fairgrave jumped from her chair and let her white linen napkin drift to the ground.

Sophie thought she'd heard the pattering of Caira's little feet as she mounted the stairs with a tray of tea for Mr. Graemer. The little one was up from her nap early and the door to their room was ajar. "Caira?" Sophie poked her head into the doorway, but she only saw the rumpled blanket left behind. "Where are you?"

A giggle traveled down the hallway along with an elderly man's gravelly chuckle. She quickened her step to Mr. Graemer's room. While her patient sat propped up with pillows, Caira curled up next to him, and she covered her eyes, then peeked out.

"Peek-a-boo, I see you." The old man smiled. "I got you again."

"Caira, I've told you. Leave Mr. Graemer alone, he's very ill." Sophie shook her head and marched over to the nightstand where she placed the small tray.

"My dear, she's no bother at all." He patted Caira on the back. "She brightens my day, as do you." He stared out the window for a moment. "How I miss my family." Light drops of rain gathered on the pane, even as clouds converged above.

Sophie puffed the pillows and poured tea from a petite green ceramic pot. "Caira, go get your picture books. Then you may look at them quietly and keep Mr. Graemer company."

"Wan' stay wif Gwaemer." Caira's bottom lip curled out.

"I mean business." Sophie tilted her head. Her daughter slid off the bed and padded out of the room and down the stairs.

Sophie straightened Mr. Graemer's bed coverings and handed the cup into his trembling hands. When she tried to help him, he insisted on sipping on his own. Once she took the cup and placed it back on its saucer, Sophie sat in Mr. Graemer's squeaky rocking chair and took up her knitting. She could hear Caira below asking Esther for help taking the books down from a shelf.

Did Mr. Graemer want to talk? She didn't want to pry, so she waited.

"Sometimes you don't realize when you're in the best part of life. Hm." He coughed.

"Another sip of tea?" Sophie sprang from the chair.

He lifted his hand. "Not right now, my dear." Mr. Graemer took as deep a breath as he could manage.

She settled back into the rocking chair, worrying her lip. He couldn't get worse on her watch.

"My sons, Lawrence and Peter, why, they were good boys, but I fretted when they fought or got in trouble at school. Worried about them getting their educations. Lily fussed over them when they had the quinsy or the grippe. I thought I should be making more money, so we were vexed about all those little things . . . that didn't seem so little at the time."

He turned to stare out the window again. "But those were the times when we laughed the most. At Christmas, our sons would help Lily string cranberries and popcorn for the tree. We lit the candles one Christmas Eve, for a few minutes, so we could sing a hymn together. A breeze blew in when one of the boys came back through the door and a curtain caught on fire. I never saw Lily move so fast with the water from the pitcher in the hall. But Peter, why he just tossed a bowl of eggnog at the tree and caught the flame just in time. She scolded him for ruining the curtains, but Lawrence, ever the peacemaker, piped up and said, 'Mother, I think the fire ruined them.' And he just took a towel and started cleaning up the mess around the tree."

Mr. Graemer swallowed and looked back at her. "I said, 'That's true, little mother.' And do you know what she did?"

Sophie shook her head. "I can only imagine."

"Lily started laughing. 'Well then, thank the Lord we didn't burn the house down,' she said. Then she laughed so hard, we all joined in and could barely stop before we thanked the Lord in prayer together. We knew we were close to being homeless on Christmas Eve. It could have been a lot worse.

"But you never think those times will someday disappear. You expect your children will grow up and marry, you'll have grandchildren, taking it all for granted. Both the boys were courting lovely girls when they went off to war. That one Christmas we didn't know we were just a few years away from things changing altogether. Don't forget to cherish the moments you have with the little one." He nodded, giving her a knowing look.

"Certainly, Mr. Graemer." She averted her gaze. What should she fear? The old man knew nothing of her history.

Caira stumbled through the door, arms full of books that once belonged to Esther's daughter. She plopped them on the end of the bed.

Sophie leaned forward. "Be careful now not to hurt Mr. Graemer." She arose and found a small chair in the hallway to place next to the bed. "You can sit or kneel on this, but don't stand on it."

"Let's see your favorite book." He gave Caira a kind but weary smile.

"Kitten." Caira picked one out of the pile.

The two looked through the pictures, Caira mimicking Sophie's reading and telling the story as though she recognized each word. Finally, Mr. Graemer nodded off.

"Come on, now, sweetie, Mr. Graemer needs to rest. You sit quiet and read your books." Sophie smiled at her daughter.

"Remember what I said, Miss Biddle. Cherish the time with your family." She jumped, not having expected Mr. Graemer to say anything more.

Caira whispered, telling herself each story she looked over. Sophie glanced toward the ill man, then out the window before returning to her knitting. Drops pelted the divided panes, making the world outside blurry. Or was it the wetness clouding her eyes? When she'd left home a couple of years before, Grandpa Morton still lived, but did he now? Or had she missed going through this dark time and saying "good-bye" with her family? And what of her mother, father, and Paul? Had Paul stepped up in responsibility in the family business? Had he found a lovely girl to court?

She and Caira had to start afresh and cherish their own family moments, make their own memories. There was no turning back if it meant facing marriage to a cruel man. She thanked God Charles hadn't found them in quiet little Stone Creek. Still, she missed her family.

Mr. Graemer had often seemed grumpy or distant, perhaps because he couldn't hear people, he didn't try hard to converse with them. Or maybe he'd been wrapped up in a world from nearly half a century before when he had his own home and family.

Caira leaned against her. "Soffie, will you read to me?" She held up her book about cats.

Sophie blinked and swiped at her eyes. She set her knitting aside. "Of course." She pulled Caira onto her lap and read not much above a whisper while Mr. Graemer snored softly.

———————•———————

Ian looked up. Gray clouds glided across the blue sky, intermittently blocking the May sunshine. The haunting coo of a mourning dove caused the chattering of robins and vesper sparrows to fall into the background. Ian took long, even strides toward Fairgrave's Boardinghouse.

He clasped his hands behind his back and shook his head, deep in meditation. No matter how long he tended this flock, it never got easier to call on the sick or the family of one who had passed on. If anything, it had become more difficult as his love for the people of Stone Creek had grown deeper.

Had a week and two days already passed since Mr. Graemer's attack? Ian sighed. Almost every day, he had gone to visit the elderly parishioner. For two Sundays now, Ian missed seeing the old man, his eyes heavy; how he'd suddenly shout out a battle cry and then calm back into a sound, snoring sleep. Afterwards, the rest of the congregation was wide-awake and listening. Ian chuckled at the recollection. When he arrived at the boardinghouse, Ian removed his hat and knocked quietly.

Esther opened the door a crack. "Oh, I'm glad it's you." She pulled the door farther open to let him in. Her face was flushed, and she mopped beads of perspiration from her face. "Such a trying day this has been. Please sit down." She motioned Ian into the parlor. "In addition to his weakened heart, Doctor Moore says it's likely pneumonia has begun to set in."

"I'd like to help in any way I can."

Esther paced and fanned herself with a handkerchief. "No one has died here since my beloved husband. So many painful memories! I hate to see the dear old man leave this earth."

Ian leaned forward, one of his elbows on his knee and his chin in his hand. He couldn't bear the thought of uttering one of those pious, expected sayings, like, *But you know he'll be better off.*" So he just listened.

Esther sniffed and blew her nose. "I don't know what I would do without our dear Sophie. Someday a man will want to marry her and take her and Caira away. What shall I do when it is as quiet as the grave around here?" She blew her nose again. "Oh dear, I didn't mean to say that." She mopped a fresh crop of tears.

He reached across to where she sat in a chair perpendicular to the settee. "This is a trying time for all of us who love Mr. Graemer. Let me pray with you." He prayed for healing and comfort and for God's will to be done. It wasn't the most eloquent prayer, but heartfelt, and there was a lump in his own throat when he finished. But the prayer for God's will had fresh meaning. Was it God's will for Sophie to marry another? His heart ached at the thought of losing dear old Mr. Graemer from his congregation, but the thought of losing Sophie, and even Caira, to another man, pained him beyond belief.

"Thank you for praying."

He looked up to see the dear widow smiling. "You're welcome. Now, I suppose I should go visit the invalid." Ian patted her hand before he let it go.

He climbed the stairs to the old gentleman's room. A strong smell, like eucalyptus or camphor, permeated the area. His footfalls echoed on the wooden steps. Ian rounded the corner of the hallway and stood just outside the bedroom door.

"Please take another bite, Mr. Graemer, just a small one." Sophie perched on the edge of the bed. She leaned toward the ill man and attempted to spoon broth into his mouth. "You must try harder."

She furrowed her brows. The delicate way in which she wiped his mouth with a napkin revealed the kind and gentle side of her spirit. Sophie pushed a strand of hair away from her face. "If you don't eat you won't get your strength back," she pleaded.

Desire to take the beautiful young woman into his arms surged through Ian, to tell her how he really felt.

"My dear, I am not long for this world," Mr. Graemer spoke in a gravelly voice.

Ian willed his hands into clasping behind his back, and he cleared his throat, hoping not to startle them when he walked into the room.

"I'm glad to see you." Mr. Graemer raised his hand with a weak wave.

Sophie turned toward him. Her eyes brightened, but she pressed her lips together, as though suppressing a smile. "Good afternoon, Reverend."

"How's our patient?"

"Difficult as ever." She shook her head.

"I just have my mind on other things besides this world." Mr. Graemer's eyes were shut and his speech somewhat labored, but he wore a grin.

Ian pulled a chair closer. "Feeling any better today?" He leaned forward, hopefully, close enough for Mr. Graemer to hear. He wasn't sure why he felt compelled to ask when the answer was obvious. He observed the older man's graying complexion.

"Much better. I'm closer to heaven. The battle's practically won."

Ian caught Sophie's worried glance. Her eyes were dewy with tears.

"He's been talking of such things all day." She swallowed.

"Ah, no wonder Esther is so fretful."

Sophie nodded.

"It makes me think of Gettysburg. Have I ever told you about that battle? I was in a Cavalry unit under Colonel Alger. General Custer was there, too. Custer kept shouting, 'Come on, you Wolverines!' Wouldn't you know that we thwarted the Rebels' surprise attack?" He paused and drew in a labored breath. "For a while there, we thought the enemy was going to win, but it was the turning point for us Yankees." Mr. Graemer swallowed and labored again to breathe.

He patted Sophie's hand. "Don't worry about me. Jesus won the battle a long time ago, and I'm about to claim victory when I get to the other side." He lifted a finger in a scolding way. "It might look like the enemy has his way now, but it's only temporary, my friends."

Ian wished all of his congregation could face death in such an admirable way. Even in his short career, he'd seen people clinging to life. They'd peer at him from the bed, looking ghostly with dark circles and pale skin. They'd grasp the edge of their sheet and the hands of a loved one, who sat through the deathwatch with them, as though they could hold fast to this world. The startling reality was that they would leave it with nothing.

Yet Ian could understand that people were scared to leave the known for the unknown. It was human nature. Mr. Graemer's faith encouraged him.

Tears streaked Sophie's face. She didn't look fearful, but sad at the passing of this dear old saint. More than ever, Ian instinctively felt a need to comfort and protect her, like that day at the Myleses' estate where they had almost kissed.

Mr. Graemer's voice interrupted his reverie. "Lily and I lost our two boys in the War Between the States. My darling wife was never the same after that. Often, she'd say, 'Ezekiel, heaven is looking brighter and brighter with the boys there.'" He swallowed hard. "I didn't really understand because she was everything on this earth to me." Mr. Graemer looked off into the distance, his eyes glassy with fever, or were they tears?

"I suppose you've wondered why I'm all alone. Well, now you know why I have no children or grandchildren to visit me. My family is waiting for me on the other side."

"I'm so sorry, Mr. Graemer, but you have us." Sophie's raised voice broke with a sob.

"That's one of the few reasons that I am sad to go. But there's more . . . I must tell you."

Ian sat, wondering at what else the old man had to reveal. Deathbed confessions were often painful. How odd. The old man smiled like he had a delightful secret he was waiting to share.

"Don't wear yourself out talking to us," Ian chided loudly while Sophie wiped her tears.

"I-I must tell you." Mr. Graemer knit his brows together. He seemed to rally for a moment and attempted to pull himself up.

"Let us help you." Ian lifted him to a sitting position, and Sophie plumped two pillows behind the old gentleman.

"I'm sorry I won't be here . . . to see your children." He grinned, looking very pleased with himself.

"What?" Ian and Sophie questioned in unison.

Mr. Graemer took a deep breath. "I-isn't what's obvious to the rest of us . . ." He paused for a moment. "Why, it should be plain to the two of you. You belong together. As much as my Lily belonged with me." He gazed out the window, looking wistful. He sighed and then wheezed.

Sophie blushed when Ian's gaze met hers. She stood. "Perhaps I should look in on Caira. She's been napping for quite a while." She paused. "Excuse me, Mr. Graemer." She spoke close to his ear.

"Yes, I can stay with the patient for a bit. Take as long as you need."

"Thank you." Her skirts swished softly as she hurried through the doorway.

Mr. Graemer's gaze locked with Ian's. "You'll have your hands full with her, I'll wager. She's a headstrong one, she is. And the little one, too." His chuckle turned into a cough.

"I'm not sure what you mean, sir." Ian felt a twinge of guilt at such evasion. If he caught Philip doing such a thing, he would have given his nephew a lecture on deception.

"What?"

Ian raised his voice to repeat his statement.

"Come, come, Reverend, we are both men. I think I can speak to you as such. That young lady is as smitten with you as you are with her." The raspy whisper left the dying man almost spent.

Ian felt the heat moving over his face. Was what he had been trying to hide so evident to everyone else?

"You'd be a fool to let her go." Mr. Graemer laid a gnarly hand on his arm. "She's fond of you, boy. And she's a hard worker. A better girl you couldn't find. She'd make a fine addition in your line of work." He looked out the window, toward the sky. "Every bit as much a good woman as my Lily."

Ian heard Esther's huffing and puffing in the doorway. "Sophie seemed a bit flustered, and I'm sure you have other work to do, Reverend. I'd be happy to take over."

Ian rubbed the back of his neck. He could feel it knotting up. "Perhaps that would be best for now."

"Think about what I said, young man." The elderly man used a scolding tone of voice. Then he looked out the window again, expectantly.

"Yes, sir." Ian felt like a foolish child who was running from what he knew in his heart was the truth.

•••)———————•——————(•••

Sophie checked on Caira, whose even breathing showed that she still slept soundly. Fleeing down the steps and out the door to the front porch, her heart pounded like a drum in a marching band. She plopped onto the seat of the porch swing, despairing of what to do. Her heart betrayed her. She had tried to hold in the affection filling her, but like a river swelling its banks, the dam could not keep it back much longer.

She hid her face with her hands, biting her bottom lip. *"You belong together . . ."* Mr. Graemer's gravelly voice echoed in her head. She had promised Gloria that she would be there to help get the orphanage and the school up and running. She couldn't just run away. And she had tried to convince herself that being close to Ian, listening to his sermons, talking with him occasionally would be enough—just to be in his presence.

But to hear Mr. Graemer's words while they sat in the same room, made her face a truth she had been running from—she loved Ian. Now, what would she do about her realization? Should she tell Ian how she felt? While Mr. Graemer had seen clear through her, surely he imagined anything he observed on Ian's side of things. If Sophie honestly faced up to her feelings, they could have a good laugh about the whole thing, shake hands, and go back to being like brother and sister. But was that realistic?

The front door hinges creaked, and she turned away, sensing that Ian had come out.

"Sophie." His voice was gentle, coaxing.

"Yes?" She could barely speak.

"I think—I believe we need to talk."

Sophie froze in her seat. Though she loved him, she didn't suppose that he would feel the same way. She was no longer pure. Surely, as a minister of the Lord, he must sense that she was the wrong kind of woman for him. He only wanted to reveal those very facts. That was what Ian wanted to talk to her about.

"Sophie, would you mind if I sit down?"

"Go ahead." She still did not turn to look at him and hoped she sounded nonchalant enough. Then the swing moved under both of their weights, and it seemed the whole porch trembled.

"I wanted to talk to you about what Mr. Graemer said."

Here it came—how nice a girl he thought she was, but how he needed a different kind of woman for a wife. She would always be like a sister to him, that the moment of closeness in the orchard had been a mistake.

"I suppose we would be foolish to think that nobody noticed that I care for you."

Sophie swung around, grasping the arm of the porch swing. "What?" She blinked. Had she heard him right? She must have, for the intensity in his lake-blue eyes must be revealing the truth.

"It wouldn't be proper for clergy to be dishonest, now, would it?" His mouth curled into a slight grin. "What I'm trying to say is that I do care for you very deeply."

Sophie's mouth fell open, still struggling to grasp what he said was real and not a pleasant figment of her imagination.

Ian took her hand and placed a light kiss on the back, which felt real enough. "Are you inclined toward me at all?"

Instead of responding, Sophie pulled her hand away again, covering her face.

"What, dearest?" He touched her shoulder.

She moaned. What could she tell him? That she loved him, but she must leave because she had some terrible secret, like leprosy? Oh, sure, she could tell him she was fleeing to a leper colony. That might work better than revealing her ruse. "There's something that's going to change how you feel about me."

His arm went around her shoulders gently. Ian leaned toward her and laid the side of his face on the top of her head. She could feel the warmth of his breath.

"Sophie, there's nothing that I could learn about you that would change how I feel. I wish you would trust me . . . completely."

•••❯————— ● —————❮•••

At least a minute passed during the silence between them. Ian waited. Surely now she would feel she could confide in him.

"Are you sure about that, Ian?"

"Yes. Do you think so little of me?"

"Never." She shook her head. "It's myself I think so little of."

"You shouldn't feel that way, no matter what has happened in your life." Ian took her hand back into his. "You still haven't answered my original question."

"Yes, I do care for you." Her gaze met his with a questioning look.

"Sophie, I didn't want to press you, but Mr. Graemer is right. I can't let you get away."

"Get away? What do you mean?"

"Perhaps this is the time for me to ask you . . ." Ian felt like a shy schoolboy. There was nothing he wanted more than to ask for Sophie's hand in marriage, but until she confided in him, he wasn't comfortable taking that step. He cleared his throat. "May I call on you?"

Sophie let out a breathy laugh.

"Well, what I mean is that if our feelings for one another are so noticeable to others, then perhaps it's time that I court you properly before someone else can." *And coax you to trust me completely.* But he couldn't form those words aloud.

"Court me? Who else would be interested when Gertrude Wringer has accused me of being disreputable? Besides, such a relationship with me would cause more rumors. And that couldn't be good for you."

Ian loved her but was it enough when secrets hung between them? Yet, other than the fact that Sophie hid that Caira was her daughter, he'd not seen any of the ill behavior Gertrude accused her of. Being worried about a perfect reputation before had only caused him regret in his life. "Sophie, I care for you very deeply. Would I declare my intentions toward you on Esther's front porch if I didn't?" The world faded around them.

"I suppose that's true. Perhaps I'm being foolish."

"Then may I pay you court, my dearest?"

"Yes," she croaked out. "I only hope that you won't be disappointed."

Now it was Ian's turn to laugh. "Never." He sat next to her, and she allowed herself to be drawn into his arms.

Sophie relaxed into his embrace. Perhaps she would tell him soon; then they could contact her parents. He'd ask her father properly for her hand in marriage.

Desire to kiss her pink lips, bowed into a smile, overcame him. "Now where were we when Maggie interrupted us at the picnic?"

Sophie smiled. "I believe—"

Gently, he touched his mouth to hers. He never wanted to frighten her after what she'd been through at the hands of an evil man. Her willingness, as her soft lips met his, surprised him.

The door flew open. "Reverend! Sophie! Mr. Graemer's taken a turn for the worse."

Ian pulled away from her. Esther blinked, looking stunned for a moment. "Well, it's about time you two figured things out." Her hands went up into the air. "But right now, I need your help."

Sophie's secrets would have to wait.

CHAPTER 22

Ezekiel Graemer died a day later. Two days after the funeral, Esther sighed and shook her head. "Sophie, that dear old man was like family." She drew in a deep breath and let it out as she darned the worn toe of a sock and sniffled. "We didn't know much about him, except that he fought for the Grand Army of the Republic, until we looked through his personal papers."

Sophie stopped stitching the back of an old skirt, where she had leaned too close to the coal stove and scorched a small hole in the fabric. She stared at an old daguerreotype of a handsome young couple and two tintypes of young men in Union Army uniforms, which lay on the parlor table. Then Sophie returned to her sewing.

She smiled as she thought of the couple. Yes, it was a younger version of Mr. Graemer, for sure, with his strong chin and aquiline nose. The young lady had dark hair swept back and covering her ears, where delicate earrings hung from the lobes. Though they had remained serious for the picture taking, their eyes sparkled. It seemed they could barely hold back their grins, so filled with love and life they must have felt—Lily and Ezekiel.

How proud they both must have been to receive pictures of their handsome sons in uniform. How many times Lily must have looked into those faces just pondering memories of her boys.

"You're awfully quiet."

"I was just thinking," Sophie said, with her head bent over her mending, "life doesn't always turn out the way you expect."

"It can be for the better or the worse. Speaking of the better, has Reverend McCormick planned on calling on you soon?"

"With the funeral hanging over him there hasn't been much time, but would you mind if I went on a picnic with him tomorrow, later in the afternoon? Maggie offered to take Caira for us."

"If you could just help me get everything set out for supper first, that would be fine."

A leaden weight suppressed the flutter of butterflies in Sophie's chest. She had to tell Ian that Caira was her daughter, the illegitimate product of being forced. But every time she tried to think of how to say it, her mouth went dry. "Ow!" She poked her finger with a needle.

Esther looked at her over the top of glasses perched on the end of her nose. "You'd best concentrate on your sewing." The matronly widow grinned.

Sophie sucked the end of the injured finger.

"Oh, I was young once. It's hard to keep your mind on much else but your beloved, isn't it?"

If only it were that simple. She longed to be courted, allowing love to buoy her, with no worries on the horizon, no fears of being rejected.

"My Clarence was quite a young man, too. Oh, not as educated as the reverend, but every bit as charming."

"I'm sure he was." Sophie forced a bit of a smile.

Years seemed to melt from Esther's face with her wistful expression. The older woman had been like a mother to her during her time in Stone Creek, not treating her as a lowly servant. Yet Sophie could not confide even in her employer.

God, you're the only One who knows. How am I going to tell my beloved? Please give me the strength to do what I must do. Tears stung her eyes as Sophie focused back on the needle and thread.

She thought it best to change the subject. Swallowing hard, Sophie asked, "Where has James been? I haven't seen him for a couple of days."

"Visiting his aunt. And it's about time he did. James won't be gone long, though. He'll be back in a few days."

"Where does she live?"

"Detroit. It'll be sweltering in the city with this patch of humid weather, but if it gets too bad, they can camp out on Belle Isle."

Detroit . . . Belle Isle. A vision of family picnics at the island park pinched her heart with a grief she tried to forget. Sophie wished she hadn't asked.

•• •)——————— • ———————(•• ••

Sophie spread the slightly moth-eaten blanket that she had retrieved from the attic over a grassy spot in the cemetery. One summer day had melted into the next. She was thankful for the breeze rustling the poplar leaves overhead as they waved like elegant green fans.

She placed clean white stoneware dishes on the blanket and put out fruit and cheese, cold fried chicken and biscuits. The idyllic picture, along with Ian's smiling face and the glorious day around them, buoyed her spirits for a moment.

"We picked the perfect afternoon, didn't we?" Ian's grin gave her confidence for the moment.

"We surely did. How kind of Maggie to watch Caira for me."

"You mean for us. She didn't mind a bit."

She set a golden piece of chicken on her beau's plate, mulling over what she must soon reveal. She reached for a biscuit to add to his meal.

"It's all right, Sophie, I'll get the rest for myself."

"My mother always served my father first. She . . ." Sophie caught herself. "Never mind."

"I think that's the first time I've heard you mention your parents." Ian raised his eyebrows. "Don't worry about serving me everything. I'm an old bachelor. My sister doesn't mind if I take care of myself, though I must say that she doesn't think I do a very good job of it." He chuckled.

After Ian said a prayer of thanksgiving, they both took a bite of the main dish Esther had provided. Usually, Sophie savored the delicious chicken, but at that moment the meat seemed as unappealing as sawdust and went down with as much ease. She put her plate on the blanket and leaned her back against the tree while Ian, sitting across from her, seemed to enjoy each bite of the food on his plate.

Sophie surveyed the area. Trees of every height grew around them, in their green spring finery. One tree, not far to her right, caught her attention. Tall with years of growth, its branches spread wide, but for one section. The deep separation and bark stripped away, like an angry scar, showed the tree had most likely been broken during a storm.

The damaged one stood in the midst of the healthy. Perhaps the exposed area would heal by itself, but it would never be the same. It seemed a picture of her life, broken beyond the most basic repair. And now she was asking the man she loved to share in this brokenness. Was she being selfish?

"Sophie, are you all right? You're awfully quiet and have barely taken a bite."

"There's something I need to tell you before things go any farther between us." She pushed her plate away. The intensity of

Ian's gaze, with an expectancy she couldn't quite read, made her stomach knot and her palms grow sweaty. She swallowed over the enormous lump in her throat. "I-it's a-about Caira. And me." Sophie glanced downward.

Ian set down his plate and moved closer to her, engulfing her hands in his. He listened, patient and unflinching as she poured out her story. At some point, as she recounted Charles' deception and attack, Ian pushed the food aside and moved closer still.

"And then, there is the reason Caira's name is spelled the way it is." She looked up into his face.

"Oh?" The word hung between them like the unanswered question it was meant to be.

"Everyone thought it was pronounced 'Care-uh', but they were wrong. I was so weak after her birth. All I had written on a piece of paper was the word 'Cairo' and Mama had misunderstood." Sophie smoothed the blanket over the prickly grass. "I'd been reading in my Bible about the Israelite bondage in Egypt. I didn't want anyone to know how angry I was about feeling entrapped, so I wrote 'Cairo' because it's a city there today.

"My parents made me feel like keeping the baby without marrying Charles would ruin my life. In fact, they believed my life was already ruined." Sophie thought back to that day. Once she had rested and was able to hold the newborn Caira, her feelings had changed. The baby girl only had to yawn with her rosebud mouth, entrance her with the sparkle of gray eyes under lazy lids, and squeeze Sophie's finger with a delicate grasp. Sophie had become Caira's slave, with her heart in sweet lifetime bondage to the child. "But once I held her, I knew I could never let her go.

"My mother had found the slip of paper with 'Cairo' written on it while I was sleeping. She thought it said 'Caira' and thought the name was unusual but pretty. It was recorded that way, so the moniker stuck. Before the birth, because of how it had come about, I had not chosen a name. I'd been sure I would be forced to give her up. I was too tired to argue about what to call her, and Caira sounded pretty. Besides, she didn't ruin my life, only changed it."

When she finished her tale, Ian stood up and began to pace.

"Are you angry with me?" Sophie stood to follow him, wringing her hands.

"Not with you, but I am furious with the scoundrel who hurt you." Ian removed his straw boater and raked a hand through his hair, averting his gaze. "I've been waiting a long time for you to confide in me. I'm hurt that you didn't trust me sooner."

"What do you mean?" Sophie noticed the tic in his jaw muscles.

"You should know . . ." Ian's voice trailed off.

"Know what?" Sophie stood.

CHAPTER 23

"I've met your mother."

"How? Where?" The sickening knot returned to her stomach.

"She came to me for prayer . . . and advice at the Florence Crittenton Home when I visited. I had no idea until she introduced herself and . . . told me some of your story.

"When she showed me your picture in her locket, why, that confirmed things."

The cawing sound of a distant crow pierced Ian's thoughts. "She's devastated, Sophie. Your mother wants nothing more than to be reunited with you."

Sophie stood there, glaring, her mouth open. "But . . ."

They faced one another, and he reached for her elbow. "Let me help you sit down."

"I'm fine." She pulled her arm from his grasp. "You've known this for how long? And you haven't told me? And I should be happy you kept that from me?" A wounded doe replaced the frightened one he'd once known. She closed moist eyes.

"I assumed you had your reasons for not telling anyone, but I'd hoped I would be the one you would trust with your secret.

It doesn't change how I feel about you." The last piece had been placed into the puzzle. Ian felt he might be ready for the next step.

"How long would you have waited? Until Caira is grown? Until my mother is dead? You would test me rather than tell me the truth—I don't understand. It's so unlike you, Ian." Sophie turned away, her shoulders shaking as she lamented over his revelation.

"You have to remember that I'm a pastor and a shepherd. I'm not free to tell what I am told in confidence." Ian wanted to embrace her, but held back. "I had such great hope that perhaps when we were at this point, you'd be reunited with your parents, and I could ask your father for your hand in marriage. Properly."

She swung around. "How dare you presume what is best for me and my family."

"Haven't your parents been deprived of their granddaughter long enough?"

"How can you say that, Ian? It's my father's fault I left."

"And what about your mother? She truly misses you."

"You're not being fair." Sophie crossed her arms.

"Sophie, I know it's a little soon, but if you are inclined toward marrying me, I want to start out right. It's time to forgive them. I think they will just be happy to know you are safe and healthy. Besides, you know we can't hide your secret forever."

"You can't possibly understand what it's like for me." Sophie picked up her straw hat in a hurry, stomping off. "My father and mother deserted me. I had nowhere to go with Caira!" Scrunching the brim of her hat, she knew she was overreacting, but even Ian had betrayed her in a sense. The aloneness swallowed her with its cave-like emptiness.

"Sophie!" The dry grass crunched under Ian's shoes. "Listen to me for a moment."

She stubbed her toe on a rock. "Ow." Sophie stood on one foot to rub the injured one. She turned away from him.

Ian stood beside her. "You and Caira are definitely cut from the same cloth."

"Are you saying that I am behaving like a two-year-old?"

Ian stifled a laugh. She peered at him from the corner of her eye. He needed to tread carefully. He cleared his throat. "I realize I'm asking a lot of you. I'm sorry." Wasn't a man of God supposed to preach forgiveness?

Still balancing on one foot, Sophie lost her balance, falling into Ian's embrace. He drew her closer. Their lips pressed together, merging in soft warmth. Her deep emotions poured into the sweetness of their kiss, blurring the reason for her anger for a moment. Then she remembered her mother's face, peering at her with sad eyes. Sophie pulled away.

"So what did you tell my mother?" Sophie fought more tears, but they spilled over, making trails down both cheeks. Anger and sadness fought to control her. Sometimes she longed to see her mother again. If only the circumstances were different. How could she make Ian understand?

"Nothing. I didn't feel it was my place." Ian held her face between his hands. He rubbed the wetness off her cheeks with his thumbs.

"So all this time you've known I'm just used goods. What do you see in me, anyway?"

"You are not used goods. *Never.* You are God's precious gift to me. And so is Caira." He sighed. "Dearest, did you realize that if Caira's name were spelled just a bit differently, it would mean 'the beloved one' in Italian? I've heard it spoken to mean that. She has been God's beloved gift to you, and to us, all along. She was not meant to be a bondage to you, *ever.*"

Sophie nodded. "I know." Though mesmerized by his aqua blue eyes, she saw the melancholy in them. "Then what's wrong?"

Ian took a deep breath. "We're at an impasse."

"You didn't feel that you could confide in me, and now you don't want to forgive your parents. I'm a minister of God. I should live an open, honest life." Even as he said it, Ian could see that she'd been wounded by his words. And conviction niggled at his conscience as he remembered his own secrets. But did she really need to know them? He averted his gaze.

Sophie recoiled, stepping backwards. "Do you think I have done this for myself? That I don't hate myself every day for living a lie? I knew that someday I would have to tell you, but it was for Caira's sake. I want her to have a chance. Do you know what people will call her if they find out the truth?" Sophie marched back toward the blanket and bent to pack the leftovers into the hamper.

"I understand your need to protect both yourself and Caira, but I thought we were close, like family. I only wish that when you were staying under my roof you'd taken me into your confidence, so I could help you." He knelt and picked up a plate to hand to her.

Sophie shot him a glance as she reached for it. "Most of which time you spent in your study."

She might as well have cut into his heart with a shard of glass. The truth hurt him, too. They'd done an odd dance, careful not to get too close so as not to bruise, but still they managed to injure one another. "Very well." Droplets of rain began to sprinkle. Ian studied the swiftly overcast sky. "Come along, now, I need to take you home." He helped her finish picking up and carried the hamper to his buggy. On the ride back to the boardinghouse, conversation eluded him.

"You're right. We are at an impasse. I don't know how I'll ever trust you again, Ian." Sophie sat next to him with arms crossed, staring ahead at the road. "How you could talk to my mother and side with her while seeing what I go through every day is unfathomable."

This was the time for a visit with Elisha. "If you don't mind, I'm going to discuss some of our situation with someone older and wiser." *Perhaps Elder Whitworth can help me find my way.*

"It will no doubt take the wisdom of Solomon, Reverend." Sophie stiffened. "You act as though you care about my daughter, but what will become of her if I go home?"

Ian heard the fear in her shaky voice. "I don't know, but I saw a grandmother who wanted to see her granddaughter, someone knitting little garments for the babies born in a home for unwed mothers. Perhaps your mother has changed."

"She will do whatever Father wants." Shaking her head, Sophie scooted farther away from Ian.

"You've let the root of bitterness take hold. I'm here to help and protect you now. And the Lord is with us." Ian waited.

Silence met his plea. *Indeed, I hope Elisha can impart wisdom such as Solomon's.*

* * *

"She's an heiress on the run from her parents? Hmm." Elisha shook his head.

"Not only that, but she was once part of a music ministry. Their talents had been quite in demand at one time, but not much has been heard about them since, well, probably since before Sophie left home." Ian paused. "I'm telling you all of this in confidence, Elisha because I need your advice." Ian told him about the providential meeting with Olivia Bidershem without revealing her identity.

Elisha took a handkerchief from his pocket and wiped the sweat from his forehead. "Have a seat then, Reverend. What can I do for you?"

Ian seated himself on the top front porch step. "I'm wondering if I made a mistake."

"Hmm, how so?"

He thought he might as well get to the point. "Sophie didn't trust me enough to tell me all this before, for one. And, quite frankly, she needs to forgive her parents." Ian removed his hat and fussed with the brim. "The fact that she's not orphaned changes things. I want to do things decently. I think that I should have her father's consent for her hand. It's only right her parents should witness it all. They should be able to see their granddaughter. I don't think we should proceed with an engagement until all of that happens."

"I see."

In the following silence, Ian felt like a child in front of his father. He half expected to find that his legs had shortened and his voice changed to an octave higher. He wanted to ask Elisha why he didn't automatically agree, but the judgment spoken in the quietness pressed its hand hard upon him. "What do I do?"

The overalls he wore accentuated Elisha's down-to-earth demeanor. The knees were smudged with dirt from his hard work. "Ian," he said affectionately, instead of the more formal "Reverend." "You're not much older than my own boys. I'd be proud to have a son like you, but you need to be honest with yourself . . . and with me." He mopped his forehead again. "Something tells me you've been on a mission to fix something, but I've never quite figured out why or what it was."

Ian had appreciated the elder's discernment as long as he'd known him, but he wasn't usually the subject. The older man sat with bushy eyebrows knit together in scrutiny of him.

Annie. Tell him about her. Ian hung his head. Had he thought he could erase his secret by doing good works? He hadn't been completely honest with Sophie, either.

"I sense something is haunting you, son."

Ian drew in a ragged breath. He went from feeling about eight years old to eighty. His shoulders slouched. "A couple of years back, at my last place of ministry in Flint, there was a young woman who needed help. Her name was Annie. No one really understood her. She needed protection." He rubbed his temple and thought of her when she was alive, traipsing through the back door of the church in her baggy brown dress with a pale face, unkempt hair, and anxious expression. "And I didn't give it to her. Oh, the Ladies' Aid Society saw to it that she had clean clothing and an occasional meal, but she needed someplace safe to stay. They were afraid of her. She seemed different.

"I had no place to put her. Being seen with her alone would be considered improper, but I saw the bruises. I should have insisted that someone take her in. I mean, shouldn't the bruises on her arm be enough proof for them that she was mistreated whenever her uncle was home?" Ian couldn't sit any longer. He stood and paced.

"Take your time, son." Elisha's gaze followed him.

"She tried to let me know how desperate she was; that she didn't know what to do. She offered to help out in the kitchen to pay for her keep, but that wasn't the issue. It wouldn't have been proper for her to be in the house with my housekeeper, Mrs. Jones, away sick.

"I could have found someone to stay with us to make things look on the level, but I was worried about finishing my sermon, Elisha—a sermon about sacrifice and loving others at any cost. I thought I was too busy doing what was important. No, I couldn't even be bothered to sleep in the shed that night." Ian stopped, gripping the porch railing with one hand and hanging his head. "I patted her shoulder, sending her away and saying I would pray for her. I told her she should come back the next day. The housekeeper would be there and we'd have tea."

"I sent her away with an excuse, and that's the last time I saw her . . . alive . . . before she drowned herself in the Flint River. At least, we assumed she threw herself into the river." The slanting rays of the setting sun cast its orange glow across the landscape.

Sandhill cranes flew overhead, their eerie cry sounding accusatory to Ian. "I'm sure she would have, rather than go on in a world missing justice and love." *When I could have been an example of charity and mercy.* The lump in his throat caused difficulty in swallowing.

Ian rubbed his fingers across his forehead, not wanting to look Elisha in the eye with his next revelation. "After they found Annie's body, they realized she was with child. I was responsible for not one, but two deaths." The power of a deep sadness and anger gripped Ian. Was the guttural sob which escaped really his? The cry of a coward?

Elisha stood, placing his hand on Ian's shoulder, much as his father would have done before he died. "Ian, I've never known a kinder man than you. You can't blame yourself for her actions. We don't always understand why things happen the way they do."

"How much better I could have honored God if I had just taken care of people instead of trying to impress everyone with a well-written sermon. The sermons that really count are written by our actions." Ian's breath hitched with emotion.

"That's true." Elisha held both of Ian's shoulders until he looked up. "Unfortunately, those actions can be done by fallible people.

"You didn't have the power to stop their deaths if it was their time to pass on, son. Well, it explains your all-fired hurry to start that ministry to fallen women and their illegitimate children." The older man let go and slapped him on the back. "Not that we shouldn't be taking care of them. Our town is a healthy haven, and their presence won't change that . . . no matter what Gertrude says."

They walked side by side and sat back on the porch. "Have you taken your burden to the Lord, Ian?"

"Many times." Ian shook his head.

"Then the time has come to leave it there."

"But there's also my problem with Sophie."

"Well, that's just it. You need to tell her your past, what you thought you had to hide. Put it behind you. Confide in her and forgive her for not confiding in you. You can be an example of forgiveness. And when she's ready to forgive her parents, maybe you'll both feel more ready for marriage."

"And just like that admit what a hypocrite I've been, hiding my secrets?" Ian's jaw tightened. His confounded pride was getting in the way again. Wasn't that what had gotten him into this pickle to begin with? Worrying about what people thought of him, a man of the cloth? He pressed his lips together, angry and disappointed with himself.

Elisha let go of a dry chuckle. "Not like I've never been a hypocrite. We all have our moments we wish we could do over. You're not alone in this fallen world." The early evening breeze stirred the humid air, which hung as oppressively as the momentary silence between them.

"I see, you think because you're a pastor you're supposed to be perfect?" Elisha scratched behind his ear as a fly buzzed between them. "Last time I read my Bible, Jesus was the only one who could claim that."

Just what did Ian really have to fear? If Sophie really loved him as he hoped, she wouldn't judge him unworthy. He stared out toward the road. Maybe he was really scared she would be so disgusted with him that she wouldn't want to marry him anymore. His heart tightened with the grief of such a thought. If he couldn't walk the road of life's journey with Sophie, he didn't want to walk it with anyone else. Sure, his life had seemed full enough with Maggie, Philip, and his parish to watch over, but having Sophie and Caira show up changed things. He now knew he'd be incomplete without them.

"You think that gal of yours wouldn't understand after what she's been through? Her eyes nearly glow when she watches you in the pulpit. I've never seen such devotion since my own wife fell in love with me." Elisha gave Ian a hearty pat on the back. "Let me tell you, Ian. If you plan on marrying Sophie, well, there's not much room for pride between two people who have to share their lives and bring up a family together."

What did he have to lose by swallowing his pride? If the congregation wouldn't back them up, so be it. The Lord would find another place for him. Ian released a long sigh as a lump grew in his throat again. "I'm ashamed I let my own self-importance get in the way of God's work in me."

"No shame, son, Jesus took that on the cross. You give Him your sin and shame, let yourself receive His grace and forgiveness completely now." Elisha's voice grew quieter. "I'd like to pray for you before you leave."

Ian nodded while he swiped at the hot tears that poured down his face. He listened to the simple, heartfelt prayer that the elder offered up. "Father, we thank you for your grace and mercy . . . strengthen your loyal servant, Ian. Enable him to receive it all. Help him to follow the path you've set out for him, bearing witness to the truth of your covenants. Help him to trust you more each day, knowing how much you love and forgive him . . ."

The shame and guilt Ian had battled and needlessly carried the last two years rolled off his back as he silently claimed the words of truth for himself. For the first time since Annie's suicide, he felt free from the bondage of the past.

Ian had hurried to saddle his horse before going out to the Whitworth farm, rather than drag a whole buggy along. When he'd decided to visit Elisha, he was anxious to talk to the wise elder. However, as he set his foot in the stirrup and slung his other leg over the saddle to return home, he wasn't as anxious to speak with Sophie.

On the one hand, his burdens had been lifted when he sought forgiveness. On the other hand, saying he would talk to Sophie sounded good, but what were the actual words he should use to tell her of his past failings? He had to admit complete honesty would be best, but not an easy way to reveal his story.

Ian pulled on the reins and Brownie halted. Across the lake, deer nibbled on the grass as a family of them gathered at dusk. A seagull swooped down and grabbed a crayfish from the shallows. The bird scudded across the surface and flew to the bank, where it landed.

Life went on, didn't it? Even when heartbreak took its toll and the people they loved had died. Nothing could bring his parents back. Perhaps that's why he wanted Sophie not to give up on hers. The days and nights would pass quickly into years. Olivia Bidershem had already missed the first two and a half years of her granddaughter's life. Caira missed out too. She just hadn't realized it yet.

Ian dismounted Brownie and patted him on the side of his neck. He led the horse toward the lake for a drink. Release from his past burdens had come like the cool evening breeze when Elisha had prayed for him. Ian knew what he had to do, so why did his pride rear up and fight him on this other issue?

Yet if Ian wanted the credibility to advise Sophie, he needed to take Elisha's advice. *"You need to tell her your past, what you thought you had to hide . . . You can be that example of forgiveness. And when she's ready to forgive her parents, maybe you'll both feel more ready for marriage."*

"Lord, what will she think of me?" Silence met him other than the sucking sound Brownie made. He tilted his face toward the brilliant orange and pink of the western sky. He kicked at a stone to loosen the object from the dirt and bent to pick it up. Feeling the smoothness of it in his hand, he then skipped the stone halfway across the water. A duck, which had been hidden in the grasses, stirred and flapped its wings.

You know the answer, son. That still small voice of the One who knew Ian better than anybody spoke to his heart in the quiet solitude. Yes, Ian knew. He was afraid that Sophie wouldn't see him as a knight in shining armor, ready to rescue her, as though he were some angelic messenger sent to touch her, riding in a chariot of fire.

Of a certainty, he knew Sophie would see the knight with rusty armor, dirty and disheveled, riding a horse fit for the glue factory. So it wasn't just pride, but fear, too? *Let go of your fear.* He picked up another stone and turned the pebble over in his palm, warm from the sun on one side, cool on the other. A verse came to Ian. *For God hath not given us the spirit of fear, but of power, and of love, and of a sound mind.*

He turned the small gray stone over again, running his thumb over the thing. "You're right, Lord, I shouldn't be afraid whether Sophie would stop loving me. The situation is in your control— always has been. And I'm sorry for the pride of wanting her to think I'm anything more than human." God's power and love could work this out if he did the right thing. And if she didn't love him anymore, their marriage wasn't meant to be.

Bless me, Father, with your strength, grace, and wisdom. Ian chucked the stone across the water, this time in a different direction than the mallard's resting place. The horse nudged his arm with a wet nose. "Yes, it is time to go home before it gets too dark, Brownie." He mounted the gentle horse once again and pointed him in the direction of the parsonage.

••◦)━━━━━━━━━ ◦ ━━━━━━━━━(◦••

Sweat trickled down Sophie's back as she took the crisp white sheets off the clothesline. She breathed in their fresh air scent. They were warm against her skin. It would have been nice to have a gentle summer breeze stir the stifling humidity. She envied the city people who flowed into the area to take advantage of the small surrounding lakes, longing for a picnic with Caira and Ian under the shade of the orchard trees at Apple Blossom House. *Ian.*

Three days had passed since they had spoken. Though she was angry he'd hidden his encounter with her mother from him, she couldn't deny the depth of emotion the very thought of him created in her. Had she completely lost the chance to become his wife? For a brief time what she had thought was impossible seemed possible.

Because of her stubbornness to forgive, everything seemed to be in jeopardy. Of course, Ian was being obstinate in this case, as well. He could at least try to see her side of things and be more patient.

Sophie bent to pick up the willow laundry basket, filled with clean linens, and carried it inside to get started on the ironing. As she pressed each sheet with a heated iron, sorrow weighed upon her heart. Biting her lower lip, she pondered her conversation with Ian. Deep within, Sophie knew that she couldn't keep her secret forever, but surely this would be the end of Ian's ministry.

Then there was the thought of seeing her parents. Even if she could forgive them, would they ever be able to forgive her? To accept their granddaughter? And yet if she did have any chance to marry Ian, wouldn't she become "an honest woman," as they'd once hoped? Unlike Charles, of whom her father approved, Ian was only a parson of modest means. He didn't come from the family of a lumber baron, possibly willing to make a friendly business alliance with a piano manufacturer. Charles had.

Ian possessed a different form of wealth. He overflowed with love, wisdom, and kindness. He'd treated her with respect for the most part.

Charles had hidden his contempt behind a handsome smile. Sophie touched her cheek. Even as she remembered the sting of his hand on that spot, heat coursed over her neck and face. When once she had been attracted by his charming ways, with a hope for marriage and family, her dreams had turned to ashes.

Her brother, Paul, had taken her in the buggy to the Warner mansion at her request.

"Sophia," Charles had fairly crooned. "My parents want to become better acquainted with you. Come for tea tomorrow."

An internal tug of war between affection and fear took place within her. Perhaps getting to know his parents would help her to see another side of Charles, which would make her more comfortable about a possible engagement. "I suppose I should get to know them, as well." Sophie gazed up and gave him her shyest bit of smile.

Her brother left her at the door, carelessly, bent on spending time with other friends that evening. Why hadn't she implored Paul to stay for the visit? Charles' parents were actually on an extended trip. He had convinced Sophie that he needed the uninterrupted time with her before telling the staff to leave them alone and closed the two of them off in the parlor.

Sophie set the iron down and put her hand to her heart. Even as she thought of how an internal alarm had gone off during the time alone with the scoundrel, her heart had set to pounding. Sophie sat in a kitchen chair, which rocked on uneven legs and fanned herself, rehearsing in her mind how she'd felt helpless to escape. *Why didn't I think of climbing out the window? Or breaking it to draw attention?* She sighed. Once her heart slowed to a normal pace, Sophie stood back at the ironing board, continuing to press the sheets, fold them, and stack them.

Heat arose from the iron even as her face had burned with anger and shame, alone with Charles in the parlor.

"Sophia, you can make this easy and nice for yourself or unpleasant for us both." He'd grasped her wrist so tightly, the skin stung under his touch as she attempted to twist out of his grasp.

"I thought you loved me."

"What makes you think I don't?"

"Please stop this. Ask my father for my hand, anything, but not—"

His mouth engulfed her lips with roughness and whisky-laden breath, making her gag. Nothing could coerce her to willingly give Charles something which didn't yet belong to him. He pushed her against the brocade fabric of the chaise, muffling her screams with his large hand. Sophie, overwhelmed, nearly unable to breathe, fainted. On regaining consciousness, the assault was over. She'd lost her innocence.

"Was it so bad, darling?" Charles sneered. "I thought you were more of a woman."

She was speechless as bile rose in her throat. Shaking, she was able to eke out a few words. "I want to go home." And vomit.

Sophie climbed into the carriage he ordered, wrapped in a shawl of Mrs. Warner's a shy maid had brought her, with unspoken sorrow in her eyes. Sophie had stood alone, avoiding the footman's study of her. She had thought it couldn't get worse, but it had.

Her girlish infatuation turned to disgust at the sight of Charles. Any suggestion of marrying the monster had brought tears to her eyes.

"Ow!" Sophie pulled her hand away. Lost in memories that had been seared into her mind and heart, she had grazed the side of her hand with the iron. She pulled butter from the icebox and rubbed the burned area with the greasy balm, soothing the pink skin with its coolness.

Plunking down in a seat at the kitchen table, Sophie found Esther's Bible left open from her morning devotions. Her gaze was drawn to the top of the far left-hand column where verse three of Psalm 147 caught her eye. *He healeth the broken in heart, and bindeth up their wounds.* How had she forgotten such words existed in scripture? Truly, she hadn't given God the chance to heal her.

But when she was tired of running, she'd found Stone Creek. And Ian. And friends.

Sophie had been busy blaming God, angry at Him for what had happened to her. Yet, in her pride, she'd never admitted she'd been a little too trusting of Charles, or perhaps naïve. Of course, that didn't excuse what he'd done to her in any way, preying on her innocence.

As painful as the whole situation had been, she went to sleep each night with a smile, thinking of Caira's antics and how much she loved her daughter. Sophie wouldn't have traded her for anything. What a precious gift her daughter was.

The Lord had allowed her to experience Ian's healing love and friendship, as well as the kindness of Esther, Maggie, and Gloria. Perhaps God wasn't as far away as Sophie thought. She closed her eyes, allowing the curative words of the verse to fill her. *He healeth the broken in heart, and bindeth up their wounds.* She swallowed against the lump in her throat. *God, I need a whole lot of healing and binding up. Please help me.*

Once the stinging on her hand and behind her eyelids subsided, Sophie blotted the butter off with a cool rag so she could continue her chores. She took the last sheet from the ironing board and folded it neatly into place in the basket with the others.

Traipsing up the stairs with fresh linens in her arms, Sophie walked as lightly as possible, hoping not to disturb Caira or Esther from their naps. She thought she would start in James' room. First, Sophie parted the curtains to let some light in. She cracked the window open, wondering how James wrote or slept in such an oven. Papers had been strewn on the floor or perhaps fallen from his tiny desk. Other sheets of paper were crumpled into wads splotched with ink. She shuffled some of them, placing them on the writing table, and sighed.

The corner of what appeared to be a Detroit newspaper stuck out from the bottom of the pile. Sophie's fingers itched to pick it up. James wouldn't mind, would he? She pulled it out. *Detroit Free Press.* She just wanted to peruse it for a few minutes, then she would fold it back up, tuck it into its resting place and get back to making up the beds with fresh linens.

Holding the paper up to the light coming through the window, she skimmed the headlines and thumbed through the paper, looking over some of the articles. One page had been dog-eared. Sophie scanned the print. A headline screamed at her.

CHAPTER 24

The heading read *"Mystery of Missing Piano Heiress."* If Sophie believed that she could've felt her heart leap into her throat, it seemed possible at that moment. She read on intently.

> *Sophia Bidershem, daughter of Lemuel and Olivia, disappeared almost two years ago with a small child in her care. Says businessman, Bidershem, "The trail grew cold awhile ago, but her mother and I haven't completely given up hope." Her former fiancé, Charles Warner, was heartbroken over her disappearance and vows to find her eventually. He believes he has a new lead, which he does not care to divulge . . .*

Sophie barely contained her trembling. She folded the paper and returned it to its place on the desk. Then she wiped the smudges of ink from her fingertips onto her apron as though wiping blood from them. Stepping back, she turned and began spreading the fresh sheet over the mattress with shaky hands. Fiancé? Lead? The bile rose in her throat to think that Charles might have any idea where she was. She was so tired of running.

Fury almost crowded out the realization that her parents wanted to see her. But she wondered if her father still wanted to press her into a union with the cold-hearted ogre who had pretended to care for her. Charles "heartbroken"? Only over the loss of marrying into money.

The other question was what to do with the paper. Had James marked the page for that article? Or another? Had *he* given Charles the lead? "No, it couldn't be." Sophie shook her head against such cynicism and suspicion. Perhaps Stone Creek was a bit too close to Detroit. Had a past acquaintance seen her? One of her father's associates may have had business in the area, when all along she thought she was relatively safe.

What do I do now, Father? Silence answered her. She waited, and as gently as a summer breeze rustling the leaves, in the tree outside the window, the words *Go to Ian; humble yourself,* impressed themselves on her heart. Sophie finished her work as fast as she could. She planned to splash some cool water on her face and change her shirtwaist, then go where she should have originally taken her concerns. The man she loved. Ian.

•••)————— • —————(•••

Sophie nearly ran all the way to the parsonage, having awakened the napping Esther to watch Caira. But when she reached the steps, Sophie stood still, gasping for breath. Ian hadn't spoken with her in days. Would he even want to see her?

"Could you make some lemonade, Mother?" Philip's voice carried through the screen door.

Sophie couldn't quite understand Maggie's reply perhaps from the kitchen. What made her think she would be welcome? She couldn't imagine what Ian might have told his sister about her. The white clapboard house had been like a second home to her. She'd dared to hope these people might become her family. But did she belong here anymore? Though humid air enveloped her, she hugged herself and purposely slowed her breathing.

Ian pushed one foot in front of another as he made his way home from the church through the wave of heat. Deep in thought, he clasped his hands behind his back. He'd been avoiding Sophie completely since his conversation with Elisha, not sure where to take back up with her. Ian had definitely made peace with the Lord over the situation, yet he wasn't sure how to tell Sophie the story. But hadn't she finally trusted him? Given him everything by revealing her secret shame? He'd judged her wrongly. He owed her the truth of his own secrets.

Forgiveness was the order of the day. He didn't want to avoid making peace with her out of misplaced guilt as he'd done with God for the past two years. Hopefully, he'd learned something. As Ian turned the corner onto his street, he saw the sweet form of his beloved standing in front of the parsonage.

Sophie turned to face him, her eyes widening. She stepped backwards and stood still, reminding Ian once again of a deer preparing to bolt.

"Sophie!" Ian picked up his pace, turning onto the flagstone path. "I'm so happy to see you here!"

She reached toward him, her posture growing more relaxed as he grew closer.

Ian took her hands into his, but it wasn't enough. He engulfed her in an embrace, drinking in the lavender scent of her hair, the softness of her form against him. Her vulnerability overcame him, and he wanted more than ever to be her protector, her husband. "I'm sorry, dearest. I have been wrong."

Her golden-brown eyes searched his face. "But I was wrong too. Whom else should I share my deepest sorrows with? And I realize now that what my mother told you put you in an awkward position. Still, I wish I'd known sooner."

Ian shook his head and placed a finger on her alluring pink lips. "But I haven't told you all of the truth. I have my own secrets and had no right to expect you to share all of yours when I wasn't willing to tell you mine."

"You, Ian?" Sophie continued to search his face, clinging more tightly to him. "I can't believe a good man like you has anything in your past to hide. I was sure that my secrets would shame you. You are so perfect, so concerned about others."

He moved his hands to grip her by the elbows with gentle firmness. "You must not think me unflawed. I'm a man, filled with faults, like any other. I let a young woman down—"

"Maggie mentioned something had happened." Sophie bowed her head.

"What?"

"When you went to the home . . . you know . . . for fallen women. She didn't say much."

Ian's ragged sigh hung on the humid air. He told her the story of the shortcoming that had torn at the fabric of his conscience and heart for the last two years. "And when they found Annie dead, it was obvious she was with child. I felt responsible for not one, but two deaths."

Sophie's eyes grew dewy. "But Ian, you're such a kind man. You would never mean for anyone to be hurt like that. How could I ever judge you, with my own sin before me? I know I must eventually come clean of it publicly. I should have told you sooner." She twisted an escaped ringlet of hair around her fingers, looking as sweet as an innocent little girl. "And you were there when Caira and I needed help the most."

Ian hurt for Sophie, wishing he could have been there to protect her from the blackguard who had stolen her innocence. He clasped her delicate hands, with their long fingers, in between his. "When I met you, I confess you and Caira seemed like a project. I believed your story, but you seemed friendless and in need of charity."

Sophie tried to tug her hands away, but he held them more secure. "But if I were honest, I would tell you there was more pulling at my heart than your situation. I could see the beauty you tried to hide, the loveliness of the person you are, your character as you cared for Caira. I know you meant no harm by your ruse. It took courage to confess, and I've waited and prayed for the moment you would tell me."

Her crooked little half grin appeared. "I did need you, Ian, but I didn't appreciate your meddling charity at first."

Ian chuckled in spite of himself. "I'm sorry, Sophie. Know that if anyone is a charity case, I am. You showed me how empty my life was without your love to fill it. And Caira sweetened the deal."

Sophie leaned against him then, resting her head on his chest and despite the blistering air surrounding them, Ian held her closer.

"I'm frightened, Ian." She shook.

"Don't be afraid, dearest, I am here."

"Caira's father, Charles Warner, may be looking for me. He's dangerous. And James Cooper may know my true identity." Sophie pulled away enough to look earnestly into his eyes as she explained what she'd found in the young man's room.

"We're going to give this to the Lord, and we'll weather this storm together." He meant it. Somehow Ian had never felt so sure. The God who healed their hearts would surely protect them. He prayed aloud for them both. "Heavenly Father, you made us from the dust to which we'll return someday, but right now this little bit of dust needs your wisdom, your help, and your shielding power from those who work against us. We need you to take our fears and give us courage . . . help us sort this out." The Lord's peace spread over Ian's heart like a blanket. Of course, it didn't hurt that the one he loved most dearly was close to being his.

After the Sunday morning service, less than a week later, Ian closed the heavy oak doors of the church behind him and strolled toward home. The gray sky threatened a thunderstorm in the ominous stillness of the humid air, which pressed on Ian. He hoped his visitors would arrive before the cloudburst.

A vision of Annie's lifeless, cold body, washed up on the shore of the river chilled him for a moment. Did he really have the right to marry his beautiful, talented Sophie? But Ian shook it off. He remembered the encouragement that Elisha had given him to rest in the Lord and His forgiveness, as well as Sophie's love and acceptance. Ian had been forgiven, but it was only after the head elder's counsel and prayer that he had become free from crippling remorse.

How ironic that his desire to help Sophie and Caira had started partially because he felt that he owed it to God to help the downtrodden. This was a debt he could never repay. He had let both Annie and God down. Yet God had given him the desire of his heart and would never let him down.

"I will be the best husband and father I can possibly be, with your help, if you allow me to marry Sophie, Lord." A light breeze stirred the moist air.

Maggie met him at the front door. "It's about time you got home. Your company should be here any minute."

"Yes, Maggie, I'm aware, but may I say that whatever you made smells wonderful?"

"Well, I wasn't going to make a roast in this weather, but I did bake some biscuits to go with our cold ham and salad. And I made a blueberry cobbler for dessert."

"I appreciate your hard work."

Maggie dabbed her eyes with the corner of her apron. "As much as I've complained that you need a wife, I will miss taking care of you, and Philip will miss having a man around."

"What are you talking about? We'll still need you."

"No, no. Sophie needs to be the lady of the house. I will gladly help her, but I've made arrangements for Philip and me to stay at Apple Blossom Cottage. Asa and Gloria have offered it to us. It's a cozy place."

"You don't have to do that."

"No, I must." She blew her nose on a clean handkerchief that Ian handed to her.

"With the fortune Robert left you, you could go anywhere."

"I came to Stone Creek to be near family. You're the only family we have. This will give me time to think about where I want to live. I'll find my own house eventually."

"And someone to help you care for it?"

"Oh, bother. For just the two of us? Idle hands are the devil's workshop."

"Whoa!" A loud voice said. Trotting horses on the street came to a standstill on the other side of the screen door.

"Oh my." Maggie primped her hair and took her apron off.

They both looked out the door at the nicely turned out buggy. "Yes, oh my," Ian added.

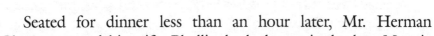

Seated for dinner less than an hour later, Mr. Herman Gloucester, and his wife, Phyllis, looked surprised when Maggie did the serving.

"Well, that's all right. I like to see a thrifty pastor. It encourages the congregation to be more frugal and charitable. Don't you think?" Mr. Gloucester raised a bushy eyebrow before he stuffed a healthy forkful of ham into his mouth.

"My husband and I are most anxious to hear more about the orphan's home and school to be built in memory of the Barringtons." Mrs. Gloucester's silvery hair glistened like the fine pearl necklace and earrings she wore. "We are so glad to be invited to hear more about your worthy charity."

"We hope to eventually build a home for unmarried mothers, too." Soliciting funds for the project gave Ian a headache.

"Yes, yes. Very ambitious of you." Herman's fork stabbed the air. "We're looking forward to seeing our friends, Asa and Gloria. Too bad they had an engagement elsewhere."

"Thank you for showing us such gracious hospitality despite their absence." Phyllis took a dainty sip from one of Maggie's best crystal goblets.

"They assured me that they would be at the church service this evening." Ian nodded and smiled.

"Well, capital." Mr. Gloucester bit off a rather large chunk of biscuit. His jowls worked over the piece. "Quite delicious. Perhaps we could get a copy of your recipe for our cook." He changed the subject. "So, I noticed that you have a Bidershem piano."

"Actually, it's Maggie's." Ian nodded toward his sister, feeling the ache move farther up the back of his neck.

"Fine instruments they are. I toured the factory a few times. First-class operation."

"Well, you'll have a chance to meet Ian's young lady tonight. She plays beautifully and has graced the keys of my piano many times." Maggie looked very pleased, not realizing how close she'd come to identifying Sophie with the piano manufacturing family.

Ian took a bite of meat but stopped mid-chew. The salty flavor spread over his tongue. He pictured Sophie sitting at the mahogany Bidershem piano for the first time, remembering how shy she seemed, and apprehensive. None of them had known that the instrument had come from her family's business. And with it must have entered many painful memories. Ian closed his eyes against the fear that niggled at the back of his mind. If the man had visited the Bidershems' company, he probably hadn't any connection with Sophie, but most likely only her father. He hoped.

"Your little town is quite charming." Mrs. Gloucester's smile lit her eyes. "What a beautiful place for orphans to be cared for, with your lakes and farms in the area."

"I agree, my dear." Mr. Gloucester swallowed and nodded. "Plenty of hearty outdoor activity for the children to partake in. Don't you think, Reverend?"

"Of course. Both my sister and I have been enchanted by Stone Creek. It's a fine place to set up a mission." Ian forced a grin, somewhat relieved the subject had changed.

"Who would be interested in some blueberry cobbler for dessert?" Maggie rose and set her napkin on her chair.

Ian contemplated whether or not to warn Sophie. Surely the Lord hadn't brought them this far to leave them in a quandary.

•••)⸺⸺ ● ⸺⸺(•••

Sophie sat at the piano when Ian arrived with his guests for the service that evening. The man, with his handlebar moustache, and the woman, with her silvery hair and square face, looked vaguely familiar.

When it was time for her to begin, she played "Jesus Like a Shepherd Lead Us." The quiet number added to the air of trust and peace Sophie felt as she smoothly played the hymn. When it was time for the sermon that evening, Sophie moved to the second pew on the left, facing the pulpit. The warm air carried the scents of polished wood and a faint odor of mildew like most buildings, which stood for many years, given by one generation to the next and reminding those present of the days past.

Ian began his time of teaching. He gripped the pulpit and cleared his throat. She could tell he was agitated and wondered what was bothering him. The worry in his eyes spoke volumes to her as their gazes connected for a moment. Ian scanned the congregation as he spoke. Was he having second thoughts about the two of them? She smoothed her skirt and turned to check on Caira, who sat quietly next to Esther, several rows back. Relieved, Sophie faced forward again to find the woman with silvery hair seated in the first pew, watching her. The older woman's brows furrowed. She twisted her head sideways and patted the back of her upswept hair.

Sophie studied the profile of the woman's husband. His moustache twitched. Where had she seen them before?

"As we continue to look at Jesus as our shepherd . . ." Ian's voice drifted into the background as Sophie was struck with an image.

There was that one time when she was six she had gone to the factory with Papa. A friend, interested in the piano business, was visiting. *"Sophia, shake Mr. Gloucester's hand."*

"Yes, Papa." She held out her little hand to be engulfed in his large, pink, doughy mitt.

"What do you say?" Papa smiled.

"Pleased to meet you, Mr. Gloucester."

The fat man chuckled. "Look what I have for you, dear." He held out a sassafras candy stick. He'd had more hair then, but she was sure it was the same person.

She thought of the times her family had occasionally seen the rich, childless couple over the years. They'd been quite kind.

"We have guests in the congregation." Ian motioned for the Gloucesters to stand. "Herman and Phyllis Gloucester are visiting from Ann Arbor. They're here to learn more about Gloria and Asa Myles' plan to start an orphanage. They are looking to be a part of such a worthy endeavor."

Sophie closed her eyes. *Dear God, not now, please. For Ian's sake. For Caira's sake. Please give us time to work this out, to approach the congregation.*

What should she do if they recognized her? Should she leave as soon as she finished the postlude before anyone could question her identity? Sophie sighed at the tiresome thought. She would just introduce herself as Sophie Biddle because of Ian, and Caira. Lying had never sat well with her, but what else could she do? Just until the wedding. Then she would have a new name and a brand new life. She would be able to come clean. Her stomach squeezed with tension for the remainder of the service.

Ian cleared his throat. "And now, Sophie will play our closing hymn."

She jumped, unready to take her cue. All eyes were upon her. She moved toward the piano. Nodding and smiling, she felt heat spread over her face.

Sophie hurried a bit through the ending hymn. When she finished, the Gloucesters got up and moved toward her, staring intently. Sophie slid her glance downward, avoiding eye contact. She scurried toward the back of the church down the side aisle and stood in back, next to Ian while he greeted the congregants. When he had a moment, she would warn him.

The flustered-looking couple pressed their way forward in line. Sophie's heart pounded like a drumbeat for someone who was being led to execution. It seemed louder as the Gloucesters drew nearer. Her palms grew sweaty inside her white cotton summer gloves.

Sophie groaned inwardly. Gertrude Wringer seemed to be making their acquaintance. Perhaps the busybody would slow them down for a moment, so Sophie had time to think.

CHAPTER 25

Ian tried to make out what Sophie whispered into his ear as she placed her hand into the crook of his arm. "What?" He leaned toward her, but Gertrude Wringer's shrill voice kept him from hearing Sophie. The nasty woman pushed forward with his guests in tow.

"Well, Reverend, I am happy to finally meet some quality people around here." Gertrude's haughty thin-lipped smile resembled a wrinkle on a prune.

For the second time that day, Ian plastered an unwilling smile on his face. "Yes, well, the Gloucesters are good friends of the Myles family and have been kind enough to consider helping them with the finances of building a school for orphans." He took some pleasure in sharing such details with her.

"I see." Gertrude's nose twitched.

Sophie trembled next to him.

"Mr. and Mrs. Gloucester, allow me to introduce you to a special friend of mine, Sophie ..."

She nudged him in the ribs.

He shrugged. "Biddle."

Sophie positively paled. "H-how do you do?" She held out her hand and leaned closer to Ian.

Mr. Gloucester took hers into his large one. "Young lady, you look so familiar to us."

"Yes, like our dear friends' daughter," his wife added.

"You must be mistaken." Ian understood. He needed to divert their attention. He put his arm around Sophie. "Perhaps you'd like to move to the lawn for the outdoor reception that's been prepared for you folks, cold lemonade and cookies?"

"No rush," Gertrude Wringer piped up. "This is quite interesting. Do tell us more about your friends' daughter."

Ian wanted to grab the spiteful woman by the arm and escort her to the door once and for all. He clenched his teeth. If only he could find a way to get Sophie and Caira away from Gertrude's examination and on the way to the boardinghouse.

"But your name, it's so close to *Sophia Bidershem*." Mrs. Gloucester touched Sophie's arm with a closed fan. "I've seen you play and sing before. I'm sure of it."

"Yes, what became of her was quite a tragedy." Mr. Gloucester cleared his throat. "Because of an alarming situation . . . well . . . let's say there's a child involved."

"Oh, Herman, really. How could you speak of such a thing publicly? I feel positively faint." Mrs. Gloucester snapped open her fan and began waving it violently in front of her face.

●●❭————— ✳ —————❬●●

"Well, since she's gone missing her parents are terribly worried. I think she needs to know this."

Sophie chose her words carefully. "Perhaps the daughter they once knew no longer exists." She lifted her chin.

"Soffie! 'Cowmick!" Caira's stubby legs carried her closer with Esther, Gloria, Asa, and Elise not far behind.

The Wringer woman gave her a hawkish stare. "Well, isn't all of this fascinating?" She licked her lips like a cat going in for the kill.

"Wasn't there something about that in a Detroit paper recently? Perhaps your friend, James Cooper, could tell us more."

Caira grabbed onto her mother's skirt. Rooted to the floor by her fear, Sophie swept the child up and held her close. Her heart's cadence grew faster like the rhythm of a train upon a track, but she couldn't stop it, as though the train was headed for a wreck and she was in the middle of it. Where could she go? What could she do?

Herman and Phyllis Gloucester looked on as Caira grasped onto Sophie's lace collar. The chestnut ringlets and almost identical facial features no doubt gave the child's true identity away in their eyes. Sophie held her breath and pressed her daughter closer. Time seemed to stop for Sophie as she awaited the Wringer woman's accusations.

"I knew it! I knew you were a fallen woman, and the child was yours all along!" Gertrude Wringer stood with hands on her hips, gleeful in her triumph. "The truth always comes out in the end!"

The congregants chatting in the foyer grew silent. Eyes turned toward Sophie and Caira. Their questioning looks darted toward Ian. Many church members stared with mouths agape. Sophie noticed James several feet away. He fussed over the brim of his hat, studying it and stealing a look toward those involved in the confrontation.

"So . . . our saintly little piano player isn't so holy after all." Gertrude continued to stand with hands on her hips and nose in the air. Her eyes brightened with her exultation over Sophie.

"I believe you've said enough, Gertrude." Ian's quiet, yet angry tone spoke volumes. His face flushed. He pulled Sophie closer and squeezed her shoulder.

"Gertrude, you have a lot of nerve accusing my employee like that!" Esther stood face to face with the nasty woman. "Whatever happened in Sophie's past doesn't matter. Her behavior in my home has been above reproach. You should have seen her caring for Ezekiel Graemer. And she has been an excellent caretaker to that precious little one."

"Well, prostitutes came to Solomon to argue over a baby. One of them was a good mother, too, but it didn't stop her from being an immoral woman. I think the elders need to see to this case." Her cold glare pierced through Sophie.

"Now wait just a minute." The large Elisha Whitworth pointed a finger at Gertrude. "You have no right to make accusations when you don't know the whole story."

"That's right." Asa Myles, half of Elisha's stature, nervously adjusted his tie.

Etta Stout joined the fray. "Our pastor has been taken in by a fallen woman."

Several people spoke at once. Sophie's throat dried. She looked into Ian's eyes. "I have to go."

Feeling numb, she pulled away from the man she loved more than her own life. She moved out the door, into the heat of the day, and toward the boardinghouse as though mesmerized. Sophie supposed she was in shock. Resignation claimed her. Grief would come later. She would leave behind those whose kindness and concern she'd come to depend on, but she couldn't think about that at the moment.

Sophie held Caira as close as possible. Her first job was to protect her daughter. Ian was right about how precious her little girl was. *Ian.* She could not look back. It was better she didn't.

With her damp dress sticking to her back, Sophie lowered Caira to the ground. "It's too hot to carry you right now, little one."

Caira let out a whine and stood still.

"You will walk with me." Sophie gave her a warning look. "Now."

Her daughter stuck out her lower lip, but she nodded and followed. Caira's plump little hand was tucked into Sophie's. The toddler's short legs pumped fast to keep up.

"Sophie!" James called to her, "Please wait!"

Sophie set her face forward. She refused to look back, but taking great strides, he caught up with her.

"I need to speak with you, urgently." He took a deep breath.

"What do you want?" She slid a glance in his direction, determined to brace up her jelly-like insides against the fear of the next few moments.

"I went to Detroit recently to see my aunt. She raised me, you see—"

"I'm well aware of that. Get on with what you have to say." Sophie kept walking, grasping onto the hand of her whining daughter.

James removed his derby, combing his fingers through his hair before returning the hat to its proper place. "I know Paul Bidershem. It seems we went to preparatory school together."

Sophie stood still, her march toward the boardinghouse abandoned for the moment.

"I ran into him. He mentioned how heartbroken his parents had been these last two years since his sister went missing."

Sophie closed her eyes tightly against the news. She was sure that a criminal being caught and returned for punishment would have the same feeling that their world was collapsing. An urge to run and hide flooded her.

"He was also concerned that a man by the name of Charles Warner had been looking for her." James paused and then spoke with emphasis. "Paul asked me that if I found Sophia, to tell her their mother and father wanted her home more than ever and she has their protection."

Sophie's eyes popped back open, and she began to make her way again toward Fairgrave's. Like the waves and the treacherous currents of the Detroit River during a violent storm, her stomach churned with the conflicting emotions she felt.

"There's something else." James pulled the derby from his head again and fussed with the brim. "I suspected you might be Sophia, so I sought Nora out to ask her a few questions. I knew she was your friend . . . I thought you might have confided in her. Gertrude must have heard me talk about my suspicions. I'm sorry, Sophie, I never meant to hurt you."

Sophie blinked against the river of tears that threatened to spill over. "It seems the damage has been done." She bit her bottom lip.

"Such an account would have made a great story to say you'd been found, but it's not worth hurting friends . . . any more than I already have." He shrugged. "You don't have to worry about that anyway."

"Thank you. I'm sure Sophia would appreciate that." She looked James directly in the eye.

·•●)━━━━━━━━ ● ━━━━━━━━(●•·

Ian knew that he had left the church in a pickle, but Elders Elisha and Asa would continue to defend him to the likes of Gertrude Wringer and her cronies.

He strode quickly, carrying his suit coat over his arm. The sun's unrelenting rays pounded down. Ian didn't look back. He cared deeply for his flock, but he had pledged his heart to Sophie.

When Ian reached the boardinghouse, he flung open the front door. "Sophie!" He scanned the parlor and dining room. Fear shot through him. Where had they gone?

He darted toward the clamor of footsteps on the stairs.

"Sh," Sophie told the whining Caira.

He met Sophie coming down the stairs with the little one in tow, carrying an overstuffed carpetbag.

The little one's eyes lit up when she saw him. "'Cowmick!" She propelled herself forward and ran to hug his legs.

Ian scooped Caira into his arms and buried his face in the chestnut curls so like her mother's. Her giggle soothed his fearful heart. "Sophie—"

"Ian, what are you doing here? What will your congregation do if they find us here?"

"Yoo hoo!" Nearly breathless, Esther tromped through the open front door. "Sophie?" She blinked. "Reverend, what are you doing here?"

"I got here just in time to talk her out of leaving."

"What?" Leaning against the wall, Esther fanned herself. "Without even saying 'good-bye'?"

Sophie stared at the floor for a moment. "I'm sorry, Esther. You deserve better."

"Would you please take Caira into the kitchen? I need to talk some sense into Sophie."

Ian placed a protesting Caira into Esther's arms though she grabbed onto his shirt. He peeled her fingers from the fabric and kissed the top of her head before he released her. Taking Sophie's bag, he grasped her elbow and bade her sit down in the parlor.

"Ian, you of all people should know that I must leave Stone Creek now. Of a certainty, Gertrude Wringer has already convinced them that I am no better than a prostitute."

"But most people know the truth."

"The whole truth, Ian? You and I are the only ones that know the complete truth. Though James seems to know a good deal of it." Sophie perched on the edge of the chaise with arms crossed.

"They know the truth about the kind of person you are inside." Ian sat next to her wanting to pull her toward him. "We'll work through this together. We'll explain to the elders what truly happened to you. I should have done this before, but I thought it would be best if we waited until . . . well . . ."

He moved from the sofa to the floor, getting down on one knee. He reached for the hand nearest him. "Sophie, will you marry me?"

Sophie shook her head. "Oh, no. You can't marry me now. I will not allow you to give up your calling for me. They'll run you out of town on a rail and then what will you do? I can't let that happen to you. Caira and I will survive. God has gotten us this far." His beloved pulled her hand from his and pushed a sweaty lock from her forehead. "If I leave now, they'll just assume you never knew the truth."

"Gertrude will see to it that I am gotten rid of for being seduced because of my naiveté. And then I will not have you *or* a church. God will see to it that my calling is fulfilled." Ian had run from facing the truth once before. As fragile as a sterling reputation might be, he could not allow his pride to get in the way this time.

Ian slipped his fingers under her chin, bringing Sophie's face toward his own. "Please, Sophie, let's give this a chance. You were an innocent victim—"

"Who deceived people."

"And who didn't want to but felt it was necessary to protect her daughter."

"And myself." Anger flickered in Sophie's moist eyes, her look indignant.

Ian sighed. She was right. Whether it had been Annie, seeking shelter from her uncle's harm or the innocent victim, God's people often feared what was different. It frightened them as they viewed these situations from their comfortable lives.

Sophie sank into his embrace as he pulled her to himself, her soft hair brushing against his chin. With all his might, he wanted to protect her, keep her from all harm, even the specter of Caira's father finding them, which had seemed to hang over Sophie. Yet he knew that God was truly their only hope in this situation. Wasn't there room for forgiveness in God's family? When it came down to it, they were all repentant sinners.

"What will happen if you keep running? You need some place to settle."

Sophie trembled in his arms. "I-I am weary of running. I wanted to stay in Stone Creek. With you." Her amber eyes sought assurance in his gaze as they pulled apart.

"Will you become my wife, then? I love you, Sophie. I can't imagine life without you." Ian entangled his fingers in her warm locks. He used his thumb to smooth her forehead, lined with worry, and then kissed the spot he'd rubbed. "I will call a special meeting so that we can deal with the situation, but either way, I will not leave you."

"Then, yes, I will marry you. I want to live an honest life and for Caira to have a father." The crooked little smile, which always charmed Ian, appeared on her face.

"One more thing. Are you willing to contact your mother at least?" Ian moved to sit next to his beloved.

Sophie nodded. "I think I'm ready for that."

"'Cowmick, I wan' up!" Caira toddled into the parlor and scrambled to get on his lap.

"Say 'please.'" Sophie smiled.

"I'm sorry, Reverend. Caira got away when I turned my back for a second." Esther huffed and puffed in the doorway.

"It's fine now." He pulled Caira to a secure position on his lap, overjoyed he would soon become her stepfather.

Esther nodded and turned toward the kitchen.

"Sophie, if you'll allow me, I would like to legally adopt Caira when it's possible."

"Nothing could please me more." She beamed up at him.

"It's about time the three of us became a little family. Don't you think?" If the Lord had seen fit to become a true Father to him, then the least Ian could do was bring Caira fully into the

McCormick clan. The little one answered by taking her thumb out of her mouth and hugging him around the neck.

"Love 'ou, 'Cowmick." Caira's head went down on his shoulder. She may not have fully understood what he asked, but her affectionate response spoke volumes to his very heart.

CHAPTER 26

The following Sunday afternoon, Sophie sat stiffly in the front pew, daring to steal only an occasional glance toward those behind her. Her heart pulsed hard in her chest. She wrung her hands in her lap. Her white cotton gloves were dampened with sweat. Sophie imagined that this was how the accused felt in a courtroom.

According to Nora, her Aunt Gertrude would have none of what the Gloucesters shared with those in the foyer the week before. She wouldn't believe Sophie was an innocent victim any more than her father had at the time. When Sophie walked down the side aisle, Cecilia and Helena held their noses in the air and turned their faces away from her. Only Nora and James held a light of sympathy in their eyes as they watched her. *Lord, I know with your grace only will I be able to do this.*

She glimpsed Gertrude Wringer seated with her sour-faced cohorts. Her timid husband grimaced and shook his head. In fact, he sat up a little straighter than usual. Sophie didn't know some of the people who had gathered on the front steps of the church earlier and poured into the back of the sanctuary.

She wanted to support Ian, to clear her name, and stay in Stone Creek—not start a riot. The crowd mumbled and pointed.

She might as well be wearing a scarlet letter, but the meeting was fair game as the evening's entertainment. Hanging her head, she attempted to take a deep breath, but her throat tightened.

Gloria slid gracefully into the pew next to Sophie, with Asa by her side. "We are with you." Her dear friend took her hand.

Sophie heard the rustle of skirts and turned to find Maggie settling in next to her on the opposite side. She took Sophie's other hand. And Caira was safe in Esther's care. Sophie had to smile for a moment about the love that had been poured out on her.

Elisha Whitworth, the head elder, walked up to the pulpit. "Let's open our meeting in prayer." He bowed his head, asking for God's wisdom and blessing.

His whiskers shook as he sniffed, his voice hitched, and he paused. Though Elisha seemed at times to be nothing more than a roughened farmer, with a face lined from hard work in the sun, his compassionate side couldn't be hidden at that moment. "I believe that Reverend McCormick has something to say in defense of his betrothed, Miss Biddle." Elisha nodded toward Ian.

"Thank you." Ian acknowledged him and approached the pulpit. A beautifully carved walnut cross, polished to a shine, hung on the wall behind him. A large Bible lay opened in front of him. They embodied God's grace and law to Sophie. By which would the people judge them? She breathed a silent prayer for God's aid.

Maggie tightened her grip and winked. "Listen to my brother."

Ian cleared his throat. He stood straight, his face set toward the congregation, both hands holding fast to the sides of the pulpit. He glanced toward Sophie, hope emanating from his eyes. He had never endeared himself to her more than he did at that moment.

"There are times in life when circumstances take place that are beyond our control. We have examples of women who were hurt by men in our holy scriptures." He paused. A murmur spread through the sanctuary.

"But even those who had been caught in sin, whether the woman caught in adultery or the woman at the well, how did Jesus treat them? He ministered to them. He spoke to those who had been banished from society, he offered them hope and life in Himself.

"My betrothed is Miss Sophia Bidershem, whom you know as Sophie Biddle. You may have heard some rumors about her, but I want to give you the facts. Shall we judge her, a young woman who did not deserve what happened to her? Sophie was a victim of a vile act done to her by someone she trusted. Yet she had the character to not desert her child." Ian reached his right arm in her direction. "She is an honorable woman, and my commitment to marry her will not change."

The congregation sat silent, but for a few gasps. Tension charged the air.

"Humph."

Sophie turned toward the noise. Yes, Mrs. Wringer stood.

"How do we know that she didn't invite such behavior?" She pointed a bony finger at Sophie. "That our pastor is not deceived by an evil woman's charms?"

Etta and Millie whispered and nodded their heads.

"Now, wait just a moment." Elisha's voice boomed from the platform. "You'll have your turn. Sit down, Gertrude."

Ian's eyebrows knit together. His eyes clouded with a faraway look. He gripped the podium and his pained gaze drifted toward Sophie. As she watched the meeting unfold, her heart felt torn piece by piece.

A reddish-purple shade colored Gertrude's face. "What is this meeting for? When are we going to show that this man is incompetent and get rid of him?"

Sophie wrenched her hands from the grasps of her friends. She stood and marched toward the front but stayed down on the step in front of the platform. "I'm sorry, Elder Whitworth, but I must say something."

He shrugged and nodded. The people's voices rose in the confusion.

"Please! Please listen to what I have to say!" Sophie straightened to her full height and stood on her tiptoes for a moment. The audience quieted. "Reverend Ian McCormick has done nothing deserving of your censure. He is a godly man. It's because of his love for the Lord that he took Caira and me under his wing." Sophie clasped her hands together, lifting them as though in prayer. "If anyone should be blamed, it is I."

"So she admits it! Do we need anything more than this sinner's own admission of guilt?" The Wringer woman sprang from her seat again.

Sophie turned to see the withering look Elisha gave Gertrude as he stepped forward. "Let Miss Bidershem finish speaking!"

Gertrude's chin went up as she defied the elder, staring back at him and pointing at Sophie. "And furthermore—"

"Th-that's enough, Gertie, dear." His voice squeaked, but Edmund stood, uncharacteristically putting his hands on his wife's shoulders in public. "Sit down and give the young lady a chance to finish." Sophie had never seen such a stormy look in this usually henpecked husband's eyes. Gasps went up around the audience.

"But—" The woman turned red with rage more than embarrassment, Sophie was sure.

"As an elder of this church, I'm telling you it's time to sit and *listen*. Now, would you want the good people of Stone Creek to think of you as anything less than the fine God-fearing, churchgoing woman you are?"

Snickers arose around the sanctuary.

Mrs. Wringer crossed her arms, all the while glaring at her husband and then at Elisha Whitworth. She plopped down in the pew, sitting with her back ironing board straight, having shrugged off Edmund's touch.

Mr. Wringer nodded toward Elder Whitworth and pulled a crisp white handkerchief from his breast pocket. He wiped visible beads of sweat from his forehead.

Had Sophie imagined it? Or did the poor man look relieved?

The head elder gestured toward Sophie. "Please continue, Miss Bidershem."

She cleared her throat. "I should never have deceived the good people of Stone Creek. You have been so gracious to Caira and to me. Please forgive me. I only wanted my daughter to have the chance I had lost . . . one for a pure and normal life. But I believed that no one would love her the way I do. Rather than put her in an orphanage, I fabricated a lie to protect our reputations. Yes, a very sorry lie with no rational excuses." She could not have stopped the flow of hot, salty tears from pouring down her cheeks, even if she wanted to. "I should have known that no such deception could ever accomplish what I hoped without consequences.

"Please don't make a mistake in dismissing this kindhearted man. He did nothing unseemly in his behavior toward me. If anything, I will leave Stone Creek. I did nothing purposely to bring on my misfortune, but I will not allow my reputation to besmirch Reverend McCormick's . . . or that of the church and any attached ministries."

A commotion stirred far in the back. A man whom Sophie hadn't noticed before stood and moved forward through the crowd. A petite woman followed him. He spoke up. "We can vouch for Sophia."

Sophie's mouth fell open. She stood mesmerized, unbelieving. "Papa?" She blinked. "Mama?" Sophie stepped back and swayed a bit.

Papa looked thinner, grayer. He nodded and opened his arms. "My daughter did nothing evil. If anything, we didn't protect her enough. I'm so sorry, sweetheart, for not listening to you."

One by one, the prickly nettles of bitterness and anger fell from Sophie's heart. Her father had come to her defense! She ran down the center aisle toward them both and into their embrace.

"My dear baby. It really is you. I've missed you so." Her mother swallowed hard. She put her hand alongside Sophie's cheek.

"Mama, I'm so glad to see you."

Her father piped up. "For this young man, your Reverend McCormick, to stand by our daughter, despite the situation, shows a measure of rare character. You'd be a fool to let him go."

"He better stand by my little sister." A clenched fist smacked into the palm of her brother's open hand.

"Paul? You're here, too?" Sophie finally noticed her brother standing near James, who wrote fiercely with a stubby pencil. Paul's face split with a large grin. They were together again as a family, except for her younger brother, Ernest, who had died from a fever as a child. As she thought of ever losing Caira, her heart squeezed with grief. Sophie noticed the tears in Mama's eyes. How much pain she must have caused her mother!

The crowd around them burst into discussion. To Sophie, only her family and Ian existed at that moment.

"How? Why did you come now?" Sophie stood with her family in a small circle and clung to their arms like a child.

"After the Gloucesters visited Stone Creek, they told us of your circumstances, and we were certain they'd found you." Mama held fast to Sophie's hand. "When James found out that your fiancé had called this meeting, he sent a telegram to Paul. Between him and the Gloucesters, we wondered if we should take a chance and see if we could make amends. We weren't sure if you'd want to see us. And then we received a letter—"

"From your young man, just in time. We're amazed that a pastor in his situation would risk his reputation like this. And we were relieved you were in such good hands." Papa drew a long breath.

"We never stopped looking for news of you, or hoping you would return." Though she smiled, Mama's tears continued to flow.

"I should have done more to look for you, but Charles tried to convince me that he'd done all he could, that he didn't need my help. The wretch. I hope you can forgive me." Paul's downcast expression revealed his humble sincerity.

Sophie remembered all too easily how Paul had esteemed Charles, admiring his confidence and style, thinking him the epitome of a young gentleman, an example to follow. Her brother had been young and impressionable himself. How could she do anything but pity him? Or forgive him for his foolishness and letting her down? They all could have been wiser, but they'd all been taken advantage of. And yet, her adorable little daughter would not have existed except for this unfortunate circumstance.

"We finally did realize that Charles' character was greatly wanting. Can you ever forgive us?" Papa's eyes conveyed his pain and regret. "I wish I could put that scoundrel in his place—"

"But that is no longer necessary. We haven't heard from the profligate in awhile." Mama squeezed her hand.

What you intended for evil, God meant for good. The words that Joseph had spoken to his brothers in the book of Genesis echoed in Sophie's mind. A mantle of peace settled on her, the kind of peace she'd not felt in a very long time.

Mama looked toward Ian, motioning for him to join them.

"Come here, son," Papa commanded him.

Ian came forward, extending his right arm. The two men shook hands.

"I believe we've met, Reverend." Mama smiled and took his hand as he came closer.

"Yes, ma'am. I'm only sorry I couldn't reveal anything sooner."

"I know. I read your letter. At least my girls have been in the best of care." Mama placed his hand atop Sophie's and let them both go.

"I move . . ." Almost everyone's attention snapped toward the usually reticent elder, Asa Myles. "I move that we retain the Reverend Ian McCormick as our pastor."

"I second that." Elisha Whitworth raised his hand. "All in agreement signify by saying 'aye.'" Dr. Moore led the many voices that rose in accordance.

"Any opposed signify by the same," Elisha finished.

The Wringer woman's eyes darkened as she surveyed the crowd. Many of the congregants trained angry stares toward her.

"Fine," she managed to croak, "but I'm sure you'll all regret this someday. Mark my words." She stood.

"G-gert, that's quite enough." Edmund rose next to her, his words came out in a stage whisper as though he could avoid embarrassing her, but at least the squeak was gone. "These people have been through enough. I think it's time for us to leave now."

"What? I wasn't finished speaking!" she shrieked.

Her husband looked toward her with an expression of resolve. "You've done enough damage here. You've heard the truth, but it's not enough for you, is it?"

"Well, I never! How can you talk to me like this?" Gertrude stood straight with her fists at her sides and stamped her foot. "How dare you?"

"How dare I? I've watched you drag this town through the muck long enough!" Edmund seemed to stand taller as he spoke with more confidence. "There'll be no more prying into other people's lives, woman. You'll be too busy at home, caring for your own laundry from now on. I'm taking you to the buggy." He stared, with brows furrowed, at his wife. Escorting her stiffly, but gently by the arm, he demonstrated his determination. She tried to jerk her arm away.

"Let's go then, Nora, " Gertrude commanded.

Edmund stopped for a moment and turned to look at his niece. "No, Nora, you stay here with your friends, the good people of this church."

The girl smiled, speechless. As Edmund pulled Gertrude through the crowd, her eye twitching, it was as though a cold chill followed her through the sanctuary.

A cheer went up. Sophie met Ian's gaze.

"Thank you, all of you. I am humbled by your kindness and God's grace." Ian, choking up, cleared his throat.

They'd stood by one another through this difficult trial. Sophie's heart had become so deeply intertwined with Ian's. She hoped the family she was beginning with him would never experience the pain of being torn asunder as hers had.

Sophie turned her attention back to her parents and her brother. "I'm sorry for running away. I was just scared."

"We know." Mama nodded.

Papa shook his head. "I should have looked further into Charles' background. He talked a good game. I knew his father, a good man, and expected the apple not to fall far from the tree, but the blackguard's reputation eventually came out. Can you ever forgive me, my dear little Sophia?"

Sophie felt like a child again, but this time it was different. Papa had changed. Instead of an overbearing businessman she saw a hurting, broken father. His eyes looked moist, but if he had tears, he blinked them back. Sophie knew Papa had to keep some of his pride.

"Oh, Papa." She put her arms around her father, hugging him tight. "Of course, I forgive you." Sophie was amazed by the grace transforming her. The Lord had worked through Ian, Maggie, and the other people of Stone Creek, wooing her back to Himself with their kindness. She knew that God had truly never been far away but had been busy showing His mercy to His lost sheep, a mercy she was compelled to show to others.

Ian had been right. They should restore family relationships before they marry. Peace moved into her heart like soft currents in a stream. Sophie looked into Papa's eyes. *Not so fearsome anymore.* One side of her mouth pulled into a grin.

"That's my girl. I've missed your funny little crooked smile." He chucked her chin, but she didn't mind being his little girl at that moment.

"Where's my granddaughter? I'd like to see her now." Papa stood straight and looked commanding. This was the papa she remembered.

CHAPTER 27

Fireflies outside Sophie's window enchanted her as they mimicked the winking stars above. The blue night sky hung like diamond-studded velvet, but for the clouds skidding across. Nearly everything seemed perfect with the momentous church meeting four days behind them. And she had so much to look forward to after she and Ian were married in a little more than two weeks.

A puff of smoke rose above a man leaning against the corner streetlamp. Did he have a pipe in his hand? The unthinkable couldn't be happening, could it? Yet, as Sophie lowered the curtain, still peeking out, the man moved, staring up at her window before he turned and walked away with an arrogant stride, *his* arrogant stride.

She backed away from the pane of glass as though a stranger had seen her in her underclothes. She wrapped her robe tighter, looking over at her daughter, sleeping on the bed. Could Charles have found her? What did he know about Caira?

Her legs lost their strength, and she grasped the nightstand just in time. A soft knock on the door brought Sophie to her senses. She inhaled deep breaths, trying to cleanse the fear from her heart.

Another knock came. "Sophie, are you all right?" Esther's voice rose above a whisper.

Sophie smoothed her robe and turned the doorknob, cracking the door open. "Do you need something, Esther?"

Esther handed her an envelope. "Albert Johnson said that someone approached him on the street with a message for you, saying it was most urgent."

Sophie did her best to keep her hand from shaking. "Thank you." She didn't mean to be rude but shut the door quietly behind her friend.

Both hands shook, and she steadied her fingers. She pried the envelope open, then stopped. If this was from Charles, did she really want to read it? Yet she must know what was going on. Letting the envelope fall to the floor, Sophie opened the folded sheet of paper.

My Dearest Sophia,

Why have you kept yourself hidden from me? Have you forgotten the passion that brought our daughter into the world . . .

Sophie swallowed down the rising bile, determined not to vomit. How could he describe what he'd done to her as passion?

How quaint that you are engaged to the local minister. If you belong to anyone, it is I. Though I'm sure if you don't want to marry me, any court would side with me as the child's rightful father, that I should have custody. If this isn't a suitable arrangement, I'm sure that you could find a way to pay me a generous sum.

I would be happy to find accommodations, perhaps in your fine boardinghouse, and stay until the wedding when we can discuss things reasonably with your parents. However, I would happily go away if I am paid in advance. Don't try to leave town. I'm keeping an eye on you. I will wait tomorrow at dusk by the lamp post for your reply.

Most fondly,
Charles Warner

Extortion? Did he think a poor girl like herself had anything to offer? How dare he imply that he would be any kind of father to Caira, yet a fit one! However, Sophie felt she had no choice but that she and Caira needed to run . . . again, even if it meant returning to her parents' home for help. She gently pushed the curls from Caira's brow and bent to kiss her forehead. "I won't let him hurt you, no matter what."

••)———————— ● ————————(••

Ian came in from the stable, feeling quite pleased with his accomplishment as he brushed sawdust from his trousers. His sister would have a fit if he left a dust trail behind him anywhere else in the house. He found Maggie as she sat darning socks by the soft light of a lamp. He would miss his sister and nephew, but looked forward to gaining a wife and a daughter. His chest puffed out with the pride of having his own family.

"How goes the rocking horse experiment?" Maggie raised an eyebrow at him.

"Experiment? I can assure you that Father's lessons in woodworking haven't been easily forgotten though I did pick up a few slivers." He thought about how smoothly he'd sanded the wood. There wouldn't be any splinters to bother the little one's legs. This was his wedding gift to Caira. He'd wanted to give her something special now that she would be his daughter, something he'd made with his own two hands.

"Just thought you might be a little out of practice." She wetted the end of a thread before pushing it through the eye of a needle. "Pour yourself a cup of chamomile tea while the pot is still warm."

"That idea has merit. Let me get a book, and I'll keep you company rather than shut myself off in the study." There wouldn't be too many more evenings they would have time to sit together in companionable quiet.

Once Ian sat in the wing chair by the fire and set the teacup and saucer on the little round table next to him, he looked for his bookmark. Maggie sighed, cleared her throat, and let out a louder, more agonizing sigh. This was worse than her absolute silence. At least then, he knew she was furious with him.

"What is it, Maggie?" He snapped shut the book he'd barely opened. "Something bothering you?"

"For heaven's sakes, you don't have to ask like that."

Ian rolled his eyes and waited.

"I suppose I should have said something earlier." A crease formed between her eyebrows. "I was at Neuberger's store this afternoon and I saw someone . . ." It was unusual for Maggie to stop mid-sentence, let alone with needle and thread in mid-air as though her mind was engaged elsewhere.

"Yes?" He tapped his foot. "Who was it?"

"That's just it. I'd never seen the man before." She stabbed the sock with renewed purpose. "I hate to judge someone I don't know, but I didn't like the look of him. He was dressed well, wearing a brand new derby and a fancy suit coat, not to mention the spats on his shoes. But something about him was odd, out of place in Stone Creek. Then there was that scar on his left cheek."

"Maybe he's an acquaintance of Asa Myles." Ian shrugged, but discomfort rose right from his gut.

"That's just it, Ian. I was trying not to be rude and eavesdrop, but I didn't like the tone of his voice. I thought I heard him ask Isaac if he knew of Sophie and Caira's whereabouts." She paused. "You don't think it was just a relative, do you?"

Ian stood and paced, still clasping the book in his hand. He thought of the day Sophie came to him with fear in her eyes, the many times she'd looked like a panicked doe, but especially the day she'd recently told him of the newspaper article she'd discovered in James' room. Could the fiend who'd assaulted her be bold enough to come sniffing around like the dog he was? Was he trying to ruin Sophie's chance for peace and her own family?

"No, I don't, but neither do I want to think about who he could be." Ian looked toward the parlor window. How many evenings had he stared out into the darkness, replaying the tragedy that once haunted him? He'd finally laid that episode to rest and thought that Sophie's difficulties were also in the past. Yet perhaps there was one more part of it that would need to be buried along with the others.

"Nor do I. What are you going to do, Ian?" Maggie stood and moved to his side.

"Pray. God's strength will have to take over my weakness. If this stranger is Caira's father, I'm going to need guidance to deal with him." Bitter words and thoughts surged inside. Tomorrow morning, he would go to Sophie, and he would trust God to help them through this.

••)———— • ————(••

Sophie moved the oil lamp away from the bed, turning its bright light down to a soft glow in the glass globe, hoping not to disturb Caira's sleep. She pulled pieces of clothing from the wardrobe and the drawers in her dresser, folding and flattening them into the bottom of an old carpetbag she'd borrowed from Esther when moving to the parsonage. How richly she'd been blessed in Stone Creek! She could leave behind her patched dress for the ragbag since she'd sewn a couple of outfits.

She smiled as she pulled out her dreary, dark brown jacket and skirt, meant to make her look like a spinster. It would be perfect for traveling tomorrow. She wanted to slip onto the train with

Caira, no questions asked. She opened a drawer where she found the little bit of cash she'd saved in addition to what her parents had given her for any needs that might arise. There would be plenty for two train tickets, and she could leave something behind to pay for the food she would pack up for them to take after Esther was asleep.

Exhausted, Sophie lay on the bed, pulling an extra blanket up over her. Caira stirred anyway. "Shh." She patted her daughter with tenderness and let her hand linger on the little one's back. Feeling her child breathe, and the warmth of her little body, comforted Sophie. They'd gotten this far. Mama and Papa would help her figure things out. "Please, heavenly Father, be merciful to us as we travel. Help us get away from . . . *him.*"

Sophie blinked, staring at the shadows on the ceiling. How could this be happening? She turned on her side away from Caira and pounded the pillow. She knew one thing. She wasn't going to let Charles take away her daughter and their new life.

How she would miss them all until it was safe to come back to Stone Creek! Esther and her motherly kindness had been such a comfort. Maggie and Gloria's stalwart friendship in the face of Gertrude's enmity had strengthened her. And the closeness she'd felt to Nora had been such a surprise. They'd both been hurt deeply, in different ways, had reaped the loneliness of those hurts, and comforted one another.

Most of all, the sweetness of Ian's love, which seemed so undeserved, had been like God's healing balm and forgiveness in one package. Why was the Lord now, of all times, letting Charles interfere? Had she fooled herself into thinking that God would forgive her deception to the good people of Stone Creek? Or that she deserved any happiness at all after all of her troubles? The whole situation confused her.

Stone Creek had grown to feel more like home than the bustling city of Detroit where she grew up. She inhaled against the inner weight pressing on her. But what could she do except run from Charles as she had all along? "We'll come back." Her words, a slight whisper in the silence of the room, were a promise she made not only to her daughter, but also to herself.

She dozed on and off the rest of the night, knowing she needed to awaken well before dawn if they were to escape on the 5:10 eastbound to Detroit.

———————————●———————————

Ian turned over and over like a hotcake on Maggie's griddle. His sheets were nearly in a knot. Multiple times he knelt by the side of bed, turning his lamp up and reading his Bible. Concrete answers evaded him. Finally, sleep weighted his eyelids shut, and when he awoke, the steely light of a gray dawn filtered in between the blinds. *Be there for her. Don't be afraid. Forgive.* The words came to him like a gentle, but persuasive nudge.

He dressed quickly in the near dark. Maggie was making her way downstairs when he emerged from his room. "Awfully early to be out and about already, little brother." A yawn interrupted her smile.

"Pray for me, Maggie. I don't want to upset Sophie any more than she needs to be, but I believe I should warn her and be there for her in case anything happens."

His sister's eyes carried such concern. "Of course."

Ian made his way toward Fairgrave's Boardinghouse, wondering if Esther would be up yet, or perhaps Sophie, cooking breakfast for the men. When Ian arrived, he slipped around the back of the house, peering into the kitchen window. No light burned on the table, but he would knock on the door anyway. He tapped gently but then grew more insistent. No answer. He turned the knob, knowing Esther rarely locked it unless she wanted to keep out a drunk tenant or she felt threatened. The door gave in more easily than he liked to see.

"Sophie?" No sign of his beloved or their little one told tales in the kitchen. He kept moving, opening the door into the dining room and adjoining parlor. "Sophie!"

He heard a heavy tread on the stairway. "Reverend McCormick! Whatever is the matter?" Esther held onto the railing, her eyes puffy with sleep and her skirt askew.

"Where's Sophie?"

"Isn't she in the kitchen? She's usually up starting breakfast already." Esther sniffed the air. "Why, I don't smell a thing cooking."

Ian didn't care what seemed improper. He pushed past Esther, taking two steps at a time, and gave a quick knock before he burst through her door.

Sophie's partially made wedding veil sat neatly folded on the bed. A needle poked through the delicate fabric and held a slender thread. On top lay an envelope marked "Ian." Next to the veil was an envelope for Esther. He tore his open.

Dear Ian,

The scoundrel who fathered my daughter by force has come to Stone Creek and threatens our safety. He wants money. I don't know what else to do but to go home to my parents for help. I am convinced they believe you are a fine man and will not press me to marry Charles, but will do what is needed to protect me.

Please try not to be hurt. In my heart, you are meant to be Caira's father. I have left the veil I have begun making, here, as a promise to return. Though I've hidden things from you in the past, please believe my promise. More than anything I want to start over and regain your trust.

The last thing I want is for our wedding to be turned into a wretched affair because of Charles' presence.

With all my heart and love.

Yours always,
Sophie

Esther sobbed by his side, holding her opened note. "Poor, dear child."

He turned and grabbed Esther by the shoulders. "We must find them. What do you know, Esther?"

She told him about how Albert Johnson had been stopped in front of the house and given the note for Sophie. What a coward! Charles Warner wasn't even willing to face her at the boardinghouse.

Thoughts bounced here and there. He needed to focus. Did he start at the hotel to intercept the villain? Or the railroad depot to catch up with his beloved before Charles got to her?

Sophie sat on a bench against the brick wall in the station, her back straight, hopefully out of the sight of the window. Pain pounded up over the back of her head, not helped by Caira's unrelenting whining.

"I hungry, Soffie." The child stood up on the bench and leaned on her shoulder.

"Shh, please be quiet." She cupped her daughter's chubby cheeks in her hands. "What did I tell you? You must be well behaved. Once we get on the train, I will give you a biscuit. How would that be?"

Caira whimpered but nodded.

"And you call me mama now, remember?"

Caira placed her head back on Sophie's shoulder. The whole thing had to be rather confusing for the little one, and the situation had been her fault.

Was fear causing the unsettled feeling in her stomach? Or had her heart fallen there in pieces? She might as well be whining like

Caira. She'd asked God *why* intermittently through the night. Why did it have to be when things were working out so well for her and Caira? Finally. They had a place to call home.

We're going to give this to the Lord and we'll weather this storm together. Ian's words, from the time she'd told him Charles may be searching for her, came to her mind as clearly as though Ian were in the depot with her. She turned her head and craned her neck despite the pain, half expecting to see him standing next to her. Nobody, except for Mr. Sims, the station manager, was visible. Sitting in his office, he hummed a vague tune, interrupted by the distant, high-pitched squeal of a train whistle.

Ian wouldn't yet know she was leaving town, but if he did . . . Sophie knew he would keep to his end of things. He would stick with her, trusting the Lord to get them through. Why was she running home then? Didn't she belong at the side of her future husband? Not back in the Bidershem nest. Ian had supported her knowing that he might lose his ministry. He'd forgiven her deception.

Sophie closed her eyes, realizing that after all he'd done, by running away she was refusing to trust Ian. The whistle sang out again, and the distant rumble of wheels on the tracks pounded in cadence with the ache in her head.

"Your train to Detroit will be here in just a minute, Miss Bidershem."

Sophie stood, picking up their bags. "Mr. Sims, I've changed my mind."

Ian jogged toward Main Street, clenching and unclenching his fists, filled with less charitable thoughts than any pastor should have. *Vengeance is mine, saith the Lord* flashed through his mind and convicted him.

"Where does this leave me, Father? What about justice? And what is right?" The words poured forth between breaths. He knew his job wasn't to be sheriff, judge, and jury, but if he had to come between Warner and Sophie and it came to blows, he certainly had just reason to protect his future bride.

Gray clouds above threatened. The wind blew, damp and chilled against the sweat under his coat. He pushed through the door into the lobby of the Pink Hotel. The darkness and silence added weight to the air. Hitting the bell on the counter, Ian hoped to wake someone.

The proprietor came to the front desk. "May I help you?" He gazed sleepily over the top of his spectacles.

Ian gasped for a breath. "I'm looking for a Mr. Charles Warner. Is he staying here?"

"Slow down, son." The man shuffled the papers of the registry. "Afraid not."

"Are you sure?"

"Would I lie to you, Reverend?"

"I suppose not." Ian eyed Mr. Markey, a man with a curly fringe around his balding head and a bit of a paunch over his belt. He wasn't much for attending church, but he'd never heard him to be less than an honest businessman.

"Need a drink of water, Reverend?" Mr. Markey motioned toward a pitcher on a tray stacked with clean glasses behind him.

"No, thanks." Ian was already heading toward the door.

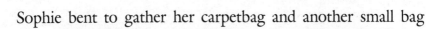

Sophie bent to gather her carpetbag and another small bag from the floor. "Beautiful child you have there, *Miss Sophia.*"

She didn't have to look to know the voice, which sent chills up her spine like a snake slithering toward its prey, was that of her tormentor, Charles Warner. Sophie straightened, letting her bags drop to the floor and gripped Caira's hand. A glance sideways around the room let her know that Mr. Sims had likely stepped outside to meet the train. Charles Warner blocked the entrance.

Father, help me. What do I do now? Remembering the Lord was ever present, strength surged through Sophie. She jutted her chin up a bit. "Fancy meeting you here."

He only looked at her for a moment, then stared at his child. "I suppose she has my eyes, doesn't she?" Tenderness passed quickly across his face. "Does she know about me?"

"Why would she? She thinks I'm her sister. She's too little to understand." His steely gray eyes commanded possession of a woman if she let them. His straight nose and strong chin fit nicely in his perfect face, with a beguiling smile he'd used to fool many, but his façade no longer charmed her. In Sophie's eyes, he was disgusting and pathetic. The scar on his face had most likely been earned.

The fleeting tenderness left. The coldness returned. "So that's how you're playing it? Well, that's going to change."

The way his hand was positioned in his coat pocket, Sophie suspected Charles pointed a gun at them. "You're both coming with me. We're getting on that train to Detroit." Charles smirked. "I'm sure your parents don't want to lose the privilege of seeing their granddaughter. What's your testimony against mine? Any court in the land would favor me as the father."

"How could you prove it?" Sophie gritted her teeth. Still, her insides felt like jelly, ready to melt under such pressure, but she had to be steady. *Give me strength, Lord.* She swung Caira up into her arms, holding her tight.

"You should know, Miss Bidershem, I have plenty of friends in high places. Now, do what I say if you want to keep the child."

Caira whined and pushed against her until Charles came closer. Then her daughter stilled and placed her head on Sophie's shoulder.

"Well, hello there." As he reached up to stroke the child's hair, bile rose in Sophie's throat, and she grew dizzy, especially as she caught the stench of his alcohol-laden breath. The closeness of the scar on his cheek. The fury that possessed his eyes. Her thoughts transported her back to the parlor in the Warner mansion as he gripped her arm. She remembered being pressed against the silk brocade upholstery of the chaise and the sweet smell of pipe tobacco clinging to the piece of furniture. Yet she couldn't call a scream forth like she had that day, and she was frozen to the wood plank floor beneath her.

"I said let's get a move on." Then the reality of the situation hit her. She wouldn't take a chance of either of them being shot, but they would get out of this yet. God had been with them through their trials. She saw this now. Caira clung closer to her, pulling away from the man who was a stranger to her.

Sophie moved forward and out the door onto the platform. "All aboard for Northville, Detroit!"

Steam hissed a warning as it billowed a menacing cloud onto the platform ahead. Sophie felt as though it pictured her future—hidden and uncertain when she thought she'd finally had everything planned out.

"Miss Sophie, I thought you changed your mind." Mr. Sims eyes widened as he looked up from his pocket watch.

"She's with me now." She could just picture Charles' oily grin as he pushed her ahead.

"And who are you, sir?" Mr. Sims, though an unimposing older man, took a step forward.

"Why, I'm *family*, not that it's any of your business. I've arrived in time to alleviate any of her travel worries. Good day, now."

Knowing Charles couldn't see her face, she did her best to give Mr. Sims a concerned look and gave him what she hoped was a slight, but perceptible shake of her head.

"Up onto the train, my dear, we don't want to miss it." She felt the gun graze her back and obeyed.

"Certainly, *dear.*" Sophie hoped the sarcasm wasn't lost on her captor. The whistle blew its final warning as she stepped up into the passenger car, not daring to look back.

———————————————————

The train inched along the track. Ian heard the train door slam shut as though his hopes and dreams had also been closed off. Still he raced to the open door of the station and looked around inside.

Mr. Sims stood just inside the doorway, scratching his head. "What in tarnation?"

Ian took a deep breath. "Have you seen Sophie . . . and Caira?"

"Something's wrong, Pastor Ian. She had tickets to go to Detroit but changed her mind at the last minute. Next thing you know some stranger showed up, said he was family and he was herding the two of 'em onto the train. But her bags are still here."

What Ian feared the most pierced his very being. Warner had kidnapped them!

"Mr. Sims, telegraph ahead to the next stop. Tell them they'll need the sheriff because there's a criminal on board! And get Sheriff Baxter over here. We may need him before this is over." As he finished, Ian backed onto the platform and turned with swiftness toward the moving train. If he hurried, he could catch the caboose.

"Don't get yourself hurt or worse, Pastor!"

"I'm not planning on it!" Ian ran alongside, gulping in air that burned his lungs as it filled them. He hadn't pushed himself this much since a boy. *I can do all things through Christ who strengthens me.* The clacking of the wheels on the track increased in speed. If he timed it just right, he could grab the railing off the back of the caboose and swing himself on. One, two, three . . . the pull nearly wrenched his arm out of its socket as he swung sideways and hooked his feet on the edge.

"Careful, mister." A barrel-chested giant of a man, wearing a suit, had opened the back door and bent out to grasp his free arm.

"Thank you." Once pulled onto the train, Ian hunched over with hands resting on his knees and caught his breath. "Have you seen a man with a young woman and a little girl, both with curly dark hair?"

"Don't think so, but they may be further up." The large man's eyebrows furrowed and he examined Ian carefully, scratching his chin. "You need some help?"

"I'll let you know if I do." This wasn't a stranger's business. Ian was pretty sure that he needed only God's strength and grace to face a coward such as Warner.

Ian pushed forward, grasping the backs of the seats. People turned to stare up at him. He figured that he must look like a wild-eyed dog hunting prey. His hat long gone, he could feel his hair had become tangled as he smoothed it back away from his eyes. "Excuse me." Through each car, he moved on, searching each face. *Lord, help me make it.* Jumping over the car couplings between passenger cars had him repeating the prayer as he aimed his feet for the platform ahead. Ian worked at not looking down toward the deadly tracks moving beneath him. The ground below rushed past in a blur.

Charles Warner pushed Sophie forward, the weapon pressed into the small of her back. "Keep going until I tell you to stop." His breath grazed her ear with his menacing whisper.

Caira whined in Sophie's arms.

"Give the child to me, so I can keep her quiet."

Sophie held her daughter close. "I can take care of her."

"We'll see about that." He pushed her along the narrow passage toward the back of the car. "Let's find a quieter spot."

How could she deter him and stay among the other passengers? "Dear me. I think I dropped . . . my handkerchief." She stopped and bent down, pretending to search the floor.

"Just leave it." Charles nudged Sophie again. A door flew open, banging against the wall.

Ian! Sophie had never seen him looking so fierce, with nostrils flaring, like a stallion ready to trample the people in his way. She would blame herself if he was shot. "Be careful!"

People around them screamed as Charles reached in his pocket, but at that moment, the train began its swing around a sharp curve, and he pitched to the left. Instead of a gun flying from his hand as he brought it out to regain his balance, a pipe clattered to the floor and broke in two.

"What?" There never had been a weapon of any sort? With Sophie caught off guard, he pulled Caira from her arms and turned to run from them. Her first instinct was to get Caira back until she felt Ian's firm hand on her shoulder.

"Let me take care of this." He pushed ahead of Sophie. *Trust.* She knew Ian had greater hope of dealing with Charles because of his strength, but this was *her* daughter who needed rescuing. She followed, not far behind Ian, praying fervently for rescue.

Caira arched her back, looking toward her mother and Ian with terror in her eyes. "'Cowmick!" And then she let out a wail.

"Shut up!" Charles pulled the child closer, but she screamed all the louder.

He wobbled, and as the train veered around another sharp curve in the track, he tripped on a cane hanging on the armrest of a passenger seat. Caira's sweater snagged on the back of the seat they were passing. Charles stumbled to the floor, catching himself on one knee.

Caira flailed her arms as Charles tried to loosen her sweater hood from the passenger seat. As he freed her, the door burst open behind Sophie. A large, burly man she'd never seen before stood before them with arms crossed and feet apart. "Need some help now?" He addressed Ian. "Thought you looked like you might be in some kind of trouble."

"As a matter of fact, I could use some assistance right now!"

Charles hadn't regained his balance before Ian grabbed a handful of his suitcoat and his right arm, yanking him backward. "Release the child!"

"Or I'll shoot!" The large man clambered past Sophie.

Charles let go of Caira once he saw the threat. Taking advantage of the distraction, Ian took a firmer grasp on Charles' arm, yanking it back and upward until the scoundrel yelped in pain. "You're not going anywhere but to jail, Warner."

Sophie reached out her arms as Caira squeezed past Charles and Ian and ran to her mother, sobbing. "Sh, sh. You're going to be fine now, sweetheart."

"Mama." Caira tucked her head under Sophie's chin after saying the word she most longed to hear from her baby's lips. Her tears wet the curly mop beneath her.

The large man had come toward Ian and Charles, offering a hand. "What happened here?"

"Who are you?" Ian pulled Charles back farther.

"Detective Perkins, Detroit Police Department. Now what seems to be the problem?"

"This man kidnapped my future wife and daughter. We have witnesses."

Several of the other passengers nodded or cried out in agreement, to Sophie's relief.

"But you're mistaken." Charles seemed to recover as Ian released his arm and handed him to the detective. The oily tone and smirk returned.

Ian grasped Warner's arm again. "Look, you're a victim of God's mercy and grace." He swallowed down the fury that boiled up inside of him. "If it had been you and me alone out there, I'm not sure what I would have done. Don't throw away your second chance, Warner. And don't ever come near Sophie and Caira again." He shoved him closer to the detective.

Any composure Charles had lost returned. He held his head high, averting any glance into his bloodshot eyes. "I'm sure it's all been a terrible misunderstanding."

Detective Perkins revealed handcuffs. "Save it for the sheriff in Northville. I'm sure he'd like to hear all about it." His exaggerated grin punctuated his sarcasm as he clamped cuffs on Charles' wrists and pushed him toward an empty seat.

"Come, let's get Caira away from that cad." Ian guided Sophie with a gentle touch to two open seats next to one another, away from the crowd.

While the feeling of melting jelly left her, Sophie shivered until settled in her seat with her daughter on her lap and Ian had placed his suit coat and his arm around her shoulders. They huddled together.

"That was a close one, but God didn't forget us, did He?"

Sophie shook her head, barely able to speak. "I apologize, Ian. I forgot all that I'd learned. I'm sorry for trying to leave instead of going to you first thing." She explained how the situation had come about.

"Sophie, I hope you know I forgive you. I'm thankful you and Caira are safe, and we can have that blackguard put away once and for all. I've done my own running from plenty of situations I didn't like."

Content to ride the rest of the way contemplating her thankfulness and the joy of having Ian with them, Sophie grew quiet again. The dust and steam billowed up outside the passenger car, leaving her in a dreamlike state. The sweet, cloying smell of tobacco lost its power to frighten her. She had a wedding to get ready for even though she'd narrowly escaped a kidnapping attempt. Caira relaxed against her, falling asleep to the click-clack of the wheels pounding out a rhythm on the track.

God had protected them, given them a means of escape. She'd seen now that He'd allowed her to face her worst fear and the specter had no more hold on her. She actually pitied the sorry man. She could begin to forgive.

···)———————— ● ————————(···

The brakes squeaked to a stop at the Northville railway station, and they disembarked to find the local sheriff waiting for them. He took Charles Warner into custody and welcomed them into his cozy office, offering strong coffee to them and stale butter cookies to Caira, who was happy to nibble the treats. Sophie gave her statement while Ian occupied her daughter.

"You're one brave woman, Sophie Bidershem." Ian took one of Caira's hands and Sophie the other as she walked between them along the boardwalk outside the station afterward.

"You're not too bad yourself, Reverend." Sophie giggled, feeling as free as a schoolgirl, but more in love than she ever thought possible for a grown woman.

Sheriff Baxter arrived to take them home in his buggy after he caught up with Detective Perkins and the local sheriff.

They arrived back in Stone Creek to a chorus of cheers. Ian turned to her. "News must have traveled fast."

Maggie waited at the front of the crowd, wringing her hands. She opened her arms to Sophie and Caira as they alighted from the buggy. "My dears, are you all right?" Her eyes glowed with tears of joy as she hugged them.

"And I am well too." Ian crossed his arms.

"You silly little brother of mine. Of course I worried for your safety as well." Maggie stepped forward engulfed her brother in a hug. Nothing could please Sophie more than to see this expression of family love, the family she would soon be married into.

The Myleses, the good Dr. Moore, Nora, James, Chet, Albert, Esther, and several others came forward proclaiming how they had prayed for them and were relieved that they were safe in Stone Creek. Joy welled up in Sophie as she realized she and Caira had arrived *home*. No more running for them. Ever.

CHAPTER 28

A week later, Sophie fingered the satin sleeve down to the cuff, trimmed with organza. Her mother had specially made the gown from a rich, deep ivory fabric, with a rose cast to it. Yes, Sophie had lost her purity. She didn't feel right wearing white, but it was such a lovely dress. Her heart quickened at the thought of donning it soon, for her wedding. Mother wanted to make sure she had time to alter the gown if need be.

Esther had been patient the few previous days when Sophie dropped a dish or when she forgot to stir the stew and allowed it to stick to the bottom of the pan. The older woman had thrown her hands into the air. "You young people, preoccupied with love." Sophie smiled at the thought.

Esther appeared in the doorway. "Ian is here to speak with you."

"Thank you." She gave her employer a hug and a smile.

"I'm so relieved to find you happy, child." Esther squeezed her hand. "You often looked so forlorn when you first came to Stone Creek."

Sophie nodded. "It was a trying time, but now I have so much to be thankful for."

"You always had a lot to be thankful for. God was always watching over you. You just didn't realize it."

Sophie smiled at the older woman's wisdom and followed her into the hallway. She closed the door as if to hide the dress from Ian, even though he was downstairs. While she didn't believe in any silly superstitions about the groom not seeing the dress before the wedding, Sophie wanted him to be surprised on their special day as she walked down the aisle toward him, to be as delighted as she was by the beauty of the garment.

She nearly ran down but stopped short when she saw Ian holding Caira on his lap. The soon-to-be father and daughter were playing a private game, smiling into one another's eyes, as though Ian had always been her daughter's father. She was doubly relieved that she no longer had to worry about Charles' hurting either Caira or herself. James had given her the news in person.

After she served Ian a glass of lemonade on the porch, where Esther allowed them a bit of privacy, they conversed easily. The chains that held the porch swing creaked with each back and forth movement.

"Sophie, did anyone tell you what happened to Caira's father?" Ian placed an arm around her shoulders. The very mention of Charles had caused a chill to slither down Sophie's spine.

She closed her eyes for a moment. Never again would she worry that some stranger may be Charles, seeking her out or looking for their child. Caira and she were safe.

"It can't be good. You look distressed." Ian rubbed her shoulder.

"One of Charles' friends in high places, probably one of his gambling cronies, sent a lawyer and put up bail for him." Sophie shook her head. "He rented a horse from the livery. Went to the saloon and became so drunk, he went out riding in the bad weather." She paused. "Of course, he wasn't steady on the horse. "

"Not surprised someone bailed him out, but I'm sad to think he might get away with what he's done."

"No, not this time." Sophie shook her head again. "The horse took off, must have slipped on a muddy hill and fell down, injuring one of his legs. Charles . . ." she swallowed. "He took a tumble off the horse and likely broke his neck. Someone found him dead the next morning." She shivered. "Just a few days ago."

Esther had taken the little one inside, but Sophie released her breath and whispered anyway. "I don't know what I'll tell Caira when she's grown. I'm glad she'll never have to see such a man again, to be claimed as his daughter. Yet someday she'll ask about who he was." Her eyes blurred.

"There but for the grace of God go I." Ian set his lemonade down on the porch and tilted her chin so her face was closer to his.

"Never, Ian."

"Ah, but you and I were both guilty sinners saved by grace and wanting a new start. God will give us the wisdom and the words if the time ever comes. We are blessed."

Sophie's fears melted as Ian held her. She knew she could count on him to protect their family with God's help. He rested his forehead on hers and then placed a gentle kiss there. "We can only forgive Charles and hope he found grace in his last moments," Ian's voice reassured her.

"I suppose." Though it was hard to imagine one so prideful would bow his knee even at his last hour.

Ian cleared his throat. "Your father came to see me yesterday."

"He did, did he?" Sophie reveled in the new feeling of joy such news brought her.

Ian nodded. "I asked him for a certain young lady's hand."

"And?"

"Just a formality, but, of course, he said 'yes.' It seems he's quite impressed with me."

"I see." Sophie raised one eyebrow.

"He offered to buy the old rundown White home, near the orphan school property so that I could begin the ministry to troubled young women."

Sophie sat up straighter. "Really?"

"Yes, but I want to know how you feel about it. It would take awhile to fix up. And we would try to train these young women with a skill so that they could raise their children. They wouldn't have to give them up—"

"Dearest, that's all I need to hear. If young women like myself could have some dignity whether they are victims of assault or have sinned of their own accord. At least if they know someone will love and accept them in the name of Christ and they won't be forced to give away their children, I can't imagine anything better." Sophie paused, shaking her head. "And you say Papa has offered to help? God truly works in mysterious ways."

They sat quietly, companionably together on the swing.

Sophie reached up and pushed his hair off his forehead. "I'll always be here for you, to help you in any ministry, as long as God gives me breath." She drew his face toward hers until warmth mingled in their kiss, heating the cool evening air. He pulled away.

Ian stroked her cheek. "Pretty soon we'll have plenty of time for that. Lord willing, we will have a long life together."

◆

A week later, Sophie looked around the Myles' ballroom. Gloria and Asa had insisted that they have their reception at Apple Blossom House.

Esther sat next to Sophie's mother as they sipped lemonade. Her father spoke with Ian's former seminary teacher, Reverend Perry, who'd come to perform the ceremony. Everyone seemed comfortable. Maggie, Esther, the Whitworths, and Moores were all there. Nora sat on a chaise, blushing while giving James Cooper her rapt attention in conversation. How wonderful that this peace had come! A year ago there had been only loneliness and chaos in her and Caira's lives.

She would be free to sew for her family and no longer had to worry about building a business. She happily exchanged that for her former dream of pursuing her music more freely as a teacher and performer. Since she'd made her peace with the Lord, she could sing out to Him with a full heart. This must have been His plan all along.

Ian sat by her with Caira on his lap.

The little one pulled her thumb out of her mouth for a moment. "Love 'ou, 'Cowmick."

"You can call 'Cowmick 'Papa' now." Joy welled up inside Sophie like a fountain filled with clear, bubbling water.

"And remember to call Sophie 'Mama.'" Ian nodded at the small child.

Caira giggled and looked from one parent to another before popping her thumb back into her mouth.

"It's going to take her awhile to understand, I'm afraid." Sophie sighed. The child slid from Ian's lap to run toward her newfound Grandma Bidershem.

Ian pointed to the lovely soft, beaded leather shoes that matched Sophie's dress. "Pretty fancy. I hope that you'll be content as a poor preacher's wife."

She had to smile. "I am richer than I ever was as a Bidershem." She kept her voice low, not wanting to hurt her parents. "Where once I thought that I was burdened, now I am free. Free to forgive, free to live in the land flowing with milk and honey. God's love and yours have brought me to the Promised Land."

"Yes, I suppose that's true. I'd never quite thought of it like that." Yet, where once he'd been plagued with thoughts of what he should have done, peace flooded his heart. Only Christ's blood could cover his sin. He'd been forgiven. They would move forward in their lives together, through trials and tribulation as well as the good times. "Yes, indeed." Ian moved closer to his lovely bride and put his arm around her. "I believe we are entering the Promised Land. And I look forward to sampling its fruits." Ian bent his head and placed a kiss on the soft pink mouth that his beloved offered willingly.

Group Discussion Questions for
Rumors and Promises
by Kathleen Rouser

1. Both Sophie and Ian are anxious to make a new start and leave their pasts behind. Why do you think they each chose Stone Creek?

2. Both Sophie and Ian are haunted by their past. How does their response to their troubles differ?

3. Bearing a child out of wedlock at the turn of the last century was considered a great taboo and unless kept a secret would most likely ruin a young woman's chance for marriage in the future. Sophie had few choices she could make. What would you have recommended Sophie do in her circumstances?

4. How do you think Lemuel and Olivia Bidershem could have better handled their daughter's situation, once she became pregnant?

5. Gertrude Wringer is correct in her suspicions that Caira is Sophie's daughter, but she doesn't know the whole story. Gossip is often started with a kernel of truth, which is twisted. How could Gertrude have been best stopped once she began slandering Sophie?

6. Sophie knows her ruse that Caira is her little sister is deceitful and feels guilty for continuing. What could she have done differently to handle this situation with honesty, yet protect Caira? What might have the consequences been if she did?

7. Ian believes he should begin a home for unwed mothers. How can someone know God is leading them into a ministry? Do you have a story to share?

8. How does Sophie's deception, and Ian hiding what he knows about her, affect the way in which they get to know each other? How does it ultimately affect their relationship?

9. Sophie often feels far away from God and Ian feels less than worthy in his calling, until they trust God, experiencing His grace and healing. What are some attitudes which keep us from trusting God more fully each day and experiencing His grace in each situation?

10. When there is a lack of fellowship between family members, relationships suffer. How did Sophie's forgiveness of her parents help to mend their relationship? And what did her parents do that helped that process?

Made in the USA
Middletown, DE
08 February 2017